GLIMMER

ASHLEY MUNOZ

ASHLEY MUNOZ
books

Cover Design/ Formatting: Dee Garcia

Editing: Amanda Edens- Jessica Hofherr- All About The Edits

Proofreading: Jessica Walenka

FOR MY SISTER REBECCA.
I COULDN'T AND WOULDN'T HAVE DONE THIS WITHOUT YOU.

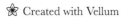 Created with Vellum

OTHER BOOKS BY ASHLEY

A NOTE FROM THE AUTHOR

BEFORE YOU EVEN BEGIN READING, PLEASE KNOW THAT THIS IS MY DEBUT BOOK. MY GENESIS, AND WHETHER YOU LOVE OR HATE IT, I BEG YOU TO LEAVE ME A CONSTRUCTIVE REVIEW, SO THAT I CAN CONTINUE TO GROW AS A WRITER. THANK YOU AND ENJOY!

ALSO, AFTER THE EPILOGUE IS A SNEAK PEEK AT ANOTHER BOOK, SO THE BOOK WILL END AT 90%

JIMMY

PROLOGUE

Five Years Ago

A STREAK of reflective light bounced off the wall, indicating that someone had pulled into the parking lot. My knee bounced as I watched the front door. The anticipation had me jumpy, but it wasn't Davis who entered; it was Tom. I let out a frustrated sigh and continued to watch the front of the bar. Waiting for Davis was testing my patience and if he were anyone else, I would have left by now. But this was what he did; he liked to play with people like they were pawns.

I tilted my left wrist and saw that it was just past three p.m. I let out a sigh and stretched my legs out in front of me. There was classic rock playing from an old jukebox perched in the corner of the room. Travis and Wilkins sat at the bar, as usual. Those two were always in here; they were widowed old men, who lived and breathed for the club. Niles, the bartender, was behind the counter, cleaning glasses, but otherwise, the place was deserted. It would stay that way until five p.m., which was why I requested this meeting before the place filled up.

I picked up my beer to find the bottle empty and set it down with a loud thud. I needed a distraction, but I had to have all my faculties for this meeting. I tapped the table irritably as I thought over my plan. It was risky and probably stupid as hell, but I was out of options. Dad warned me that Davis would have a bigger agenda, and not to get caught off guard. After all, I was nothing but a pathetic game piece to be moved and shoved around as he saw fit. I checked my phone for a distraction and saw that I had a new text from Jackson, my closest friend, and someone I considered a brother.

Jackson: Done?

He was anxious for this to work, but I could tell he was also worried.

I punched out a reply: *Still waiting.*

I lifted my head and glanced around. The stale smell of cigarette smoke and empty beer bottles filled the room. The two oldest members of the club still hadn't moved, and the melody of '*Dream On*' permeated the dark space. The irony of the song wasn't lost on me. Tom must have gone somewhere in the back because he was nowhere in sight.

I shifted in my chair a fraction and pulled my legs in, dragging the worn-down heels of my boots along the faded wood floor. The chair creaked because it was old, like the tables and everything else in the bar. It was an older joint, so everything inside had nicks of history fixed into it. I peered over my shoulder at the booth near the back, where Lisa and I hung out for the first time. That large, faded American flag was still on the wall above where she sat. I could still see her twirling the ice in her drink with that huge, red straw. Just the memory had my stomach churning. I forced my myself to turn my attention back to the entrance, just as my phone vibrated with another text.

Jackson: Shit, get out. He must know something is up.

I had considered the same thing after Davis was thirty minutes late, but now that an hour had passed, I was almost positive he knew what I was planning. Anxiety simmered inside me. I stood and shoved the chair behind me just as the front door opened, revealing Charles Davis, leader of the Brass. His silver hair was greasy, with pieces falling on his face, and as usual, he wore his leather vest over a white t-shirt. He was tall and walked with the same cocky gait that I had seen him use my whole life. He had a cigarette tucked behind his ear, with two other members clad in the same leather vests trailing behind him.

I clenched my fist and released it several times as he drew closer; took a steadying breath, counted to five, and made sure my emotional mask was in place. If I lost my temper now, everything would go to hell, and I'd end up dead. I could hold my own in a fight, but I was vastly outnumbered, and Davis didn't fight fair. I caught a look from Kendrick, one of the men following Davis, his eyes narrowed, softening a bit as he flicked his gaze to my wedding band; pity flashed across his stern face. Everyone in the club had heard about what happened, I'd been catching that look from several of the guys for the past few weeks. I didn't want pity; I wanted out.

Davis pulled a chair back and sat down. His light eyes that almost looked gray sized, measured and sifted me. Even now, years later, the weight of his stare still had me reconsidering my actions and filled me with fear. No grown man wanted to admit he was afraid of another man but, deep down, Davis scared the hell out of me.

I sat back down as well, not wanting to give anything away. Davis waited for me to begin, so I leaned forward, leveling him with a stare of my own. Keeping my words clear and short, "I need to leave."

Kendrick and Gables, the two with Davis, gave each other

a look. I couldn't tell if it was worry or surprise, maybe both, I didn't really care which. Davis didn't seem fazed. He sat back, pulled the cigarette from behind his ear, and lit it. After he took a long drag, he considered me, leaning in he asked, "how long?"

He hadn't said no, that was good. I held back the urge to relax in the chair.

"Not sure. But I need to get out of the city for my kids. Stay away for a while." My voice was relaxed, steady and sure, almost like I wasn't terrified that he'd tell me no, and I'd have to fight my way out. He took another long drag and looked down at the table. A second went by, maybe two. His gaze made its way back up as he squinted at me like the sun had suddenly invaded the room.

"We're your family. We can help. You can stay put, and we'll put you on better-paying jobs," he suggested, with a slightly menacing tilt of his head.

Better-paying jobs meant illegal jobs, something I'd so far avoided since being a part of this particular chapter. No, I wouldn't risk getting locked up or killed. I needed him to agree to this; otherwise, I'd be hunted down by every member of the Brass in Chicago.

The Brass started a few decades ago, as a small group of men who rode together and worked at the same factory. The factory's owner thought it would be acceptable to skim a little off everyone's paychecks, assuming the bikers were too stupid to realize what was going on. They knew, and they responded. What started as a fight for absolution, turned into a movement and grew into something far more superior than any of the original members thought it would. Now it was the largest chapter in Chicago, with over 500 members. They had to split up throughout the city, which caused friction with several other clubs. Eventually, we established a new territory and took what we wanted. Some called us a Biker Gang, others called it a

Brotherhood, and some just called us a Motorcycle Club. I didn't care what the hell people called it; I couldn't do it anymore, and I needed out.

"You've given special treatment to other members in the past, depending on circumstances. We're family, right? We trust each other and have one another's backs," I stated firmly. I was hoping to remind him that he once had empathy in that wicked heart of his, even if it was a lifetime ago. Davis tapped his cigarette on the table, letting the ashes fall, and leaned back. He had faded tattoos all down his arms, almost like a second skin. His fingers tapped the table; the word 'KILL' spread out in dark ink, across his knuckles. I remembered seeing that tattoo for the first time when I was eleven. I asked my dad about it, and he merely said it was a code that Davis lived by.

"Look, you're in a rough spot. We all heard about what happened, but I can't let you just take off. I wouldn't want you to get any ideas, like your old man." Davis gave me a crooked smile while he signaled Niles for a beer. My dad had cut ties with the Brass when my mom died two years ago. He was heartbroken and trying to live out his late wife's dying wish. She hated this life, hated what it did to him and eventually, what it did to me. So, she asked him to cut ties entirely and leave the group, once and for all. It wasn't an easy thing to do in a club as large as this one. He managed to disappear for a while, but the Brass were relentless, and you don't leave without getting Davis' blessings when you're a blood member.

Dad managed six months of peace before they found him, but he was ready. He sent back three members in body bags and left two in a coma. Nobody was sure what would happen after that, but Davis said my dad had fought and won his freedom. He respected him for standing his ground. After all that, no one ever pinned him leaving on me, but that didn't mean there weren't a few guys who tried to get revenge over it. I needed to convince Davis that I would never desert them, and that legacy mattered to me. Which was total bullshit. The only legacy that mattered to me were my two children.

"My dad's actions are his own, and we haven't kept in touch since he left. It's not the same thing, but I do need some space to get sorted. I need time. I'm asking for a sabbatical from club business, from meetings, from all of it. Just for a while," I lied through my fucking teeth. Niles chose that moment to bring more beers for everyone.

Davis took a long swig of the cold beer before setting it down across from my empty bottle. Then he drew in a silent, deep breath, and relaxed his shoulders into the chair. After he waited for what felt like forever, he finally gritted out, "You burn me, and I'll kill you."

He sat forward and pointed his finger at me. "I won't hesitate, and if your dad ever sets foot in my city again, I'll kill him as well. For the time being, I will let you have your sabbatical. Take some time, figure out your shit."

I nodded my head in acknowledgment. "Understood."

Relief rushed through me. I stood from the table, not wanting to risk him changing his mind. It wouldn't do me any good to say thank you to Davis, since he considered gratitude a form of weakness. Before I made it to the door, Davis yelled over his shoulder at me.

"But, Jimmy Boy, remember that we ain't done. Not by a long shot."

I gave him a quick nod and left the bar. I knew I wasn't done, but for the time being, I was free.

ONE

Ramsey

SHADOWS DANCED through the canopy of green and golden leaves above me. It was the perfect day for driving. The sun was peeking through vast, puffy clouds; the air had cooled to a comfortable temperature and all the trees were changing. I ached to pull over and run my fingers along the bark of the large Black Tupelos, or the beautiful Slippery Elms; to try and feel the change in the season or, in some way, connect myself to it.

Yeah, it was strange, but it was also tradition. A lifetime of road trips with my mom had taught me to always pull over, take time to breathe in the air, feel the trees, even take off my shoes and feel the cool ground beneath my toes. She always told me that it would connect me to God in a way that nothing else could.

I checked my rearview mirror that was tilted a tad too low and caught a glimpse of the feminine face that stared back. I looked like her and now, every freckle that I had, or smile I cracked, would be a living reminder of what I was going to lose. I blinked, trying to ease out of the memories of my mother sitting next to me with a pair of oversized sunglasses on her face, telling me stories and making me laugh.

I focused on the road and the blue jeep in front of me. I was traveling the stretch of road from Belvidere, Illinois, where I had relocated from Chicago after learning of my mother's diagnosis. The revelation of her condition was oddly synced with the termination notice that I received from my job, days before the call came: *Stage four liver cancer and less than a year to live.* So, I packed my life and moved two and a half hours west of Chicago to take care of my mother.

Belvidere was a small town, roughly thirty thousand people. It was a mixture of old buildings, historic landmarks, and small-town charm and majorly lacking in employment opportunities. Well, not entirely; it was lacking in any jobs that would appease the rigid line of pride I still held regarding my bachelor's degree from Northwestern University. Begrudgingly, I started looking outside of the small town; being away from my mother was difficult and every mile I was forced to put between us hammered away at what was left of my breaking heart.

The blue jeep in front of me hit its breaks, bringing me back into the moment. I turned the music down in my mom's '99 Ford Explorer, the overwhelming tan interior goading me to turn around and go back home. I always hated the interior of this car. Everything was tan. The tan steering wheel was cracked, from the years of sun, and it was practically black now with how much leather had been removed.

The tan seats were wrinkled and stretched, and the car was so old I had to use an auxiliary cord converter in the form of a cassette tape just to listen to music from my phone. I was irritated with the car, but not for any of the color or worn-out related reasons. I was haunted by the memories in this car. Memories of my mom picking me up from school, taking me to soccer practice, memories of sitting in the passenger seat holding a large map, while I charted the course for our impromptu road trips. It was always just the two of us, so we were free to go where we wanted, when we wanted. She'd only ever had this car, and now I was driving it away from her to try and find a job. *So, I could live my life, even though she was about to lose hers.* I squeezed my eyes together to prevent the onslaught of tears that had been held at bay for the last two weeks.

My phone's GPS dinged with the distance remaining to Rockford where I was headed for an interview. It was only fifteen miles from Belvidere, but fifteen miles drove like thirty minutes. *Fifteen miles was better than two and a half hours.*

I needed a job. Six months of turning down those low-paying occupations had finally caught up with me, and if I didn't find something soon, I wouldn't have a way to buy groceries or pay the bills.

Changing tactics from my usual interview prep, I decided I should focus on my skill set instead of pumping my fist to Halsey's newest release. I read somewhere that if you verbally encouraged yourself out loud, along with listing any accomplishments, it would make you more successful. *Here goes nothing…*

Inhaling a sharp breath, I began, "Bachelor's in Business Finance and Accounting from Northwestern University, where I worked my ass off. Remember those long nights, when I wanted to give up and work on a cruise line? Five freaking rough years as a tax accountant at Dyson and Reed, Inc., where men ogled and belittled me because I was the only accountant who wore lipstick." I held my thumb out, uselessly in the air, keeping my eyes on the road but my mind on my success.

"I tended to multiple company mergers and brand purchases, maintained business relationships with smaller branches and assisted with company buyouts, which wasn't easy to do when the contact person, Daryl, repeatedly asked me out. Today, will make it all worth it."

I was verbally spouting off self -encouragement while I cautiously tapped my breaks to increase the distance between the jeep in front me. Since I took the bus or rail system most days while I lived in Chicago, my driving skills were a little rusty. Careful, nervous, and borderline dangerous was how my mother described my driving, but I didn't care. I was safe, dammit.

With my left hand on the wheel and my right hand in the air, my thumb out, I added my pointer finger and then another as I started to decamp from the resume specifically, and focused instead on my overall awesomeness:

"I am a tall person, so I can easily reach things on top shelves and I won't need to ask for help. I am a go-getter, I normally have a great attitude, and am eager to start assignments. I am strong, I am confident, I can do anything!"

I was starting to feel empowered, energized and ready to go as I rattled the facts off louder and louder, until the rumble of an engine interrupted my little pep talk. I glanced in my side mirror at the motorcycle behind me. I had about zero knowledge of motorcycles, but this guy's bike seemed extra loud, like he was revving up his engine on purpose to get my attention. I double-checked my speedometer and tried to take comfort at the sight of the black needle hovering right over the sixty-five mark, but at the sound of his revving engine, I was nervous again.

Motorcycle Guy was tailing the hell out of me. Whether I was a cautious driver or not, that shit was rude. I situated my rear-view mirror, so that I could see him better. He was making me so nervous that I couldn't focus on mentally psyching myself up or do anything other than watch him. Because if he rear-ended me, so help me!

He couldn't pass me. There was a solid yellow line and even if he could, the car I was behind and the traffic coming from the opposite direction would make it impossible. I stopped myself from looking down at my speedometer again.

"I'm going with the flow of traffic, asshole," I said to my mirror, as I continued to watch him. What was this guy's problem? He wasn't wearing a helmet; instead, he had a black bandana folded around his head. It wasn't covering his hair, which I could see was a dirty blond color. He had a leather jacket that looked simple and classy. To top it off, he was wearing motorcycle boots and dark sunglasses. Typical, gorgeous bad boy. *Whatever.*

I put my focus back on the road and tried to ignore him. I cleared my throat, "where was I?" Putting my thumb out again in an attempt to count off what made me a great candidate, I tried to ignore the man behind me, until he started drifting.

"What the hell?" I asked out loud, getting way to comfortable with talking to myself. He started drifting from one side of the lane to the other like it was a joke to him, or like I was wasting his time. He lowered his legs from the foot bar and had them hovering above the ground while we were still pushing sixty-five miles an hour. "Is this guy crazy?" I whispered, as my stomach knotted with anxiety.

I had no idea how to make this guy go around me. "Just ignore him, don't look behind you again," I muttered to myself. I stared at the blue jeep in front of me, assessing our distance then biker guy throttled his engine… again, and now I was looking at him… again. I flicked my gaze to the oncoming car in the opposite lane just to be sure there wasn't a chance this guy would try something when I saw movement in my rear-view mirror.

Biker guy was going around me. So fast, it all happened in a blur. All I heard was his loud engine and, in a split second, I realized the oncoming car was too close. The car in front of me was too close, and motorcycle guy was trying to squeeze in… oh my gosh. *I was going to die!!*

I SLAMMED ON MY BRAKES, CAUSING MY WHOLE BODY TO JOLT against the seatbelt. I gripped the wheel, but felt my car slightly lose control as I tried to stay within the lines. Tears built in my eyes and I was positive the car behind me was going to hit me as he laid on his horn. I barely saw the motorcycle asshole jump in front of me, because I was watching my side mirror.

Thankfully, the Honda Accord behind me only had to swerve slightly to his right to avoid hitting me. My heart was hammering, but I ignored it as I tried to regain my speed and position on the road. I double-checked and saw that it was still a solid yellow line in the middle of the road.

"Shit! You asshole! It was a double line!" I slammed my hand against the steering wheel and screamed at the motor-cycle in front of me. He couldn't hear me, but he likely had a good view from his side mirrors of my crazy eyes, and insane hand gestures, including the middle finger that I slipped him several times. I committed the back of the bike to memory: it was a solid black frame, except for two silver wings that fanned out on either side. I swore, right there in my seat, that if I ever saw this man again, I was going to rip out his throat. Which was an exaggeration, of course. Sort of.

My face and neck were red and blotchy, I could tell from the heat that was locked inside my chest. I wanted to calm down. I *needed* to calm down, but that asshole started to casually swerve from side to side in front of me, as if he hadn't just nearly ended my life.

My grip tightened on the steering wheel in rage. I had this dark part of me that wanted to ditch my interview and follow him, track his ass down, and taser the shit out of him.

I huffed out another long sigh and tried to regain some composure. I finally lost sight of him after he passed another two cars and I had to take my exit. Once he was out of sight, I began a few breathing exercises and tried to relax my shoulders. I took in the beautiful scenery along the exit for the shopping complex. Tall, green trees were modestly spaced alongside the road as I came down the ramp and turned right. I knew that I was close, but just to get back into the right headspace:

"Ranked MVP two years in a row in women's college soccer, winner of the Landry cup my senior year, averaged most shots per game for two seasons straight..." I finished by listing off a few more soccer stats from my glory days in college because soccer could always make me feel better about myself. I needed a big dose of confidence after that shit show of an almost car accident.

Just as I pulled into the parking lot, a brief flash of sunlight glared off a piece of chrome, snagging my attention.

No. No freaking way was that asshole here!

He was sitting there on his bike, staring at a cell phone. I plastered on the World's Creepiest Smile and let out the most murderous laugh. I knew that I needed to reel in the crazy leaking out, but I was too far gone. I parked a few spaces away from him and unbuckled my seatbelt. Before I exited the car, I pulled the skinny flashlight taser out of my purse and held it in my hand, you know, just in case.

I breathed in and out a few times and dug deep for some courage.

I was wearing ballerina flats instead of heels because of the long drive, but my strides were cut short because of the gray pencil skirt I wore. Even so, I walked towards this seemingly dangerous stranger, completely undeterred.

He was standing near his bike, taking his bandana off and unzipping his coat. He was wearing a white, V-neck t-shirt underneath, and he had tattoos running along his arms as well as one that traveled up from his chest, onto his neck. I hated that the tattoos made me curious. I didn't need to be curious about dangerous strangers.

Once he caught sight of me, he did a double take, lowering his head, then lifting it again, his eyebrows furrowed in confusion. Without his bandana, he looked younger than I thought; I could see that he was probably in his late twenties or early thirties. Without the sunglasses or cloth on his forehead, it left his face smooth and clear. I could tell from here that he had dark green eyes. He seemed tall too, broad shoulders and strong arms.

His gaze took me in from my feet, all the way up to my hair, where he paused, causing me to feel a twinge of self-consciousness as I closed in on him. My hair has always been thick like a sheepdog's, but light chestnut brown and way past my shoulders. I took the time to dry and straighten it this morning, which was no small miracle, but a freaking huge one. I also twisted two braids to look like a headband on the top of my head. I thought it looked cute, since I pulled my entire look from Pinterest, but the way he was staring at me made me think I overshot it.

I was just a few steps away from his bike now, and I realized too late that I was too close. I could smell the man, and I will note that it was not a bad smell but for safety reasons, I backed up a few steps. Then I planted my feet, looked the jerk square in the eyes, and laid into him.

"Hey!"

There was no response, he merely continued watching me, like I was crazy.

I pushed past my nerves and continued, "You nearly ran me off the road back there." My voice came out shrilly and louder than I intended; I sounded like a panicked teenager.

He continued to stare for a second longer before his gaze skimmed behind me, where my mother's Explorer sat. He had this squinted look in his eyes, like the sun was blinding him, except that the sun wasn't currently out, it was hidden behind an assortment of clouds. He didn't say anything, so I kept going.

"Seriously, what is your problem? You passed me on a double line and nearly caused a really ugly accident. Do you even know how to ride that thing?" I gestured toward his bike, hoping to get him to respond.

He looked at my hand that was stretched out toward his bike, then back up at me. He sighed dramatically, like he was irritated beyond belief. *Screw you, buddy.*

"Listen, lady, I don't know what your problem is, but you can chill the hell out and lower your voice," he snapped at me. His face had angry lines digging into his forehead and chin, all portraying a level of frustration, that screamed "stop, don't say anything else."

It was a red flag and I was the bull. Amped up, ready to go.

I clenched my fists at my sides, squeezing the taser tighter, and took a step closer.

"My problem? My *problem* is that you don't know how to drive that stupid bike, and you nearly caused me to wreck my car when you whipped in front of me. I think you owe me an apology."

As a rule, I normally hate those people who spout off exactly like I was doing right now, but my anger had taken on a life of its own. The motorcycle jerk looked like he might kill me. The side of his jaw kept ticking, and his eyes were narrowing in on me. My hand was getting sweaty and I felt like the taser might fall out completely, so I gripped it again, resisting the urge to wipe my damp hands on my skirt. *Pull it together Ramsey.*

"Well, as far as I am concerned, you owe *me* an apology for not passing the idiot in front of you when you had the chance and kept going ten miles under the speed limit. I had an appointment to keep, and I like to honor my arrangements, not that I owe you even that much. Why don't you get out of here and go pick up your kids from soccer," he clipped, and then he turned on his heel and walked inside.

His words actually stung a little. I hated to admit it, but they did. I looked back at my car and realized that driving my mom's SUV with a soccer ball sticker in the back window from when I was in high school, was probably not the best idea. I should have just called a taxi or an Uber, except I didn't have the money for one.

My face felt flushed and I tried to ignore the dig of being compared to a soccer mom. Not that being compared to one was embarrassing, but the fact that I wasn't even in a relationship and I was going to be completely alone once Mom died; made me realize how truly sad I was. How broken. I needed to shake his comment off and get back in the zone. I decided to head to the bathroom to check my face before stepping into my interview. Hopefully, I wouldn't run into that guy again. I couldn't be held accountable for what I did, if I ever encountered him again.

I made my way through the parking lot and took a second to look around. There were three large cottonwood trees that lined the oval-shaped lot, green grass ran along the ground that bordered it, and tiny purple flowers were still peeking through the back brush. The bar that I was applying at was in a secluded corner of the shopping complex. Further down, I could see a gym, coffee shop, small grocery store, and a burger joint. Since this was a bar, I could see why it was further out.

I was applying for their accounting position, but I would take anything they gave me, even the bartending slot that I knew was available. As I crossed the black asphalt and started walking on the smooth sidewalk, I noticed how nice the outside of the bar looked. It wasn't old or haggard-looking, like some bars tended to be. It was all whitewashed stone with massive glass windows, it had fresh clean trees and well-trimmed bushes out front with those same purple flowers scattered everywhere. Above the doors, sleek black signage displayed the word "Jimmy's."

I walked through the shiny glass doors and silently padded into the entrance. I stopped mid-step because the entire space was absolutely stunning. Soft lighting fell gently over the darkly-stained wood floors, and the walls were the same white-washed brick as the entrance. I saw a long, curved bar that was black and contrasted nicely against the wall of liquor with glass shelves and white paint opposite of the bar. The lighting was strategic and inviting, there were tables, soft couches, and chairs spread throughout the room, with another bar on the opposite side.

The entire back wall was encased with windows that looked like they opened to the back patio, where more seating was laid out. It was so nicely put together that my head started pounding as adrenaline hit my system. This was exactly where I wanted to work. I noticed a black sign that said 'Restrooms' and headed toward it. There were a few servers milling about and one or two customers lounging at the bar, but no sign of the jerk. *Good.*

Once inside the bathroom, I gripped the black countertop and stared into the mirror. I looked the same five feet, eight inches, but swore I felt shorter after my verbal sparring match with the jerk. I exhaled, then wet a paper towel to pat my face down. My watery blue eyes looked darker than normal with my black tank, white sweater, and my tanned skin from the recent summer sun. Although since I was half-Cambodian, I usually had a tan, regardless of summer, thanks to my mother's heritage. My hair still looked fine, no flyaways or frizz, so I applied some more lipstick, double-checked my teeth, and exited the bathroom.

I flagged down one of the waitresses. "Excuse me, where can I find Jimmy Stenson?"

She smiled and pointed me down the hall opposite where the bathroom was.

"Thank you," was all I got out as I headed for the hallway she had gestured towards. I gave myself a quick mental pep talk about how to be awesome and reminded myself how badly I needed this, then I fixed my skirt and stopped outside a black door that said 'Manager.'

I knocked and heard a muffled yell that sounded like "Come in," and since he should be expecting me, I opened the door and walked in. The office was smaller than I expected; a modestly-sized desk sat in the middle with a laptop perched on top, there was a fancy water cooler sitting in the corner, and a few black filing cabinets that lined the back wall.

I focused on the center desk, where I saw a white piece of paper sitting in front of the man I just yelled at in the parking lot. I felt my gut tighten and my face flush, then inwardly I hoped that maybe the guy I yelled at was Jimmy's cousin or a bartender using Jimmy's desk. Maybe Jimmy the owner was late, or in the bathroom?

I cleared my throat and while he was still looking down at the paper in front of him, I decided that even if this guy was Jimmy's cousin or bartender, I would be professional and push through. I stepped forward, and with a strong voice, said, "Hi, I am looking for Jimmy."

The man nodded his head, still focusing on the paper in front of him, "You found him, you must be Ramsey, I was…" His voice trailed off as his head tilted up and he saw who was standing before him. I didn't know what to do. I stood there, frozen, as he looked at me. His stare turned into a mean glare, and he gawked for a second or more before his eyes returned to his laptop where he continued to type like I wasn't there.

I gathered the courage to speak, "Is the interview over then?"

Jimmy, I guess is the jerk's name, owner of the bar, looked at me again, but still didn't say anything. I turned my back to him slowly, and just as I was about to walk out, he spoke up and said, "Are you still holding your taser, or did you leave that outside?"

How did he even know I was holding one? My face heated but I tried to ignore it. I turned back around to face him and replied with hesitation, "I, uh, put it back in my car." It was actually tucked in the back of my skirt, like you would a gun, and my sweater was covering it up, but I felt like he might call the cops if he knew that.

He seemed to smirk, but it quickly disappeared. "You're here, we might as well interview."

This was so awkward and weird, I just wanted to leave. I couldn't possibly work for a man like this, but I wasn't a quitter and I already went through all of this just to be here, so if he was willing to let me do the interview, then I would take it. I took a seat in front of his desk while he was shuffling around some papers that seemed out of place. He scanned down one page, and then looked up at me with those gentle green eyes.

"I have to trust the person doing my books, completely, without question. I don't get that vibe from you, and I see here that you were fired from your last job. That tells me the rest of what I needed to know. Sorry, doesn't look like this is going to work out."

His words echoed through me and clamored around like a small stone, skipping over rough water. The memory hit, like a punch to the gut.

"Doesn't look like this is going to work out," my mother said to the room, then looked up at me, making sure I heard her declaration. She was informing me that she was done.

Unwilling to acknowledge her or her declaration, I moved my eyes to her gown. It was white with small blue symbols splattered everywhere. There was no order or structure to the blue symbols, they just seemed to exist wherever they were printed. It was chaos.

My gaze lifted and roamed her face; her skin was pale, her beautiful eyes tired and red, her gorgeous hair was thin and straw like. This was supposed to be her next big shot at beating the cancer. They said she could start chemotherapy. They said she had a chance, a weapon, a tool, something to use against the disease destroying her liver.

I took in the clipboards, the whispered words, the sad glances in our direction, and the throats clearing. I knew it too, just like my mother; this wasn't going to work out. But I wasn't ready to give up. My eyes moved up and searched the doctors soft blue hews for any hint of hope. There was none.

"I'm sorry, when we last checked your liver, it was a good candidate for chemotherapy, but things have progressed, and we no longer see that as a viable option." The doctor delivered the news hesitantly, like we didn't already know that my mother was a walking time bomb. Like we'd erupt for entirely different reasons instead. It was that simple. No chemo, no help, no hope. That was it. She was done trying, didn't have any fight left.

That was two weeks ago.

The sound of someone clearing their throat brought me back to the present, but I was still caught up in my memory and my throat started to burn. The walls I had erected to hold back those tears for the last two weeks were breaking. *No, no, no. Not here. Anywhere but here!*

I closed my eyes and desperately tried to clear away the painful lump in my throat that had formed. It didn't work, the tears were coming anyway. I looked up at the ceiling and tried to count each and every white square that outlined the room. I blinked and blinked but still the tears cascaded down my face. I heard movement and then Jimmy cleared his throat.

"Sorry, are you...are you crying?"

His voice was a mixture of shock and doubt. No concern was present whatsoever. I lowered my gaze and saw that his face was twisted with derision, confirming that he didn't care that I was crying, he just couldn't believe that it was actually happening. With one last attempt at clearing my throat, I managed to cough instead. *No, not this.* The coughing escalated into a relentless stream of tears. *Sweet Jesus, please make it stop!* This entire thing was a total nightmare. Since my mother's diagnosis, random bursts of emotion would hit me, and if I tried to repress them, it would inevitably turn into a horrific coughing fit.

Jimmy wrinkled his eyebrows, and now looked genuinely concerned as he asked, "Are you okay?"

I didn't respond, I physically couldn't. After half a minute of my coughing fit, he cursed and jumped up to grab me a cup of water from the water cooler. He carefully set the cup in front of me, then hesitantly started hitting my back to help clear the blockage. I realized through a few more coughs that he was touching me. It dawned on me how close we were, then my brain finally caught up: he was going to feel or at least see my taser and call the cops.

I jumped up so fast that I bumped into his desk and spilled the water, which traveled down the middle of his desk, heading straight for the laptop, my resume, and that random pile of papers. All at once, I took my sweater off and started mopping up all the water, while he dove for his laptop. He was holding it above the desk, my sweater was soaked, and, for one brief moment, we just stared at each other.

The silence between us was heavy and since my pride already went to die out in the parking lot, I decided to be professional and leave with my head held high. I shook out my sweater and gently folded it over my arm, straightened my skirt, and wiped under my eyes to clear the black streaks I was positive were running down my face.

"Mr. Stenson, I am disappointed to hear that you won't be considering me for the position, however, if anything changes,

please let me know. My contact information is on my resume."
I jerked my hand out straight in front of me, practically
jabbing it at Jimmy, but he didn't accept my attempt at a handshake. Instead, he just stared at me as if I'd just grown two
heads, so I dropped my hand down and walked out of his
office.

TWO

Ramsey

My DRIVE back to Belvidere was a quiet one. I didn't play any music, or do any talking, I just drove, thinking and trying to figure out how it all went so horribly wrong.

This just goes to prove that I should most definitely *not* follow my impulses, I should think things through and let them go. If I hadn't said anything to Jimmy the Jerk, then I might actually be employed right now, and I wouldn't have had an emotional breakdown in his office.

Although, in the back of my mind, I would always resent him for that one time that he nearly killed me. Once I was back in Belvidere, I decided to pull into the local bar, which looked nothing like Jimmy's gorgeous establishment; instead, this one was called, 'Sip' N Sides.'

I laid my head against the steering wheel. I was exhausted from crying and coughing. My eyes burned, and my throat ached. I wanted to go home and cry some more, but I needed time before I faced my mother. She was always so hopeful about me landing jobs, I hated letting her down and I was actually pretty sure that I'd land this one.

I hopped out of the car and headed into the bar. The dim

lights inside offered some sanctuary and protection from the world seeing the failure that lurked behind my eyes. I weaved my way through the few pool tables and bearded patrons that crowded around each one and found a place at the bar.

I ordered myself a beer but the bartender must have picked up on my mood because he put a shot of tequila next to my drink. I stared at it, and decided, what the heck? I threw it back and set the glass down.

The bartender was an elderly man with graying hair, and he wore a plaid shirt that he rolled up to his elbows. I imagined my dad maybe looking like that, although I wouldn't know. I haven't seen him in twenty years; no cards, no random visits, no friend request on social media, nothing. He up and left my mom and me one night when I was eight years old, just leaving a note behind, explaining that we deserved better. Well, I guess we did if he was going to just leave us.

The elderly bartender's gaze narrowed on me, his soft blue eyes watching me. It was a pleasant look, but I'd seen it enough through my mother's sickness to know that it was a look of pity. He came over with his rag in his hand and took my shot glass, then he gently asked me, "You okay, hun?"

How does one answer that? I smiled at him and asked, "What is your name sir?"

He smiled back and threw his rag over his shoulder. "They call me Ripper around here, but you can call me Theo."

I felt my dry lips crack as I gave Theo a smile. It felt like he was offering me friendship, and I had exactly no friends in Belvidere. I put my hand out as I introduced myself, "Hello there, Theo, I'm Ramsey Bennington."

He chuckled to himself. "Ramsey, huh? What kind of name is that for a girl?"

It didn't sound rude, just like he was amused. He had a point. I really had no idea how I ended up with the name Ramsey, but I have never stopped getting that question.

"I don't know, I like to pretend that I am somehow related to the famous Gordon Ramsay, but the spelling is all wrong, so my theory usually ends there. My mother always just shrugs when I ask her about it."

Theo smiled and continued his questioning, "So, you okay, Ramsey?"

I decided to go with the truth, I mean, why not, if this was my one and only friend in this town? I might as well vent. I spilled out the whole, long story to Theo, about the trip to Rockford, the almost accident, the person—Jimmy the Jerk. All of it, and I told him about how unfair it was that I didn't even get a real interview, and that Jimmy didn't even let me explain that I wasn't fired, I was phased out; it's different.

Theo leaned on the bar, fist under his chin, eyes intent, listening. I told him the sordid details, skipping over why I started bawling like a schoolgirl. After I swiped a few peanuts and took a breather, Theo rocked back on his heels and asked. "This place that you interviewed at, didn't happen to be a bar, did it?"

I drank some water and nodded, not sure exactly how he knew. Theo stood up, shaking his head back and forth, as he started wiping down the counter space around me. He turned away from me to talk to a customer a few seats down. I took the opportunity to swipe even more peanuts. A moment later, Theo left the bar area through a door toward the back. I wasn't sure if he was coming back and I needed to get back to my mom. I started to get up to leave, but a second later, Theo returned with a basket of curly fries.

"Looks like you need some grease, sweetheart, not alcohol," he said as he moved the basket in front of me. This man was quickly becoming my favorite human being. I reached for the fries, then remembered how much I spent on the beer and realized I really couldn't afford such a luxury.

"Thanks, Theo, but I can't really spend any more money tonight."

Theo laughed out loud. "Do you really think I would listen to a story like that and actually charge you money for these? Sorry, sweet pea, but your story is one of the saddest that I have heard, and the whole town has heard about your mama's sickness. Please, take these, it's the least I can do."

I swallowed that familiar lump in my throat that liked to surface when people were really nice to me, or when they mentioned my mom. I started eating the fries and instantly felt better. Theo leaned forward on his elbows, watching me carefully, like he was settling in for something.

"Now, since you've told me a story, I feel it only fair that I share one of my own." He smiled and started in- not giving me a choice about it one way or another, "once, when my son James was eleven, he had this girl that he liked. He was so nervous and embarrassed by the fact that he liked her but didn't know how to talk to her that instead of trying to approach her, he spied on her."

I choked on my water. "Spied on her?" I asked, my mouth tilting up into a smile.

"Oh yes." Theo shook his white head while looking over my head, as if his memories lingered there. "He would follow behind her to school, to tennis practice, and anywhere else she'd go. He never went to her house, thankfully, but still, I reached out to the girl's dad, just so he didn't do anything if he found a little gangly kid following his daughter around.

"Now, the girl's dad was the police chief, and once I talked to him, we made a plan. One day, James started to follow the girl and her friends to a movie. The chief followed them and pulled up behind him, turned his lights on, and used his loud-speaker, commanding him to freeze, like he was a criminal. I was in my car, watching the whole thing from across the street, and nearly died of laughter at how red James' face turned. The police chief ended up introducing my son to his daughter, thinking it would help the two to actually speak, but after that, James was too embarrassed to ever talk to her again."

"No. Theo, that's the worst." I leaned forward, laughing, my stomach aching from the intensity of it. It felt good to laugh. Theo laughed with me, then swiped a few fries before he continued, "Oh, it gets worse. When James was in high school, he thought he could hide the fact that he had failed a class from his mother and me. He would intercept phone calls from the school, throw out the mail, and even faked a report card showing that he had a passing grade. Of course, my wife and I knew the entire time, but thought we'd see how far he'd go until he assumed he was home free. We decided to team up with his teacher for the class that he failed, and one day the teacher explained that she had wanted to share a special presentation with the class about parental dynamics and how to overcome adversity. So, the teacher rolled in a TV cart and played the video that my wife and I had recorded, where we talked about the way we met, fell in love, and of course, our baby boy, James. We had baby pictures. I guess he was so mortified that he ran to the TV and turned it off and fessed up to the teacher on the spot. He ended up working off his bad grade in school with extra homework and he worked off his deceptive behavior here in this bar for an entire month straight."

Theo finished with light laughter at his memories, his face was bright, and his smile was wide. He didn't just look happy. He looked fulfilled. It was the kind of look that I could only hope for someday. I took a sip of water and waited a moment before I responded.

"Sounds like you have an amazing family. Your son James must have grown into a great man with such fun and attentive parents," I said, while drawing circles in the bar from the condensation of my glass.

Theo clicked his tongue and started wiping down the counter with force. "He definitely hasn't stopped surprising me, that's for sure, but his mama passed a while ago, about seven years now. That really messed with him." Theo finished while looking off into the expanse of the bar again. I could tell this topic was painful for him.

"I'm sorry to hear that, Theo," I said, while watching his face. He gave me a warm smile and patted my hand.

"It's okay, she's in heaven now and died peacefully in her bed, surrounded by her loved ones. No better way to leave this earth," he finished, while squeezing my hand, like he was trying to infuse hope into me with just his grip. I looked down and fought against the pain rising in my chest. I needed to get back to my mom and make her dinner. I gathered my purse and was about to say goodbye to Theo, when he placed his hand on my arm, "Wait for just a second, honey."

Theo disappeared in the back, and when he returned, handed me an apron. "I know it's not a fancy accounting job, and I could only afford to pay you minimum wage, but you would get tips. You can tend bar for me, and serve, bus tables, whatever you want to do. You can also eat and drink for free here. What do you think? I could really use the help."

I was speechless, I really didn't know what to say, but as I looked at Theo's hopeful face, how could I tell him no? I would be just down the street from my mom, and maybe it wouldn't hurt to just accept something. I swallowed and replied with a smile, "I would love to. What time should I start?"

Theo replied with a big grin, "Three would be great. See you tomorrow, sweet pea."

I couldn't get the smile off my face as I walked out of the bar. I wanted to run into Theo's arms and hug him like I would imagine most girls would do if their dad had just made everything better for them. Maybe it wasn't a good idea to keep comparing Theo to my dad, but I was too far gone already.

I drove home and pulled into the single car driveway that was a mixture of grass and gravel. I walked down the path to grab the mail from the box and surveyed my mom's house from the street. It was a modest three-bedroom home with a lighter blue color and white shutter windows. It looked like it belonged to a happy family, a whole and healthy family. Not a dying one, with a broken mother who was being taken care of by her failure of a daughter.

I left the SUV in the driveway, like I usually did, since her garage was chock-full of my stuff from my apartment in Chicago. I kicked my flats off by the door and made my way into the kitchen, where I found my mom at the stove, stirring some soup. Guilt reached in and wrapped around my heart, holding it hostage. I should have gotten home earlier so she didn't have to make herself anything.

"Hey Mom, how are you feeling?"

She smiled like always and said, "fine sweetheart, how did your interview go?"

I blushed. I didn't want to tell her how it went. I looked down at the white, outdated linoleum, trying to find some courage there in its shiny patterns. "I didn't get the job, but I was hired at the local bar here in town."

I moved past her to the fridge. Hopefully, she wouldn't see my face.

She wiped her hands on her nightgown and stepped closer to me. "How do you feel about that?"

I grabbed a can of soda water, and cracked it open, finally meeting her dark brown eyes. I told her the truth, "well, I would have preferred the other job, but I just need something right now, so I am thankful."

She smiled, and then came closer and held my wrist. "My sweet girl just do what makes you happy. Promise me, you'll always do what makes you happy."

I hated when she did that. When she talked like she was

leaving me verbal goodbye notes, like she wouldn't get the chance to tell me these things later. I would never tell her that though, it wouldn't be fair, so I just smiled and nodded my head.

I poured her soup into a bowl, placed it on her TV tray, and got her some water. There was a strong chance that my mother wouldn't even eat the soup because she felt sick, but I liked that she was at least attempting it.

Once she was settled, I headed for my bedroom to call Laney. I needed to decompress with my best friend. I tossed the phone on my bed while the speakerphone rang. I stripped out of my clothes, threw on my comfy sweats and sleep shirt and moved toward the bed. I briefly recalled that it was a Thursday and I had every intention of going to sleep directly after my phone call. I winced at the memories of my old life, that Thursday night meant date night, or book club with a new flavor of wine, or something else equally as fun. The ringing finally stopped reverberating through my room as Laney answered.

"Hey, I was wondering when you were going to tell me about landing the badass accounting job!" My best friend excitedly yelled.

An ugly red color marred my cheeks as I responded, "Ha, yeah no, I didn't land it."

"What! No way, you were way overqualified for that job, what happened?" Laney's shock slowly led into disappointment. For the second time that night, I told my sad, pathetic story. The only thing she managed to wrangle from the story was, "good-looking jerk who happened to smell good," which made me immediately regret telling her anything.

"What's his name again?" she asked, curiosity coloring her tone.

"Jimmy Stenson…" I breathed out while turning on my TV and getting under the covers.

She clarified, "The bar is called Jimmy's?"

"Yep," was all I could manage as I fluffed my pillows behind my head and grabbed the day-old glass of water that sat next to my bed. *Was it gross to drink day-old water?*

She was quiet on the other end. I heard some typing, then, "He's hot."

I spit out some of the water. "What?"

"I looked him up. Huh, looks like he has kids."

Of course he did, because he was handsome and successful and probably had a wife that could easily be mistaken for a supermodel. I pinched the bridge of my nose and listened as Laney kept going. "It doesn't say that he is married, and I don't see any pictures of him with a woman. He hasn't posted anything for over a year, though, so who knows?"

I was actually thankful I couldn't see what she was seeing. I deleted my social media accounts after I was phased out. I didn't need to see an endless feed of happy ex-coworkers getting drinks and not being unemployed. I decided I didn't really need to decompress as much as I thought I did; instead, I just needed sleep.

"Laney, I gotta run, just wanted to catch up with you for a second."

She sighed. "Okay but call me tomorrow and let me know if you are going to be able to make it over here for Thanksgiving."

It was only September, so my answer to that was a simple, "Okay Laney, love you."

Once I ended the call with her, I did my best to relax. I didn't want to think about Thanksgiving, and how it would probably be my last one with my mom. Laney meant well, but she really couldn't understand how hard it was for me to leave my mom, or even take her anywhere. The treatments she did get took too much out of her, and our time together was so precious, which made the realization that I would be spending the next evening away from her so much more difficult.

So right there, in the darkness of my room, I let those tears fall free. Everything hurt, I didn't want to lose my mom, but a huge part of me felt like she was already gone.

THREE

JIMMY

"EIGHT, nine, ten! Ready or not, here I come!"

I let my voice ring through the house, so my little boy could hear me. If I didn't, then he would make me count again. I knew this because I had made that mistake twice now, and that was how we found ourselves playing hide and seek at nine thirty at night.

I bent down to look in between the side table and the loveseat. He was only six, so he still fit in awkwardly small spaces, but wasn't tall enough to fill in bigger ones. I caught sight of his toes and legs behind the coat rack near the door. I wanted to let the game go on a little longer, but one glance around the room confirmed that I needed to put him to bed, so I could clean up.

I snuck up to where the coat rack stood and grabbed Sammy's legs, while yelling like a monster. He screamed as I threw him over my shoulder, then headed upstairs to his bedroom. "Okay, mini Stenson, are you ready for bed?"

Sammy didn't reply, he just kept talking about his next hiding spot, and how it would be even better the next time.

I hit him on the back of his legs. "Hey, are you listening to me up there?"

He giggled. "Yeah, Dad, I'm ready, thanks for playing." I threw him on his bed once we reached his room. After tucking him in I kneeled next to his bed and began to pray.

"Dear Lord, thank you for this day, thank you for our family, keep us all safe, and bless our home. Amen," I finished, then Sammy added in like he always did, "And please keep my mom safe, wherever she is out there."

I froze, like I did every time he prayed for her. I didn't want to pray for her, didn't want to think about her, I didn't even want her name mentioned in the house. Sammy had such a good heart though, and I never wanted to crush that part of him, so I always let him say his prayer. I kissed him goodnight and headed towards Jasmine's room.

Jasmine was laying in her twin bed with her pink comforter pulled up to her stomach. She had her necked propped up by pillows while she wrote in her journal. I smiled as I made my way to the side of her bed. She never asked to pray, and she especially didn't talk about her mom like Sammy did. I didn't mind that, but I knew that she still struggled with the anger she held towards her mother. Therapy could only help so much, especially at her age. She had just turned nine and asked to stop going last year. I obliged and figured we were past the worst of it, or at least I hoped we were.

"Hey sweetie, you ready for bed?" I gently asked.

Everything between us was so fragile, it seemed. She got upset with me and even her grandpa, more than she ever did before. I'd received emails from her teacher, letting me know that she wasn't making friends very easily because she seemed to be mad at the world. I didn't want to confirm anything for anyone, but here's the truth: she *was* mad at the world. She was mad that she didn't have a mother and she was mad that her hair looked like a man did it every day, because one did, and she was mad that all the other little girls rubbed it in her face.

I patted her head, stroking her blonde hair, wishing so badly that I could fix her, fix all of it.

"Yeah, I'm ready, Dad, goodnight," she squeaked out.

I kissed her on her forehead and turned off her light. As I walked back downstairs, I heard the front door open and knew my dad had just walked in. He lived in our renovated basement, which was a huge help with the kids since I was doing this parenting thing alone. He was kicking off his shoes in the entryway and made his way towards me.

"Hey Dad, how was your night?"

He set his shoes in their place and wiggled his sock-covered toes.

He smiled, but then after a second or two, he frowned. "It was interesting. How was your day, get the position filled?" Like I needed one more reminder of the disastrous interview that took place earlier in the day.

"No, I didn't get it filled. The girl who showed up to interview for it ended up being a little off." I grabbed my neck, trying to rub the stress out of it. Dad didn't need to know the whole story, but she was. She may have had a reason to tell me off, but it was still ridiculous that she actually did it, all while gripping a taser. Then the crying. *What a shit show.*

Dad looked down at the floor while his hands rested on his hips. He was wearing one of his signature flannel shirts, rolled up to his elbows. His gray hair was losing the battle against the white that was invading his scalp and face. He looked like a peaceful grandpa who played bingo twice a week and went fishing on the weekends. You'd never know that he was once a ruthless member of a biker gang. You'd never know that he had to kill men once, just to be free of them. He was stronger than me, braver. Shame slammed into me at the reminder of what he did for his freedom versus what I did. I was a coward.

Finally, he spoke up, stalking toward the kitchen. "Well, that's too bad."

I remembered that I wasn't the only one who has a business to run or a position to fill.

"Well, what about yours? Did you find a new bartender?"

I heard him yell from the kitchen pantry, "Sure did, with a pretty little thing. Should bring in some good tips, and maybe get some more regulars in."

That was surprising. Dad usually hired men or older women. It was an older bar, so I wasn't sure what his angle was with hiring a younger "pretty little thing."

I replied, "well, that's good, you needed some help, right? Hopefully, the new girl knows what she's doing."

He chuckled. "Yeah, I think she can handle herself, plus, she's a sweetie. It will be nice having her around as I get ready to tie things up there."

Another surprise. For an entire year, we had gone back and forth about him retiring. To hear him bring it up for a change was nice. Maybe I could finally start moving forward with my plans of flipping the bar and actually turn the dump into something that could pull in a profit. I wouldn't share that with him, though; it would spook him and probably encourage him to stay on forever.

I joined him in the kitchen and began putting the dishes in the dishwasher. My suburban, three-story house was snuggled neatly in the nicer part of town. Honestly, it wasn't something I ever thought I'd be able to afford, but two years ago, after I opened the bar, things just took off.

I placed the final plate in the bottom of the dishwasher and started it, turning toward my dad, I was about to ask him about his retirement comment, but he beat me to it and asked a question of his own.

"So, when are you going out on a date? It's been over a

year since your last relationship of any kind, and that ain't healthy."

"Dad, not this again." I let out a loud sigh. Normally, my dad and I would go around and around on this particular subject. I didn't have it in me to argue tonight, so I gave in. My voice dripped with exasperation as I asked, "Dad, who do you want me to go on a date with?"

He laughed, turning to face me fully and crossed his arms. "Don't play coy with me, boy, I know for a fact that you have at least half a dozen women asking you out on a regular basis."

He wasn't wrong about that, it was just that the types of women were all wrong. Usually, women would approach me in either my bar or my dad's. If it was in my bar, they approached me because I was the owner and they knew it. If they approached me in my dad's, then it was usually because of my connection to the Brass, the motorcycle gang I was still technically tied to.

Although the women who hit on me were usually hot as hell, it turned me off when they'd bring up my bar while pulling on their necklines or talk about the Brass while running their hands over my tattoos. I was looking for something different. Something I didn't think I even deserved. I had a rough history, and the one-night stands were fine for a while, but I was tired of it. I wanted more. I wanted someone I could bring home and introduce to my kids.

The image of a dark green SUV with a soccer ball sticker in the back window started forming in my mind then it wandered to the gorgeous brunette attached to it. It irritated me beyond reason that my thoughts went back to that woman. That frustrating, opinionated, beautiful woman.

Even from the moment she walked up, and I saw her hair. When I saw those braids, something inside me stirred. I'm not even sure why, I guess because I thought maybe a woman who had braids in her hair wouldn't care about me being the owner of a restaurant or about my position in the Brass. But thinking those kinds of thoughts about a complete stranger, was dangerous, it made me all the more glad that I didn't give her the job.

I answered my dad with the only thing I could think of to get him off my back. "Dad, find me a babysitter and I will find a date."

He replied with a hearty laugh, "Deal."

I left dad to make his dinner and went into my office to tackle bills. It was still so foreign to not feel anxious over paying them. Before the bar, I was barely making ends meet. After I left the Brass five years ago, I came to Belvidere where my dad lived. He still had his two-bedroom condo that he owned with my mom. He took me and the kids in, just like we planned. I'll never forget the way he looked at me that night as I pulled up to his house.

It was late, nearly midnight. The kids were asleep in the backseat of my shitty little Honda Civic. I had managed to shove everything I owned into that little car, minus any furniture of course. But everything that mattered was there. Dad came out of the condo to help me, his silvery-gray hair shining with the light from the porch. I went to grab one of the kids when he stopped me, gripped my shoulder, and looked into my eyes, worry and curiosity flooding his gaze. I stared back at him and nodded to his unspoken question; I was out, and with Davis's permission, so no one was coming after us.

My dad hugged me so tight that I thought my back might crack. He whispered in my ear, "I'm proud of you, son. It's time for a fresh start."

I worked construction and odd jobs for the first three years, saving every penny that I could. I shared a room with my two children and slowly but surely began to embrace the fresh start that I was supposed to have. It wasn't easy, and nearly every night I laid awake, staring at the ceiling, wondering how I was going to do it. Being a single parent was never supposed to happen, not to me, at least. Not to my kids.

I pushed the onslaught of memories back and tried to focus

on sorting the bills for my house. Once that was through, I focused on the restaurant. I needed an accountant. One that doubled as a personal assistant, and I needed one as soon as possible. I was really banking on Ramsey Bennington working out; based off her resume, she was my top pick. I lowered my head into my hands and pulled at my hair. *Shit.* I needed this position filled today, and now I was even further behind than before.

I thought back to when I passed Ramsey on the road. I was in control and knew what I was doing but still, I did feel like a prick for scaring her. I would have apologized too, if she had given me a chance.

I rolled my office chair closer to the desk, and aimlessly clicked through a few emails. There were two new ones requesting an interview for the accounting position. Hopefully I'd have better luck with one of them tomorrow.

FOUR

My first official day of work was starting, and I felt relieved. It wasn't Dyson and Reed, and it wasn't Jimmy's, but it was work and, more importantly, money.

Once I got to Sip N Sides, I clocked in at exactly three p.m. in the back office. I made my way to the lockers along the back wall of the breakroom, found an empty one, and put my things inside.

I wasn't exactly sure how I was supposed to dress, so I settled on wearing a pair of black skinny jeans, white Tom's, and a plain white t-shirt. The black apron Theo gave me last night, I already had fastened around my hips. My hair was in a few loose, big braids leading into a high ponytail. There was a black V-neck t-shirt that had two white S's on the right pocket hanging near the last locker in the row, which I assumed was for me. I rubbed the black cotton fabric between my thumb and pointer finger, assessing it.

I tilted the collar so I could see it better; S for small. I tilted my head back, closed my eyes, and sighed. I wore a medium. I righted my head and with determination, I tried stretching the shirt out a few times. I made a mental note to ask for a bigger size the first chance I got.

THEO WAS ALREADY OUT IN THE BAR AREA, WHEN I CAME OUT. There was light making its way through a few windows to the side, but most of the establishment was dark and smelled of stale cigarette smoke. I navigated around a few slot machines until I was closing in on the bar.

Instead of elderly customers lining the stools, or anyone of legal drinking age, I saw two kids. One was a girl with beautiful blonde hair that was put into a side ponytail, around nine or ten. The other was a boy, around six or seven, with messy brown hair, and a smile full of missing teeth. Both kids nearly took the breath out of my lungs with how cute they were. They were just sitting there, eating fries like it was the most normal thing in the world that they were in a bar. I walked up next to Theo, catching his attention. He turned toward me with a large smile, wearing another flannel over a white t-shirt.

"Aw, Ramsey! Perfect, you're here just in time to meet my grandkids."

This was too cute. I cut towards the kids and smiled. I received a big smile from the boy and half of one from the girl. I stuck my hand out to each of them.

"Hi, my name is Ramsey, what's yours?"

The boy giggled and drank some chocolate milk, leaving a large mustache behind on his face. "What kind of name is Ramsey for a girl?" he joked.

"Shut up, Sammy, that's rude. I think it's a pretty name, it's better than my stupid name," the girl squeaked out.

"I don't think that's possible. What's your name?" I asked the girl. How could she not like her name?

"It's Jasmine," she replied in a small voice, then shook my hand.

I took my hand back. "Jasmine, you have a beautiful name, it suits you. You are a drop-dead gorgeous girl. You definitely need a pretty name like Jasmine."

She blushed a little, then looked up at my hair. "I wish I could do that with my hair, but I don't know how to braid."

I touched my hair. "Oh Jasmine, you and I are going to be great friends. I can do your hair anytime you want, if your mom doesn't mind me messing with it, of course. But I don't have any kids of my own, and I would love to try out some hairstyles on someone willing."

She stared down at her fries then looked away, and I worried that I said something wrong. Slowly, she turned her head back towards me and replied in a soft voice, "I don't have a mom... so I would like it if you wanted to try some hair stuff on me, as long as my dad or grandpa says it's okay."

Theo looked at us both and then smiled. "Ramsey consider it a part of your hourly wage. In fact, I was going to mention, if you are interested in making some extra cash, their dad is looking for an occasional babysitter, so he can go out some evenings. He pays really well... is that something you'd ever be interested in?"

Theo had his fingers drumming on the counter, and a sneaky look on his face, he was simply adorable. I didn't have anything against becoming a babysitter at twenty-eight, especially to kids as cute as these.

"Yeah, absolutely. It will give Jasmine and me a chance to try some hairstyle ideas. I don't know what Sammy likes to do, but I am a pretty talented hide-and-seeker, and I love playing tag."

Sammy lit up like a Christmas tree, and yelled, "Those are two of my favorite games! I am really good at hiding, and my dad always gives up too soon. Would you really play with me, if you come over?"

I smiled at him, snagging a fry off his plate. I loved that I had made a total of three new friends in less than a twenty-four-hour period. There was just something powerful about having people care if you show up somewhere.

"Yes, of course. If your dad decides to let me babysit, we'll play all the games, bud."

Theo added, "Well, their dad asked me to find a babysitter since I originally was going to do it, but the evening he needs it, there's a big bingo tournament going on down at the VFW hall. So, you would really be helping me out."

I smiled at him and patted his shoulder. "I got you covered, boss, what night do you need me?"

He looked over his shoulder and seemed to think about it. "Would tomorrow night around six be too soon?"

I beamed. "Not at all, that's perfect." Then I internally cringed at how happy I appeared. I made a mental note to seem less available, as if I actually had a life.

I talked some more with Jasmine and Sammy before Brenda came over to train me. I waved goodbye and promised to see them tomorrow. Was it normal for people to trust strangers that soon? Was it normal for me to trust kids that soon? What if Sammy and Jasmine were only nice in front of their grandpa? What if they were secretly like the evil kid next door on *Toy Story*? I needed to calm down and just stop. They were probably amazing, especially if Theo was their grandpa.

THE NIGHT WENT ON PRETTY SLOW, UNTIL AROUND NINE. THEN the customers started pouring in, and my wrists already ached from how often I was grabbing glasses and pouring bottles. Sweat was beading at my brow because I had to run down the bar from customer to customer. I was moving just to keep up with the crowd. How did this many people even live in Belvidere? I was astonished as the front door just kept opening and more people walked through. The training Brenda gave me basically covered where things were located, since I already knew the basics of tending bar and mixing drinks. So, she left me to fend for myself at one end of the bar as she covered the other.

I was right in the middle of making two whiskey sours when I felt a hand on my ass. I turned around so fast that I nearly fell. It was a guy my age, with dark hair, massive arms, and he was beyond drunk. He'd reached over the bar to get my attention, but I couldn't really understand anything he was trying to say because of the rage that was rolling through me. I mean, who just grabs someone's ass?

I wasn't sure what to do. I wanted to tell this jackass to never touch me again, then maybe bend his hand backward to prove my point, but I didn't want to get fired. The drunk guy was slurring his words. It sounded like he was saying sorry, and something like, "I just wanted to get your number, baby," which further pissed me off, because the reason for his grab wasn't even drink-related. Brenda saw the exchange from the other side of the bar and gave me a sympathetic look but didn't offer any help. I pushed the guy's shoulders back away from the bar and told him he was cut off.

He started laughing. I realized he was with a group of friends, and the debauchery was some big joke to him. Two of his friends started yelling something at him, but I couldn't hear what they were saying over the rage still burning in my system, I was shaking and needed to recover if I was ever going to hack it as a bartender.

I was pouring out the head of the beer and re-filling the pint glasses when I felt something touch my ass again. I whipped around, startled to find that the jackass that had touched me before made his way behind the bar. He was standing right behind me, slurring something disgusting like, "Baby, I want your number, give it to me." He said the "give it to me" with a little moan.

I gagged a little in my mouth, and silently wished for my taser as panic settled in. I didn't want Theo to think I couldn't handle this, but then again, Theo had left hours ago. Still, I didn't know what to do, so I decided to go with my gut. I shoved the guy out of my space and continued pushing against him, trying to get him out of the employee area, but the more I pushed, the more he stood his ground and pressed into me. He had impressively solid footing for a drunk asshole. When he grabbed at my shoulder, I nearly lost it.

"Knock it off. Get the fuck off me!" I yelled, but he didn't budge.

I tried to get better footing, but I had started to fall back on my heels. I took an awkward step back but ran into something solid. I twisted around, but all I could manage to see was muscular arms covered in tattoos. I tried to switch my angle to get a better look, and only gathered to see the side of a hard jaw, and a white t-shirt. Whoever was behind me put his hands on my shoulders and slowly positioned me to the side.

From this view, I could see him better. Then again, maybe my eyes were too strained from the low lights, or the few shots the cute redheaded guy bought me earlier had started to hit my system. Because standing there, with a look that could kill, was Jimmy Stenson, or, as I had so affectionately named him in my head— Jimmy the Jerk.

I followed his deadly gaze and realized it was pinned on the drunk guy who was causing me trouble. I froze, caught now in the silence between the two men; it was like Jimmy was trying to hold back by the way he clenched and unclenched his fists. A moment, two, then all hell broke loose, as Jimmy unleashed whatever he was holding in and let it all out on the drunk guy.

"Get the hell out of here," he stepped forward, anger rolling off him, "don't ever fucking touch her again."

I flinched at his words, and his tone. Why did Jimmy care

either way if this guy ever put his hands on me again? Why was he even here?

The drunk guy wasn't getting it, he pushed against Jimmy the Jerk and told him in all kinds of slurred words that he saw me first and that my "ass" was his.

Jimmy grabbed the drunk guy by the shirt and began pushing him forward until they were both out from behind the bar. He kept pushing him until they got to the door, where Jimmy threw drunk guy out, directly on his ass. I stopped watching, remembering that I had customers and drink orders to fill. I focused on the small glasses in front of me. The group of friends with drunk guy were still gathered near the bar and within listening distance.

"Shit, man, do you know who that is?" a blond guy asked, while looking over his shoulder to where his friend had been dropped.

"Bartender chick's boyfriend?" A few of them laughed.

"No, fuck face. That's Jimmy Stenson," the blond one quipped, as if that were enough explanation.

I found myself searching needlessly for more limes as I tried to get closer to their group, so I could hear better.

"So?" the tall one drew out. I looked up to watch the exchange, paying close attention to the one who seemed to know more about Jimmy. I wanted to know why it mattered too.

"You ever heard of the Brass? It's a fucking motorcycle gang in Chicago. Jimmy was nicknamed 'The Fist' for a reason. I'm getting out of here, I don't want any beef with them."

He slammed a twenty on the counter, threw back the rest of his beer, and took off. His friends laughed and watched him go, their mumbles no longer interesting to me. I was buzzing with adrenaline, curiosity, and confusion. I couldn't figure out what the hell just happened.

I took a second to look around, as if the room could give

me the answers I needed. Just as I started to fill a few more drink orders, I noticed movement behind the crowd and saw Jimmy pop back around the bar. He started filling drinks like he worked here. *What the hell?*

I kept filling orders as they came in, and I didn't ask or even look at him. I purposely reorganized my thoughts to call him Jimmy from now on, not Jimmy the Jerk since he did just come to my rescue, but my mind was still spinning as to why he was even here in Belvidere to begin with. Obviously, since Brenda didn't bat an eye at him being in the employee area, he must be a friend of Theo's or something. Maybe because they were both in the bar industry? I didn't know, and I really didn't care, I just wanted to get through my shift. Finally, around midnight, things calmed down. I was wiping down the counter and refilling the limes when my gaze wandered and caught Jimmy drying some glasses. I put down the towel and walked over to him.

"Thanks, by the way, for earlier, with that guy." My voice came out shakier than I intended.

He didn't look at me, just kept drying. Then after a few more glasses, he started in on me. "What in the hell are you doing working here anyway?"

Why did he always sound so pissed off?

I ran my hand down the length of my ponytail and let out a sigh, hoping my attitude would come off more jokingly as I replied, "I had a job interview that didn't go so well, and I came in for a drink before I went home. I met Theo, and I'm pretty sure he liked me, since he offered me this glamorous job."

I held my hands to show off the room and cracked a smile to lighten up the mood.

He pivoted to face me, his hands still on the glass. He was wearing dark blue jeans that fit him perfectly and a white t-shirt. His jeans were more on the thin side and made his boots stand out. He looked like a model, which wasn't fair at midnight. I'm sure my look was more like, sweaty 90's reject.

He put down the glass and narrowed his eyes on me, "Theo?" He let out a little scoff, "I can't believe this. Of course you're who he hired." He pinched the bridge of his nose, then let out a sigh before he continued, "look, I'm sorry, but you can't work here anymore. Go get your stuff ready and head home."

For the first time in a while, my face didn't turn red, it turned completely white. What the hell was going on?

How on earth did this guy keep popping into my life and ruining it?

"What the hell is your problem with me? Look, I'm sorry for telling you off yesterday, I didn't realize I would make an enemy for life by doing so, but I need this job." I hated how desperate that made me sound, how vulnerable I was in front of him, again.

He looked down at the floor, and unapologetically said, "not this job."

I used to be calm under pressure. I used to handle awkward moments with ease and professionalism. In just two days, Jimmy had exploited the fact that I couldn't do either of those things anymore. I was an emotional basket case now, and I was about to cry in front of him again.

"This isn't even your bar! You managed to keep me out of yours, but you can't kick me out of this one, you don't have the right!"

I was making an embarrassing spectacle of myself for the customers who were present, but this guy had a way of making me feel like a schoolgirl being bullied on the playground.

He threw the towel on the bar with force then told me, "I own half this bar, and hold weight in hiring and firing, and you just got fired. So, go get your shit and get out!"

I untied my apron, tears now streaming down my face. I

threw the apron on the bar and ran into the back. I did exactly as he said, I grabbed my stuff and left. I couldn't think of much as I made my embarrassing getaway, but one thing was for sure.

I officially hated Jimmy the Jerk.

FIVE

JIMMY

My Friday started rather normal...

I got up, made the kids breakfast and drove them to school, went back to the house to get my bike, then rode to Rockford and started work. The bar was normal, I interviewed a couple more people for the accounting job. They were idiots or, if I was honest, neither of them held any of the credentials that the resume I carried around in my jacket pocket had.

Ramsey had wiggled her way into my head. I had looked over her resume at least twenty times, dissecting it, weighing it, and trying to find something wrong with it. I had even spoken to three of her old bosses, including Richard Reed of Dyson and Reed. Once he heard that someone had called inquiring about Ramsey Bennington, he demanded to speak to me himself and told me that I was the biggest idiot in Illinois if I didn't snatch her up. It was a similar sentiment from all her other references, who I didn't even need to talk to. I kept thinking I would find at least one person who would confirm for me that hiring her was, in fact, a bad idea.

I learned that she had earned a full ride scholarship to Northern Illinois University for soccer. She could have gone pro, according to her coach. Which was why she was scouted for Northwestern only two years into her college career. She transferred schools, and even graduated with honors, but seemed to be completely fine with leaving the soccer career behind, because of her obsession with numbers and massive talent for keeping businesses afloat. I really was an idiot for letting her go, even more so than Dyson and Reed.

After the lame interviews and research that I devoted to Ramsey, I folded her resume up and returned it to my pocket. I got home, had dinner with my kids and, around nine, dad asked if I would mind stopping by the bar to check in on his new employee. I didn't mind getting out if he was going to stay home with the kids. Dad had already mentioned that he found me a sitter for tomorrow night and although I had found my date, a part of me still wondered about the available women that might be at Dad's place tonight. Did that make me an asshole? I just wasn't sure how it was going to go with Sarah from the coffee shop.

I hated that I'd gone for an easy target, someone who'd already flirted with me a million times, just waiting for the day that I finally caved. I didn't quite care for her three seasons in one outfit look, with her little snow boots, shorts and flannel, but she wasn't ugly. She looked similar to most of my one night stands; too much makeup, hair too straight and shiny, tan skin, tight clothes. I was exhausted from this monotonous routine, but I wanted dad off my back about this whole dating thing, so it'd have to do.

"Don't forget to tell Brenda that she needs to place the supply order tonight," Dad yelled at me from the kitchen, bringing me out of my thoughts.

"Okay," I threw back at him from the top of the stairs. I tossed on some jeans and a t-shirt and headed out on my bike.

I pulled into Sip N Sides, a name I was eager to change as soon as my dad was willing to retire and saw the full parking lot. There were usually at least ten spots available during any given night that the place was open. Tonight, however, there wasn't a free spot in sight. I ended up pulling up outside the door and parking on the sidewalk. I walked in and the smell of stale cigarette smoke and beer assaulted me.

My parents had this bar for as long as I could remember and even now, as a thirty-three-year-old, I couldn't walk in without seeing my mom at the bar wiping it down, laughing with the regulars. I smiled at the memory and walked further in, past the pool tables, and clumps of men and women. The music was blaring, classic rock, like usual, and the dim lighting helped cover the stained carpets and deteriorating decor. I wanted to change this place so badly, but dad wouldn't budge.

I was trying to find Brenda, the shift supervisor, so I could talk to her about the new employee, but the bar was crowded. There was a mixed group of older men and younger, college-aged guys standing around the bar, blocking my view so I couldn't see who was serving. I recalled how dad joked about the pretty little thing he had hired, and figured he was right about drawing in more customers. That was, until I saw her.

I noticed her hair first; it was braided, again, and again something inside me stirred at the sight of it. She wore it up, which gave her long body even more length. My eyes were taking on a life of their own and they were greedy. I took in her high cheekbones, her plump lips, then her tight t-shirt that moved something entirely different in me. Lastly, I noticed her tight jeans, but right as I was enjoying the view, someone's hand landed right on her ass. I stopped short. I watched the hand on her and followed it up to the dark-haired college-aged asshole that was leaning over the bar, trying to get her attention. *What the hell was happening to me? Why was she here?*

. . .

I HAD NO IDEA WHY RAMSEY BENNINGTON, MY JOB APPLICANT— no, my *failed* job applicant—was here in my dad's bar. And I had no idea why I felt this rage simmering under my skin at the sight of someone touching her. I shook my head to try and clear it. This was bullshit and just my desperate need to get laid, that was it. I tried to think of Sarah, my date for tomorrow. I didn't need to think protective or have any kind of thoughts about someone who chewed me out, cried, and spilled water in my office.

This was stupid. I let go of the chair and moved forward. I glanced around the bar again, this time catching Brenda's eye. She nodded at me, and went back to work, making drinks. I carefully moved closer to the new employee, planning to be professional and helpful.

Except now I saw the same guy who had put his hand on her ass back behind the bar, reaching for her. I saw Ramsey push him away and heard her scream something at him. I clenched my fists and squeezed so hard that I thought I might break one of my knuckles. I made my way behind the bar and let Ramsey center me as I placed my hands on her perfect shoulders. *Since when were they perfect?*

Ignoring my growing list of issues, I moved her aside, never taking my eyes off the asshole who had touched her. I grabbed his shirt, shocked that it wasn't his neck, and pushed him through the bar, and groups of people, until we were outside. I pushed him onto the ground and placed my boot on his chest, shaking with the urge to hit him.

"Don't ever come back to this bar, and if you ever see that girl somewhere, keep your damn distance. You get me?" I yelled down at him, my boot making an imprint into his skin.

He barely shook his head in acknowledgment but the fear in his eyes told me that he understood. I let him up and watched as he walked off, then I took a few minutes to breathe and calm down. What the fuck was going on with me? I pulled my hand through my hair and sat on the curb. I hadn't felt this kind of rage in years. Now it was back with a vengeance, and over a stranger? A crazy one at that? This was insane. I hated how much Ramsey affected me and that I seemed to have no control over it. She was like a virus working her way through my system; compromising everything in her path.

After a few minutes, I walked back in and decided to stay and help, and be sure there weren't any other zealous customers. We worked in silence, mostly because I didn't trust myself not to do something stupid, like kiss her or yell at her. I was angry that she accepted a job here, with her qualifications; it was an insult to her hard work and intelligence. With the shirt, she was wearing she might as well have been working at some sleazy strip joint. I was angry that she lowered her standards and angry that she was putting herself in a position to be manhandled. I realized that we hadn't spoken at all until I heard her soft voice, and all my anger from the night just spewed out on her.

I was pissed at myself for putting her in this position to begin with, that I felt anything for her already and I had only seen her twice. I was pissed that I didn't hurt the asshole who touched her ass. I was just angry, and she caught the storm brewing inside of me. I watched her face twist in pain after I told her to leave. I hated the heavy rise and fall of her chest as she worked to contain her tears when I told her that I owned half the bar. I hated the realization that sunk in when her shoulders slumped as I told her to get out.

I didn't want her here, maybe I could have calmly told her that, but I didn't, I just yelled at her. And I knew that I went too far. I couldn't do anything to stop it, I had to get her out of the bar before I lost it. Letting her hate me would be worth it. Fuck it; I planned to fix it later, when I'd offer her the job at my bar. I just had to hope she'd hear me out, but even if she declined it, I wouldn't have to see her again.

. . .

AFTER HELPING BRENDA CLOSE THE BAR, I HEADED HOME. IT was a little past two in the morning, and I wished that I had driven my Tahoe instead of my bike because it was loud, and having kids had made me considerate of my neighbors. I clenched my teeth as I wheeled into the driveway and pulled out the garage opener from my backpack. I cut the engine and walked inside.

I crept through the door leading into the house, quietly sat down in one of the kitchen chairs, and took off my boots and jacket. After Ramsey left the bar, I couldn't stop replaying the look on her face. She hated me. I lowered my head into my hands and let out a sigh. I really screwed things up, just like I normally did. That was the reason Lisa left, after all. I could still picture that damn note, taped to our bedroom mirror.

"JIMMY, I CAN'T DO THIS ANYMORE. NOT WITH YOU, NOT WITH the kids. I thought I wanted this life, the Brass, all of it... I was raised to want it but when you went to jail, I realized I want more. I'm not strong enough to love you through all that you'll face as a member. I'm too afraid of being alone. I hope my absence inspires you to be the best person you can be for the kids and for yourself. Don't hate me, but I never wanted this, I have dreams and if I stay here any longer, I know I will never see those dreams come to life. - Lisa"

FIVE YEARS HAVE GONE BY, AND YES, I WAS A SHITTY MAN BACK then. I landed in jail for three months for losing my temper at a bar, Sammy was only a few months old then. Aside from the hurt she caused me by leaving, and the agony she caused our daughter who ended up blaming herself for her mother's absence, I still had a hard time grasping that Lisa had pinned

55

her getaway on me. It took quite a few counseling sessions to let that shit go and become the father I am now. Yet, here I was screwing up again.

I ran my hands through my hair a few more times before getting up and grabbing a glass of water. I set my it down on the counter and started heading for the stairs when I heard a click and saw the corner of the living room illuminate. Dad rubbed his eyes from the oversized chair he dozed in. I stood there awkwardly for a second, hoping like a little kid that he might fall back asleep. I didn't want to talk about the fact that I just fired Ramsey, with him. He yawned, slowly getting to his feet, stretching before he walked towards me.

"Son, you just getting in?"

I just nodded my response, the words were stuck in my throat, along with my admission. He looked back up at the clock, then at me again, a look of confusion and worry crossed his face. "Everything go okay at the bar?"

I faced him and crossed my arms. "Actually, no. I walked in on your new employee getting grabbed on by a customer, twice. She didn't seem to have control over the situation at all, so I helped and ended up letting her go after the crowds died down. I don't think that bar is really her scene."

I brought my hand to my neck and I didn't even have the balls to look him in the face while I spouted off the nonsense, so my gaze fell on the floor instead. Then I even had the audacity to yawn and try to move past him and say goodnight. "Well, Dad, I'm…"

He cut me off, waving his hands and shaking his head like he was trying to erase what he just heard. "No, no, no, you didn't fire that sweet girl. You couldn't! Even you have more of a heart than that!"

He raised his voice on the tail end of his comment and my stomach sank. I knew this was going to be hard, but honestly, why did he care so much?

"Dad, you weren't there, trust me, that bar isn't the right place for her," I tried to argue with him.

He glowered at me, with his hands on his hips. "I don't care, son. I handpicked her, and it's my bar. I expect you to make this right. Unless you plan on giving her the position at your bar, do you hear me? Either way, that poor girl is going to be employed!"

He was yelling again, and I was flinching because if Sammy woke up, then I wouldn't get any sleep. He would want to sleep in my bed, and he was a kicker.

"Okay Dad, I promise. After this weekend, I will fix it," I said in a hushed tone, so he would remember that the kids were asleep.

He gasped like he couldn't believe what he just heard. "You aren't letting that girl live with this kind of thing all weekend, you will fix it first thing in the morning!"

I wasn't exactly sure how I managed to feel like a twelve-year-old boy getting caught sneaking in after curfew, but that was exactly how I felt. I placed both hands behind my head and ran my fingers down my scalp, blowing out all the extra air in my lungs. "Okay, first thing tomorrow."

With that, I made my way around him and started up the stairs. I couldn't look at him anymore and see that look in his eyes; it was the same disappointment he had when he came to see me in jail for the first time. Or the look he gave me on my wedding day…

Dad walked into my bedroom, the one at his house that Mom had turned into an office. I looked in a full-length mirror as I straightened my tie and caught Dad's reflection in the mirror. He looked sad, had his hands shoved in his pockets, almost like I was heading towards a funeral, not a wedding. We stood silently until he asked, "Does she shine for you, son?"

My chest tightened, because I remember swearing that the day I got married, it would be to my 'glimmer.' Lisa wasn't my glimmer, she didn't shine for me, but we were having a kid together. I was a screw-up who needed to make an honest woman out of her. I turned to face Dad and walked past him while I muttered, "She shines enough."

Then I left to marry the woman who would later abandon me and my children.

I hated letting him down, and for some reason, he was protecting the hell out of Ramsey. Yet one more sign from the universe that Ramsey was special, and I shouldn't have treated her the way I did. Now I had to figure out exactly what I was going to say to her to try and make up for the complete asshole I was to her at the bar.

SIX

BRIGHT RAYS of sunshine danced across my closed eyelids. It was nice, warm, and inviting. It was the kind of sunshine you'd feel closer to midday, not early morning. I cracked my eyes open and scanned the room; indeed, the white light coming in was not from the early morning sun. *Shit, it had to be late.* I fumbled for my phone to check the time.

"Twelve thirty? That can't be right," I wondered out loud while looking around my room. The 'Are you still watching?' Screen was still displayed on the TV from my Netflix binge the night before, and the big pile of clothes on the floor that I kept promising myself I'd go through was all lit up with the afternoon glow. Wow, I had really slept in past noon. I made a sound that came out like a scoff, or a disappointed laugh and laid back down. *Screw this day and everyone in it.*

I was pulling one of my large pillows over my face when I realized that my mother should have woken me up.

Panic surged through me.

She'd never let me sleep in this late. Cancer or not, she would always come into my room and start 'cleaning' if I slept past nine thirty. I jumped up from the ball of blankets that I was tangled in and made my way into the hallway. I began charging towards the other side of the house, where my mom slept.

"Mom?!" I yelled, hoping to hear her tender voice soothe my worry.

What if something happened? What if I could have helped her? My throat was starting to close as I thought about what could have happened to her or why she hadn't woken me, and why I'd overslept, to begin with. I winced as I remembered last night's disaster. I couldn't sleep. I tried. It wasn't like I wanted that pathetic mess running like a bad TV marathon in my head.

I was desperate to settle my mind, so I turned on *The Office* and drowned my sorrows in the hilarious life of Michael Scott while I ate dry Captain Crunch from the box. Sleep must have claimed me at some point because I was just now waking up and it was already noon. *Freaking noon!* I've never slept in this long, not even after a game. The panic and concern for why my mother didn't wake me surged back with full force and filtered into every hard-footed stomp I made towards the living room.

"Mom?" There was still no answer, but then I heard my mother giggle. I knew it was her because, she did a little snort at the end. Then I heard a male laugh, not a giggle, but a deep tenor laugh, husky if you will. It made my arms erupt with goose bumps, like my body was warning me to get the hell out of there. I slowed my pace and started creeping down the hall while moving my head carefully around the corner until I could see.

The only problem was, once I was able to see, I realized too late that whoever the laughing stranger was would be able to see me as well. My mom was looking at me like I was a deranged lunatic, and my brain slowed down, and heart stopped as I took in the other face. Jimmy the Jerk couldn't actually be sitting in my living room. Except that he was.

Jimmy stopped talking to my mother and slowly stood, his blue jeans straightened, and his dark green shirt pulled tight against his chest with the movement. *That color shirt matches his eyes.* Shit, I shouldn't notice that. All those tattoos were hidden by the blue zip-up sweatshirt he wore.

Jimmy the Fist. I thought of what I had heard last night at the bar and wondered how accurate the rumors about him were. My eyes lingered on the barely visible black scrawl that climbed up his neck. *I wonder what it says?* I hated that I noticed that damn tattoo again, or how he looked. I hated even more that I liked how he looked.

My mother cleared her throat while staring daggers at me. Her eyes squinted, and her lips thinned into a line. I followed her angry gaze and realized it was zoned in on my chest. I knew that look; it was the same look she gave me growing up when I wanted to wear ripped jeans to church or a spaghetti-strapped tank. I quickly looked down at what had offended her and saw that I was wearing a neon green tank top with the letters 'STD' printed on the front. A hilarious college joke from the student tech department, which at the moment wasn't funny, and I suppose neither was the fact that I had charged down the hallway in boy shorts underwear.

I instinctively pulled the hem of my tank down to cover my legs, but it caused the scoop neck of the tank to dip further. My mother's eyes jumped to my face then my boobs. Shit, I wasn't even wearing a bra.

This was a nightmare.

I glanced at Jimmy the Jerk for a second to see if maybe he was looking away or doing anything to help me through this awkward moment, but when I caught his gaze, his green eyes drilled into mine. He was standing with his hands in his pockets, feet spread apart, and his jaw locked in place. I didn't look away; I wanted to challenge him, see how long he'd watch me. I quirked my brow as his stare roamed down the length of my body.

I withheld the urge to pull a Vanna White and move my hand vertically along my half-naked body, as if it were some prize. *Take it all in buddy; you'll never see this train wreck again.* My mom moved to stand, then approached me slowly.

"Ramsey, you're finally awake."

I gave her a tight-lipped smile while I moved my arms to my chest, I had given up on the hemline. I refused to think about my hair, or face, or how either of them currently looked. My mother gently touched my arm as she looked back towards Jimmy. I noticed that his blond hair was neatly combed to the side, and as much as I didn't want to admit it, he looked good —really good. I studied the way his long hair on top fell across his forehead. I wanted to push it off his face and run my fingers through it.

What the hell? I hated him. I needed to remember that I hated this man. *But even villains can have great hair.*

Speaking of villains, I could feel my face finally catch up to the shame of being seen like this by my new mortal enemy. His stare was still cold, calculated, and frustrating. He wasn't looking away from me or moving to leave. I could only imagine the things he thought of me now. *No, I didn't give a shit what he thought of me.* I just wanted him gone, both out of my house and out of my life. The anger that was so dominant from the night before started to surface again.

"What are *you* doing here?" I seethed, trying so hard to keep my anger in check. I wanted to scream at him, shout, possibly throw something. Whatever it took to get through his stupid, beautiful head that I didn't want him here. His face paled and he shifted on his feet. He seemed like he was struggling for a response.

Finally, he managed to get out, "I came here to talk to you.

Could we go somewhere, uh, private, like the kitchen or something?"

I liked that he was nervous and stammering like an idiot. Mom took that as her cue and yawned, then gently closed the space between us and kissed my cheek.

"It's time for my afternoon nap, sweetie." She looked at Jimmy and smiled wider than I have ever seen her smile. *Traitor.* "Jimmy, it was nice to meet you. I look forward to seeing you again."

He smiled back at her and nodded. "Same here, Ms. Carla, thank you for the iced tea."

So, it was possible for him to be nice. Who knew?

Jimmy's gaze cut back to me, and the smile he gave my mom fell away from his lips. He watched me with a measured reluctance, like he was waiting for me to make my move. I wouldn't give him the satisfaction. My arms were still crossed, and my spine was straight as an arrow. I refused to look weak in front of him. Messy, crazy, and possibly like a hoarder, but not weak.

He looked down at the carpet, pulled his hands from his pockets, and placed them on his hips like he was thinking. "Ramsey, look, I'm..."

I put my hand up to stop him before my brain could even catch up. *Fight or flight, I was going to fight.* I was already on edge, and since I refused to give him the chance to explain, or the benefit of the doubt, I stopped him from speaking. He would get nothing from me, not even the courtesy of me hearing him out.

"Jimmy, let me stop you there. I don't know why you came to my house, why you didn't take the fact that I was asleep as a cue to not come inside, and to leave me the hell alone. But I don't want you here, and I don't want to talk to you, so please leave."

He looked shocked, his eyes wide and his lips parted. He

had one hand on his hip, and the other out, like he was waiting for a low five or just still frozen from trying to talk. Then he began to rub his jaw. He coughed before he replied, "look, I know I have been a bit of a jerk, but just give me a chance to explain."

My arms grew tight as I pulled them closer to my chest, like armor. "No thanks, Jimmy, I don't need to hear you explain. Your actions have spoken louder than any words you could possibly utter. I won't go back to Theo's, and I won't go back to your bar. As far as I am concerned, our business dealings are done. We can both act like we never met each other, I don't want to see you again after this. If you see me in the store, go the other way, don't say hi to me, just leave me alone."

I paused, looking down, and gathered what strength I had left to kick the man out. I had never been this mean or forceful with another human being before, so it all felt like a rush. I lifted my head and stared straight through him as I said, "Please let yourself out."

I turned and walked back down the hallway, shut myself in my bedroom, and waited to hear him leave. As I paced by the window, I found my phone and began sifting through the text messages that had come in that morning. I had two new numbers who texted me, one was from Jimmy, the first coming in at nine a.m.

HEY, IT'S JIMMY STENSON. I GOT YOUR NUMBER FROM YOUR *resume, I need to talk to you. Would it be okay if we met somewhere?*

THEN ANOTHER AT TEN A.M.

HEY, I KNOW YOU'RE PROBABLY PRETTY UPSET ABOUT LAST NIGHT,

I would be too. I really need to talk to you about it though, please call me or text me where we can meet up.

THEN, THE LAST ONE, AT NOON.

OKAY, I ALSO GOT YOUR ADDRESS FROM YOUR RESUME. I AM coming over. See you in a few.

I WAS SUCH AN IDIOT. WHY WAS TODAY THE DAY THAT I SLEPT like the dead? I could have met him on neutral ground and possibly avoided looking like an emotional basket case, yet again in front of him. I looked back down at my phone and saw the other text was from Theo. All it said was: *Babysitting tonight. Address is 1256 NW Tenth St - Come by around 6:15.*

Theo probably didn't know that his business partner had fired me. Guess I needed this babysitting gig more than ever now.

I leaned my head against the window and texted Theo back: *See you then.*

SEVEN

JIMMY

I STORMED out of Ramsey's house, angry and pissed off. I didn't know why I had pictured her listening to me, maybe forgiving me. I originally didn't want to see her, and only planned to talk to her after the weekend, but the more I thought about it, or *her* rather, the more I realized that dad was right. I needed to fix things. But more than that, for some reason, I *wanted* to fix things with her.

I got on my bike and carefully pulled out of the driveway. I might have been angry, but not angry enough to disrespect Carla by spitting gravel everywhere. I actually enjoyed spending the half-hour with Ramsey's mom on the couch, drinking tea and talking about Ramsey.

I was a little panicked when Carla told me that Ramsey was only sleeping so long because she was stressed out.

I asked what she was stressed about, hoping it didn't have anything to do with me.

She sweetly declared, "It's the cancer. It's in my liver, but it's no matter because Jesus will heal it."

I didn't even know how to respond, but I had respect for Ramsey, taking care of her mom like that. She didn't run when things got hard, she turned around and embraced it; that was something insanely attractive to me.

I DECIDED TO BLOW OFF SOME STEAM AND TURN LEFT, TOWARD the back side of Belvidere, instead of turning right towards my house. I needed to clear my head, and riding was the best way for me to do it. As I rode, I felt more at peace, less angry, and as the frustration surrounding Ramsey left, something else took its place. I couldn't get the picture of Ramsey coming out of her room, wearing practically nothing, out of my head.

She was beautiful. Her chocolate hair was bundled on top of her head, but she had these tendrils falling all around her neck, and it made me want to walk over and brush them behind her ear. Her eyes were a mess of blue water colors, hidden behind a dark rim of smudged mascara and eye makeup. Something had physically shifted in me at the sight of her. Something I hadn't felt or wanted in a long time. Something dangerous.

I knew I was in trouble when all I could think of, when I first saw her standing there in her pajamas, was how perfect she would look coming down the stairs of my house like that. With messy hair and that cute little outfit, moving through my house on a Saturday morning, making coffee. I pictured those bare feet on my hardwood floors, and those long, lean legs curled up on my couch. It was a miracle that I didn't walk her back towards her room to have our conversation, because everything in me wanted to tell her exactly how sorry I was, just not with words.

Talking with Carla answered a few questions that I had about Ramsey. She told me that Ramsey was single, she didn't have any kids, and she still had several friends back in Chicago, but none local, except for a friend named Theo that she had recently met.

I didn't explain that Theo was my dad. It sounded like Ramsey was lonely here in Belvidere and that revelation made me reflective. She didn't party or go out every weekend. She spent most of her nights at home and in bed before nine at night, according to Carla. It was like she was reading my invisible dream journal for my future wife. My heart beat a little faster at the thought of finding someone with substance.

I LOOPED BACK AROUND TO THE FIRST EXIT OF THE CITY AND started to make my way back home.

I continued down the street and waved at a few neighbors, and as usual, they shook their heads in disappointment. They didn't approve of the bike, and they really didn't approve of me not wearing a helmet. They might have a point, but most of the appeal of a bike was getting to feel the wind on your face.

I parked the bike in the garage, putting it away for the evening. Stopping in my office, I checked my email. I was about to head upstairs when my phone rang.

"Hey, what's up, Rav?" I asked, while pulling off my boots.

"Hey, boss." Rav hesitated, which caused me to pause.

"What is it?"

He cleared his throat before continuing. "I got a call today..." He paused again. I waited and another big sigh of reluctance followed. "It was Davis. He said to tell you he has something you've been looking for."

My gut tightened. I hadn't heard anything from Davis or the Brass since I left five years ago. I was still technically a part of the club, and I knew it was just a matter of time before they called me up, but I hoped it wouldn't be so soon. I grappled with all the thoughts at war in my head as Rav spoke up.

"You ok, boss?"

I shut my eyes and tried to focus.

"Yeah, just thinking, is all."

Davis may be the leader of the Brass and a twisted son of a bitch but for all his evil and contorted faults, lying wasn't one of them. Which meant he knew about the search for my ex-wife and likely my lack of information regarding her where-abouts. If he wanted a meeting with me, then he wanted more than I would be willing to pay for the information. But I had been searching for over two years, and if he knew anything, then I needed to meet with him. I realized that Rav was waiting for my response.

"Thanks, Rav. Go ahead and set up the meeting."

"You got it, boss." Rav hung up the call and I rested my face in my hands, hoping I wasn't making a colossal mistake.

THE REST OF THE AFTERNOON WENT BY FAIRLY QUICK. I TOOK the kids to the park and played soccer; Sammy really needed to work on his penalty kicks. Once we got home, the kids settled and started watching some cartoons in the living room, but dad was nowhere to be found. I checked the clock and saw that it was already after five, so I reluctantly ran upstairs and jumped in the shower, afterwhich I stood in my walk-in closet and stared at its contents. The glow from the light in the ceiling cast just enough light for me to see a variety of blue, gray, and white dress shirts. I had somewhat of a large selection of shoes on the rack below.

Owning a bar had widened my wardrobe considerably but still, I sifted through each one with reluctance. None of it felt right, I didn't want to give Sarah the wrong impression. I'd agreed to go on a date with her, but I didn't have plans to pursue anything with her past tonight. I winced at how much of a bitter asshole I'd become, but it was true. Plus, it didn't feel right to try and impress Sarah when my thoughts hadn't left Ramsey. Which was concerning. Why the hell did I care about

Ramsey? She wasn't exactly pleasant today, and didn't even give me a chance to explain myself. I should be glad that I wouldn't be seeing her anymore. Bringing my hand to my neck, I let out a sigh and settled on a black t-shirt, blue blazer, and some nice jeans.

I checked the time again and saw that it was already past six. I opened my door and started to jog downstairs. Dad was in the dining room, trying to fix his tie. I guess he was trying to look nice tonight, although he swears he'd never try to pick up on the ladies down at the bingo hall. I went over to help him when I heard the doorbell ring. I figured it was the babysitter, so I started towards the door. Just as I took a step, dad put his arm out and physically pushed me to the ground, and ran past me. *What the hell?*

I LAY THERE, TRYING TO FIGURE OUT WHY MY DAD JUST DID that, when I heard voices. I vaguely recognized the first voice, which came through soft and sweet. The other, of course, was dad's, then I heard the high-pitched squeal of excitement coming from my kids. A stampede of small thumps resonated through my floorboards as they ran toward the door where the babysitter was. It took me a second to realize what name not one, but both, of them were screaming. Then all at once, as clear as day, I finally registered the words.

"*Ramsey! Ramsey!*" I jumped up and turned my head towards the door, but dad and the kids were blocking my view. My mind was racing, there was no way that it could be her. Then the bodies broke apart and I saw her.

She was wearing a patterned sundress, that looked kind of bohemian, and over her shoulders was a small jean jacket. Her hair was in a messy, long, beautiful braid, with tiny pieces framing her face. She was here, in my house, and she was dragging Sammy on her leg; he was wrapped around her like a koala bear. Jasmine smiled so big that I thought her face might break. The two girls were already deep in conversation about hair and something that sounded like "interest."

Ramsey's eyes were locked onto Jasmine's, so she hadn't had a chance to see me yet. She continued to carry Sammy further inside, I wanted to hide, but realized it was my house, and my kids, and at some point, she might need to meet me, the dad. So, I just stood there and waited for the shit to hit the fan, because it most definitely would when she noticed me.

My guess was that she had no clue these kids were mine, or that the babysitting gig she agreed to do for her beloved Theo was actually for me. How did my kids already know her? None of this made sense, but shit, I liked the look of this woman in my house, and with my kids. She had no idea what she was doing to me right now.

Once she made her way into the living room, Sammy jumped up and walked over to me. Jasmine was still talking Ramsey's ear off, but as Sammy got my attention, Jasmine noticed and stopped talking. Ramsey's eyes left Jasmine's and found mine. Her body lurched to a stop and froze.

Her eyes went big, and I could tell that her breathing had become erratic. Sammy grabbed my hand, and then hers, and looked between us. She was still frozen. Sammy spoke up in his cute little voice and said, "Dad, this is Ramsey, our friend. She has a funny name, but she is really nice and likes to play hide and seek."

He let go of our hands and ran off, then we were left standing with Jasmine between us... Until my Dad called her into the kitchen.

Ramsey just stood there and looked at me, and I did the same to her until she whispered, "Is this some kind of sick joke?"

She sounded hurt.

I shook my head. "I didn't know you were the babysitter

Theo hired. I swear I wouldn't do that to you. You made your-self clear this morning," I tried to reassure her.

She crossed her arms over her chest again. Her eyes roamed my house as her face turned red. I noticed her foot had started tapping too.

I stepped a little closer, slowly, like I was approaching a dangerous animal, and cautiously said, "Look, I get that you didn't know what you were walking into here. Let's just call this whole thing off and you can go home. I wasn't really…"

She countered in a panicked voice, stopping me mid-sentence, "No. I already told Jasmine and Sammy that I would be here!"

Well, shit. She was just claiming more and more of me by the second.

I smiled at her, and then forced my body to take a step back, so I didn't make her nervous.

"Okay, then if you don't mind staying and still doing this, I can go over some basics with you."

She unfolded her arms and seemed more comfortable. She stopped tapping her foot and gave me a solid nod of agree-ment. I turned towards the living room and walked over to the coffee table.

"This controls the TV and volume. The kids have their own profiles set up on Netflix, whatever you do, don't ask which one you should use. Just choose mine and select a kid's movie from the search bar," I informed her and went to move on when she held up her hand.

"Yes? You don't need to raise your hand, by the way," I clarified for her. She just lifted one of her perfectly shaped eyebrows at me in question.

"Why do you give them their own profiles if they aren't allowed to use them?"

I considered her question and felt the slightest irritation at her tone, and suggestion that I didn't know what I was doing. Or maybe I was just sensitive.

I cleared my throat. "Because it makes them happy to have their own." That's all I was going to say because I wasn't ready to talk about how they would try to impress her with their very own kid's profile or how Jasmine and Sammy would spend a ridiculous amount of time showing her the type of shows they liked. I wouldn't go there because, to my kids, having people accept them and like them was a big deal, and I didn't want to give Ramsey any pointers. She could learn those things about my kids herself. *Why did I care?*

I left the remotes where they were and walked around the coffee table, through the living room. We walked upstairs together and stopped at the top. I gestured with my hand towards the first door on the right and told her, "this one is Sammy's room, he will need to go to bed no later than ten." Then I walked forward a bit and signaled to the door directly across the hall on the left. "Here's Jasmine's room, they both have the same bedtime." I noticed that she looked anywhere that I gestured with my hands, but she wouldn't look at me.

Once we were back downstairs, I pulled out the emergency card with the kids' info on it.

"Here's my dad's cell phone number." Ramsey glared at the card, then cut a glance towards the kitchen where my dad was standing out of sight.

"Your dad?" She looked confused by the way she rubbed at her temple, frustrated. "You're James?" She asked accusingly, like she'd just heard of a legend or myth. I nodded slowly; no one had called me James since I was a teenager.

"I prefer Jimmy," was all I eluded to. Her eyebrows drew together, and her lips thinned as she glanced one more time towards the kitchen.

"Anyway, the kids don't have any allergies, but they won't eat any kind of pizza but pepperoni, so just save yourself the headache and order that." I eyed her carefully as she stood holding her elbow, watching the table.

"I'm taking my date to a local place nearby, so just text me if you need anything or have any questions," I finished, placing a twenty-dollar bill on the table for pizza.

She pulled her bottom lip in between her teeth, and I was nearly paralyzed by the movement. She didn't seem to be thinking about what she was doing. She cut another glance back towards the kitchen, then back towards the table. As I put my wallet back in my jacket, she finally spoke up.

"I don' t know of any pizza places around here. You'll need to tell me which one you usually go through." She was still watching the table, then sliced another glance towards the kitchen.

I was getting frustrated. She wouldn't look at me, and I didn't want to come off as an asshole again. So, I just decided to put an end to this whole thing, and walked into the kitchen with her on my heels.

Dad was on his phone, talking with someone, when his eyes went big watching Ramsey behind me. I looked back to see her face; it had twisted into something cruel and her eyes had transitioned into something deadly. Dad quickly ended his call and placed his hands up, like he was surrendering.

"Now, Ramsey, hang on a sec, honey. Let me explain," dad pleaded with her, but it was in vain.

"Please Theo, tell me another cute story about your son, James. I'd love to hear more, but maybe you should wait until he fires me again or turns me down for another job interview. I'm sure it's bound to happen again soon." Ramsey's voice was a bit shaky, like she might be on the verge of tears, or just really pissed and nearly ready to kill my dad. I winced at her words as she included me in her rant.

Dad looked down at the counter as red filled his cheeks. He was ashamed. If Ramsey knew who my dad was, knew who he was in the Brass, knew who the Ripper was, then she'd appreciate this moment so much more. Dad was about to say something again, but Ramsey spun on her heels and walked back towards the living room. I watched my dad as he eyed Ramsey's retreating form and quirked an eyebrow at him. Serves him right for trying to play matchmaker.

I turned to try and find Ramsey, hoping to smooth things over with her, when Sammy ran into the room, screaming, "Pizza, pizza, give me some pepperoni pizza!"

He was throwing his arms out on either side of him, like he was trying to stop traffic. I walked back through the house, with Sammy attached to my arm, to where Ramsey was sitting in the living room. She said she wanted to spend the evening with the kids, and had that look on her face, like if I told her to leave, she'd fall apart. Choosing to let her stay, regardless of how upset she seemed, choosing to trust a perfect stranger with my kids, I grabbed my keys, hugged the kids, and walked out the front door. Praying, and hoping yet again, that I hadn't just made a huge mistake.

EIGHT

I should have known. Ever since driving to Jimmy's bar and having my bizarre interview with him, it feels like I can't seem to shake him. That feeling only proved to be correct as I stood on the doorstep of Theo's house. Theo, the scoundrel. His omission about James felt like a betrayal and honestly, a cruel joke. Why wasn't he just honest about Jimmy being his son? Then knowing Jimmy would come to his bar last night. What a bunch of jerks. I let out a long sigh and stood up from the couch. The kids were outside and barreling their way to the screen door.

I pushed all my frustrations aside and focused on having a good time with them. They might have drawn the short straws for a grandfather and dad, but that wasn't their fault.

I headed into the kitchen to call in the pizza order, then went to find the kids. They were both in the living room, watching some show about teenagers who were also superheroes. I stood against the archway of the kitchen for a second, watching them together. They laughed and joked as they watched the show, while they both pretended to use superpowers on each other. I silently wondered what it would have been like to grow up like that. With someone to play with, someone to laugh with, and shoulder the heavy burdens of life with. I grew up completely alone. I had no one, except my mom.

Shoving past the emotions that were swelling up, I walked towards the couch. Jasmine smiled up at me from the floor and asked expectantly, "hair time?"

I smiled and nodded my head, crawling behind her. Thankfully, my dress was floor-length and stretchy, so I easily crossed my legs and sat behind her head. I brushed out her whole head of hair, then began gathering a few strands together in the front of her head and worked my way to the back. She sat patiently and would only speak to ask me a few off-handed questions here and there that made me laugh.

One was, "Do you have a husband? Or a boyfriend?"

I laughed at her blunt nature; it was kind of refreshing.

I replied with a little humor, and drew out my syllables, "no to either one."

She let out a sigh that sounded like relief, then she asked me another question, "so if you were to have a husband, what would you want him to look like?"

I hated that the first person who came to my mind was her dad, Jimmy the gorgeous jerk himself. I shrugged my shoulders, even though she couldn't see it. "I don't know, I haven't thought about it," I lied and kept pace with braiding her hair as I continued, "I'm not too picky, as long as he has long arms to wrap around me, and a big heart to keep me, I am a happy girl."

She seemed to let out a sigh and forcefully flipped a page in her notebook, crossing out a line of words. I looked down and noticed that she was writing my answers down in a journal. I smiled at the notion. So, freaking cute. She continued with her questioning, not satisfied with how I answered, "but if you had to be specific, would you want someone with dark hair or light hair?"

I gathered a few more strands of hair and decided I would play her game, I had a fairly good idea where she was going with this. "I like light hair, but not too light, it has to be a combination of both," I said with a smile.

She wrote something down, then asked, "do you have an eye color preference?"

I laughed out loud, and replied, "Jasmine, are you trying to find me a date?"

She dropped her head and I could hear the embarrassment in her voice when she answered, "no, not at all, I just thought maybe I could find someone you might like if I wrote down all the things you like in a boy...or a man, I guess."

I smiled, letting out a big breath, and responded with, "Well, when you're grown up, you stop looking at how they look as much as you notice how they act and treat people. That is what I would look for in a man, Jasmine. If he treated me like gold, but looked like a troll, I might just marry him."

She seemed defeated, then responded with, "Kind of like Beauty and the Beast?"

I bent my head down and kissed her cheek, and said, "Exactly!"

I heard the doorbell ring, signaling dinner had arrived, and I jumped up to grab the pizza.

We ate our huge slices outside on the back porch because there was still a warmth that lingered in the air from summer. Jasmine kept her journal with her, and asked a few more silly questions, writing them down. Sammy finished his pizza, with sauce smeared across his face, then jumped down and begged me to play hide and seek.

"Ramsey, you promised me, now you stay here and count, I am going to go hide and blow your mind," he said excitedly before running back inside.

God, this kid was hilarious. I did exactly as I was told. I counted to one hundred and then went inside. I found Sammy hiding on top of the laundry room shelf, and the few times after that were pretty easy, but then it got a bit more challenging. Like when he hid in the dryer and shut the door. *Talk about heart attack.* Or the time he shoved his small body into the crevice between the wall and the fridge. Every time I found him, I would scream out, "Got you, hamburglar, now give me all your cheeseburgers!" Then I would tickle him.

Jasmine was laughing so hard at how hard Sammy would laugh that she finally wanted to join us, and I would do the same thing to her every time I found her.

Playing hide and seek while babysitting somewhere new was always fun because it gave me the chance to snoop in any room of the house. I always liked to do this when I was a teenager, because it made me feel better to know that there were no secret torture rooms or creepy rooms filled with dolls. I didn't feel the slightest bit bad about snooping, if it was just looking, and not actually going through people's things.

I quietly crept upstairs and pushed open Sammy's door.

"Sammy?" I whispered while I lifted his Captain America blanket that had fallen off the side of his bed. I peered underneath, he wasn't there, but neither was much of anything else. What kind of kid didn't have junk under his bed? My own bed at the moment had at least fifteen pairs of shoes, two dinner plates, and half a dozen socks. I shuddered at the image I had of my own room. I needed to clean, and promptly, because a six-year-old was showing me up, and that was just bad form.

I stood and looked around Sammy's room, appreciating the cleanliness but also how nicely it all was decorated. His room was inundated with all types of Captain America paraphernalia. Curtains, pillows, posters—it was a big mass of red, white, and blue, with a hint of gray. I pulled his long curtains back to confirm he wasn't hiding there, then moved to his closet.

Clean, organized, little clutter. Still no Sammy. I left his room and ventured towards Jasmine's, and began inspecting the purple and pink room like I did his.

"Sammy, are you in here?" I asked, while pulling back the clothes in Jasmine's closet. Her room had a variety of animal posters everywhere and her bed was covered in a large pink comforter. I checked under her bed, and again found it neatly-organized with a storage tote, and a few Barbie containers. Sammy wasn't there. I headed towards the last room down the hall.

I was nervous to look in Jimmy's room. I stood at his door and waited. Did I want to see where he slept? Where he dressed? It felt like such an invasion of privacy to a man that I had vowed to hate. I looked around the hallway again, then pushed the door open.

"Sammy, little man, are you in here? Please don't make me look through your dad's room," I pleaded, while my eyes moved around the room. Bright light filled the space, even from the sun nearly setting. A large, king-sized bed sat in the middle of the room with a dark mahogany wood frame, covered in a white duvet. *Interesting.* I wouldn't have pegged him for a white sheets kind of guy. I moved closer to the bed and ran my fingers along the soft covers while scanning the rest of the room. Black and white canvas photos of Jasmine and Sammy covered one wall near the window, and a large over-stuffed chair sat in the corner. A flat screen TV sat on top of his mahogany dresser. I walked further into his room until I was standing in his walk-in closet. *Holy hell.* Jimmy had style, and an insane amount of clothes and shoes.

"Sammy?" I yelled again, just in case someone walked in. I left the walk-in closet and sauntered into his master bathroom, wishing immediately that I hadn't. Big was the only word that came to me. Big bathtub, big shower, big space, just big. The whole bathroom was bigger than my entire bedroom. Why did such a mean person get such a nice bathroom? It didn't seem fair or right. What was worse was how impeccably clean it was. Maybe he had a maid because what I knew of men, was that they were messy. I glanced behind his toilet, no grime or stray hair. My ex was a pig and left his beard hair all over the place after he shaved. There was no way that Jimmy was this clean. I refused to believe it.

"Ramseeeeeeey? You give up?" I heard the faint sound of Sammy's voice coming from somewhere down the hall. I ran back through the room and shut Jimmy's door behind me. I flung open the hall closet door and there, on the top shelf, was Sammy folded in half, giggling uncontrollably. He jumped into my arms, then we made our way downstairs. I headed towards my favorite room in the house; the kitchen. I loved his kitchen.

I loved the huge island where the kids sat while I searched the cupboards for plates. They giggled at me as I opened and shut at least three before I located the mismatched set below the silverware drawer. *Who puts plates in a bottom cabinet?* I loved the corner breakfast nook that had large windows around it. I loved more than just the poorly-organized kitchen, I loved the entire house. The large, spacious living room that was big enough to fit an entire baseball team inside. It was exactly the kind of home that I would want if I had a family...a husband. I knew that I should stop with those thoughts, especially associating Jimmy's perfect home with my dream home, but I couldn't seem to stop myself.

You just met him, and he fired you… twice… Kind of.

After we played three different variations of tag for about an hour, I made the kids get their showers over with. While they did, I had the chance to reflect on what happened between Jimmy and me earlier that morning. He wanted to talk, to explain himself. What did that mean? I hated that I was regretting not hearing him out. Hated that I hoped he'd give me another chance to listen. I had found fresh flowers beside our couch where he was sitting, after he left. He brought me flowers, and I didn't even give him the chance to give them to me. I've never actually been given flowers before, not even by any of my old boyfriends. Face in my hands, I mentally battled what to do. Guilt tugged at me inside and hope blossomed in my chest when I pictured seeing Jimmy again. Why was there hope? What was happening to me?

"Ughhhhhh, this is stupid." I sagged against the wall and slid to the floor. Pride was telling me to stand my ground, but loneliness pulled at me to forgive.

I needed to apologize so I could keep seeing his kids, if they wanted to see me that was. I'd even be willing to forgive Theo. I wanted friends, people in my life, who might help me shoulder the burden of losing my mother. It was settled. I was going to apologize. I didn't know if Jimmy would accept it, but maybe we could start being friends? Acquaintances? I didn't know, maybe nothing, just not enemies.

Sammy's loud singing had stopped at the same time as the water. Jasmine was already in her pajamas and was headed out of her room with a brush and some small rubber bands. We sat down, and I braided her hair into two, symmetrical, braids down her back. Then Sammy came out of the bathroom in matching Batman pajamas, his hair was in the shape of a Mohawk, and he was smiling like he just made the funniest joke.

ONCE WE WERE ALL READY, I GATHERED SOME BLANKETS AND told the kids to follow me outside to the trampoline.

We crawled on and snuggled under blankets while we stargazed and talked about the Avengers being aliens. Then, out of nowhere, Sammy asked, "If moms leave their families, do they still get to go to heaven?"

I stayed silent for a second and didn't exactly know what to say, so I redirected with, "Do you think moms who leave their families should get to go to heaven?"

I rolled over to watch him; this was such dangerous territory. I didn't know anything about their mom except that she wasn't here, but the topic of her felt like a landmine. Sammy let out a big breath and said, "I think so. I think everyone should be able to go to heaven. Right?"

I smiled at how sweet this kid was, then responded, "Yeah buddy, I think you're right."

He smiled, looked at me, and said, "I wish you could be my mom, Miss Ramsey."

"Shut up, Sammy!" Jasmine yelled. *Oh crap.*

If I could make a stealthy exit, I would. Instead, I stayed silent. I didn't know what to say. Thankfully, I didn't have to say anything because I heard a door shut from inside the house and then a figure filled the doorway leading to the backyard. The shadow, that I already knew was Jimmy, started walking towards us. I heard his smooth voice ask...*Normal voice, Ramsey...*

"Is there room for one more on that thing?"

THE KIDS BOTH SCREAMED, "*YES*! COME UP HERE WITH US, Dad."

I was sandwiched between Jasmine and Sammy. *Small miracles.* I wasn't ready to lay next to him, especially under starlight. I knew that I could speak up about needing to head home and maybe I should, but I decided to stay and try this friendship thing. I let out a silent breath as I tried to calm my heart rate because the sight of Jimmy crawling towards me was almost too much. I wasn't too proud to admit that Jimmy was good-looking, and the whole "single dad" thing was somehow making him look even hotter than normal.

I tried to focus on how I was going to form my heartfelt

apology instead of blatantly staring at Jimmy's steady movement toward us. Then I remembered that he just got back from
a date. He was dating someone. That helped put things into
perspective.

The kids were busy telling him all about our night and
everything we did as he took his spot next to Sammy. His body
was overwhelming. Even though Sammy was between us, his
body heat emanated from where he laid. *Dear Lord, his smell...*
Jimmy smelled like fresh laundry, and spice, with a hint of
mint. *So good, damn it.* I didn't need to be feeling heat waves or
smelling spice and mint—he could keep his heat, and smells to
himself and his date. Not that he was trying to share them but
still.

I kept my gaze on the sky, Jimmy's gaze was down on his
son, listening to Sammy talk about our epic round of hide and
seek. I tried to blend into the trampoline, or blankets, anything
really so that I was invisible because, for a brief second, I was
picturing my life as Mrs. Jimmy Stenson.

Sammy's comment about me being his mom had lodged
itself in my brain and no matter how hard I tried, I couldn't
shake it loose, but with it was also Jasmine's loud objection.

"Sounds like you guys had way more fun than I did, I am
so bummed that I missed such a fun night," Jimmy said with a
sigh, like he was actually upset.

Then Sammy piped up, "Let's have another night where
we do exactly all the same things, but this time let's have you
here, Dad, and Ramsey!"

Jimmy laughed, then let out another sigh before he continued, "Aww, buddy I don't know that we could ask that of poor
Ramsey. You two are quite a handful."

I could punch this guy in the stomach. He was the handful,
not them. I didn't want the kids to think, even for a second,
that I felt that way, so I spoke up and said, "No way, guys, I'd

come back here and steal your cheeseburgers any day of the week."

Sammy laughed again, and Jasmine was quick to join him. Suddenly, Sammy shot up like a gopher and lurched to the edge of the trampoline. There was a weird dip when he jumped, making Jimmy awkwardly slip toward me. He was basically on top of me. We were too heavy to escape the drooping center. I completely ignored him, or so I tried anyway. I distracted myself by searching for the North Star, but I couldn't remember which part of the Big Dipper was pointing at it. My chest was rising and falling fast, my heart in my throat. With Jimmy lying there next to me and my hips just barely touching his side… this whole situation was too much to handle. Sammy was bouncing around the edge, loudly humming some weird song, and I felt like a victim in his cruel game. We were all being knocked around. Out of my peripheral, I caught Jimmy looking over at me with a genuine smile on his handsome face.

His eyes were like pools of murky water. My eyes had already adjusted to the dark, so with the stars as our light, I could see the glint of deep green that was in them. I was a total sucker for moments like these. I wanted to apologize for earlier, but the timing seemed off with the kids here. So, I just stared at Jimmy awkwardly instead, but he was staring right back. He was so close that just a little lean from either one of us and we would be close enough to kiss.

Suddenly, Sammy jumped right on top of us, trying to wiggle his way back into his spot. The indent we made with our bodies was too deep and we couldn't seem to make room for him. So, Jimmy grabbed Sammy and stuffed him under his arm on his other side. Sammy fought against him and started arguing, "No! I want to be next to Ramsey too, Dad!"

I laughed and reached my arms toward Sammy, and he awkwardly jumped into them, kicking his dad in the groin as he did it. Jimmy lurched to the side in pain. Since I was sitting up to grab Sammy at the same time, Jimmy's face landed directly in my chest. Sammy was wedged between our legs, and we were in the most awkward position ever. Jimmy threw his head back and started apologizing. Sammy was laughing, Jasmine was yelling at Sammy, and Jimmy was still groaning in pain.

I started laughing because I couldn't help it, and as soon as I started laughing, Jimmy did too, and then Jasmine joined in, and we were all laughing like Sammy. We just laid there, laughing in our pile of blankets under the stars.

It was the most blissfully perfect moment that I'd ever felt in my life.

It made my heart race and hope gained even more territory there, blossoming into something full and beautiful. Then, through bits of little laughs, I heard Sammy whisper to his dad, "Ramsey's shiny, Dad."

Jimmy laughed and messed with Sammy's hair but didn't respond. I figured it must be something just between them, but then I worried that my face was all oily and shiny from eating pizza. I gently touched my temple to see if he was right, but I couldn't feel anything, so I just let it go.

AFTER A FEW MORE ROUNDS OF LAUGHTER, SAMMY AND JASMINE started arguing and I knew that was my cue to leave. Jimmy must have had the same thought because he grabbed Sammy by the waist and told him it was time for bed. We all started to climb out of the trampoline, the netting around it only gave a small, child-sized opening, so it was quite a feat to climb out.

Once I made it to the ladder, Jimmy was there with his hand, ready to help me down. I looked at him and then placed my hand into his as I climbed out. Once on the ground, Sammy ran and jumped from the porch, launching himself into my arms. I managed to catch him like someone would catch a large dog. I situated him until I could hold him properly and carried him inside. As we walked, I couldn't stop myself from taking a mental picture of how cute we were, with Jimmy carrying Jasmine, and Sammy in my arms. We looked like a family.

Stop it, Ramsey, he's dating someone.

As we walked, Sammy whispered in my ear, "Don't forget to think about what I said earlier about you becoming my you-know-who."

Then he winked at me. I laughed and let him down, watching him run up the stairs.

Jasmine was tired, I could tell, but as Jimmy was about to walk up the stairs with her, he stopped and looked at me. "Do you mind waiting for just a second?"

I shook my head, then Jasmine sat up in her dad's arms and looked at me, yelling, "Wait! What if my braids fall out tonight? When am I going to see you again, Ramsey?"

I shattered just a little over the panic in her voice. I looked at her with a half-smile, not sure how to respond because I wasn't sure Jimmy wanted me back or not.

I answered the best way I knew how. "Jas, don't worry, I will talk to your dad about coming back and babysitting. He's a good-looking guy, I am sure he's bound to have lots of dates, which means lots of chances for us to hang out."

The words were out before I could process what I was saying. My face flushed red and I could only hope the dim lighting in the house covered up how embarrassed I just made myself. I just called him a good-looking guy to his nine-year-old daughter, and insinuated that he was a player. I glanced at Jimmy's face, his jaw was set and ticking, like the other day in front of his restaurant. He was angry.

Shit. Not again.

I wanted to fix it, clear up what I meant, but just as I went to speak, Jimmy jogged upstairs with Jasmine.

I turned away, ignoring the stinging in my chest, and started looking for my purse. A second later, I heard Jimmy yell from the top of the stairs, "Don't leave!"

I looked up at him, locked my gaze on his, and felt the intensity in his words. I gave him a slight nod and continued towards the door. I found my purse and my jacket, and stood near the entryway, waiting for the awkward moment when I got paid for babysitting. Like a fifteen-year-old. The funny thing was, I didn't even want money for watching them. I had the best moments of my life tonight, and I couldn't stomach getting paid money for it.

After a few minutes, Jimmy came back down the stairs. His jaw wasn't ticking, but his lips were still in a thin line… still displaying the frustration from earlier, and maybe because I was standing near the door—ready to make my quick escape.

He walked only as far as the couch, leaving me alone in the entryway. He was goading me back into the living room, probably to talk about how awkward I was and how I shouldn't imply that he was a player in front of his kids. I was hoping to apologize quickly, kind of like ripping off a band-aid, then he could just slip me money if he absolutely had to, and I would be on my way. I guess my plan wasn't going to happen if we needed to sit.

I reluctantly crossed my arms over my chest and walked towards the couch. He moved enough to let me by while I took a seat at the end of the couch. He walked around and sat on the chair across from me.

His face transformed under the lamplight. Gone were his thin lips and furrowed brow, and their place was a smile as he took his seat. "Do you want anything to drink?" he quietly asked.

I didn't want to move around the chessboard of our

emotional conversation any more than we already had, so I shook my head. "No, thank you. I'm okay."

He gave me a slight nod, then placed his hand behind his neck. His eyes wouldn't meet mine. Instead, they searched the carpet, like some thread of fiber down there would give him what he was looking for. Finally, his green eyes met mine.

"Ramsey, look, the reason I went to your house today was to apologize for how I acted at the bar."

Crap, he took my moment. I tried to recover. "No. It's me who needs to apologize. I should have heard you out today. I'm sorry for how I acted. I hope that we…"

I stopped, not sure how to say it, and I realized too late that by asking this, I was being vulnerable with him. Still, I needed to say it, so I tried again. "I was hoping we could start over, from the bar, my house, the interview, all of it. Can we do that? I know I was a jerk in the parking lot, but…"

He cut me off. "No, I was the jerk when I reacted to you and didn't give you the interview you deserved."

I smiled at him, it wasn't often that I got to see guys like him apologize. I stuck my hand out, like a dork, hoping he would understand the gesture. "Friends, then?"

He looked at my hand, then my eyes, leaned forward and put his hand in mine. "Yeah, I'd like that."

He smiled, shaking my hand, and I was feeling butterflies in my stomach over it. It took me off guard, so I pulled my hand back and rummaged through my purse for my phone. I didn't know how else to end the moment, and I felt like a total coward.

His white teeth flashed as he let out a soft laugh. He looked around the room and pulled his arms in across his chest. My eyes were drawn to the tattoos that were on display on those lean arms. He had black lines running down each bicep, like a leaking flag. Below each line was a small number, then below that, was an insignia of some sort—a skull with wings, the word 'BRASS' within it. I cleared my throat and moved my gaze to the TV instead of his arms or tattoos.

I regained my train of thought, asking him, "So when's your next date or night out? Maybe I can come hang out with the kids." I watched as his face transformed from easygoing, even relaxed, to angry again. His jaw ticked, and eyebrows drew together, it was like watching a storm. Beautiful and terrifying. Maybe he didn't want me to come back after all?

"Sorry that was a little presumptuous of me, I shouldn't have asked that," I corrected, while internally kicking my own ass for throwing myself out there like that.

His eyebrows shot up and his green eyes searched my face as confusion washed over his own. "No, that's not it at all, I just —" He stopped and looked back down at the carpet for a moment before continuing. "I hate dating. I won't see the girl I took out tonight again. I don't have any future plans, but my kids clearly like you, so maybe…"

He trailed off and let out a big breath of air. "Maybe we could just have you come over and spend time with us? With them, I mean, or us. You know, Theo seems to like you too, regardless of how he chooses to express that."

I scoffed lightly at the memory of Theo talking about his son the other night. I definitely didn't see myself sitting in front of that same son, discussing babysitting wages and hanging out.

Jimmy spoke again, mistaking my silence for reluctance. "I could pay you each time you come over if you want, or you could just accept the accountant job at my bar."

He slid that last part in so smoothly, I nearly missed it. I was already looking at him, because I was trying to be extra polite while he was talking, but as soon as I fully registered the seriousness of what he said, I began stammering. "What did you say?"

He smiled and leaned up from his chair. "Look, Ramsey, I

did my homework. You're quite the catch—professionally, I mean—and all the other idiots I have interviewed didn't come close to having as much experience as you. Would you please, at least consider it?"

Consider accepting my current dream job? Ha! I tried to come off as unaffected, cool while I calmly replied, "Yeah, sure, I'd like that."

Jimmy smiled, his teeth flashed again, and his eyes lit up, I would assume he might be on the verge of laughter when he asked, "Is that a yes? Or, an I'll think about it?"

I smiled back and stuck my hand out again. "Yes, I accept the job offer... officially." *Why did I keep holding out my hand?*

Ending the handshake rather abruptly, I stood up, adjusted my purse, then started for the door.

Jimmy followed me. "So, just show up on Monday at nine a.m. Oh, and let me pay you for tonight," he said, reaching for his wallet.

I put my hand on his arm to stop him. "Jimmy, honestly, I couldn't take money for hanging out with your kids. I only suggested more babysitting gigs here to see them." I pushed some hair behind my ear and swung my purse forward in an awkward movement, then added, "You have really great kids."

He gave me another big smile. "I do have great kids. Well, they're smitten with you, both asked me some very interesting questions about you," he finished with a snort.

I smiled weakly and tried to join in his joking, but it was all feeling too real. "Yeah, Sammy has propositioned me for a spot here and Jasmine seems to be trying to find me a perfect date, so I'm not sure what they're planning." I said, while laughing. I took a step toward the door and reached for the handle, but Jimmy casually beat me to it, then lightheartedly asked, "Oh yeah? What exactly is that position here that Sammy's offering you?"

I looked down at my feet. "Uh, maybe you should ask him

that." Then I turned and walked out the door, giving Jimmy a quick wave and a sweet, "Night."

As I walked to my car, I noticed that Jimmy was watching me from his doorstep. It was like everything had changed. Not just between Jimmy and me; in a weird way, it felt like my whole life had just changed and now I was officially employed. I could dance with how happy I was right now, but I'd wait until I was clear of Jimmy's driveway. You know, for appearances.

NINE

JIMMY

IT WAS Sunday afternoon and I was supposed to be cleaning up the books for the bar. I didn't want Ramsey to walk into a complete mess and assume that I was just a lazy business owner. But balancing figures wasn't my strong suit, especially when none of the totals were matching up. It also didn't help that I couldn't get the previous night out of my mind.

I kept replaying moments, like when Ramsey stared at me while lying next to me under the stars, or how she looked sandwiched between my kids on the trampoline. I couldn't get the feel of her hand in mine out of my brain. I felt like I was in middle school again.

I closed my eyes and tried to clear my head so that I could just focus on cleaning up the books, but if I was being honest with myself, it was difficult to not have any promises of seeing Ramsey today. I only met her a few days ago, but I was already trying to figure out a way to see her again. I realized that's not healthy at all, and I should resist it.

I lowered my head into my hands and let out a long, frustrated breath. These intense feelings were dangerous, and seeing Ramsey with the kids, hearing the kids talk about her, it was just too much. The look on both Jasmine's and Sammy's faces when I tucked them into bed last night showed how affected they were by her too. The conversation with Sammy was on repeat in my head.

"Daddy, don't you think Ramsey is pretty?"

"Yes, I do Sammy, what does that have to do with you going to bed?"

"Nothing, but I like Ramsey, and I think she's pretty."

"Yeah, I think so too buddy, but you need to go to bed."

"If you're looking for a shine, Dad, why don't you pick her?"

"Sammy, we just met her. It's way too soon to be talking about that type of stuff. Besides, how do you know she's worthy of you guys?"

"Because she played hide and seek with me, Dad, duh…"

IT WAS MESSING WITH ME, AS I REMEMBERED A SIMILAR conversation with my own father when I was close to Sammy's age. One that changed the way I would look at women forever, and more importantly, how I would love them.

I shifted in my office chair and tried to keep my eyes off the framed photo of my mother. She died shortly after Jasmine was born, and I haven't stopped missing her a single day since. My mother was the type of woman who knew what she wanted in life, regardless of how broken, misshapen, or weird. If she wanted it, she'd get it and nurse it back to life, until it showed all the beautiful potential she knew it had from the beginning. I held the black frame in my hands and traced the lines of my mother's beautiful face with my eyes. It took me back to that conversation I couldn't seem to shake. The memory of it, so intense and clear.

"Daddy, how do you know that you love Mommy?" I asked while climbing into bed and getting settled under my covers.

Dad started laughing. I wanted to roll my eyes at his laughter, but I didn't. I didn't want to get in trouble right before bed. He always laughed when I asked big kid questions, but I felt pretty grown up these days, espe-cially after today.

"Jimmy, you're seven years old and you already have women prob-lems?" Dad joked, but he didn't know how right he was. I shimmied down further into my bed, trying not to get embarrassed as I talked about Nora, the girl who kissed me.

"Well, I have questions about girls, not problems," I mumbled, while looking over at my Ninja turtle lamp, hoping he'd ignore the growing color in my cheeks.

Dad ran his hands through his dark hair and got that far-off look; it's the look he got when he thought about my mom. As if she heard him silently calling her, Mom made her way into my room, holding a laundry basket full of clothes.

Dad looked up at her and gave her that smile. It was the one I noticed he used only on her.

She caught it, like she always did, and smiled back, pushing her dark blonde hair out of her face. My mother was the most beautiful woman in the world, even prettier than Nora Clark.

"Boys, what are you up talking about so late? Don't you have school tomorrow, young man?" she asked, raising her eyebrow while looking directly at me.

Dad laughed again. I liked seeing his big white teeth flash when he laughed. He held out his hand and pulled on my mother's arm until she landed in his lap, causing her to drop the basket. Then he wrapped his big arms around her.

"Jimmy's curious about how I know that I love you," Dad said, while looking up into Mom's eyes. They were green, like mine.

"Well, Jimmy, that's easy. It's because of the glimmer," she said happily while jumping up, turning around, and kissing my dad. Then she leaned forward and kissed my forehead before leaving the room. I remember Dad lovingly watch her leave the room and continued to stare at the door, as if lost in thought. He was sitting on the edge of the bed, slightly leaning forward with one elbow perched on his knee and that bright Mom-grin on his face.

I stared up at my plastic glow-in-the-dark stars that covered my ceiling and asked, "What's the 'glimmer,' Dad?"

Dad rubbed his dark beard while thinking, then leaned in. "You know how we light fireworks on the Fourth of July?"

"Yes, it's my favorite holiday!" I yelled back at him. I had a good feeling about this glimmer thing, if it had to do with fireworks.

Dad laughed, then kept going. "Well, you know those fireworks that we light and right when we think they're done, it lights back up and keeps going?"

I nodded. "Those ones are our favorites," I told him, thinking back on the last time we had one do that.

Dad nodded. "Well, the glimmer that your mom mentioned, it's like one of those fireworks." He leaned in even closer and started almost whispering, like it was a secret. "When you find that one special person that you love more than anyone else, you see this wonderful light, and even when you think it's done for and it might go out, it lights back up again and keeps going."

Dad cleared his throat, like he swallowed something hard to get down, like maybe he needed some milk. I did that when I ate peanut butter and jelly sandwiches too fast.

"Your mama would just keep shining for me, even when I thought we were done. She led me home with that glimmer, her light. That's how you know; when they keep glowing and you find your way home." He trailed off and then rubbed his beard some more as he added, "Love is a funny thing, son. It's not always perfect, it's not always fun. It takes work and finding the right person who's worth it," Dad said with a twinkle in his eye and a small smile on his face. "Your mother had something no other woman had for me. She'd shine, but when things got tough between us, her light would dim, but never go out. It was like a glimmer, a faint and wavering light, always there, willing to shine no matter the darkness." He then leaned in and kissed my forehead. I smiled up at him, not really knowing what to say. He must have known because he ruffled my hair, then turned my lamp off and left my room.

I didn't understand much after the firework part, but it still felt nice to have some kind of explanation. I liked Nora, but she didn't feel like one of those fireworks.

I shrugged my shoulders and snuggled back into my bed. I pictured myself following one of those green tank fireworks down the street. It was all lit up and the cardboard wheels on the side would spin, rolling past house after house until it led me back home.

I smiled, happy, knowing what a glimmer meant and knowing that one day, I would find my own special light.

I SWALLOWED THE GOLF BALL-SIZED LUMP THAT WAS STARTING to form in my throat at the memory and put my mother's picture back. Suddenly, that need to see Ramsey, to have her included in our weekend, was overwhelming. So much so, that I broke down and pulled out my cell phone. I pulled up Ramsey's contact info and sent off a quick text.

ME: *HEY, IT'S JIMMY...SORRY TO BUG YOU ON YOUR DAY OFF, BUT I'm trying to prep the books for you to take them over. I was wondering if you'd be against me asking you for help?...I need some clarification on a few accounting terms.*

It was only eleven in the morning, and she might not even be awake yet. Hopefully, she wouldn't read too much into it.

But then again, maybe I wanted her to read too much into it. I needed coffee, or to go for a drive, I needed to get my mind off her. *She's too good for you and your Brass past, idiot.*

I closed my eyes and tried to shut out the images of the Brass and prison. Images that still liked to haunt me and remind me of how much I didn't deserve in this life. How much I'll never have.

I tried to focus back on the computer screen in front of me when my phone dinged. I looked down and saw an incoming text.

Ramsey: *Ha ha, my day off, I see what you did there. Yes, I would be happy to help, would you consider coming over here to talk? Mom is actually really struggling today and could use the company. Maybe the kids and you could come, and maybe even your dad if he's free? I was going to barbeque, no pressure though.*

I PUNCHED OUT THE REST OF MY REPLY AND HIT SEND.

Me: *We would love to come over. The kids have been bugging me all day about when they were going to see you next, so this is perfect. What can I bring?*

I jumped up and ran to my bathroom to get in the shower. Once I was out, I double-checked my phone to see what I might need to bring with us and nearly fell over from laughter. There were several more texts from Ramsey,

RAMSEY:
  11:12 am: "Just bring your body"
  11:12 am: "Crap, autocorrect. Your bodies!!"
  11:14 am: "Wait, that sounds just as weird, just come."
  11:14 am: "Agggghhhhhh, dang it."
  11:16 am: Let me try this again. Please feel free to bring anything you'd like, but really just showing up with whoever can make it, would be fine.

I TOOK A SCREENSHOT OF THE TEXTS, JUST SO THAT I COULD look back on this conversation anytime I might need a good laugh. I shot her another text and had a really difficult time not flirting with her, especially because she was clearly embarrassed that it came off like she was flirting with me. I typed and retyped my response; the desire to blur the lines with her was frustratingly strong. I finally just decided that I needed to keep it clean.

Me: *Do you have any idea how hard I just laughed at you? Anyway, we will bring our bodies and some chips, what time would you like us there?*

She didn't reply for about half an hour, and I was getting antsy. What time did people usually start barbeques, or was it only a dinner thing? I needed to see her before dinner. Just as I was about to round up the kids and head to the store, she finally texted back.

Ramsey: *Sorry, had to jump in the shower. Come by whenever. I will start prepping the grill soon. Make sure the kids bring some toys or something. We don't have much here for them to do, except Netflix, and a backyard.*

I forced my eyes shut at the image she just put into my mind and shoved the phone in my pocket. This was going to be more work than I thought. I bounced around the idea that I should maybe go on a few more dates with some cute baristas just to get Ramsey out of my head. Especially before we started working together. Then again, the date last night with Sarah the barista was a total failure. The poor girl wore a tiny cocktail dress and six-inch heels to the movies and dinner. She must have confused me with some corporate jerk who ate at five-star restaurants. Reggie's was a straight three-star establishment with ripped up booths and the best fettuccine alfredo in the state.

To say that she looked a little bit out of place and very much like a hooker would be putting it delicately. Not to mention, everything she did made me wonder if it was something Ramsey would do on a date. The comparing and wondering drove me crazy as I considered if Ramsey liked spicy food, or Italian food. I wondered what she would wear on a date, specifically what she would wear on our first date. When Sarah ordered beer with her dinner, I wondered whether Ramsey drank wine like a normal person, or if she was a beer girl too. The poor barista could tell that I wasn't into her, and the night ended pathetically early.

I yelled for the kids to load up in the car and ran down the basement steps to talk to Dad. He was reading in his oversized leather chair with his thick black-rimmed glasses perched on his nose; the man was getting old. I gently knocked on the door frame, he looked up at me, then closed his book.

"Hey son."

I smiled and crossed my arms over my chest. I was suddenly shy about extending the offer to him, I didn't want him to think I had a crush. Even though I did.

"Hey, we were invited to a barbeque at Ramsey's house with her and her mom. She wanted me to be sure to let you know that you were invited."

Dad smiled and looked down at the floor. "Oh, I bet she'd like me to be there, she still hasn't reamed me for lying to her about the babysitting gig," he said with a laugh.

"Dad, I doubt she'll ream you. She and I ended things on good terms last night, which is why we've been invited to her house for a barbeque. Would you like to join us or not?" I said with a little bit of frustration in my voice. He was wasting my Ramsey time.

Dad sighed and stood up, then grabbed his flannel shirt and headed towards me. "Keep your panties on, son. Do we need to bring anything?"

I smiled at the memory of Ramsey's earlier text. "Yeah, some chips. We're headed to the store now."

Once Dad was in the car and the kids were buckled up, we headed out and made our quick stop at the supermarket. I had picked up more flowers for Ramsey, but figured if I handed them to Carla, then it wouldn't seem like they were a weird gift from her new boss. I didn't even know if she liked flowers, and I assumed that she didn't see the ones I had left the day before when I went to her house; that, or she threw them out.

I threw the chips down on the floor by dad's legs and as I put the flowers on his lap, I caught the look on his face but tried my best to ignore it. I started the Tahoe and pulled out of the parking lot when I heard Dad clear his throat.

"Hmm, mighty fine flowers you have here, son."

I knew where he was going with this and I wasn't in the mood.

"Yep."

I kept my eyes on the road, thankful that our drive would only afford him possibly one, maybe two more questions before we arrived at their house.

"And Ramsey is a mighty fine-looking woman, don't you think?" Dad said, while looking out his window, clearly trying to be slick. He wasn't even a little bit.

"I hadn't noticed. She's my employee now, so I can't notice those kinds of things. These flowers are for Carla, Ramsey's mom."

Dad looked back over at me, and smiled. "You gave her the job?"

I kept my eyes forward on the road. "Well, she was the most qualified for the position. So, yes." I situated my body in my seat a little differently, his scrutiny made me uncomfortable. I glanced over at him when he didn't say anything else. I assumed that he would have more comments up his sleeve, but he was just looking out the window, a huge grin plastered on his face. I rolled my eyes, he could think whatever he wanted. Nothing was going to happen with Ramsey. It was a crush, and now she worked for me.

I came around the corner of Cherry Loop and gently

pulled up to the curb of Carla's house. The kids jumped out, and I noticed that Sammy had grabbed his soccer ball, while Jasmine had grabbed her journal and a purple bag with a brush handle sticking out of it. I admired the coincidence that some of the kids' favorite hobbies were things Ramsey was naturally talented in. Dad grabbed the chips, and I brought the flowers, and we made our way towards the door.

My palms were sweaty as I readjusted my shirt collar for the fifth time. I normally just wore regular t-shirts, to keep it simple. However, something had me reaching for a nicer navy-blue dress shirt today. I also decided to go with some tan, knee-length shorts; it was still warmer outside, so I took advantage.

Dad knocked and we all just stood there, waiting for a few seconds until the door swung open and Ramsey stood in front of us. She had a huge grin on her face, I tried to focus on her smile, and not let my eyes wander but I failed. I couldn't stop my greedy gaze from roaming down her body. She wore jean shorts and a simple black tank. It was all modest, but anything on her body would be measured inappropriately by me.

She had a pair of tongs in her hand and hair from her braid had fallen in her face. She was gorgeous. I smiled at her and as hard as I tried to keep it a friendly smile, I really couldn't help but give her a "I think you're sexy as hell" kind of grin that she probably got from guys at bars all the time. I couldn't help it. She smiled back and blushed a little, then looked at my kids, and that was like a bucket of cold water in the face. No, this was not a date, and my children were standing directly in front of me, what the heck was my problem?

Ramsey moved to the side to let us in, and we all pushed through, into her house. I made sure I was last. I handed her the flowers and selfishly waited to see the expression on her face. She locked eyes with me, her smile reaching her eyes, and I noticed just a hint of red coloring her cheeks. She was definitely affected by me, which was a good thing, but also terrible at the same time. As if pulled back to reality by the thought of why her being affected by me was a bad idea, I cleared my throat and looked down at the flowers. "These are for your mom."

I took a step back to create some distance and noticed a new shade of red coloring Ramsey's face, but this time, I had a feeling it might have been from embarrassment. I was a selfish jerk. I should have just been upfront about the flowers to begin with, but I wanted to know if she felt at all the same way as I did.

She put a loose strand of hair behind her ear and moved to shut the door, then turned and led the way for everyone to follow her through the house. The floor plan was fairly open, the entryway led into the living room, but the living room was also connected openly to the kitchen and right next to it was a big dining room, which had French doors that opened to the backyard.

A cream-colored couch sat against the large window in the living room, and two deep sunken red chairs framed the rest of the space out. They also had a large, flat screen television set inside on top of a thin TV stand. I looked over the walls and found several pictures of Ramsey through the years. There was a large, golden-framed school photo of Ramsey in a soccer uniform, from what looked like when she was in grade school. Her hair was in a thick braid, and she was missing three of her top teeth. My eyes roamed the kitchen next, there was a large island in the middle, and near the sink sat a window, below which sat the flowers I had brought to Ramsey the day before.

So, she had noticed them after all.

The kids found their way to the backyard and started playing soccer. Dad found Carla, and they were already discussing some bingo fundraiser event, while Ramsey was still in the kitchen getting a vase for the flowers. I decided to plop down into one of Carla's patio seats and watch the kids until I knew how I could help.

A few minutes later, Ramsey emerged from the house with a tall vase full of flowers and placed them in front of me on the glass patio table while she yelled out, "Mom, look what Jimmy brought for you!"

I saw Carla look over from where she stood next to my dad. I noticed now how frail she looked, she wore just a simple track suit and slippers on her feet, with a glittered, hat that I'd only seen a twenty-something wear, the word, "Slay" was printed on across the front. On her, it was more than adorable. Still, the weathered look on her face was heartbreaking.

Carla sweetly said, "Thank you, Jimmy, they're beautiful," before returning to her conversation with dad.

I chanced a quick glance at Ramsey and caught her staring at her mom like I just was. A look that I was all too familiar with passed over her face. Starting at the corners of her mouth, her lips sagged and her eyes watered. Her forehead creased and then she wiped absently under her eyes. I knew what it felt like to lose a mother, so I knew that Ramsey was barely holding it together. I had this strange urge to wrap Ramsey in my arms and tell her it would be okay. That the pain of losing her mother would gut her, but she would recover. She would take the strength her mother had and carry it within her, but I couldn't. I barely knew Ramsey, I had to stop this desire to fix her life, and more importantly, I had to stop the ever-constant desire I had to make her a part of mine.

In the yard, Sammy and Jasmine started fighting,

"Stop it Jazzy! It's no fair! You can't always win every time, you have to let me get the ball over there sometimes!" Sammy was practically shrieking across the yard.

"Yes, I can! Dad told me that I have to try my hardest, no matter who I am up against, and you are just a sore, baby loser!" Jasmine shouted back, crossing her arms over her chest.

She seemed tough, but I knew that Sammy was getting to her by the way Jasmine was idly kicking at the grass and how red her face was turning. The idea of seeming unfair or mean, or really anything like her mother at all, scared Jasmine, so she tended to be overly cautious with people, even to a fault.

Just as I stood up to address the kids, I heard Ramsey say from the grill, "Well, for one thing, I know that I could really use the muscles of two very strong Stenson kids with this food. And the second thing I know is, that I am dying to play some soccer with those same kids, and maybe…" She started to trail off, then turned to face me as she finished, "Maybe we can get your Dad to play and have two against two, maybe even girls against boys?"

She jutted her hip to the side and placed her hands on them, tongs in one hand; grease getting everywhere. She was being so adorable, and I had some not-so-adorable urges starting to surface. I felt the need to go over to her and wipe some of that grease off that had splattered onto her collarbone, near the strap of her tank top… She'd probably try to fight back if I went over there and spread that black mess over more of that perfect skin. I'd start by grabbing the tongs from her hands, so no weapons were involved, then from her collarbone, I'd make a trail down her…

"Jimmy, did you hear me?" Ramsey had moved closer to me, her eyes dancing between mine and her hands were out now, like she was waiting for a response.

"Ugh, yeah, soccer, right?" I fumbled while heading away from Ramsey and towards my kids, where my focus should have been to begin with.

"No, ugh." Ramsey smiled, holding back a laugh as she tugged on her braid. "I said, you should head inside with the kids and help them get the stuff from the fridge."

"Right, sorry." I turned and followed the kids inside.

I grabbed the hot dog buns and the chips we had brought,

Carla came in and took some watermelon out of the fridge. She handed Dad a clear glass bowl that was filled with potato salad, and together, we all headed outside.

I stared at the kids with watermelon juice dripping down their chins, and my dad laughing while throwing back a Pepsi, with Ramsey's hair catching pieces of sunlight as she picked at the potatoes in the salad; it was perfect, and I didn't want it to end. That same familiar pang of desire hit me in the chest, and I breathed with a little extra force to try and clear it away.

After the epic round of two against two soccer that was clearly unfair from the beginning, because of Ramsey's extensive skills, we had ice cream and watched as the kids raced each other in the yard. The sun was setting, and I had yet to open my laptop to talk to Ramsey about the accounting terms. I knew I had to do that at some point, so not to lead her on or make her think that my text earlier was somehow a way to weasel an invite out of her. But it was later than I'd intended, and the kids had school tomorrow.

I looked at my exhausted dad, and asked, "Would you mind taking the kids home and getting their baths started? I am going to review a few of these accounting terms with Ramsey really quick, and then I will walk home when I'm done." Both kids dropped what they were doing and walked over to say goodbye to Carla. She grabbed them as tight as it seemed she could, then placed a big kiss on each of their faces. Then the kids walked over to Ramsey, who was resting her hip against the kitchen counter. They both went in for a hug and she scooped each of them up individually and hugged them tightly. Sammy laughed, Jasmine squeaked, and I melted a little.

Jasmine looked sad and whispered to Ramsey from where she stood in front of her, "Ramsey, I have, um, a dance tryout thing at the high school. It's a big thing for fourth graders, and I was wondering if you could help me with my hair?" Jasmine finished, while playing with her fingers and wringing them together. I had to turn away and pretend to wipe down the table; I couldn't admit that my little nine-year-old daughter had just split my heart open.

I felt relieved that she had someone to ask, otherwise Jasmine would try it on her own and as usual, end up looking like she lived with two men who didn't know the first thing about doing girls' hair. That, or she would just choose not to go, like she had for several other dance-related events. Being the girl without a mom, grandma, or even an aunt proved to make her an outsider rather quickly. Her tomboy clothes and unkempt hair gave too much ammunition for the other girls her age.

I didn't see what Ramsey did, but I heard: "Jasmine, it would be my honor, and I would be so sad if you didn't let me not only do your hair, but take you out for a full day of pampering. Dance tryouts are a big deal, and we will have you looking your absolute best."

I turned back around to catch Ramsey pulling Jasmine up into a hug. There was something that came to life inside me at the sight of my daughter in her arms. I quickly looked away before anymore emotions could take root, but a few already had and I was worried those would lead somewhere I wasn't ready to go.

DAD TOOK THE KIDS SHORTLY AFTER, WHILE CARLA HAD GONE off to her bedroom with a big smile on her face. I was set up at the dining room table with my laptop open, and Ramsey walked over and placed a cup of coffee in front of each of us. Then she settled in, sitting across the table from me.

I looked up and noticed her face; even after a full day of smoke, grease, and sweat, she looked gorgeous. Her cheeks had some color on them from the sun, it made her light blue eyes stand out. She looked perfect. I had to swallow the lump in my throat and turn my focus to the computer screen and the accounting terms I had typed on a spreadsheet. My focus was split, however, as I noticed that she had a soft smile playing on her lush, pink lips.

I SMILED AT HER AND SHE SMILED BACK, AS SHE SIPPED HER coffee. "So, can I ask what happened to your last accountant?"

She sounded nervous as she asked it, but still confident.

"Ha, yeah, that is actually a great question. Jackson, my best friend, did it for me, for an entire year, while he was also opening and running his own restaurant. I was still so new, he wanted to help me out, but after a year, he released them back to me with some tips and a few video tutorials. I have been slowly sinking ever since," I finished with a bit of a laugh, hoping she wouldn't think I was too pathetic.

"So, Jimmy's is fairly new then?" she asked with a hint of concern.

"Uh, yeah, it's just barely two years old this October," I responded with an equal amount of concern. She was the professional here; maybe I was already in trouble?

I waited for a cringe or wince, but she just looked thoughtfully at the wall behind me and then down at her coffee. "Interesting, I thought you'd been open a bit longer than that. The place looks amazing, you and Jackson must have done something right," she said with a laugh.

"Yeah, well, I took out a pretty big loan to make it look so amazing. Jackson backed me for forty-percent of the company, he really stuck his neck out for me." I had my fist under my jaw, looking at her as I thought about my best friend taking the biggest risk of his life on me.

"He sounds like an amazing guy, it's rare to find friends like that," she said, while staring into her mug and running her index finger around the rim of it.

"Speaking of friends like that, your mom mentioned that you had some still back in Chicago? That must have been difficult, to leave them behind?"

Her eyes wandered to the wall behind me again, as if she was lost in thought. A moment later, she looked back down at her mug.

"I have Laney, she's my best friend. We still keep in touch every day, so it's not too difficult and Chicago is only a few hours away."

I smiled at her, then dug in a little deeper. "Yeah, sounds like you left your whole life behind. No husband or boyfriend waiting for you in the Windy City?" I knew what her mom said, but part of me had to hear it from her. Even though pursuing anything with Ramsey was completely not possible, I still needed to hear that she wasn't with someone.

Ramsey turned a deep shade of red and moved her cup of coffee to the side and then back before she answered, "I've been single for a while. My last boyfriend tried to take our relationship to the next level by asking me to move in. Which I agreed to, only to come home one day to find him with someone. That was the end of that. Shortly after, I got the phone call from my mom telling me about her diagnosis, so I took that timing as a sign to get over here to help her. The rest is history, albeit a short history so far."

She finished the tail end of her story by lifting her arms out with a subtle shrug, as if this house wasn't exactly where she wanted to be. My eyes followed her gestures around the house, and I nodded along with her sentiment. I slowed my gaze as I came back around, tracing the mellow curve of her wrist up her arm, to the wispy hairs curled along the back of her neck, and my eyes fell on the tiny dimple on her cheek. Even from her profile, I could tell she had this proud, yet solemn, look about her.

"What about you? You seemed upset last night, any time I brought up you going on another date," Ramsey asked, gesturing with her chin.

My eyes jumped to meet hers, alarmed that she picked up on my frustration last night.

"Upset?" I deflected, trying to figure out a way to explain my frustration last night without giving away the real reason, which I still didn't fully understand yet.

"Well, frustrated at least," Ramsey hesitantly clarified, while pushing hair behind her ear. I drummed my fingers on the table and decided that I'd give her a little background instead.

"I met my ex when I was a teenager, we got together when I was twenty. We were good together, then we weren't, we did a lot of stupid stuff back then. I finally asked her to marry me when I knocked her up with Jasmine." I stopped for a moment, reminiscing about that day and that time of my life.

"Did she say yes?" Ramsey carefully asked, quietly, like she was worried about my response.

I smiled and continued, "Yes, she did. We had the quaintest shotgun wedding. And I was happy. Happy about our kid, happy about our life, but once Jasmine was born, things changed. I was doing more jobs for the club, legal jobs, which were hard to come by, and if you did snag them, they usually required longer hours, so I was spending more and more time away from Lisa and Jasmine. Soon enough, every time Lisa and I saw each other, we fought." I paused to take a drink of coffee.

"That sounds really hard," Ramsey whispered, after sipping from her own cup. "What happened?"

I rubbed at my chin, not sure how much to tell her. I wasn't ready to scare her off, but I also felt at ease talking to her. More at ease than I ever thought I would be with anyone again.

"My mom died. My emotions were everywhere. I entered a few street tournaments for fighting, and was actually making decent money from it, but I was gone even more than I was before. The fighting eventually landed me in jail for a few months, where I sorted through my grief and had decided to turn my life around.

"But when I got out, Lisa wasn't there waiting for me. I should have known then, but we struggled in our marriage for another two years, until I woke up one morning and found a note on our bedroom mirror, letting me know that she couldn't wait around for me to go to prison again. There were a lot of reasons my marriage ended but that's the short version. Sammy was barely a year old, Jasmine was four."

I had to stop because I didn't want to think about what it was like to have my children's mother abandon them.

Ramsey was quiet, so I glanced up at her and saw tears heavy in her eyes, ready to fall any second. She tucked her head down and swiped at them before responding, "Sorry, that's just heartbreaking. I'm so sorry about your mom." She swiped at more tears before continuing.

"I'm sorry if I'm out of line, but how could Lisa leave her babies? Sammy was so young. How could she leave you?" she asked and threw her hand towards me, then continued with her tirade, "I just don't get it. I know I wasn't there, and God knows if I will ever be there with the whole husband and kids thing, but I know that if I am ever blessed enough to get it, someone would have to kill me before they took it away. I'm so sorry you guys went through that."

I felt this kick in my heart and a lump in my throat. I never liked getting pity from anyone about what happened with Lisa, but I could feel it for my kids and for one tiny second, I wanted to feel it for me. Hearing Ramsey's confession proved what I already knew to be true about her; she was no quitter. She would never quit on her family, the one that she would one day have. The kids that she would one day love, and the husband that she would stand beside. The thought of Ramsey getting the perfect family unit made my stomach twist with something stupidly close to jealousy. *Why was I jealous?*

I had to control my emotions so that she wouldn't see the treacherous feelings reflect on my face. "Ramsey, of course, you'll have a husband and kids someday. Are you kidding me? My own kids already love you and they've only known you for a few days," I said with a little laugh, to try and lighten the serious ache that was attached to those words.

She smiled and dropped her hands to the mug in front of her, cradling it. With a smile on her face, she said, "Well, your kids are exceptional and if I am lucky, even a little bit, then my kids will be half as fun as yours."

I was staring at her with an intense look, I knew that I was, but this conversation had to end. I was frustratingly too invested to joke around about Ramsey's future kids. I knew that eventually, I would find it funny, eventually the novelty of how beautiful and fun Ramsey was would wear off, but tonight, it was just a blunt steak knife to my gut. So, I threw my wrist in front of my face and looked at my watch, already aware that it was getting close to nine at night. But I declared it to Ramsey like a new revelation.

"I should probably get going. It's getting late, and I have a new employee starting in the morning," I said, as I stifled a yawn.

Ramsey slowly stood and started stretching her arms above her head, even that was sexy and went down on my list of what not to allow Ramsey to do while at work. Yes, I had a list. Her wearing jean shorts was on the list, holding barbecue tongs was on it, licking her lips was a definite no-go, and now, stretching her arms above her head was on there.

She looked apologetic before she said, "I'm sorry we didn't get to the accounting terms, but I promise that I am very good at what I do, and I kind of love the idea of walking into something that's not perfect. I like to see how much progress I can make on something."

I smiled at her and waved my hand over my laptop while scooping it up off the table. "Well, that's good to hear because it's a mess. You will have your work cut out for you."

Ramsey laughed, then walked over to the counter and grabbed her keys. She turned towards me, while pulling on a knit sweater, and said, "Let me drive you home, boss."

I wasn't in the habit of letting my employees drive me home after dark, but I also wasn't in the habit of walking home with a twelve-hundred dollar laptop fastened around my shoulder. So, I smiled and followed her out the door, liking the idea way too much of Ramsey headed to my house at night.

TEN

It was Monday morning and I was beyond excited. My alarm was set for seven, but I was up by five. I was finally going back into the field of work that I loved and like the complete nerd that I was, I could feel the buzz to crunch numbers and figures surging through my veins. Maybe that buzz was actually from the three cups of coffee I downed before I did twenty minutes of a half-assed morning yoga routine, which consisted mostly of bed making and jean shimmying.

Jean shimmying was a new term I used when referencing those poor unfortunate jeans that fell victim to the dryer and shrank. That was the only explanation as to why my favorite, denim skinny jeans would barely button. It wouldn't have anything at all to do with the fact that I had sat on my ass for the last six months, watching cooking shows, and learning how to survive in the wilderness with just a bit of black string and a few twigs. I was now convinced that I could not only survive in the jungle, but also cook up something fantastic while out there.

Now that my skinny jeans were officially on and securely fastened, I stood in front of my closet and flipped through several hanging shirts. I was battling a serious case of first day jitters, as well as possibly crushing on my new boss. The second part was definitely a problem, which brought me back to the shirt predicament. I wanted to look professional, still be cute, but not too cute as though I was trying to lead him on.

I pushed my hair off my neck and let out a strained sigh. I reached for my black blazer and a white shirt. There; fancy-ish, without being slutty.

Now, for the shoes. I let out another sigh and I went into a crouched position, then eventually laid completely flat, half under my bed. I let out a groan as I pushed things out of my way. I cursed as I recalled how I was supposed to clean under the cramped space. I pushed those negative thoughts aside and kept searching for my black, slingback heels. *Come on, stupid shoes!*

"Aha!" I slowly made my way out from under the bed and pulled the shoes free. I held them in the air, like a prized trophy. I double-checked my face in the mirror; my makeup was fresh from a video tutorial, my wing-tipped eyes and shadowed lids were perfect. I had chosen a smooth red lipstick color, to match my darker complexion.

I walked into the living room and found my mom doing some yoga video on the television. It was an old DVD that she had. As I watched her, I couldn't help but smile because if I were given less than a year to live, there was no way in hell that I would waste any precious time exercising, even it was just yoga. But that wasn't my mom. No, she began every morning with as much physical movement as she could manage, half a grapefruit, and a large glass of lemon water. She must be so disappointed with her Cocoa Puff-eating, coffee drinking, fake exercising daughter. Shaking my head to clear my self-deprecating thoughts, I walked into the kitchen to grab my thermos, and filled it with even more coffee. I grabbed my toast and made my way to my mom.

"Mom, I'm headed to work. I should be home, around five, I think. I haven't asked yet, but I think five. I will call you if it's later," I said, while placing a kiss on her cheek.

She smiled and touched my shoulder as she said goodbye. "Have a good day, sweetheart. Tell Jimmy hello for me. If he asks you out to dinner tonight, don't hesitate to say yes. I have some leftovers still, or June from next door keeps bugging me to come over for dinner. Either way, don't deny that boy," she scolded me, like I was fifteen again.

I knew my mother way too well to even put up an argument. But I was curious why she thought he'd ask me, so I asked while grabbing my purse. "Why do you think he's going to ask me to dinner, Mom?" I checked my phone and offhandedly added, "Besides, he's my boss now."

Mom gave me a smile, took a drink of water, and replied with a shrug, "I saw the way he looked at you. That boy likes you, my sweet girl, so don't deny him!" She walked towards me and, instead of a hug, gave me a swat to my shoulder.

I rolled my eyes but didn't have time to hear the same speech that she'd been giving me over the last six months; she wants to see me get married and have kids before she goes to heaven. I kissed her cheek and headed for the door.

During my drive, I kept picturing what I would do if Jimmy *did* ask me out to dinner.

He had been a little flirty with me since the night I babysat for him then after last night, when he stayed to talk business but didn't actually end up talking business. I saw through that the moment his text came through that morning, but my Mom was lonely and struggling with depression, so in the end, it really did work out. Still, it caused me to toss and turn all night about this working arrangement.

Why was Jimmy so flirty if he was going to be my boss?

Surely, he knew that we couldn't date. Besides, right now, with my mom, all my time and focus had to be on her. Except for work, I needed the job in order to eat. I had to remind myself that Jimmy just apologized for being a total jerk, and I needed to transition into trust, not just throw it at him all at once. It felt too easy to like him and to allow his flirtatious nature to reel me in. I checked my odometer— eight more miles before I pulled into Jimmy's.

I played back the conversation we had last night about Jimmy's former wife and then what he said about his best friend. He had opened up, and in a big way. I paired what he had told me with what I overheard at the bar. *The Brass. Jimmy the Fist.* I didn't have all the details of his past, but from what I did know, I was able to get a clearer picture. He seemed like he had a few skeletons in the closet and definitely some baggage, all signs that I should stay the heck away from him.

The early morning light nearly blinded me as I drew closer to my exit. I pulled the visor down and thought back to the sad look on Jimmy's face when he mentioned his mom's death.

I felt that little part of me that wanted someone to share the burden of losing my own mother, reach out and try to grab on to Jimmy. That little part of me wanted to take solace in the fact that he had lost someone and managed to work through it. I wanted him to tell me how he did it, how he got through it, and then I wanted him to tell me he'd be there for me as I faced the same fate. All things I could never put on him or ask of him. But for just a brief moment in time, I wanted to.

I hit my head back against the headrest and knew that I needed to stop trying to create scenarios in my head that would give me permission to say yes to dinner. That is, if he asked. I blinked my eyes closed and reopened them as I put my blinker on for my exit. This was going to be a long day. I decided that my answer would be no if Jimmy asked me to dinner. In fact, any romantic advances would be shut down and not encouraged, because I needed to be there for my mom.

I pulled back into that same parking lot that I had last week. I looked at it now with fresh eyes, and without the sting of anger or frustration. I found Jimmy's bike already parked, along with a few other cars. Worried that I was late, I double-checked my phone for the time, since the dash clock hadn't been updated since the last spring forward.

Relieved that I was on time, I got out of the car and started towards the front entrance. I made my way to Jimmy's door and knocked, but there was no answer. After a few seconds, I knocked again, and again I was met with silence. Frustrated, I opened the door and checked his small office space. Clear desk, clean, organized floor, but empty. *Where was Jimmy?*

I glanced down at my cell phone; it was now five minutes past nine. I could feel the heat of confused irritation rising in my chest. I always hated being late, and not knowing the official sign-in procedure here was making me panic. I didn't want Jimmy thinking that I was irresponsible. I could feel the warmth of panic traveling up my throat.

I walked back down the hallway and glanced around; there was no one at the bar or even in the room. So, I walked behind the bar towards the kitchen doors. I gently pushed them open to a splendor of pristine white and chrome. There was a smaller kitchen area off to my right for prepping food and a commercial kitchen more towards the back.

I crept forward, a little nervous to run into someone I didn't know, and worried that I might have to explain that I actually did work there. Maybe this whole thing was a giant joke and Jimmy was just really vindictive and wanted to play the world's meanest prank on me. I would die of embarrassment if that were true, then I would torch this place to the ground, just for good measure.

I continued creeping forward, hearing voices echoing in the back. I rounded the corner and peeked through the serving window to see Jimmy perched on the huge stainless-steel counter in the middle of the kitchen, swinging his legs back and forth like a little kid. Across from him stood a large man, wearing a white apron. He had a shiny bald head, and had deep blue eyes that made his blond eyebrows stand out. He had tattoos all down his arms and up his neck. He and Jimmy were joking and laughing back and forth, while Jimmy was snacking on something from a small white plate.

I walked in a little further and saw several white plates behind the bald man, each with a different kind of pastry sitting on it. My mouth automatically started salivating. I was about to step into the room to introduce myself when I heard my name. I stopped cold right there.

"Ramsey will care, so don't do it anymore, okay," Jimmy said to the bald baker man.

What were they talking about? The balding man was rotating his arm, like he was stretching it out, and replied while letting out a loud sigh, "Fine, consider it dead, boss, we won't do it anymore."

Curiosity got the better of me and since they were discussing me, it wasn't like it wasn't any of my business. I rounded the corner fully and smiled at Jimmy, who stopped swinging his legs at the sight of me. The bald man stopped stretching and followed Jimmy's line of sight. I cleared my throat and waved. "Hi, sorry to interrupt you guys, but what exactly won't I like?"

There I just said it. They could ignore me, but at least they'd know I heard it.

The bald man let out a loud laugh and slammed his hand

down on the counter in a playful manner. "So much for clearing it up before the famous Ramsey found out, boss."

Jimmy turned a little red in the face but recovered easily. He dusted his hands and placed the plate next to him and jumped off the counter. He looked really good, in black dress pants and a white, collared shirt. I felt vastly underdressed. He reached over to the counter with all the plated pastries and grabbed one, then walked towards me and handed it over.

"Sorry, Ramsey, I was trying to clear up some spending disagreements with Rav here, before you take over the books. There are some things that I understand these guys do in the kitchen, but I know that it will drive you crazy, so I told him to stop."

I took the plate from him and picked the scone up, investigating the bite-size treat. There were little crystallized orange twists sprinkled across the top. It was still warm but before I bit into it, I asked Rav, "What kind is this? Looks, uh, interesting."

Rav grinned. "It's a new recipe, love… Crystallized orange peel with a Madagascar vanilla glaze."

I bit into the heavenly triangle and responded, "Holy crap, Rav, if you make these every day, then I don't care what you do with the books." I swallowed the perfect piece of heaven and looked at Jimmy, "If Rav made this, then I don't care what he does."

Rav gave me a big fat, happy grin then walked towards me, put his arms around me, and lifted me off the ground, like I weighed nothing. "Can I keep her, boss? Better yet, why don't you keep her, if you know what I mean?" Then he winked at Jimmy.

Real subtle.

I let out a laugh and squirmed until the giant baker man let me go. I finished my scone in an embarrassing amount of bites, then waved at Rav as I followed an eye rolling Jimmy from the kitchen. Once I could breathe again, I caught up with him, then let out a little laugh.

"Sorry, but those scones are powerful negotiating tools. How bad could he be anyway?"

Jimmy peeked at me from over his shoulder with a look that clearly said, "just wait," then opened his office door and took a seat. He laced his hands behind his head and stretched back as he explained, "Rav and the kitchen guys are all old friends of mine. Either I have known them, or my dad has, so we run things a little differently with them. It's a mess, and you'll hate how they spend money." He leaned forward and leveled me with a serious gaze.

"Basically, they use their own money, then turn in receipts when and if they remember. Or they'll use the company credit card that I gave them, but forget that they are using it when buying their personal groceries, and then they turn in receipts for that. Or they will all go out to lunch together and try to use the kitchen budget to cover it. I usually let it slide, but I was telling Rav that he needs to follow our original policy, which was following a budget, making the menu, planning the ingredients, writing it down, then taking the company credit card on company time to go get the groceries. Or order through a larger vendor, but either way, what he's currently doing isn't going to cut it anymore."

I GULPED AND COULD FEEL A SMALL BEAD OF SWEAT FORMING ON my brow. These guys were monsters. Who on earth conducted business like that? I would have to go unfriend my new friend by telling him that there was no way in hell that he could keep doing that. It was literally any accountant's worst nightmare. I noticed a small smile started covering Jimmy's face, who must have picked up on my panic. He leaned in further and said, "Told ya. How do those scones taste now?"

I placed my hand on my throat, remembering the sweet taste of throwing caution to the wind, and said, "Yeah, there is no way they can keep doing that. I will go crazy and probably end up making everyone hate me. I don't want to be hated, Jimmy." I said the last part a little panicked.

I sat back, and Jimmy finished his little laughter fest, and then started with my first-day introductions. He showed me the "office" that I was already familiar with; it was an awkward feeling to be back in that chair and not get a little queasy. Jimmy handed me form after form to fill out, made a copy of my social security card, took a voided check from me for the direct deposit, gave me a key, and then went over their "Open for Business" times versus their "Open to the Public" time.

"We can do whatever we want, wherever we want until ten thirty a.m., at which point we start getting ready for the public. We officially open at eleven a.m." Jimmy started typing something on his computer.

"Why do you open so early, if your peak hours aren't until after five?" I asked, a little curious to the workings of a fancy bar like Jimmy's. He smiled from over his computer,

"We get several business meetings that take place here. Mimosas and scones are more popular of a combo than you might think."

"Interesting. Well, what should I be doing during that time or, better yet, where's my office?" I asked, while crossing my legs, then uncrossed them as soon as I remembered how tight my jeans were. *Holy crap, I needed bigger clothes.*

Jimmy stopped typing, and his eyes jumped to mine, then darted back down as a slow blush crept into his face.

"Actually, about your office. You don't exactly have one," he finished, while grabbing for his coffee and taking a large drink.

I leaned forward. "Ok, so where exactly should I go during open business hours?"

Jimmy sat back and lounged in his chair while throwing his arms open. "We are going to share this office. I know it's not much, but you'll have whatever you need and up until eleven, you can spread out anywhere you'd like."

The idea of getting to spread out with my work on the back patio that I vaguely saw through the back windows played in my head, and I found it agreeable. Jimmy must have sensed my acceptance because he grinned and continued.

"There's another part of this job that I haven't covered with you yet. You'll be splitting time between here and my dad's bar." He paused, perhaps evaluating my reaction. "And I'll also need you to help me as a personal assistant. But it won't be much, I promise. I just know that you'll get bored once all the books are balanced and organized."

I was so focused on the Sip N Sides part of this conversation that I didn't really care about the other part, and doing PA work didn't bother me; it was just one more thing I could add to my resume. I had forgiven Theo and invited him to my barbeque, but we still hadn't talked about anything, just the two of us. I was still a little mad at the guy, but that wasn't Jimmy's problem, and this was my job, so I would get over it and be professional.

JIMMY GAVE ME A MORE DETAILED WALK THROUGH OF THE BAR with him. Once we headed outside, I fell in love. There were stringed lights all along the back pergolas, and a few fire pits scattered the patio, along with cushioned seats and wood tables. They framed a large dance floor that was placed in the middle of the outdoor space. I loved it. The changing trees offered shade and the beauty of Illinois surrounded the area, like a fantasy or a dream. I knew, at nighttime, it had to be magical. I would definitely dub this as my office space.

Once the tour was done, we walked back to his office. I took a seat, a little star-gazed from how beautiful everything was.

"So, this all sounds good, and I'm fine with sharing the office or finding my own space, but do I clock in somewhere each day, or is it electronic?"

Jimmy gave me a quizzical look. "You are salary. So, if you really don't want to come in, you don't have to. I would like you to come in, though, so if there are any questions or anything to clarify, then you are here on the premises."

I was salary!

I must have lit up like a Christmas tree; this was the perfect scenario, since mom was so sick. I could still take her to appointments, and even be home with her if I needed to. Jimmy must have seen my wheels turning because he gently spoke up and said, "Yeah, I figured it might help with your mom and stuff."

I smiled up at him and responded, "Yes, it's perfect. Thank you for thinking about that. I appreciate it."

He just nodded, but had a serious look on his face, then he asked, "How is she doing, by the way? I didn't get a chance to ask yesterday, without her hearing or it being weird."

"She's a fighter," I replied, smiling just thinking about her. "She has her good days and her bad days, she has her sick days and her sad days, but she also has her happy days, like yesterday ended up being for her. She originally was only given six months, but that was six months ago, and her new diagnosis says up to a year, so we are just trying to be grateful for the time we have."

I swallowed the lump that was forming in my throat. The air was thick, and I just wanted to talk about anything else.

Jimmy must have sensed it, as he turned around and pulled

out a large white box and placed it between us on the desk. "This is your laptop. You will use this for all your accounting and PA needs." I stood up, rotating the box to look at the specs on the side. While I was pulling off the tape and other things to free my new toy, Jimmy spoke up again, "By the way, I know it's hard to talk about, and I don't ever mean to push or to pry, but I'm here if you ever need to talk about it, okay?"

I looked over at him and couldn't help but give him a smile that spoke louder than my words could. It was one of those smiles that we women have to be careful with because it's not merely conveying our thanks or appreciation, but reflects the deep part of our souls that might show the more intense feelings we have as well. Mine, I'm sure reflected that I was a little more than infatuated with how sweet Jimmy was being. I tried to correct it quickly and hoped that he sensed my appreciation as platonic. But maybe, if I was lucky, he would read my deep craving for another one of those amazing scones.

The rest of the day flew by, telling jokes and laughing with Jimmy, and it felt like I wasn't even at work. I met the rest of the staff, and instantly fell in love with who Jimmy had selected to be on his team. I charged and started configuring my new work computer. While that started, I took a quick glance at Jimmy's computer, and the books, to see what I was up against. It was rough, but not horrible. I already had some ideas on what I would do to tighten things up and how I could help.

Before I knew it, it was five, and the bar was busy and full of people. I figured that would be my end time, although I never did officially ask. I was eager to get back to my mom and cook her dinner. During my earlier lunch break, I busied myself with finding new recipes to try, since I did nothing to prep for the week over the weekend. I decided to leave for the day, and as I was slipping my brand-new work laptop into its accompanying leather bag. Jimmy showed up at the door, leaning his large shoulder against the frame. As soon as he saw me packing up, he looked a little defeated.

"Oh, you're leaving?" he asked, as I pulled my blazer on.

I felt a little strange; he looked so hopeless, like he didn't want me to go. But it was five p.m., and nine to five was a respectable work day. "Uh, yeah, I figured I would head out since its five. Is that okay?"

"Of course. But I thought maybe Rav could make us something, and we could talk about how your official first day went?"

Oh damn. How did Mom know? Butterflies were fluttering in my chest. Of course I wanted to have dinner with him, but I had already self-talked my way out of any romantic situations, and going to dinner would just confuse our relationship. I cleared my throat and looked down at my shoes as I kept fixing my jacket. "Uh, I would love to normally, but I really should get back to my mom tonight. Raincheck?"

I was a total sucker; I could have just said that we shouldn't go to dinner because he was my boss and I was his employee. Although, I did happen to read the employee handbook, or rather, I specifically went out of my way and looked up 'Romance in the Workplace,' on page twelve. Anyway, I didn't see anything in it against Jimmy dating one of his employees. Still, it could complicate things, and I was way too attracted to Jimmy for it to not get complicated.

He smiled and put his hand behind his neck as he said, "Of course, yeah. Actually, why don't you grab some dinner from the kitchen on your way home? I'm sure your mom would love Rav's cooking."

I loved that idea. "Okay. I will, if that's okay? I would really like to share this place with her."

He smiled again, but his smile looked different, it looked...*shit*...seductive, with the way his eyes lit up and the corners of his mouth curved. He came forward and leaned into my space. In what felt like slow motion, he brought his hand up next to my chin, then reached up to my neck, and softly pulled my hair out that was caught in the jacket collar. I swear, time stopped, or maybe I was sucked into a black hole, because everything froze as his fingers grazed the top of my exposed shoulder.

Once my hair was free from the collar, he gave the curls a little tug on the ends, while that promiscuous grin stayed on his face. I got goose bumps, but I rejected the urge to shudder with delight. I stared up at him, wide-eyed from the shock of him being so close. His expression was saying, "Let's get dinner and do more than eat." He was being sweet all day with his kind words, but now I knew what was really on his mind.

Shit. Shit. Shit. He was practically a big fat marker, coloring all over my lines and not caring how much ink he was getting everywhere. I cleared my throat and squeaked out a "Thank you."

I shifted my weight to my toes a little bit, and he thankfully stepped to the side. If he hadn't, I might have stayed glued to the floor all night because I didn't have the guts to ask him to physically move out of my way.

He walked behind me, putting his hand on the small of my back, and said, so close to my ear that I could feel his lips, "Let me walk you to your car. This place can get a little crazy in the evening."

Not minding the feel of his hand on my body, I let him walk with me to the parking lot. I was so nervous that I kept asking about his kids just to fill in the silence.

I wanted to stay with him, to have dinner with him, to get to know him, but I couldn't mix our signals up or lead him on. I had to focus on my mom; my whole life was a mess right now and I had no business bringing anyone into it. I pushed away the warm sensation in my chest at being near Jimmy, and forced myself to wave good night as I climbed into my SUV. I drove away, feeling conflicted and even more jittery than I had at the beginning of the day.

Once I turned towards the exit, I saw two men on motorcycles, wearing leather jackets, heading towards Jimmy's. I was curious because these guys didn't look simple and classy, like Jimmy. They looked rough around the edges. Both had long hair and full beards, and they too didn't wear helmets. Their leather jackets had patches all over the place. Something settled in my stomach, like a rock. It felt like fear or dread. Was Jimmy still part of the biker gang?

Uncertainty churned in my mind and warred with my nerves. It was like a big warning alarm, which I needed to listen to because as much as I liked Jimmy, I didn't actually know him at all. And I didn't need to do anything that put my mother's life at risk, more than it already was.

ELEVEN

JIMMY

RIGHT AFTER RAMSEY DROVE OFF, I heard the sound of two Harley's making their way down the offramp. *Shit*. It was probably nothing, but I knew better than to assume that, especially after Davis' call. I walked over to my bike, away from the entrance of my bar and my customers, and waited for whoever was coming towards me. Sure enough, two sets of headlights made their way into the complex, accompanied by the sound of two loud engines, roaring as they drew closer.

Wilkins and Thompson stopped in front of me and turned off their bikes. Thompson looked like he had seen better days. He was about my age, had long hair that was always tied behind his head, but now it was a tangled mess that sat below his shoulders; he also had a bit of a beard growing. Wilkins was in his late sixties and looked it. He had no hair but a full, scruffy, unkempt beard. They glanced at each other, then Thompson leaned to the side while still on his bike.

"Long time, Jimmy." His brown eyes looked red and irritated.

I nodded at him. "Thompson." Then I looked over and regarded Wilkins. "Old age finally catching up with you, old man?" I smiled, so they knew I was kidding, and hopefully lightened whatever message they were sent to deliver to me.

Wilkins laughed and shook his head. "The ladies don't seem to think so."

Thompson shook his head too, laughing. I didn't want to wait all night for this, so I dug in. "How can I help you, gentlemen? Or rather, how can I help Davis?"

They gave each other a brief look, so fast I couldn't make it out, but I caught it. Wilkins turned off his bike and kicked his legs further out, as if he was settling in. Thompson cleared his bike and turned it off. The sound of his kickstand scraping the asphalt was the only sound between us. He pushed some of his knotted hair off his face.

"Jimmy," he drew out, while he gripped his leather jacket and looked around. "Nice place you got here. Why not invite us inside, order us a drink?" I glared at him. I didn't have time for this.

"Cut the shit, Thompson. Why are you here?" I responded dryly. Thompson reared back as if he was offended, and Wilkins shook his head with a low chuckle.

"Why, Mr. Stenson, that wasn't very kind of you. If I didn't know better, I'd say you were trying to get rid of us and even, perhaps, keep us dirty vermin out of your fancy bar?" Thompson drawled in a fake southern tone, while spreading out his arms.

I took a step closer and itched to loosen my tie. Thompson watched my fingers twitch and took half a step back. Maybe he was remembering that time I smashed his cousin's face in. Or maybe he was recalling the reason I received my beloved pet name, The Fist. Either way, I was glad he backed up. I didn't need a scene in front of my bar and that's exactly what this asshole wanted.

Thompson cleared his throat and crossed his arms. "Davis

expected you to set up a meeting by now. He's getting tired of waiting for your response."

I narrowed my gaze on the two of them in confusion. "I told Rav to set it up."

They looked at each other again, and Wilkins exhaled while he situated his larger body on his bike.

"You should know better than anyone that when Davis says he's ready to set up a meeting, that means you show up in person and pay your respect. Don't make him go through your damn secretary," Thompson spat at me, while looking me up and down.

He took a step to the side and drew his hand up to run his fingers over his messy hair, looked around and took a sidestep back in my direction. "He gave you five fucking years, Jimmy. Now he's not only found your bitch of a wife, but kindly asked for you to meet with him, and you put him off." His face was twisted with anger, like he was ready for a fight.

I waited to respond, getting my anger totally in check. My hands were casually in my pockets as I leaned forward.

"I meant no disrespect. It was an honest misunderstanding. But let's be clear; I didn't ask Davis to find Lisa. I am thankful that he used his resources to aid me, but I didn't ask for the favor." I zeroed in on Thompson. "And, if Davis is that worried about this meeting, then why the hell didn't he straddle his Dyna and ride down here himself?"

Wilkins grimaced at my tone and Thompson began breathing through his nose so hard that I thought he might hyperventilate. He was pissed, and obviously working on keeping his own anger in check.

"Next week: The Brass, nine p.m. Don't be late," Thompson threw at me as he got back on his bike and started it up. Wilkins followed and gave me a hesitant look, like he wasn't sure what to do. I nodded at him and watched as the two of them drove away.

I let out a sigh once they were gone, and looked around. Thankfully, Ramsey had missed that. This part of my life-my past, was something I never wanted her to see. I knew for sure if she ever did, she'd abandon any notion of something happening between us. Not that she was showing any interest so far, but I had hopes that she'd come around.

I walked back towards the restaurant, intent on grabbing dinner for Ramsey. I realized that she had forgotten it after she drove off. I went into the kitchen to find Rav tying up two plastic bags. "I wrapped up the 'Tuesday night' special for your lady friend, boss." Rav handed the bags to me. "A quart of basil-tomato soup and gouda grilled cheese on sourdough. I thought you might want to ask her to eat with you tonight, but when she left, I assumed maybe you'd drop it off," Rav finished with a sly smile on his face, and I laughed.

"Smooth, and very perceptive. What made you think all that?" I asked, while reaching for a small piece of pita bread that was left out from an earlier meal. Rav laughed while reaching over the counter for some green garnish. "I have eyes."

I grabbed another piece of bread to evade answering and shook my head at him while grabbing Ramsey's dinner. I considered bringing up the interaction that just took place in the parking lot, but reconsidered when I thought of what might happen if Rav brought it up to someone. Seemed Davis wasn't particularly happy about going through our third party to communicate. I left the restaurant and secured the meal in my backpack, and headed to Belvidere.

WHILE I RODE, I THOUGHT BACK ON HOW I HAD STARTED THE DAY with absolutely no plans on pursuing anything with Ramsey. I had a plan. We would not be in the same space at the same time, she would not share my office, I would not invite her to dinner. But just like always with Ramsey, as soon as I saw her, I buckled. She looked like sin in a church, walking in with skin-tight jeans and high heels. Her lips were blood red and damn, it looked good on her.

Her hair was down, but I still looked for the braid, and it drove me crazy all day trying to find it. I knew that she had at least one somewhere in her hair. I even began to doubt how perceptive I thought I was about her, until lunchtime. I saw her flip her hair and there it was, a small little braid tucked under it all. I fist-pumped the air because it proved that I knew something about Ramsey that probably no one else did, or very few other people did; she wore at least one braid every single day. She didn't even know that it was my favorite thing about her when I first saw her.

I was two seconds away from running my hands through her hair while I looked over figures with her, but I could only imagine what she would have done if I did. The idea of her hair fanned out behind her on my bed was playing through my mind, and I lost all sense of time and direction. I wanted her. The responsible and grown-up part of my brain was scolding me, telling me that I didn't even know her, but the immature and very lonely part of me was screaming for me to take her and make her mine.

Before I knew it, I was already pulling into Belvidere and onto Ramsey's street. I took in a few calming breaths, hoping it wouldn't bother her that I showed up after she had already requested a raincheck from me. I parked my bike, pulled the bag of food out of my backpack, and walked up to her front door. I rang the doorbell and waited.

Carla opened the door, wearing a black and silver tracksuit with a small beanie on her head, her eyes wide from seeing me on her stoop, dark circles riddled the area underneath each eye, causing me to wrinkle my forehead in worry.

"Hey, Carla, sorry to show up unexpected, but Ramsey forgot her dinner at the restaurant."

I held up the bag for emphasis, and Carla's whole face lit up. "Jimmy come in! Ramsey was threatening me with some type of meat that I know she doesn't know how to cook."

Moving toward the table, I tried to swallow the lump in my throat that had started to develop every time I thought of Carla's sickness and her leaving Ramsey too soon. I set down the bag down on the kitchen table, while looking around for Ramsey. I didn't see her in the kitchen or dining room, which must have meant that she was in her bedroom. I was about to turn around and head home when Carla rushed up behind me and grabbed my wrist, pulling me towards a chair.

"Sit, sit, stay. Eat with us."

I smiled at her, but had no intention of staying. Then again, Ramsey mentioned the raincheck because she needed to be with her mom and since she was here, maybe she wouldn't mind?

"No. Thank you so much, Carla, but I have to get home." I didn't want to assume that Ramsey wanted me here, regardless of how tempting it was.

Just as I finished talking, Ramsey walked out. Her hair was piled on top of her head with loose strands falling around her face, and she was wearing a tank with tiny pajama shorts. I had to sit back down for a second to be sure that no one saw how much the sight of Ramsey all dressed down affected me.

She stopped mid-step at the sight of me, confusion and surprise marring her face as her beautiful eyes widened in surprise, then her eyebrows drew together a second later.

"Uh, Jimmy, what are you doing here?" she asked while pulling her shorts further down, as though she was trying to stretch the fabric to cover more of her gorgeous legs.

Oh nothing, I just thought we could have dinner together after all.

Excuse my very persistent behavior. And maybe before we eat, I could walk you back to your room and we could get better-acquainted?

"Jimmy?" Ramsey had taken a step closer, her eyebrows were hugging her forehead as she questioned my silence. *Shit.*

I looked down at the plastic bag then held it up again. "You forgot your dinner," I declared with a small smile. I waited for her to light up, like she did before. Or to walk towards me and smile. But she just stood there, not saying anything. Carla spoke up and broke the tension between us.

"Well, Jimmy, that was so sweet of you to bring it all this way. Will you join us for dinner then?"

I almost accepted this time, almost pulled out a chair and sat down, but I wanted to wait for Ramsey to agree with her mom that I should stay. I waited, one second, then two. Ramsey stood watching me, then looked around the room, but she didn't encourage me to stay. I should have just left her alone tonight. It wasn't about a raincheck, she just didn't want to have dinner with me.

I messed with the sleeves of my dress shirt. "Sorry, I can't, but I hope you ladies enjoy your evening. Ramsey, I will see you tomorrow at work."

I smiled at her and turned to leave. I didn't see Ramsey move towards me, but once I was to the door, she appeared behind me to walk me out.

She had her arm pulled across her chest, holding onto her elbow. She was looking at the floor as we moved from the entryway, through the door, and outside.

"Thanks for bringing this, and …um…"

She tucked a few strands of hair behind her ear, trailing off, like she wanted to say something else. I stopped and turned towards her to try and encourage her question, but when I looked at her face, and saw the red on her cheeks, all I could focus on was how that heat traveling up her body had to start somewhere, and I wrestled against wanting to discover exactly where. *She just rejected you, idiot.*

She wasn't saying anything else, so I finished up our conversation. "It was no problem. Enjoy your dinner, Rav packed it for you."

My voice came out harsh as the sting from her rejection started to hit. She had both arms crossed and her eyes darted to mine as my comment landed.

"It's not that I didn't want to see you for dinner, I just had to get back to my mom. She's my priority right now. Nothing else, no one else, just her. She has to come first and be my whole world."

I heard what she was saying—no dating until her mom got better, or worse, her mom passed on. Either way, the living part was solely dedicated to her mom and only her mom. She was also ignoring the fact that she had the opportunity to have dinner with both her mom and me tonight, and yet, she still didn't want to.

I smiled and turned back towards my bike before saying goodbye. "I understand, Ramsey. Please let me know if there is any way I can make things easier on you at work with your mom."

I didn't wait for her to respond. I got on my bike and drove off. Ego bruised, and pride pricked, I inhaled the cold air as I put some distance between Ramsey's house and myself. I needed to let this go; get over this crush or whatever the hell this thing was.

TWELVE

I RECEIVED AN EMAIL BEFORE WORK, requesting that I spend my day in Belvidere at Sip N Sides. It felt like a slap in the face because Jimmy had already mentioned that he would see me at work today. That was, until I stood there like a silent idiot, not inviting him to eat dinner with us, then spouted off some bullshit about why I didn't. I slightly hated myself for what I told him because obviously, I liked him and wanted him to like me back, and wanted to be asked out to dinners and brought flowers, and the whole thing. But how on earth could I possibly be happy and dating someone while my mom was dying? And what if he had illegal stuff going on? I didn't want to get mixed up in anything like that.

I closed my eyes and let out a strained breath.

I made the right decision to tell him to back off; my mom needed to come first, no matter what. Still, it would have been nice to continue to be his friend, but based off the look on his face last night and the new arrangement this morning, it didn't seem like I was going to have a choice.

I walked back to the closet and reached for a regular white, cotton t-shirt to pair with not-so-tight-that-they-might-explode blue jeans.

I pulled my hair into a simple French braid, dragged out some ballet flats, and checked the mirror. My jeans were still skinny, but not plastered, and no lipstick today. I kissed Mom on the way out, desperate to ignore her glares since last night. I thought back to how badly last night ended, not just with Jimmy but her too.

I WALKED BACK INSIDE AFTER JIMMY LEFT AND GRABBED THE plastic bag off the table.

"You know, Theo told me that Jimmy hasn't dated anyone in a really long time. It was a big deal for him to put himself out there like that," my mother threw at me from the kitchen while she hastily grabbed two bowls. I stayed silent, knowing it was pointless to try and argue.

"That boy drove all the way over here to bring you dinner, and the least you could have done is to invite him to eat with us." She had made her way to the table. I bit back my retort about him driving all the way over here, when our house was on his way home. She cut a cold glare in my direction before continuing.

" I won't be here for much longer, darling. I want to see you happy, and I think you could have something with him, but now we'll never know because of how rude you were to him."

Her dramatic tirade had finally stopped, or so it seemed. Silence filled the room as we took out the containers of soup and grilled cheese. Finally, I braved speaking.

"Momma, I don't want to date right now. Especially not my boss, and especially not someone who has kids and drama. It's just too much for me now."

"No, it's not. I know you better than anyone, and I know when you're just being stubborn. You two have a spark, a light that others can see, but you're too blind," my mother scolded while she pushed around her soup.

I reached for my water glass and took a sip, to help clear away some of the words I wanted to scream at her. I realized it was pointless to tell her how she should be my priority or how little money we currently had in the bank, and how me not screwing up my job was a big deal. Or how my heart was in no position to be handed over to someone who might damage it. So, I shut my mouth and ate my dinner. Eventually, she gave up on trying to eat any of the food, and just went to bed without so much as another word to me.

I knew she hoped that I would apologize to Jimmy and try and go out with him, but I wasn't going to. Sucks for her, but I wasn't going to fling around romance and be happy while she was puking up her guts in the bathroom.

ONCE I PULLED INTO THE BARELY-KEPT-TOGETHER PARKING LOT of Sip N Sides, a vast change from the gorgeous parking lot I had pulled into yesterday, I slid out and trudged in. I was in a crap mood and I needed to get out of it, Theo deserved better. So, while I made my way to his office, I decided to focus on happier things. I gave the brown door in front of me a soft knock and waited. Nothing happened. I knocked again and heard a small cough, but still, no one was opening. I eyed the doorknob and wondered if I should just go in, when a moment later Theo opened the door and gave me a big smile.

"If it isn't my prettiest employee!" he practically yelled, sounding almost happy.

Weird.

"Hey, Theo, what's going on?" I asked, a little confused. I figured today would be strange for Jimmy and me, not me and Theo.

He opened the door a bit wider, and I noticed his office was much bigger than Jimmy's. It had a large oak desk with an old computer perched in the corner, along with a mess of papers scattered across it. There were two worn green leather chairs in front of the desk, and old blue carpet on the floor. It was outdated, to say the least. I crept forward and sat down in one of the green chairs while Theo settled across the desk in his own chair.

He cleared his throat and answered loudly, "Well, I was just thinking how nice this arrangement is. I originally wanted you to work here, and now here you are. I have never had a daughter, Ramsey, but I feel like if I did, she would be like you."

My brain was fried. It had to be, because what I just heard was the equivalent of a madman rambling. I fixed my stare on him, watching his body. There was no shaking or jitterbugs, no random nose swipes or ear pulls. He didn't seem like he was on anything, but still, he was being weird.

"Theo, is everything okay? You just seem a little off?" I asked, while giving him the side-eye.

"No, why? Is this about the whole omission about Jimmy thing? I can explain that." He shuffled a pile of papers and set them atop another pile. "People are just people at the end of the day, and we aren't all perfect. I just didn't want to freak you out by telling you I was his dad or associate myself with him until he had a chance to redeem himself."

He turned on his computer and glanced at the screen while moving his mouse around; the whole thing was ancient, so different from Jimmy's space.

"Theo, it's okay. I'm over your little omission. Although, getting publicly fired wasn't my favorite thing, and I would have loved a heads-up on that, but it's okay."

Thinking we'd moved past his awkwardness, I took out my own laptop and started it up.

Theo clapped his hands together and rolled his chair closer to his desk. "Look, Ramsey, I know I'm running a million miles a minute, but I am truly glad you are here. Jimmy may come off as a jerk, and I wanted to put my hands on the boy after you told me your story of him nearly running you off the road, but he has a good heart, and I was hoping you could work out seeing that for yourself."

Maybe I just needed to realize that Theo was odd. Or that something was off with him and he didn't want me to catch on.

I held back the urge to roll my eyes and tried to focus on today's task. I thought about his greeting today and how he kept bringing up Jimmy. We were still practically strangers, so why was he pushing the Jimmy topic so hard? Theo was up to something and I suddenly wondered if it wasn't Theo's choice that I work here as an accountant. Maybe I was just paranoid, but it felt like he was trying to keep me distracted from something, and I had a very strong feeling that he didn't want me peeking at those books. This should be interesting.

It HAD BEEN AN HOUR. ONE WHOLE HOUR SINCE I HAD requested to see Theo's books for the bar. Theo started his evasion by distracting me with stories. He leaned back in his squeaking, old wooden chair, and laced his fingers together on his stomach.

"Did I ever tell you that time Jimmy nearly lost an arm?"

That was how he hooked me the first time. Because, of course, I hadn't heard that story. I hadn't heard any stories, except for the ones he shared with me that night in his bar. I sat forward, laughed, and even asked questions as he told me tale after tale. I didn't want to be rude, but I was getting irritated. I was even getting to the point where I wanted to write out an email to Jimmy to beg for some advice on how to get through to his dad, and then add in a little tidbit about how this was my job and I shouldn't be made to feel like the dirty IRS peeking around. I wrote it out and then deleted it five times.

Finally, once I started playing his game, asking about his

late wife, and grandkids he gave up and let me view everything I needed to see, which answered my earlier question about why he was so weird. He didn't want his son Jimmy involved in his books, because Theo was loaded.

The revenue from the bar was decent and covered paying the few employees he had, as well as utilities. The building itself was paid off and he didn't have any other loans out. He was fine on budgeting and keeping up with his orders. The bar on its own was doing fine, but it was the overwhelmingly large cash reserve that caught my attention.

I scratched my neck and then began to rub my temples. My gut started to turn at the idea that Theo was probably into something illegal. It was no secret that Sip N Sides was a local favorite for its cheap liquor and greasy food. It was also well-known that the pool tables were old, the carpet faded, that was barely held together and even ripped in some places. Duct tape held most of the stuffing in the seats. It didn't exactly scream steady income or big money. The regular customers were mechanics in greasy coveralls, biker guys in their leather cuts, or some flannel-wearing truckers. So, as I stared at all the zeros in the cash reserve, I kept coming back to the same conclusion: Theo was doing something illegal. I pictured Theo running drugs or maybe he had killed someone. Was this his payout? *"They call me the Ripper..."*

Oh my gosh.

I suddenly pictured Theo ripping into bodies and hiding drugs in their chest cavities. *Ewww.* I needed to stop. But what if it was true? What if Theo was into something illegal? Would I turn him in? I pictured Theo as a grandpa and thought about how some of those nice people get caught up into mob life situations. How the mob was a family business, and I pictured myself keeping Theo's secret, so he wouldn't go to jail. I mean, I couldn't do that to Jasmine and Sammy. *No Ramsey, you'd just go to jail. No big deal.*

I looked at Theo and waved my hand towards his computer from my spot across his desk.

"Theo, do you have something you would like to tell me?"

I didn't want him to think that I would snitch, so I took my legs down slowly, leaned forward and steepled my fingers under my chin. Giving him my most intense look possible I continued, "I mean, if there is something you need to tell me, you can trust that you are only telling me, and I have a pesky habit of deleting things."

I was entertaining the idea of winking, to really get my point across.

I could be in the mafia.

I could totally do this.

My pulse was jumping, doing massive overtime, just thinking about some guy named Vinnie walking through the door any minute.

Theo's thick white eyebrows drew together in confusion. "What?" he tried to clarify with me, "are you implying that I'm hiding something?"

"Aren't you, though? Isn't that why I'm here?"

He was frozen. Mouth open, eyes wide, hair in his face, hand on the mouse, frozen. I was starting to get uncomfortable as he just stared at me. Finally, he broke his weird staring match with me and looked at his computer screen. Letting out a huge breath he started, "I guess you would find out sooner or later, girl. This is why I didn't want Jimmy to put you in here, poking around."

I knew it. I just knew it, and now we would have this secret, and I was going to be officially in the family business. That, or I was going to die because I knew too much. Definitely one or the other, and I was really hoping for the family business one.

I realized I was being too quiet and in my own little world when Theo called my name again.

"Ramsey, did you hear me? It's not what you think."

Oh. It's not what I think…then that means…

"Theo, if it's not something illegal, then where did all this money come from? You can't blame me for being a little surprised. I mean, who has over one hundred grand sitting as a cash reserve for their mediocre bar?"

Theo threw his hands forward and laid them on the desk. "Look, Ramsey, when my wife died, she left me a life insurance claim, as well as part of an inheritance that she had received from a deceased relative. Jimmy knew about the life insurance claim and demanded that I put all the money away for retirement. He wouldn't even take a dime of it to start up his bar."

Theo was running his hands through his hair, but his eyes looked strangely peaceful, like it was taking a load off of him to share this with someone. I relaxed, hopefully to encourage him to continue.

"The life insurance claim paid for Loretta's medical bills and funeral mostly, and I tucked some of it away in my retirement fund, but in her will, Loretta made it clear that the two-hundred-thousand dollar inheritance was to go to Sip N Sides, so that Jimmy could take it over with a clean slate and be debt-free, and make it into something great. She had always wanted something that stayed in our family, something that would go on for generations. That's why she didn't leave the money for Jimmy personally; it's strictly for Sip N Sides."

I was leaning forward, with my hand propped under my chin, in full on listening mode. What a sweet gift that Loretta left them. I was getting caught up in the story when I realized I was utterly confused. "Wait, why all the secrecy then? Why don't you want Jimmy to know what is going on over here?"

Theo moved forward a few inches in his rolling chair. "Jimmy has always hated Sip N Sides. He has never really shown interest in owning the bar, and I was always hesitant to bring him into the business anyway because it was such a debt magnet. We were never in the black, always running red in the books. It was an embarrassment, and when Jimmy worked here as a teenager, he knew it was a money pit. It took a few years to get things balanced, for the banks to release the money and for the IRS to take theirs.

"The day I planned to tell Jimmy about the inheritance for the bar, he told me about his idea to start his own in Rockford, and laid out his entire business plan. He told me about how Jackson had already fronted the money, and I couldn't stop him. I couldn't do it to him, I didn't want to keep him here and hold him back from starting something on his own, and I knew then, that if I had offered him Sip N Sides, he would feel like he didn't earn it. He would feel like he was just getting a hand-out, so I shut my mouth and just kept it a secret, waiting to decide what to do. You might not know this, but Jimmy is trying to push me to retire."

I couldn't understand why Theo didn't want to retire; shoot, I would be on an island somewhere if I had a hundred grand to float by on. "So why not retire, then? Why not sell? I know Loretta wanted it in the family, but you can't force Jimmy to take it."

Theo had this look on his face, the type of look that said he had a plan, but wasn't going to share it with me, and I didn't have another four hours to try and get it out of him. Still, at least he responded, "I have a plan, it will just take some time. Meanwhile, I get to hire pretty new employees like yourself."

I smiled at him, cheeky bastard.

"Yes, and hopefully update some of the nasty carpets around here," I said with a laugh. Theo slapped the desk and let out a laugh. "Not a chance, darlin', not a chance."

I knew he was trying to move the conversation forward, but I couldn't help but ask. "Doesn't Jimmy already own half the bar? That's what he told me when he fired me."

Theo folded his hands and creased his eyebrows. "Technically, he does, but he's a silent owner. He doesn't check in or anything, maybe that's why he put you here, to feel better about it."

That made sense, I guess. This whole thing seemed strange, but I just shrugged and decided to let it go.

After our talk, I couldn't stop smiling, I knew something that Jimmy didn't know, and it made me feel closer to Theo, and cooler somehow. I always liked feeling cooler than other people.

The rest of the day flew by rather quickly. I asked Theo a little bit more about the origins of the bar, and a few more financial questions, then fell into an easy silence, until he spoke up again.

"So, your mother and I are both attending the big bingo bash this weekend in Chicago. It's a big night on the town, they even booked us a group of rooms at a hotel near the hall. I guess it's a championship of some kind, should be fun."

My eyes shot to his in surprise. I didn't know that my mother agreed to go. I had heard her say something about Chicago and bingo, but I didn't catch any of the details. My face must have betrayed how worried I was because I felt Theo's hand gently land on mine.

"What's wrong, hon?"

He probably knew what was wrong, but didn't want to put his foot in his mouth by assuming. I searched for the words to say, to explain how worried I was about her leaving without completely falling apart.

"I'm just... I'm worried about her. I'm worried something might happen..." *Damn tears. Damn them!* I blinked to keep them away, but the more I thought of something happening to her while I was away, the more they crept in. I swiped under my eyes and sat up straight. "She needs someone on standby; medically, I mean. If something happens..."

I looked down at the nasty, outdated carpet, not ready to face Theo's assuring face. He patted my hand and kindly said,

"Since the senior center is setting it all up, they have three RN's tagging along. She'll be okay. I'll call you immediately if anything comes up."

His assurances worked for now. I knew my mother was stubborn and was going to live what life she had left, so asking her not to go was out of the question. I also knew she'd step up her matchmaking game if I tried to tag along. So, it helped knowing that Theo was going and that he would watch out for her.

"I know my mom is excited, and it means a lot that you are going as well. Just… watch out for her."

"Of course. You know that I will, Ramsey. What will you do with your weekend since you are suddenly free?" Theo asked, while shuffling a few small piles and placing them onto larger ones. I cringed at the chaos and directed my focus back on his word choice.

I loved that this man said the words, "Suddenly free," like I actually had a life of some kind. He didn't need to know that, though.

"Oh, you know me. I'm sure I will get some kind of invitation for fun from one of my billion friends here." Maybe I should go see Laney.

"Well, I'm sure a pretty girl like yourself will get an invite to do something," Theo said with guarded confidence, like he didn't want me to go have fun with a date, just like a dad would sound with his daughter. My heart melted and my eyes stung. He was making this whole hating Jimmy thing so difficult because they were all a big package. Him, his dad, and his kids —they lived together, and were affected by who Jimmy dated together. I let out a quiet breath so that Theo wouldn't hear me. I didn't want to respond, but I did anyway.

"Yeah, I'm sure I will get something." Something vague, oddly hopeful, and completely a lie. Me and the local stray cats knew that I was working with absolutely nothing.

THIRTEEN

JIMMY

It was Thursday. Grocery shopping day. I set odd hours to avoid the masses and it happened to oddly be the slowest day at the bar out of the entire week. I normally didn't mind shopping, normally I liked the peace I felt during the monotonous task.

But today, as I walked down the cereal aisle, I couldn't help but feel irritated. I had somehow managed to keep Ramsey at bay all week by keeping her at dad's bar. I started this whole mess by sending her to Sip N Sides, all because I felt rejected. I actually understood where she was coming from.

It wasn't that she rejected me, though; it was that she affected me, and that was dangerous. I liked her, but I also wanted to stay far enough away from her, that she couldn't hurt me. I couldn't actually date someone seriously unless I was just that—serious. The kids deserved stability, and I wasn't entirely sure I was ready to trust someone to that degree again.

I steered my cart to the side of the aisle and grabbed a box of honey nut something and chocolate puffs, then headed towards the canned goods. I was worried that I had set up a new wall between Ramsey with the whole email thing.

I needed to clear up some of the stuff I tried to put on her and just be her boss, and hopefully her friend. The problem was, I had no idea what to text, except to ask her to come back to Jimmy's. So, I pulled out my phone in between the chili and the diced tomatoes and punched out a text.

Me: *Hey Ramsey, I know I have had you helping dad all week, but could you come into Jimmy's tomorrow at nine?*

I stuffed my phone back into my jeans and kept going down the aisle. I piled in at least ten cans of chili and then headed towards the produce. I wasn't even staying on track with a list today, I just knew we needed food in the house, and I couldn't help but gravitate towards the comfort kind. I started steering the shopping cart to the frozen food section when a small voice piped up behind me.

"Jimmy, dear, is that you?"

I turned around and saw Carla standing there in one of her adorable tracksuits and a green beanie.

I smiled at her and leaned down to give her a hug. "Hi, Miss Carla, how are you?"

She smiled but it quickly turned into a frown. "Well, I'm okay, but"—she shifted on her feet and turned her body more towards me, like she was ready for a serious conversation—"I will tell you, Jimmy, I am worried about Ramsey."

Her eyes darted around, like we were sharing a secret. I felt my stomach flip a few times.

I leaned forward, sensing that she wanted our conversation to be discreet. "What do you mean, is she okay?" I asked, trying to shove down the panic in my voice.

Carla let out a sigh. "Yes, she's fine, but this week, she has been in a mood and I still haven't forgiven her for—" She stopped, her eyes roamed back and forth over my face as if she might find her next word there. "Oh, never mind. She's just been in a mood, and I worry that she's not thinking clearly about specific people or situations."

Her voice had taken a bit of an 'I told you so' tone to it.

I wanted to laugh at the obvious situation she was speaking of. I checked the aisle we were in to be sure we weren't blocking anyone.

"Carla, you know that Ramsey just wants the best for you, right? I can understand why she might be hesitant about specific people or situations."

Carla gripped her shopping cart and her eyes darted around; I could tell that she wanted to say something more. She opened her mouth then shut it, then opened it again. "I know she worries, but she doesn't understand how badly I want to see her happy before I leave this earth."

Tears started in her eyes and I had to look away, I didn't deal with tears very well. Especially not from dying mothers thinking about their children. She wiped a few of them away and then continued, "Well anyway, I should be heading back… can't stay out too long, or else I get tired. I need to rest up before my big bingo trip this weekend."

She said the last part with so much hope that it broke me a little bit.

I smiled at her. "Well I hope you have fun this weekend, you deserve it."

She gave me a gentle smile back, "oh, and Jimmy?" pausing mid-step, she said, "Ramsey will be all alone this weekend, I would love it if you checked in on her. She won't admit it, but she could really use a friend right now." Carla finished with a waved and walked off.

I felt my phone buzz in my pocket. Pulling it free, I found an incoming text.

Ramsey: Sure, whatever you need, boss.

I GRABBED THE KIDS FROM SCHOOL ON MY WAY HOME. ONCE I was done, and the kids had put their stuff away, they both settled into the breakfast nook.

"So Sammy, how was school today?" He was digging into a pile of peanut butter with an apple wedge.

"Today was the best, Dad! Seriously, the best. We got to hold snakes in class today, and one of them was so big that the snake guy told us that it could eat our class hamster."

Sammy had one knee bent under him while he stretched his hands out, demonstrating just how big the snake was. I didn't particularly like snakes, but if my kid liked it, then I wanted to be happy for him.

"Awesome, bud. Did you wash your hands after you touched them?" I asked, looking up from the meat I was browning. Sammy froze, and his eyes darted to either side of the room, in his very famous "Oops" face. I threw my arm up and pointed toward the downstairs bathroom. He hopped up from the table to go wash his hands.

Becoming a dad turned me into someone I would have made fun of a few years ago. I would never have cared about touching snakes and washing hands, but now, as a parent, I cared. While Sammy was gone, I looked over at Jasmine and continued prepping dinner.

"So Jaz, how was your day?"

She was quietly eating her apple slices and staring at the table, which was her famous "I had a bad day" face.

She took a minute but finally responded, "It was fine, have you heard from Ramsey? I want to make sure that she is still going to help me before the tryouts on Saturday."

Thankful I had cleared things up with Ramsey, I nodded my head, but realized she would probably need some words to attach to the nod. "Yeah, sorry, sweetie. She will be at work tomorrow, and I can check in with her. But I don't think she forgot, she asked me about it on Monday."

Remembering that brief conversation, before she climbed into her car on the night she rejected me, made my neck feel tense. I looked over at Jasmine, and noticed that she was still silently eating her apples, looking worried. Poor thing, I knew she was panicked about the tryouts. I thought having tryouts for nine-year-olds was ridiculous. They seemed a little young to be that competitive, then again, I thought of some of those reality dance shows and realized how wrong I was. Still, I hated how nervous it made my little girl.

Trying to improve her mood, I placed my hands on the counter and faced her. "Hey, I have an idea, Jaz. Why don't we have one of our famous theatre nights on Friday, get your mind off things?"

Right as I said it, Sammy ran back into the room. "Theatre night?!" he yelled, and then jumped back into his seat.

I let out a little laugh at my spastic kid. "Yeah bud, let's do a theatre night. I heard there is a new superhero movie that came out. Or we could always do a classic; we haven't done one in a while."

Jasmine had her elbows up on the table, facing me. "Why not a princess movie? I never get a princess movie, Dad." She wasn't wrong, but there was a reason for it. I hated princess movies with every fiber of my being.

Sammy jumped up on both of his knees, hovering with half his body over the table. "Let's ask Grandpa and see what he wants. I bet you a million bucks he won't want a stupid princess movie," he snidly argued with Jasmine. She sat up tall, about to yell back, when I cut in.

"Actually, Grandpa will be gone this weekend on his bingo trip, so it's just us." I thought that would excite them, but of course, they both shrank in their seats, looking defeated.

It was silent in the kitchen for a few glorious minutes while I finished preparing dinner, then Jasmine spoke up. "Is it the same bingo trip that Ramsey's mom mentioned at the barbeque last weekend?"

I kept my eyes on the meat that I was prepping as I responded, "Yep, the same one, sis."

She started kicking her legs back and forth in front of her, another one of her famous tells, that said, "I have a plan."

Sure enough, I heard a little cough from her, then saw her take a sip of water before she stood up. "If Miss Carla is going to be gone, then that means Ramsey will be all alone, won't it, Dad?"

I didn't like where this was headed. "Um, I don't know, Jaz? She might have plans."

Jasmine eyed me as I kept prepping dinner, rubbing her hands on her jeans, continuing, "Well, let's say she *is* all alone. Wouldn't it be nice to invite her to our theatre night?"

Crap.

This was all Sammy would need; he was like a dog with a bone when people put fun ideas in his head, and he wouldn't let go until you either yelled it out of him or gave in. Sure enough, his eyes got big, he jumped off the bench and ran up to where I was standing.

"Yes, please, please, please. Invite her, she will come, I know it. She likes us, Dad."

He was hanging on my arm now, as I tried to keep working on dinner. I knew my kids well enough to know that they weren't going to give up. I faced them both and held my hands up in surrender. "Okay, here's the deal. You kids make her an invite. On it, put the movie we are watching and what time, and I will hand it to her at work tomorrow. That is all I can promise, okay?"

They both nodded their heads and ran upstairs in search of craft supplies. Something told me this was going to be yet another Ramsey-filled weekend.

FOURTEEN

IT WAS FRIDAY, and my temporary banishment from Jimmy's was finally lifted. I could be immature about the fact that Jimmy had froze me out all week and stuck me at Sip N Sides as some sort of emotional punishment, but I chose to rise above it. After all, Sip N Sides was a part of my job. Thinking back over the last few days at Sip N Sides, it was actually quite fun.

I had walked out to the bar area to grab a soda when I gently mentioned, "You know, these bar stools are nice." I walked over to the duct tape-covered stools to make sure I landed my next point. "Except, I actually overheard some customers talking about how they had to pick some duct tape residue from their pants the last time they were here."

Theo's eyebrows drew together as he walked over to check out the object in question. Sure enough, he moved towards the other barstools, inspecting each one as he went.

"Darn it. This duct tape has gotten a bit out of control, hasn't it?" he asked, taking a few steps back to get a better view of the seating area.

I ran my hand along one of the padded seats. "Yeah, I think it might be time to swap 'em out." I briefly looked up to catch Theo's face as I said it. Surprisingly, he looked thoughtful as he ran his hand over his light beard.

Encouraged, I kept going. "In fact, I was just looking on this website and saw a few ideas for Sip N Sides, would you want to see them?"

Theo let out a sigh, put his hand out, and said, "Lead the way."

That's how our week went, and exactly how I managed to talk him into not only upgrading the bar seats, but the carpet and a few of the light fixtures as well. I showed him how cost-effective we could be, and how little of a dent it would put into Loretta's money if he chose to upgrade. Best of all, I showed him how Sip N Sides wouldn't turn into Jimmy's fancy place, simply by investing a little money into it.

However, as much as I loved designing and shopping for Sip N Sides, I was ready to get back to actual work. Jimmy's really did need my help and God only knew how much worse things had gotten over the last few days.

I was pulling my black V-neck sweater over my head just as my mother walked into my room; or rather, barged in. She didn't have much of an opinion on privacy, except that kids who lived in her house shouldn't have it. I straightened my sweater and faced her. She was holding the door with one hand and a small suitcase handle in the other.

"I just wanted to say goodbye before the van came to pick me up. I wanted to remind you to please reach out to Jimmy if you need anything this weekend."

I held back the urge to roll my eyes at her and just smiled instead. I guess me living on my own since college held no weight in her eyes.

"Mom, I promise to reach out to Jimmy if I need anything, but I was thinking about maybe going to visit Laney this week-end, since you were going to be gone."

I walked over to my closet and grabbed some boots, then glanced back at her. She faintly smiled, then moved both hands to her suitcase. "Just be careful, sweetheart, with whatever you decide to do. And remember that your life on this earth is limited, so enjoy it, and I hope you have fun."

I was shocked. No matchmaking scheme, or lecture on meeting someone and making her grandbabies before she died? My mom might need to get out more often, if she was going to be this agreeable. As soon as that thought entered my mind, so did a big batch of guilt. What if something happened? What if I missed something?

I turned away from her, so she wouldn't see my conflicted emotions. *She'd be fine. This was her choice and it was good for her.*

Turning from the closet, I stepped forward and wrapped her in a hug just as a horn honked outside. Mom patted my back and grabbed her suitcase, then walked out. I trailed after her to make sure she didn't need any help and to make sure that whoever picked her up was actually young enough to drive; crazy world we lived in when that started making a difference.

Outside, a big white, fifteen-passenger van was in our driveway, and Theo himself walked up to the house to grab Mom's suitcase. He smiled at me and then winked, reminding me not to worry. I thought of his words from the day before, to "take this weekend and let go." I knew that he didn't mean it in a "wet and wild" kind of way, but a "find your peace" kind of a way. I smiled back at him, hugged my mom one last time, and then watched as she took her spot in the van.

Once she took off, I jogged back inside, noticing that it was getting close to eight thirty. I was going to be late if I waited any longer. I threw on my black knee-high boots and grabbed my coffee, heading out just as my phone rang. I fumbled my way to the car, answered, and put the phone on speaker.

"Ramsey Lenae Bennington, you still haven't answered me about Thanksgiving, and more importantly, you told me that you would come to visit me this weekend!" my best friend half-yelled, half-panted into the phone. Knowing her, she was probably in midtown, walking to her office.

"Laney calm down," I started to scold her. "First of all, it's only September—"

"Mid-September. *Mid*, Ramsey," Laney cut in. I slowly brought the SUV to a stop as I waited my turn. The clicking from the turn signal in the car was the only sound as I chose my next words wisely. It wasn't smart to argue with Laney, nor was it prudent to get her riled up before work. These were just little facts about who Laney was. She was my best friend and I loved her dearly, but she was ferociously competitive. It came from her being raised with four older brothers. It might also have something to do with her being a redhead, but I have no idea if there's factual evidence in that or not. I still blamed her brothers. They weren't just regular brothers either. They were the kind that would prank you in the middle of the night, and then film you waking up in it.

"Fine, it's mid-September," I agreed, as I drove towards the outskirts of town, before I gently tried to explain my delay in scheduling. "Secondly, I *am* considering this weekend. I just want to be done with work before I make any final decisions, and I haven't really had a chance to double-check my calendar."

She laughed, the whore. "Ram, come on. I'm your best friend, and it's been three months since I've seen you." The eye roll was evident in her tone.

"Lane, I know, trust me. I want to come see you. I need to see you and Chicago, I miss you both equally, but I still need to check." I couldn't shake the feeling that I was forgetting something important.

"Okay, fine. Just call me when you know, okay."

I let out a silent breath that I had been holding. "You got it, Vainy Laney, I will call you soon."

I didn't like letting people down, especially her. Laney was more like a sister to me, so our relationship looked much different than regular friendships. We were allowed to be our true selves, no matter how ugly or tainted. We always forgave each other, and eventually moved past any indiscretion the other made because we considered each other family. I even spent Christmas with her entire family, two years ago, and fell victim to a few of her brothers' pranks. Which is why I now sleep with a flashlight and bug spray near my bed.

I WAS ON THE HIGHWAY TO ROCKFORD NOW, TURNING INTO THE complex, where Jimmy's bike was already parked. My adrenaline spiked at the sight of it, which proved that I wasn't as free and clear of any emotional entanglements as I thought. *Shit.*

I'd just be professional, sure of myself, and ready to work.

I walked confidently down the hall until I landed in front of the manager door. I paused, deliberating only for a moment whether to knock or not, before grabbing the handle and pushing it open. This was my office too, and I didn't need to knock. Jimmy sat at his desk, his laptop open in front of him. He wore a Cubs baseball hat and a long-sleeved, Henley. He looked like he was headed to a ballgame.

Once I made my way to his—or, our—desk, he looked up at me and gave me a kind smile that spread to his green eyes. "Hey Ramsey, how are you today?"

I am confused and frustrated, and lately, I've been secretly writing Stenson at the end of my name.

"Oh, not too bad, how are you?" I said, as I settled into the only other chair in the office. "Good, just gearing up for the weekend, actually. I am taking off today around

noon." He said the last part while looking down at his computer. I began pulling my laptop out as well.

I felt a little odd, like maybe he only asked me to come back because he was going to be gone. I wondered if this was going to be our working relationship now? My stomach sank at the thought. "Well, sounds like you have a big weekend planned," I rattled off, as my computer powered up.

He looked back up at me, "Yeah, nothing too big, just trying to get Jasmine in the right headspace before her big tryout on Saturday."

I FROZE. MY HEART MAY HAVE EVEN STOPPED. HOW COULD I have forgotten about her?! I mentally scolded, kicked, and maimed myself for forgetting about his beautiful daughter's big tryout day. Thankfully, he was looking down at his computer and hopefully, that meant he just missed everything that went on in my head that might have made its way to my face.

I slowly let out a silent breath and responded calmly, "I bet she is so excited, but so nervous. I was actually going to talk to you today about what time I could pick her up Saturday to do our pampering thing?"

Hopefully, I saved that. *Please, dear God let me have saved that*! I carefully watched his face while trying to seem uninterested in anything that had to do with him. He sat up suddenly, then reached down into a bag on the floor.

"Actually, Ramsey, I have something for you from the kids." He handed me a white piece of paper that was folded in half. It had blue and red construction paper cut out and glued to it, to make it look like a giant movie ticket. I opened the paper and inside, I saw six-year-old coloring and nine-year-old hand-writing.

"YOU'RE INVITED TO THEATRE NIGHT!
We will be watching an Adventurous Princess Movie
Time: 6 PM

When: Friday night
Where: Our house
From: Love Jasmine and Sammy
P.S- Please come
P.P.S-
Pleasssssssssssssssssssssssssssssssseeeeeeeeeeeeee
Come."

I COULDN'T CONTAIN THE LAUGH THAT HAD BUILT UP IN MY chest. Those kids were the sweetest thing on the planet and I didn't deserve them, especially not after I forgot Jasmine's tryout. I had to go, just to mentally make up for the fact that I forgot her. I folded the paper in half and stuck it into my purse.

I stared at my computer as I responded, "So who do I have to RSVP with? And should I eat before I come, or can I offer to bring some Chinese food?"

He shook his head and looked up at me from his screen. "We are making mini pizzas. You will have your own dough and can make one with us, if you want. If you don't want mini pizzas, then eat before you come. And you don't have to RSVP, just tell me if you plan on coming or not, so we know to save room for you in the theatre."

I looked at him square in the face as I tried to process what he just said. "I'm sorry, the theatre? Do you have a theatre down in the basement or something?"

Jimmy laughed, and I wanted to set the sound as my ringtone or bottle it up somehow; it was like melted butter on a delicious pancake. "No, we make a theatre in our living room, out of blankets and pillows and stuff. It's fun, and it's tradition. We try to do a theatre night at least once a month, or around a special occasion, and Jazzy's tryout is our special occasion."

I felt humbled and honored but, just to be clear, asked, "And they asked me to come?"

Jimmy grabbed his chin and rubbed the stubble as he answered. "Yeah, they wanted you there, and I don't know, Ramsey?" He began to trail off, and then grabbed the back of his neck.

"I wanted to apologize to you, again. Looks like I am doing that a lot. I can't quite explain why I asked you to stay in Belvidere all week. I know I thought we had this connection the other night, and I went for it and overstepped a boundary between us. I hope you can forgive me and come to this theatre night for the kids. They would really love it if you came."

My tongue felt thick and my neck was hot. Jimmy was so vulnerable and sweet, and so different from the guy who nearly ran me off the road and fired me from Sip N Sides. I looked at my computer screen again, then once I was sure there was no gleam or damn hearts in my eyes, I glanced up. "Of course I forgive you, and of course I will come to theatre night. I feel honored to have been invited. Should I bring anything?"

Jimmy smiled so wide that I saw every perfectly straight and sparkling tooth in his beautiful mouth. Then I wanted to slap that smile off his face when he responded with, "Just your body," mocking me from my unfortunate text mishap from last weekend.

My face burned red as he laughed at me. "Just joking, I couldn't resist."

I smiled, and we fell into an easy banter as he went over information with me about the books. It wasn't until he asked about his dad's books that things got awkward again.

It was close to noon, and I was hoping that once he brought it up, he would just leave and go set up everything for this famous theatre night. He was perched half on the desk with his leg hanging down and his hands in his lap as he asked, "So, how bad is my dad doing? Is it still a total money pit?"

I rubbed my hands on my thighs and straightened my spine, ready for some serious lying that was about to happen. If

Theo didn't want me to tell Jimmy the truth, then I wouldn't. "Your dad is doing fine. Not a pit, just making ends meet." Not exactly a lie, but also not outing that his dad has way more money than him.

Jimmy's eyes narrowed on me and his eyebrows drew together, making him look confused. "Are you sure he's doing okay? I worry about him, but every time I try to peek at his books, he freaks out and shuts me out."

I bent my head down just a little, letting the pieces of hair that were out of my braid fall over my face, so that hopefully he didn't pick up on my deception. "Yep, nothing to worry about with your dad."

I could feel the heat of his stare as he sat there in silence, but I just kept looking at my screen like nothing was wrong.

I must have a terrible poker face because the next thing to leave his lips was, "Then you wouldn't mind if next week we sit down and go over his books together?"

Crap. Double Crap.

I smiled sweetly, looked up at him, and said, "Not at all," then quickly turned my gaze back to the computer screen. Maybe I would have enough time before next week to tip off Theo, so he would have a game plan because even though Jimmy might not be great at accounting, something told me that he'd notice over one hundred grand in Theo's cash reserve. Jimmy lifted up off the desk and adjusted his baseball hat.

"Well, I am going to head out, text me if there are any issues. You are welcome to leave as soon as the books are balanced, and we have a set budget for the kitchen and bar for the weekend."

I had requested to set the budget for the kitchen because those animals had no clue what they were doing. I also requested to oversee payroll and basically anything finance-related. Jimmy agreed faster than I expected, but the money side of things wasn't his expertise.

I smiled at him again and responded with a simple, "You got it, boss."

THE REST OF THE DAY WENT BY FAIRLY QUICKLY. IT WAS amazing how much work someone could get done when there was no one else in the office to bug you. During my unofficial lunch break, I called Laney to let her know I wouldn't be coming this weekend. While I waited for the phone to ring through, I took a few bites of raspberry scone.

"Hello?" Laney answered her office phone like she was genuinely confused. She always did, and it never ceased to amuse me.

"Lane, it's me. I have an update about this weekend," I said, through a thick mixture of scone crumbs and saliva.

"Great, what's the news?" Laney asked with a positive tone. *Crap, this wasn't going to be easy.* I took a sip of water to clear out the rest of the scone I foolishly tried to finish, before braving the news.

"I can't make it. I totally forgot that I promised Jimmy's little girl that I would do her hair for her dance tryouts on Saturday."

Silence. I waited with bated breath. Laney might yell, or she might cry, or she may be totally fine with it. It usually depended on what time of the month it was, and whether or not she got a late notice about her student loans.

"Seriously, Ram? Are you sure you can't come after or something? I could really use a girls' weekend with you." Laney sounded desperate, which surprised me and threw me off a bit. I felt guilty and really wanted to figure out why it was desperation in her voice and not anger, but I already knew that I wouldn't want to drive almost three hours to Chicago, only to have to turn around the next day and head back.

"Laney, I know and I'm so sorry. I totally suck, but her tryouts are later in the afternoon. I wouldn't make it to Chicago until late, and then I'd have to turn around and head back to be here in time for my mom to get home," I finished, trying to sound lighthearted, but I knew she was upset. I hated this long-distance thing.

I heard a loud sigh and a clicking noise. "Fine. I understand. But promise me you will try and come soon. There's a guy who I need to dish to you about."

There it was. Something was off, and I knew it had to do with whoever this guy was. "Really? Do we have to dish in person, can we do a phone date later?" I begged.

Laney laughed, and then covered the phone to answer someone else. "Ram, of course we can dish on the phone. I'll call you soon, okay? I gotta run."

"Love you, talk soon," I assured her while I snagged another scone. I hung up and looked around the bar, until I saw that Rav was staring at me. He was cutting a few limes at the counter, shaking his head back and forth.

"What?" I threw at him from my spot across the room.

"Eat a salad, or a sandwich. You can't just eat scones, it's not good for you," he argued while chopping more limes.

I grabbed my things and walked over to him. "Rav, it's not my fault you bake the best scones I've ever tasted. Plus, there's tons of ingredients in them, making them a perfectly acceptable meal." I took another bite, proving my point. Crumbs fell down onto my shirt. I looked down and wiped them off in frustration. Rav saw my movement and rolled his eyes.

"Eat a salad!" he yelled over his shoulder as he walked back to the kitchen.

Not a chance, baker boy. Not a chance.

. . .

I FINISHED UP AROUND FOUR AND EXCITEDLY MADE MY WAY through the mass of people that had already gathered near the bar. On my way home, I thought over the movie night at Jimmy's. I began to overanalyze it, wondering if there was some hidden agenda behind it. Then I realized how trivial I was being and decided to just accept it for what it was—an invitation from his kids. I completely melted at the idea.

I parked Mom's old green SUV in the usual spot and wrangled the house keys from my purse. It felt so weird coming home to an empty house, even though I had been living on my own since I was eighteen. Over the last six months I'd gotten used to living with another person. I padded past the living room and headed to my room, ignoring how loud the silence was in the empty house.

After showering, I stood in front of my closet, paralyzed. I hated being *that* girl, but I believed every girl had some part of her that would stand in the closet and worry about what she was going to wear over to her boss' house, to have a movie date with his kids, when there might still be some romantic type feelings still happening between said boss.

At least there were on my end. No matter how frequently I talked myself out of going for anything with Jimmy, my mind still betrayed me with images of us together. We would be the cutest couple, my mind decided, and I would be the world's best stepmother that had ever existed.

I grabbed a hold of some distressed jeans in one hand and held up my yoga pants in the other. Finally, I decided that regardless of where the movie was being watched, no one wanted to curl up to a feature film in jeans, it just wasn't comfortable. So, I pulled on my yoga pants, a sports bra, and then an oversized, off the shoulder college shirt. I was going to be comfortable, and it was time that I pushed past the need to look cute in front of Jimmy. I pulled my hair into a fishtail braid, threw on some flip-flops, and headed out. I was excited to spend the evening with Jasmine and Sammy. We had fun last weekend, and I was eager to get to know them better. They made me laugh and they managed to brighten up any space they filled. People like that were rare, and I needed some brightening in my life.

I STOOD IN FRONT OF JIMMY'S DOOR, SLIGHTLY BEFORE SIX. "Don't make it weird. You turned Jimmy down and he put you at Sip N Sides all week. Now you're just acquaintances, possibly friends, but that's it!" I reminded myself before I knocked on the door. Jasmine answered, wearing a purple princess gown and a plastic crown on top of her blonde head.

I smiled at her as she grabbed the hem of her dress and swayed to the side of the door frame to let me pass while practically yelling, "Welcome, Princess Ramsey, to our royal theatre night!"

I half-bowed, half-curtsied, then made my way past her saying, "Wow, Jazzy, you look gorgeous!"

She beamed and led the way into the kitchen where Sammy and Jimmy were. They were covered in flour and had two round crusts in front of them, covered in red sauce.

I put my purse down and slid onto one of the stools. "Did I miss the pizza making?"

I asked, trying to break the ice. For some reason, I was nervous and felt shy. Jimmy smiled at me and then handed me a big lump of dough.

"Nope, you are just in time. Jazzy just put hers in a few minutes ago, Sammy is next, and depending on how fast you are, it's either you or me after him."

I felt the dough in my hand, then hopped off the stool, and walked over to the sink. I placed the dough on a paper towel and then scrubbed my hands, trying not to notice that Jimmy hadn't moved to make space for me at the sink. He kept his place, crowding me, while his eyes focused on the dough in front of him. I breathed in his spicy smell that blended with the aroma of baked crust, and tried not to groan at the irresistible combination. I wanted to place my nose in his neck and inhale until it hurt.

Ignoring my strange urge, I dried my hands and went back to my stool. I glanced at Jimmy for a brief second, just to see if he would betray some look to show that he had crowded me on purpose, but when I looked at him, he was still focused on his pizza.

Maybe I imagined it?

I grabbed some flour and threw it down in front of me, and began working on my mini pizza. After several attempts to flatten and shape my dough into something that might resemble an actual circle, I finally settled on an odd-shaped, uneven, and lopsided patch of dough. I threw some red sauce on it, and some mozzarella, then claimed the next spot in line behind Sammy for the oven.

Jimmy stared at my handiwork and laughed. "Not much for fine detail, are you?"

I creased my brows and stared at my not-so-great master-piece. "Not exactly, unless of course, there is math involved."

He let out a loud laugh at my lame sentiment, then placed his perfectly round and flat piece of dough on the counter and lathered it in pizza sauce and mozzarella cheese.

I stared at it and sighed. "Good thing it wasn't a competition."

He laughed again, then surprised me by saying, "Don't worry, Rams, we'll turn you into a pro when it comes to making mini pizzas."

I smiled and tried to hide the fact that I was geeking out over him including me in his long-term plans. Pushing back some unruly hair, I asked, "Now why would I need to become a pro?"

I don't think he thought through his response when he said, "Because Stensons don't settle for anything less."

Then he turned around and started answering Sammy's questions about his pizza. I let myself off the stool and headed into the living room to find Jasmine. My mind was a freight train that had taken off. I was surely overthinking Jimmy's response about how "Stensons don't settle for anything less." It felt a lot like he was calling me a Stenson, and if he was, it was obviously in a platonic, sisterly way... right? I needed Laney or a reference guide for complicated relationships.

Jasmine came over and started tugging at the end of my braid. I looked down at her to answer her unspoken question, then took the elastic tie off the end of my braid. I sat down on the floor and relaxed as Jasmine's small fingers pulled on my hair. I took the moment to look around and admire the huge fort that Jimmy had set up.

The whole living room was encased in hanging sheets from the ceiling with little stringed lights that hung alongside each panel. It looked like I had died and gone to fort heaven.

I had this need to be inside of it, like I was a little kid again, so I turned my head slightly towards Jasmine and said, "Hey, let's move inside the fort."

Jasmine held tight to my hair as I slowly stood, and we made our way through two large, white sheets. Once inside, we readjusted to a comfortable sitting position and she continued braiding. There were four little bed rolls laid out in front of the TV, with a pile of pillows set up behind them. I touched the blankets under my legs and smiled. This was the coolest thing I had ever seen and really close to transcending my trampoline moment from the other night.

Something warm settled in my stomach—it felt like coming home. I tried to shut it down, I tried so hard, but a small part of me didn't want to because I loved being near this family. That same part of me admitted that I didn't just like the family,

I liked Jimmy. I thought back over the moments I had with him —the firm set of his jaw when he was frustrated, and the few times things hadn't gone exactly smooth between us. Then I thought of all the moments that did. The easy smile he got when he looked at his kids, the way he pulled the hair from my jacket that first night of work. The way he brought me dinner. The dips and flips in my stomach when I saw him or he came near me.

Shit, I totally liked him. How did that work in with my "no dating" plans? My mom's sickness hadn't changed, she was still my biggest priority. Panic set in with a whole lot of fear because I could not fall for Jimmy Stenson. I could not. I could not fall for his kids, or his home theatre forts, or his mini pizza skills, I could not. I began to breathe in and out slowly, so that Jasmine didn't catch on to the fact that I was slowly drowning in the idea of being a part of their family.

Jasmine bent to the side to peer at my face, while still holding firm to my braid. "Look, Ramsey! I actually braided! I did it!" she started jumping up and down with excitement.

I wanted to cry. Instead, I threw my arms around her and pulled her into my lap. "I knew you could do it. See, practice makes perfect."

Pieces of hair were falling from the braid, and I could feel how loose it was, but I wasn't going to say anything; this moment with her was perfect. Jimmy and Sammy came in, ducking their heads through the sheet entrance with our pizzas and some sodas. Sammy looked at Jasmine's position in my lap and immediately abandoned his pizza to find his own spot.

"Move, Jasmine! I want a spot too!" Sammy whined, while wiggling his body into place on one of my thighs.

I threw my head back and laughed as I grabbed onto both of them and squeezed. Unfortunately, my eyes found their way up to Jimmy's. He stared at us. At me. His look seemed to have about a million layers to it. My pulse raced as his green eyes danced with mine. *Look away. Look away!* I internally demanded, urged, even threatened myself, but in the end, I didn't look away; I just stared back.

It felt like a romantic moment, as we stared into each other's eyes, and it might have been one, except for the loud and very painful crack that came next. *Ouch, holy hell, owww!*

"Sammy!" Jimmy yelled, and grabbed for his son to pull him away from me.

Holding in my pathetic cries, I tried to grasp onto what had just happened to my face. A small elbow landed, powerfully in the corner of my eye. Sammy was apologizing, while holding his hand to his mouth.

"I didn't mean to, I'm sorry," he said, on the verge of tears while moving further away from me with his dad's guidance. I hadn't yelled or said anything, so I was surprised at his concern. Then I realized that I hadn't opened my eye yet. I was sitting there, holding in my breath, as tears threatened to fall and profanity threatened to spill from my lips.

"It's okay, bud. Don't worry about it. I'll grab some ice and be good as new." I carefully stood up and limped towards the entrance, in search of some ice. Why was I limping? I had no clue, but for some reason, the fact that I couldn't open my eye made my legs not function properly.

"Hey. You okay?" Jimmy asked, while tugging on my elbow. I glanced down at his hand with my good eye. Was it weird that I liked his hands? They were warm and felt really nice in comparison to my throbbing eye.

"Yeah, just going to grab some ice real quick," I replied coolly, covering the frantic tone that was trying to surface through the pain. He moved in front of me, then led the way back to the kitchen. I focused on my posture instead of the two, very defined lines of muscle that ran down Jimmy's back that shifted under his t-shirt. He stopped in front of a drawer, grabbed a small baggie, then moved to the freezer to fill it with ice.

Expecting him to hand it over, I held out my palm, but to my surprise, he invaded my space and held the bag of ice to my face. In an instant, I felt heat rush through my body. He was too close, with his scent and his warm hands. I held my breath and waited for his inspection to be done. His warm thumb ran over the corner of my eyelid. He tried to pry my eye open, but it wouldn't budge.

"Trust me. I just need to make sure your eyeball is still in there," he whispered, his warm breath fanning my face. I didn't realize I had shut my other eye as well. I opened the good eye and then let him work on my wounded one. It hurt like hell, but once he pulled the eyelid open he did, in fact, verify that I had my eyeball and there was no permanent damage, in his opinion. Then he shocked me by gently blowing on my wounded eye. Which, at first, confused me because air in the eyes wasn't normally a good feeling, but with my eye closed, the air felt soothing. He had the ice pack still held in place and with his other hand, he was holding the back of my head. He was so close to me, all I would have to do is tilt my head up a fraction, and we'd be kissing. With my good eye, I caught his gaze and saw by the way his eyes focused on my lips, he was thinking the same thing.

"I think you'll live, but keep this pack on once you get situated in the fort, okay?" Jimmy broke the moment, handing me the ice pack. He took a few steps back and then headed towards the fort. I nodded my head absently in understanding and gripped the bag of ice, following after him while wondering what exactly might have happened if he hadn't ended that moment. Or if he had any plans to ever ask me on a date again? I pushed those thoughts way, way out of my head, and ignored my racing pulse as I situated myself on my designated blanket spot.

I had taken the furthest spot in the fort and pulled on Jasmine's arm to make sure she took the spot next to me. Not that I didn't want Sammy, but I wasn't quite ready for anymore accidental elbow jabs. And I figured as long as someone was between Jimmy and me, then these butterfly feelings that kept erupting in my stomach would settle down or go away. The fact that I was maybe falling for Jimmy was a problem, so sitting next to him while we watched a princess movie was absolutely out of the question.

THE MOVIE WAS OVER, OUR PIZZAS WERE EATEN, SODAS GONE, and everyone had fallen asleep. Everyone but me. It was dark, save for the twinkle lights that ran along the edge of the fort. I tried to enjoy the moment, but Jasmine was sleeping on my arm, and it was starting to fall asleep. I wasn't sure what the best way to try and wiggle free was, so that I could head home without waking her, but the pins and needles in my arm demanded I just get it over with. No matter how smooth I moved, or how slowly, she still woke up. *Great.*

She yawned and stretched her tiny arms outward, pushing against me. Then she slowly got up, claiming she had to pee, and ran out of the fort. I was lying there, hoping no one else would wake up, when I heard a loud "Pssst" off to my right.

I turned my head towards the sound. Jimmy was laying similar to me, with Sammy on one arm, but he was gesturing for me to move closer to him with the other. Not wanting to give up my spot that was positioned away from him, I cupped my ear to encourage Jimmy to say what he needed to say from where he was. Jimmy looked down at Sammy, then back at me. That glowing light from above made him look dreamy, handsome, like a prince. *Shit, that princess movie must have really done a number on me.* Giving up on him, I stared up at the soft ceiling of hanging sheets and waited for Jasmine to come back. Then I heard it again.

"Psst."

I looked over again and saw Jimmy waving his hand for me to move closer.

Reluctantly I rolled over, filling the spot Jasmine had been in, so I could hear him. Once I was close enough, he asked, "Are you leaving?"

I kept an eye on the tent entrance, so I would be fast enough to move so Jasmine wouldn't lay down on the wrong side of me. "I don't know... I was thinking about it," I whispered.

Jimmy looked so peaceful and at home in his plain white t-shirt and gray sweats. He looked too good, like a dream that I couldn't afford to have. He leaned forward and gently placed his free hand on my arm, then murmured, "You should stay."

I looked down at my arm just as Jasmine stumbled back in from the opposite side of the tent, and laid down where I had been before, causing me to stay in between her and Jimmy. I let out a panicked breath and whispered to Jimmy, "Okay, I'll stay a little longer."

Until Jasmine fell back asleep, that's what I planned. Maybe I could discreetly move her body over mine, so I literally had a buffer between Jimmy. Otherwise, who knew what would happen if we stayed next to each other, while I was secretly planning our wedding in my head.

FIFTEEN

JIMMY

I woke up inhaling sugar and lilac, a smell that I had picked up on that night I fired Ramsey from Sip N Sides. I lay frozen, with my eyes closed, before I moved my nose closer to her smell. I loved that scent. I ran my nose along the mass of hair that was just below my chin and breathed her in, memorizing her. I opened my eyes and saw that she was sleeping on my chest. Her arm was draped across it and her leg was thrown over mine. I had my own arm wrapped around her, practically holding her against me. She was snoring, and from the damp spot I felt on my shirt, she was also drooling.

She was perfect. I was falling, way too fast, for Ramsey, and it scared the hell out of me. From the looks she kept giving me all night, it made me think she was feeling it too. Regardless of what she said about priorities and her mom, she felt something for me.

I looked over and found Sammy upside down and nestled in near my feet. Over Ramsey's shoulder, I saw that Jasmine was cuddled up with her back against Ramsey's. Both kids had us pinned in. I had no idea what time it was, but I could tell it was early; there was a little bit of pink creeping through the window at the back door. I looked back down at her body on mine and carefully tugged her closer. I wanted her here, even if she wasn't sure about it. And I wanted just one moment alone with her before the kids woke up.

One moment where she saw me and felt my arms around her, so she knew what this meant to me, what *she* meant to me. I moved my hand a little until it was cupping her hip. She squirmed, bringing her leg higher. *Shit, not that.* I adjusted her on my chest, reorganizing my thoughts to ignore the growing need stirring in my sweats. We didn't need that this morning. Finally, I felt her head move. She gently raised it, and I tightened my grip on her hip, so that she knew I wanted her there.

Slowly, her eyes opened and drifted up my chest to my face. There was surprise and something else in her expression. I knew it would only be a few seconds before she noticed how she was positioned on me or worse, realize that she had drooled, so I had to act quickly. I stared at her with all the emotion and heat I could muster, hoping she'd notice exactly what I wanted. I squeezed her hip. She tensed up for just a second, and then relaxed, almost melting into me. I waited for her to react, to show that she wanted this. I needed her to show that she wanted this. Wanted me.

Her hand made its way up to the side of my face, she ran her fingers along my day-old stubble, then traced my lips. Her eyes followed the movements of her fingers. I leaned forward, placed my hand behind her head, and pulled her towards me. I led her lips to mine and as we connected, her chest rose, her fingers found my hair and gently tugged me closer.

God, this woman.

She had set me on fire and burned me from the inside out. Just as I was about to deepen the kiss, someone knocked on the front door.

Ramsey immediately pulled back. She didn't get off of me or up from where she laid, but she pulled far enough away that it ended whatever moment we had. Her cheeks were flushed, but it was nothing compared to the moment she saw the large wet spot on my shirt. Her eyes went wide as she slowly brought her hand up to cover her mouth. I smiled at her to try and put her at ease, but whoever was knocking on my door at this ungodly hour of the morning knocked again.

I looked at Ramsey apologetically and got up. I pushed the sheets aside and climbed over a pile of pillows until I was free of our little fort. I grabbed the door handle, probably with too much force, and came face to face with my best friend.

Jackson stood there, wearing aviators, holding a duffel bag in one hand and a large coffee in the other.

"Hey, man, sorry to stop in so early... but I did try to text you last night... but you never responded."

He said this while trying to look past me, and for some reason, knowing that Ramsey was inside suddenly had me territorial as shit. I moved to block the entryway, so he couldn't see and crossed my arms over my chest. "Sorry man, I was really busy last night, and as you can tell, this morning. I was sleeping. What time is it anyway?"

Jackson smiled and turned his left wrist towards him. "Five thirty in the morning."

"Sweet Jesus, why are you here so early?!" I whisper-yelled at him.

Jackson had never done anything like this, not even after Lisa left. So why the hell would he just show up like this?

Jackson looked at the ground, then finished off the last of his coffee. "Look, man, I'm sorry, I'll tell you over breakfast. Mind if I stay here this weekend, and get out of this frigid cold weather? My balls are going to fall off."

I didn't want him near Ramsey, but maybe I could figure something out where she stayed hidden. "Yeah, of course, man. Come on in."

I moved aside and let him through, knowing I needed to

change my attitude. Ramsey wasn't mine and knowing Jackson, if he knew that she was here before the sun even rose, he would stay away.

I shut the door and we walked quietly back through until we were in the living room, where we found Ramsey bent over trying to find her sandals while attempting to not wake up the kids. She was half out of the fort and had her sweatshirt pulled over her head, and her hair braided to the side. Her ass was facing us and again that urge to punch Jackson and tell him not to look was right there. I didn't know why it hurt so much to see that she was leaving, but it did. Whatever stupid notion I had of us eating breakfast together, as a family, was gone. Because we weren't a family and she wasn't staying, and ultimately, she didn't want this. Otherwise, she wouldn't be looking for her sandal right now.

She finally found it, then having pulled it on, she quietly crept towards us. Her eyes got big when she saw Jackson. No surprise there; everyone's eyes got big when they saw Jackson. He always looked like he had just walked out of a photo shoot. Then her gaze quickly moved to mine, her face flushed red, and it made me physically weak. I wanted this woman so badly it hurt.

She tucked a piece of hair behind her ear as she continued to walk towards me, then she whispered, "Hey, I'm going to head home, and I will be back around ten to grab Jazzy. Is that okay?"

I smiled, even though I was disappointed that she was leaving. "Yeah, of course, see you then."

I wanted to thank her for coming, for staying, for wrapping her body around mine last night and giving me the honor of waking up tangled with her, but I didn't. She quietly crept towards the door and left.

I felt like the air was trapped in my lungs as the door closed; we had a moment and didn't talk about it. Part of me filled with fear and anxiety over the idea of not knowing what she thought of the kiss, or if she would just pretend like it never happened.

"Dude, what the hell?" Jackson asked, pulling me out of my thoughts. I turned to look at him. He had taken his sunglasses off, and had his arms crossed loosely across his chest, with a look on his face that clearly said, "Spill it."

I briefly remembered that the kids were sleeping, and if they woke up, they would start wondering where Ramsey went, so I headed into the kitchen, with Jackson following after me. I went straight for the coffee pot and started pulling out the filter and grounds. We never converted to one of those newer forms of making coffee, with the pods and things. Dad tried the one I had set up in the breakroom at his bar once, and told me he'd break any I bought for the house on principle, if I ever even thought of getting rid of our old one. Jackson settled in on one of the stools; I could feel him watching me, but I wasn't ready to talk yet.

He cleared his throat and started again. "Man, what in the hell is going on? Since when do you have women sleeping in your house? With your kids? Who look like that?" He drew out each point that he made, speaking slowly and trying to make it seem like a bigger deal than it actually was. Although, from his perspective, I could see why he was confused.

I looked at him and decided that since he was my best friend, he had a right to know, but as I started to speak, something just shifted inside of me and I couldn't bring myself to be honest about her. "It's hard to explain but it's not what you think."

Jackson stared at me, not saying anything. Then he looked down at his hands and blew out an obnoxiously loud breath. "Man, it looks like you have started dating again. And from the way you looked at her, I would say you might even be on your way to..."

"To what? You honestly think I'm that careless?" I threw at him from over my shoulder. I hated how perceptive he was, but I wasn't going to admit anything or give into it, because the fact that I was feeling rejected again proved I *had* been careless.

"No, man. I don't think you're careless. I think you haven't cared enough, if anything," Jackson assuaged while rubbing his chin.

"Well, it's nothing. She babysat the kids last weekend, and they grew attached to her, is all. Like a big sister thing, they invited her to theatre night, and she accidentally fell asleep... she's also my new accountant for Jimmy's and Sip N Sides." I said the last part while grabbing a mug, covering my face with the cupboard and giving myself a small reprieve. I didn't want to see his reaction, because I knew, just as well as anyone, how stupid of an idea it was to have an employee stay the night at your house, especially one that looked like Ramsey.

Jackson stayed silent for a while longer than I would have liked. Once I looked back over at him, he had his fist under his chin.

"So, you and she aren't a thing then?" He used a tone that insinuated he didn't believe me at all.

So, I made sure he did. "Not at all, man. You know that I'm not that stupid after everything I have been through. The kids like her, she's an insanely good accountant, but that's it. Oh, and dad loves her, so she's kind of everywhere."

Jackson stood up from the stool and stretched his arms over his head. I could tell he wanted the questions and answers to stop with me because, for some reason, he was at my doorstep at five thirty in the morning. I wanted to jump in but he beat me to it.

"Then you wouldn't mind if I asked Ramsey to dinner tonight?" He said it like he was trying to call me on my bullshit.

I drank a huge gulp of coffee, hoping it would somehow

give me the strength to not punch my best friend in the face. I hated that he knew me so well, and he was only suggesting he ask her out to call my bluff, but I couldn't let him win and think that he got to me. So, I gently placed my mug on the counter and looked him square in the face. "Nope."

Jackson gave me a shit-eating grin that clearly showed he was going to enjoy torturing me. To take my mind off of what it was going to be like seeing Jackson flirt with Ramsey, I decided to turn the questions on him. "So, what in the hell brought you to my house so early anyway, man?"

Jackson grabbed onto one of the barstools with his hands and leaned forward. "It's a long story, but the short answer is; I needed to get out of Chicago. The sooner the better, and I remember you saying that Jazzy had something this weekend. Besides, I haven't talked to you in a while about the bar, so I figured there was no time like the present."

It was a piss-poor excuse for interrupting the moment I had with Ramsey, but I had a feeling he wasn't telling me everything. Just like I wasn't telling him everything. We were a shitty example of friendship.

I nodded at him, and that ended our little pre-breakfast conversation. He stretched again and then nodded at me. "I'm going to go pass out for a bit, if that's okay? Is the guest bed made up?" He started heading towards the basement, and I didn't want to yell because of the kids, so I just nodded.

Once he was downstairs, I went back into the fort with the kids. I laid back down and stared at the ceiling of blankets and sheets. I hated how empty it felt now without Ramsey, and more than that, I hated how I would never be able to experience theatre night again without thinking of her.

SIXTEEN

I TRIED to fall asleep once I got home, but my mind was in full freak-out mode. So, I gave up on the idea of it. Around six thirty, I just decided to consume as much coffee as possible and count down the seconds until it was deemed the 'not too early' kind of early to call Laney.

I needed to talk about that kiss with someone. Anyone, really. I was almost desperate enough to find some radio show looking for callers, to call in their questions about complicated relationships. I started at the beginning, in my mind.

First, I didn't mean to sleep there all night. Second, I didn't want to be next to Jimmy, because I knew that I was an insane spider monkey sleeper. I should have just moved Jazzy after I agreed to stay. When I woke up and noticed my leg, and then saw the wet drool spot, I wanted to die. Of course, I would have only noticed that spot after he kissed me.

I shoved my face into a pillow and groaned. My first kiss with Jimmy, and my mouth probably had horrific drool breath or crusted spit on the side of my face. God only knows how my hair looked. I pulled my cell phone out and peeked at the time. I saw that it was six forty-five, and decided it was late enough to call Laney. I hit my favorites tab and tapped her face, then waited patiently through each ring until she finally answered.

"Hello?"

She was groggy and probably hungover, and most likely pissed, but I didn't care.

"He kissed me." I didn't even respond with hello, I just went for it.

I was biting my thumbnail, waiting for her to respond. She coughed a few times, and then everything was muffled, like she was trying to move blankets around. "He kissed you? As in, Jimmy? As in, *your boss?!*" She was trying to yell, but her voice was raspy, like she had been yelling and now she was out of steam.

"Yes, that Jimmy. He kissed me."

"Whoa, back up, start from the beginning. How did this happen?" She sounded thoroughly confused, and I let out a sigh.

"So, I told you his daughter has a dance tryout today, right?" I waited for her to respond, so I knew she hadn't fallen back asleep. Wouldn't be the first time either, if she did.

"Yes, the reason you aren't here right now. Go on," she rasped.

"So, in order to try and cheer her up, Jimmy put together this theatre night, and the kids invited me to come watch a movie with them. It got late, and I accidentally fell asleep there." I stopped, thinking that was enough info for her.

"And? How did you end up kissing? Come on, Rams."

I bit my nail harder as I launched back into my night. "Well, I should tell you that we almost kissed before the movie. Or maybe we didn't, I don't know... he helped me with an ice pack and was really close to my face, and we had this moment where we stared at each other." Everything was coming out cluttered and chaotic.

"But he didn't kiss you?" Laney clarified, fully engaged now.

"No, he broke the moment, and I thought he was going to just act like we didn't have this crazy chemistry because I turned him down when he asked me out last week."

"He asked you out last week?!" Laney yelled in my ear. Shit, forgot that I didn't tell her that.

"Not the point. Listen!" I reprimanded.

"So, everyone falls asleep and he asks me to stay. I agree, but his daughter had gotten up to pee and left the spot next to him open. So, I accidentally fell asleep next to him, and when I woke up, I was wrapped around him, like a—"

"Crazy spider monkey. Oh, Rams," Laney lamented. She knew how I slept because every time we had been in a situation where we had to share a bed for any reason, she woke up with me wrapped around her and drool leaking down her arms or in her hair. I was tall, and she never stood a chance.

"Yes, but I didn't even have a chance to see the drool before he tightly gripped my hip, gave me this dreamy, crazy sexy look—"

Laney interrupted me with a scoff because she apparently can't keep her inner bitch in check so early before coffee.

"Anyway, dreamy look, then we kissed," I pushed on, regardless of her bitchy tactics. I told her about the gentle and perfect kiss, and then the interruption.

"So, he kissed you, then answered the door, and then you left because his best friend showed up?" She was replaying all the facts back to me now.

"Well yeah, I mean, I figured if his friend was there, then it would be awkward if I was there. So, I left... Do you think that was the wrong thing to do?" I asked, a little panicked.

She took a few seconds to respond. "Why did you really leave? What if his friend just stopped in for a few seconds and was about to leave?"

That took me a second to process. With anyone else, I might try to hide my real feelings, but not with Laney. She knew too much about me to ever pull one over on her.

"I guess I was worried that with his friend showing up, that he would apologize for the kiss and take it back." I paused, played with the strings on the pillow in my lap, and waited. When Laney didn't say anything, I continued, "I guess I felt like his friend interrupting us would pull him back to reality, and I didn't want to be rejected."

She made a sound of acknowledgment. "I thought so. How do you think he felt about you leaving?"

I was getting a little irritated, even though this was exactly what I needed. I was starting to feel a little guilty for taking off. I shifted on the couch.

"I don't know, maybe relieved that he didn't have to deal with me? His best friend doesn't live around here, so I didn't think it was going to be a quick visit."

She started in gently, "Look, Ram, you know I love you, but I think you are so afraid of getting hurt that you run from it. What are you going to do when you see him next? What if he does apologize for the kiss?"

I thought about that for a second. She was right, I didn't want to deal with anymore heartbreak since my mom's news, which was partly why I rejected Jimmy's dinner invite in the first place. "I don't know. I don't know what to do or what I will do," I gently said, but I lied. I knew exactly what I would do when I saw Jimmy again.

No surprise, though; she guessed it.

"Just don't jump the gun and apologize for the kiss before he does, just to avoid rejection, because it sounds like you have already rejected him once."

I stayed quiet. I *was* going to apologize for the kiss until I realized I couldn't because I didn't kiss him. *He* kissed me before his friend knocked, so he held all the power, the ball was totally in his court.

She spoke up again through my silence. "Look, I think you leaving right away may have sent him the wrong message, so just roll with it when you see him. Don't be weird or freak out. But I think, if he wants to push it or talk about it, you should let him be honest with you."

She was right, and I knew that she was, it just terrified me. I smiled and agreed with her. "You're right, I will just let it play out and not overreact. Thank you, Laney, I love you. How did you end up spending your night? Ready to dish about that guy? Or are you hungover?"

She laughed. "No, I'm not hungover, I wish I was, though. I actually had a weird night. A weird week, really. We got a new client. I've been working with him, and he's a freaking nightmare, Rams. I don't like the term hate, you know that I don't, but this guy is seriously making me think about using it. We were doing fine until yesterday, when...I lost it." She went quiet, like she was afraid to tell me anything more. Probably because her saying she lost it was a big deal. Laney was a lethal weapon in more ways than one. She was about five-three, one hundred and ten pounds, and a half-lit stick of dynamite on a good day. But that competitive streak nearly always got the better of her.

I waited, not sure what to say or where to begin with her. She hated losing it.

"What did he do?" I hesitantly asked.

"He just kept questioning everything I said and changed three things behind my back without talking to me. He asked for someone more experienced, I found out in front of the entire team and was so humiliated," she said, sounding exasperated, which I knew she was. That would be the one thing to say to her to piss her off.

She let out a long sigh. "And I don't know, Rams. Originally I thought he and I had this connection or something, he has these moments where he's sweet and God, he's gorgeous, but yesterday, it all just went to hell, and I felt so stupid for thinking he might like me or might ask me to dinner," she sounded defeated.

This was worse than I thought. Laney pissed was one thing; Laney pissed and embarrassed was a totally different thing. She had a big heart, but she defended it like a gladiator, so I actually kind of felt for the guy and the earful he must have gotten.

"Laney, he's an idiot. I'm sorry he hurt you, but I know you probably more than got him back," I tried to encourage her, even though I knew it was kind of futile at this point.

"I know, and thanks. I love you, girl. I'm going back to sleep, call me after the tryout thing, I want to know how the aftershock goes."

I felt better after processing with her, but now I was nervous about seeing Jimmy. I glanced at the time. It was only seven, and since I was going crazy over the what-if scenarios with Jimmy, I decided I should pass the time by cleaning.

I cleaned as much as I could until nine, and then I hopped in the shower. This time, I would be taking my time, and making myself look cute because it mattered to me, and because I wanted that kiss to mean something.

It was ten minutes until ten when I pulled up in front of Jimmy's house. I had everything planned out. I would be flirty, but not overly flirty with Jimmy as I picked up Jazzy, and then she and I would leave to get pampered. Then, at her tryouts, during all the excitement, I would kiss Jimmy again, that way words would not be necessary to show him how I felt. And although I still wanted and needed my mother to be my first priority, I realized that I needed to reconsider the idea of dating. Maybe, if I was with the right person, I could enjoy my mother's life *and* my own, so that she could see me happy.

I stepped up to the door and knocked. I felt pretty, my hair was down and curled, with a few tight braids on the side of my head. I wore my skinny, distressed jeans with boots and an off-the-shoulder sweater. Jasmine opened the door; she was grinning so much I thought her cute face might break. She hugged me as I stumbled forward into the house, then we straightened out and walked in further, towards the manly laughter that was coming from the kitchen. My stomach was dipping and flipping at the sight of Jimmy again. He leaned against the kitchen counter, his feet crossed at the ankles, while eating a banana. His friend, who I knew was Jackson from a picture I'd seen, was standing opposite of him, with a bottle of water in his hand. Both men stopped laughing when I came in. My eyes landed on Jimmy's, but as soon as he saw me, he looked down.

My heart did a little lurch as panic settled into my stomach. Maybe he was going to apologize for the kiss? I glanced up at Jackson, who was smiling at me with a sexy, brilliant grin. He was handsome, but he wasn't Jimmy. I smiled back and waved a little.

"Hi." My voice came out all high-pitched, and nervous.

Jackson leaned over, with his arm stretching towards me from the side furthest away from him, so it made his whole body turn towards me.

"Hey, I'm Jackson… Jimmy's best friend," he said, his voice all smooth and velvety.

I quickly glanced at Jimmy for a clue as to what was going on; Jackson was giving me bedroom eyes and Jimmy didn't seem to care. No, he seemed completely disconnected and was looking at his phone.

I took Jackson's hand and introduced myself. "I'm Ramsey, Jimmy's new accountant."

He held my hand longer than he needed to, then replied, "Oh good, Jimmy finally found someone to replace me."

I started laughing, softly, not meaning to sound flirty, but

Jasmine must have picked up on it, because suddenly, she was right next to me, pushing me closer to Jackson. *What the hell?*

"Uncle Jax, isn't Ramsey pretty?" Jasmine asked, while pushing on my back. I looked back to Jimmy for some help, but he was still looking at his phone, so I turned and grabbed her shoulders and directed her towards the living room.

"Hey Jazzy, we have a pedicure appointment. Go get your shoes and coat on, okay?"

As she ran off, I looked back over at Jimmy, who was still looking at his phone, totally detached, uninterested, and weird. *Why was he acting like that?*

I cleared my throat, hoping for some courage as I approached him. "Hey, so I thought maybe Jazzy and I could just meet you guys at the school, since she has to be there by three. It starts at five, so I'll just hang with her those two hours so you guys don't have to. If that works for you?" I added, with a little bit of caution in my voice, suddenly feeling insecure.

Jimmy was looking at me, but his eyes were distant and almost pained. His gaze drifted to my lips before he responded.

"Yeah, of course, that's fine." He glanced back up and met my eyes briefly before he turned and headed towards the fridge.

Seriously, what was going on?

I lowered my head and began to turn around towards Jackson. He was smiling again and as I walked past him, he placed his hand on the small of my back, guiding me back towards the living room. I drew in a sharp breath at the contact and quickly, before I thought too much about it, glanced back at Jimmy. His eyes were locked on my back, where Jackson's hand was, and he didn't look happy. I threw my head forward again and kept walking until Jasmine ran into the pathway and grabbed my hand, leading me towards the front door.

Right as I was about to open it, Jackson gently grabbed my arm and leaned in to whisper, "It was nice meeting you,

Ramsey. I hope I have the chance to get to know you better after the tryouts."

I didn't know what to do; I felt like I was caught in some weird Twilight Zone. I just smiled and nodded at him, then walked out. My gut twisted; whatever I thought was going to happen with Jimmy clearly wasn't happening. I just needed to change my perspective on a few things, and realize that I screwed up. Jimmy didn't want me anymore, that much was clear.

I opened the back door to my SUV so that Jasmine knew to get in. I tried to clear my thoughts and focus just on her; it was her day, after all. I smiled really big and turned my head to see her as she buckled up.

"Okay girl, we are going to get our nails done, then we are going to head to Target and do some shopping. Then I think we should have lunch, and afterward, we'll head to my house and get all ready. How does that sound?" Thank God for coupons, gift cards, and credit cards, otherwise this trip wouldn't be happening.

She lit up, and threw her arms over her head, shouting, "It sounds awesome!"

I put the car in drive and headed away from the house. I had to roll my eyes at myself and how selfish I was being; today was Jasmine's day, and I wanted to make sure she had a good one. So, I focused my eyes on the road and planted a smile on my face as I headed to the nail salon.

WE WERE IN THE JUNIOR SECTION, WITH OUR NEWLY-PAINTED nails, where I tried to let Jasmine roam and look at what interested her without being overbearing. Jasmine had walked over to the training bra area, while glancing around nervously, as though she was afraid to be caught. I hated that this would be another area of her life where she wouldn't have someone to help her. I made a promise to myself that even if things with Jimmy didn't work out, I would be there for this girl. I would be her person until, of course, Jimmy did remarry. That thought sent little pinpricks of pain into my heart, like little shards of glass. I walked over to Jasmine while she looked at the bras.

"You should go try this one on," I encouraged Jasmine, as I held out the small, black sports bra. Her face turned red as she looked around, showing how mortified she probably was. I knelt down, out of the way, so the bra wouldn't be on display to everyone at my height.

"Look. Whether you want it or not, bras are going to be in your future, and soon. It's important to have a good one, and you definitely don't want to have to have this moment with your dad or grandpa, do you?"

Jasmine shook her head, while her face remained red. I grabbed a few more bras for her to try on, then held out my hand for her to take. She followed me to the dressing room area.

"Here, go in this room and try these on, and if you have any questions about anything at all, or how they're supposed to fit, just yell for me. I won't move from this spot." I gestured toward the red bench to signify my position. She smiled and ducked into one of the rooms.

Jasmine ended up loving all three that she tried on, so we bought them all. We also got bracelets, hair stuff, lip gloss, shoes, and some clothes. Then we headed back to Belvidere.

Once we got to my house, Jasmine changed into her practice clothes, and then she sat down and let me do her makeup. That's when things got tricky. She had acted like she wanted to talk to me about something all day, but never said anything. Now, while her eyes were closed and I was applying eye shadow, she started in.

"Ramsey?"

I continued to mix colors and replied, "Yeah?"

She kept her face still. "I was wondering something?"

"What's up, you can ask me anything." I smiled, even though she couldn't see me.

I could tell that she was struggling to say whatever it was. "Well, um, do you like my dad?"

She had no idea that I had picked champagne and pink as me and her dad's wedding colors for our nonexistent wedding, just this morning. "Yeah, sweetie, of course, I like your dad. He's my boss, I think I have to like him."

She opened her eyes and rolled them. "Not like that. I mean, do you *like* him, like you could love him kind of like?" she asked, a little frustrated.

I thought of how she had pushed me towards Jackson and not her dad earlier, and wondered where this conversation might lead, but I responded with, "I'm not sure, honey, why do you ask?"

She looked relaxed once I said that. Her shoulders lifted, and her lips turned up into a smile. "I don't know. I just wasn't sure because you work with him, and we keep seeing you together."

I blended her makeup and added eyeliner. "How would that make you feel if I did like him?" I cautiously asked, not sure if I was out of place or not.

She scrunched her face, oblivious to my attempts of straight lines or careful handiwork. "I don't know? I hadn't thought about it." She paused and added, "Ramsey it's just that... I just... um, I want you to be my best friend. You have no idea how fun today was for me, and I have never had this before..."

She started to tear up, like she was going to cry and I knew that if she started to cry, then I would start to cry. It made me hurt for my own mom and all the mother-daughter moments we had shared over my lifetime, and how painful it would be not to have her be a part of my moments anymore.

I wrapped Jasmine in a tight hug and promised her, "Jasmine, I have no idea what will happen with your dad and me, but here is what I promise. I promise to be this person for you, no matter what. I will take you shopping, I will take you to get your nails done, and I will take you to lunch, so that we can talk about boys. I'm here for you, okay?"

Then she started to cry again. "But what if you move away, and have kids, and forget me?"

I rubbed her back and responded as gently as I could. "Then you will be the best adopted older sister my kids could ever have. And if I move, then I will be back on weekends to take you to do fun stuff."

We leaned away from each other, and I carefully wiped her eyes and face, so her makeup didn't smudge. As we settled back down, I braided her hair around the crown of her head so that she looked like a Greek goddess. Then our time was up, so we grabbed all of her stuff and headed to the school.

I got to watch Jasmine practice her routine for about an hour before I had someone sitting next to me in one of the metal folding chairs set up for parents. I looked over my shoulder and found Jackson sitting there, in an army green jacket with a black V-neck shirt underneath and worn-in blue jeans. I hated mentally admitting that he looked good, very good, but he still wasn't Jimmy, and he still didn't have those two extra humans attached to him that I was starting to love. He wasn't looking at me, he was staring past me at Jasmine. So, we sat and watched, until he placed his arm behind my chair.

He leaned towards my ear while still looking forward and said, "How was your girls' day with Jasmine?"

His breath was warm on my skin. I kept my eyes forward as I answered him, "It was great. How was your man day?"

I have no idea what came over me; thankfully, he wasn't

watching my face because it was probably red from being an idiot. *Man day?!*

He chuckled, which I felt all the way down to my toes. "We had a good day, except Jimmy seemed like he was all pissed off. Not sure why, but he's in a mood today."

That made me feel like crap. Was he mad about the kiss?

I kept my face forward before I responded, "Huh, that's strange. Where is Jimmy anyway?"

He turned his head a bit, so when he spoke, his breath was on my neck. "He's still at home. I remembered you saying that you'd be here early, and figured I would sneak away and see if I could talk to you."

I wanted to turn and look at him, to see what his face looked like, because he was being really flirty and coming on pretty strong, but I kept my eyes on Jasmine. I waited a minute to respond, choosing my words and inflection carefully, "why did you want to talk to me?"

He leaned in again. "You're the new accountant, my godchildren seem to love you, my best friend seems to be… something with you. We seem to have a lot in common, and I'd like to take you to dinner tonight to explore whatever else we might have in common."

It should definitely say something that the only thing I picked up on was the "my best friend has something with you" piece of his little offer.

I realized I hadn't responded when Jazzy ran over, all excited, and jumped onto Jackson's lap. She was more than a little hyped up. I turned to her as Jackson wrapped his arms around her and said, "Looking good out there, Peanut."

She beamed up at him. "Thanks, Uncle Jax."

She was so cute with her lip gloss and fuschia-colored cheeks. I had already taken a million pictures of her, but I wanted a million more. He scooted Jasmine to fit in his lap a bit better, then quizzed her. "So what happens at this tryout of yours?"

She giggled. "We have a routine we follow, and get points for everything we do correctly."

He laughed and kissed her on the forehead. "Well, I already know that you're going to get all the points and show everyone else up."

Jasmine blushed. "Uncle Jax, I haven't won yet."

"So what happens if you do win? Is there a team you're on… or a squad?" Jackson asked, scrunching up his face like he really couldn't understand the idea of a sport like this.

Jasmine started picking at her shirt while she answered, "Well, if we do well enough, then it means we get to advance into a higher class, plus it's just fun, Uncle Jax."

He jostled her around, then hugged her. It was cute seeing their dynamic; I could tell that Jackson was important to them.

A woman with glossy blonde hair and blue eyes grabbed a megaphone and started yelling at people to get into position. Jasmine jumped up just as Jimmy and Sammy walked up behind us. Jimmy went straight for Jasmine, wrapped her in a big hug, then kissed the top of her head before she ran off to join her group.

Parents were directed to head into the gymnasium and find a seat.

We found a bleacher seat about three rows up from the floor. I followed Sammy in and Jackson walked behind me, which left Jimmy at the end, far away from me. I was getting ready to say yes to Jackson's dinner offer, if only to show Jimmy that his regret over the kiss wasn't getting to me, even though it was. Music started, and kids stood in a line on large, thick blue mats. I kept my face forward, refusing to try and catch a peek at Jimmy.

A few seconds later, Jackson pulled a vibrating phone out of his jacket and stared down at the screen with a concerned look on his face. "Excuse me guys, I have to take this." He walked down the bleachers, leaving a large vacant spot between Jimmy and me.

I didn't look at the empty spot, and I didn't look at Jimmy, but I felt him next to me a moment later. I could feel his body heat and I saw out of the corner of my eye, his dark denim jeans, his perfectly white t-shirt, and the Cubs baseball hat on his head. I was focusing so hard on keeping my head forward that my neck started to ache. Then Jimmy broke the silence between us by dipping his head towards me and gently talking in my ear. "Jasmine looks perfect. I can't thank you enough for helping her today, I know it made a huge difference in her confidence."

I felt heat flood my chest because his words hit my heart and no matter what I was feeling towards Jimmy, I would never ignore a comment about his kids. "It was so much fun. We had a good time today, and I hope that maybe I can do it monthly with her," I said, a little breathy. I hated this awkward tension between us.

Jimmy didn't say anything for a while; his face was like stone and his eyes were serious. *Maybe he was just thinking again about how much he regretted kissing me?* A loud shout came from below for the girls to stick their turns. I rolled my eyes, hating how immature I was being. I carefully checked Jimmy's face again; still stone-like. *Maybe he was trying to figure out a complicated math problem?* Great, now I was wondering how I could convince him to share it with me. I needed to stop.

I sat up taller and focused on the mats, where Jasmine was doing a routine with punches, somersaults, and cartwheels. Jasmine's routine was almost finished, and right when I thought Jimmy was going to stay stony and silent, he spoke up. "I actually wanted to talk to you…"

He leaned in close, then abruptly pulled back when we heard, "Hey, sorry I had to leave, it was work. What did I miss?" Jackson squeezed back into his spot, right next to me, and Jimmy let him. I was so frustrated, I could punch something. Jimmy was going to talk to me about something, and yes, it could be to apologize for the kiss, but maybe it wasn't.

Jasmine's group was nearly finished. To make more room in the small gym for families, they'd requested we leave as soon as our kid's group was done. The girls were in a large huddle and some of the parents were beginning to leave. That's when Jackson chose to ask me again about dinner.

"So, Ramsey, did you decide about us going to dinner?"

I sat forward enough so that I could see Jimmy. I glanced at him briefly while I worked through my hesitation. "Um, well. Jackson, I don't really know you, I'm not sure…"

I kept my eyes on Jimmy, so that I would be able to tell if he wanted me to say no, but as it was, he wasn't doing anything but looking at Jasmine.

"Just ask Jimmy, I'm a good guy, right?" he said, turning towards Jimmy.

Jimmy gave a little half-smile and then turned half his body towards us and agreed. "You should go, Ramsey. He's a good guy."

Okay then.

If I thought that Jimmy had any romantic notions whatsoever about me, he just more than proved that he didn't. He just suggested I go out with his best friend. My heart physically hurt, which was so irritating because I still barely knew Jimmy, and yet that damn body part of mine felt like it had claimed him. Stupid heart.

I looked down at my shoes, trying to hide the rising heat I knew was climbing my neck. Once I felt some semblance of control over it, I looked up and smiled at Jackson.

"Okay then, if Jimmy thinks it's a good idea, then let's go. Let me just say bye to Jasmine and give her a hug, and then we can leave."

I leaned over in the other direction to give Sammy a hug, then messed up his hair and told him I would see him later. I stood up and walked past both men to wait for Jasmine.

I discreetly looked back up towards Jimmy and saw a flash of hurt cross his face as he stared at Jackson. I couldn't hear what they were saying, but Jackson looked defensive; he was holding his hands up like he was getting robbed. Jimmy's face was red, and when Jackson looked over at me and smiled, Jimmy followed his stare. I locked eyes with Jimmy for just a few seconds before he looked down. He seemed upset, he looked hurt, and angry, but if that were true, then why the hell did he just pawn me off on his friend?

No, I was the hurt and angry one. He kissed me this morning, and now he was probably trying to get someone else to act interested in me, so that he wouldn't have to deal with the clingy girl. Well no problem there, buddy, I had no plans to cling whatsoever.

I kissed Jasmine on the head and hugged her fiercely. She wanted us all to go out for pizza, but I told her I had dinner plans with her Uncle Jax. She beamed at me for a few seconds, then slumped her shoulders and walked off.

Jackson appeared then and held out his elbow for me to grab. I somehow managed a smile and followed him out of the gym.

SEVENTEEN

Jackson drove us in his brand-new jeep to an upscale burger joint. I was actually relieved since I wasn't able to change into something date-worthy. He had looked over at me a few times with a seductive smile on his lips, and it made me want to cry. I was such a mess, and all I wanted was to tell him to turn the car around so I could go make Jimmy talk to me about what happened. I forced a weak smile for Jackson and then turned to look out the window. Once we were in the restaurant and we received our meals, Jackson took a small bite of food and wiped his hands.

"So, how did you meet Jimmy? I've heard bits and pieces about it, but I would love to hear your rendition."

He smiled again and leaned forward on his fist, waiting for me to respond.

I took a drink of my lemon water and began to tell him my Jimmy story, which again struck at me because I *had* a story with Jimmy.

Not wanting to overshare or bore the poor man, I stopped my story right after I didn't get the job, on that first interview. Jackson took another bite of his vegan burger, which offended me on so many levels; why did he even want to go to a burger joint? Once he drank a few sips of water, he smiled at me, but it didn't reach his eyes. It was pretty obvious that he wasn't actually trying to charm me, which changed things a bit.

"So how on earth did you end up babysitting his kids on accident then?" he asked with obvious curiosity. It occurred to me that if, in fact, Jackson was interested in me, then he wouldn't only be asking me questions surrounding Jimmy and his kids. Relief swept through me because this wasn't a date; it was an interrogation. He tricked me.

I couldn't help the smile that came over my face. "That is a funny story," I said, laughing a little at the memory of that night with Theo. "I was so upset about my interview with Jimmy that I went to get a drink at the local bar in my town, Sip N Sides. I met Theo, he took pity on me, heard my sad story about the jerk from Rockford, and by the end of the night, he had offered me a job. He never once mentioned that he knew Jimmy Stenson from Rockford, by the way."

Jackson let out a hearty laugh. "Yeah, Theo can be a little troublemaker when he wants to be."

I drank more water and continued my story about getting asked to babysit Theo's grandkids, and then about that night, and getting fired again. Jackson finished off his meatless burger and wiped his hands.

"So, Ramsey? Where are you from?" Jackson asked sternly, like he was preparing for an argument. I drank more water.

"Chicago," was all I gave him. I didn't want to waste time, when I knew I was only here to be interrogated.

"So why here? Surely there are better paying accountant jobs in Chicago, why did you settle in Rockford?" He was being nice on the surface, but under his tone, he was accusatory.

"I didn't. I'm in Belvidere," I answered coldly. This was getting ridiculous. How long did we need to carry on like this? I wasn't about to have him pick apart my entire life.

I could sense that Jackson wanted to say something to me, but he was hesitant, I took the opportunity to put him at ease. "Look, Jackson, I like the Stenson family. They are helping me through a rough time with my mom. They're becoming my friends. Real ones. I don't know what you're looking for, but I won't hurt them."

I was tracing a line around the top of my glass as I finished my last sentence. Jackson was staring at me, clearly mulling over everything that he had just heard. "You know what they've gone through then?"

I looked down and nodded. "Jimmy told me about his ex-leaving, about how old the kids were, how alone he was, how heartbroken."

"Yes. He was completely shattered, and Jasmine didn't stop crying for a month. She didn't understand, and she didn't know what she did wrong. The second month, she refused to acknowledge her baby brother because she thought he was the reason that her mom left. By the third month, she just didn't talk at all. Months, Ramsey. It took months to put her back together, and Jimmy took years."

Jackson explained, while trying to be quiet, so not everyone heard, but I could hear the intensity in his tone.

"I see the way he looks at you, and I haven't seen him look that way at any woman ever, and that includes Lisa. You're dangerous, and I know that you've figured out why I really brought you to dinner, which is good. That means we're on the same page.

"I can't allow another person to tear that family apart. Because even though I don't live here, that is *my* family and I would do anything to protect them. You seem nice, but you also seem unsure of what you want, which is a big red flag to me."

He was staring down at me, like I had just stolen his wallet or something. It made me want to squirm and leave, and never make him angry again. I pushed my empty plate forward and folded my hands in front of me.

"I know. I may not have lived through that hell, but I can still feel remnants of it in each of them. If I seem unsure, it's because I am. My mom has less than a year to live, she is my priority right now, she has to be. Otherwise, I would have accepted Jimmy's dinner request last week, but I turned him down because I am a wreck right now. I am barely keeping it together enough to bring in a paycheck.

"When I get home every night from work, I am broken. I cry myself to sleep because I have to watch my mom wither away, and once she's gone, I am all alone. I have no one. My best friend lives in Chicago, and I have Jimmy, Theo, and the kids. That's it. Of course, I'm unsure, but I would never ditch those kids. I have already promised Jasmine that she's stuck with me, one way or another." I let it all out, feeling lighter and more confident now.

Jackson leaned forward. "I don't blame you, Ramsey, for being unsure, and you seem honest. I feel in my gut that you are good for him. Just promise me that you will be kind to him, and that you will protect him from himself. He still has demons that come out to play every now and then. Jimmy doesn't believe that he deserves the whole package deal—a wife that loves him and his kids, one that accepts his past. He'll push you away if he gets the chance because he's afraid." He squeezed my hand, then pulled away and went to stand up.

He pulled his jacket on as I stood up as well. We walked together to the checkout counter and paid the bill. Jackson dropped me off at my car that was still in the parking lot at the school.

Once I hopped out of his jeep, he leaned towards me and said, "Ramsey, I was glad to meet you. I am headed back to Jimmy's, but I will be gone by morning. Give him time, he will explain himself."

Jackson drove off, and while my car warmed up, I thought about what he said; that Jimmy would explain himself, and I knew eventually he would have to, we worked too closely together for there to be any awkwardness between us. I thought about that all the way home, but I couldn't help pulling into my mom's driveway and feel lonely with the dark house looming in front of me.

I wanted laughter and life, I wanted the pitter patter of little feet, I wanted warm fires and the sound of the dishwasher running; I wanted a family. If I was purely honest, I wanted Jimmy's family. The space between my chest ached for what I didn't have, it was at war with the feelings of selfishness over wanting all that when my mom was dying. I hated how conflicted I felt about it. Why couldn't I just fall in love and my mom have a promising future ahead of her, so that she could plan with me, dream with me, and hope with me? Life was so often not fair and at this precise moment, I hated it.

I dragged myself out of the car because the exhaustion from the day was finally hitting me. I walked up the driveway until I was safe in the warm, empty house, then headed straight for the hot shower, where I stayed until the water ran cold. I changed into sweats and a tank top, and then went back into the living room to watch something funny and hopefully pass out. I didn't want to come to terms with how pathetic I was, or how sad. I face planted on the cushions and wrapped the massive blanket around my body. I was about to officially call this Saturday night to an end when I heard a knock at the front door.

EIGHTEEN

JIMMY

I WAS PISSED. Beyond pissed. I had been pacing back and forth for the past hour, waiting for Jackson. I knew that this whole, shitty thing was on me, but he shouldn't have pushed it so far. He was my friend, and knew something was going on.

Finally, around nine, he walked in. He still had his jacket on and a somber look on his face, like he had a terrible date. *Good.* Without waiting, I walked up to him and punched him square in the face.

"That was for pushing me so far today, knowing things between Ramsey and me are complicated!" I shouted at him as I rubbed my knuckles.

He adjusted his jaw a bit while he stared intensely at me. He slowly peeled off his jacket, then his shoes, and walked past me. "I'll watch the kids and put them to bed. You should go talk to Ramsey, I think she's waiting to hear from you."

What the hell did that mean? How would he even know? Jealousy surged through me. I hated feeling like this, feeling this ownership over her like she belonged to me when she didn't. I didn't even respond, because honestly, I had been waiting to talk to Ramsey all day, and I wasn't going to wait for another second if I didn't have to. I pulled my shoes on, grabbed my keys, and headed out.

I parked my car, not wanting to be too loud with the bike, got out, and stomped up Ramsey's driveway. Her house was dark, but as I got closer, I could see the television was on in the living room. I suddenly worried that she was asleep, and that I would have to wait until tomorrow to talk to her. That thought made me panic, and that, added in with my earlier anger, wasn't good. I knew I needed to cool down before I knocked on the door, before I faced her, or worse, didn't face her… but my hand had a mind of its own. It balled up into a fist and began rapping on her door. I held my breath while I waited for her to answer.

I couldn't hear anything behind the door, and just as I was about to knock again, I heard the deadbolt unlock. Hope surged through me as a sleepy Ramsey slowly pulled the door free. She carefully peeked out through the opening, as though she was trying to be careful, as well as establish a boundary. I looked at her, then the size of the gap that she allowed, and gently placed my hand on the door while I spoke. "Hey, I thought we could talk. Is now a good time?"

She pushed her lips together and scrunched her eyebrows, like she was thinking about saying no. I could tell our relationship was about to suffer a major backslide. But she surprised me by swinging the door wide and carefully moving her body to the side so that I could enter. I stepped through the door, walking a little further into the entryway, and into her living room. She had secured the door and as I looked back, she was adjusting the massive blanket that was wrapped around her. She had her wet hair piled on top of her head, in a way that showed off her long neck. The blanket had slipped a few times, and I knew that she was wearing a sleep tank with tiny straps, and sweats. Comfortable; she looked comfortable. There was no makeup on her face, no attempts to be something other than just who she was. I craved that kind of authenticity in a woman, and there she was, standing right in front of me.

She made her way to the couch and curled up under the blanket, waiting for me to take my seat. I sat down across from her on one of the chairs. Her face was expressionless, and it made me uneasy. She blandly asked, "Can I get you anything? Coffee, water, or tea?"

She didn't get up or even move, so I knew she was just trying to be polite. "No, I'm good," I replied, a little softer than I normally would. My earlier anger was starting to dissipate, just with her being in the room with me.

She was still staring at me, and I realized after a few seconds that she wasn't going to yell at me, which made me feel strange. I think a part of me wanted her to yell and wanted her to be mad at me, just like I was with her. Finally, I spoke up and decided to be the man that I wanted her to see me as.

"So, I wanted to talk to you all day, but things... got complicated after our kiss."

She adjusted herself on the couch and looked down at the carpet; the movement made her seem irritated. I had to keep going though, otherwise, I would lose my nerve.

"I wanted to apologize for what happened this morning, with the kiss."

"Just stop. Please," she cut in abruptly.

I looked probably as confused as I felt but waited for her to continue.

"I have worried all day that you would apologize to me for that kiss, and I don't want an apology, Jimmy. Surely you know that no woman on Planet Earth wants the guy to apologize for kissing them," she deadpanned, and sounded incredulous all at once, like I was a small child. She wasn't doing it to be harsh, more like trying to make a very important point.

I kicked my legs out until they were stretched in front of

me, and leaned back in the chair. My pride was swelling a little bit that she didn't want an apology for the kiss.

"Of course I know that no woman wants that, and I wasn't going to apologize for the kiss, Ramsey. I mean, I am sorry in the sense that I am your boss and I shouldn't complicate things for us, but I thought long and hard about that kiss, and I didn't do it on a whim and I wouldn't take it back."

She was staring at me now, and I noticed a little heat that was now touching her cheeks. She practically whispered, "Then why did you act the way you did today?"

I looked down at my hands. "I don't know...I just didn't want to confront how badly it hurt to see you leave this morning. I mean, I guess I get it. I may not have regretted that kiss, but it seems like you did."

She looked a little taken back, and sat up a little straighter. "I didn't regret the kiss! I took off because your out-of-town best friend had just walked in, and I didn't want to make things weird for you," she yelled.

"You could have stayed, Ramsey, you could have waited to talk to me!" I yelled back. Feelings of abandonment were surfacing from old wounds that I thought had healed. I needed to get a hold of things, and fast.

She was leaning forward and had released some of her blanket as she continued, "Wait for what? For you to pull me aside and tell me that you regretted it because of our jobs, or because of the kids, or because of the million other reasons I know that you have? I didn't want to be rejected, Jimmy, not again from you."

"Me reject *you*?! Excuse me, wasn't I the one who asked you out on a date and got rejected, not even a week ago?" I responded to her, just as incredulous as she was earlier with me.

She was staring at the carpet, but her face had morphed into pure rage. "I rejected you because my mom has cancer,

Jimmy. I was trying to do the right thing. You have kids, I can't just date you on a whim because I want to. I have to think about you and the kids and, more than anyone, my mom! Sorry if you can't understand that."

She blew out a huge breath and was also standing now, pointing at me, the blanket completely forgotten. I would appreciate the moment more if she wasn't so angry at me.

I was about to respond but she beat me to it. "Now I *am* starting to regret that kiss. Everything with you is so damn complicated, Jimmy. Why is that?"

I wasn't hurt by that statement, or rather that question, I was stunned. Then good ol' self-preservation kicked in like an emergency raft in the ocean, and I felt the walls that had begun to recede away from my heart reinforce with more strength than ever. I stared at her, realizing that she was still standing, and I was sitting, so I stood, because I had every intention of leaving. I knew I needed to salvage what I could for our work relationship, but I emotionally no longer felt safe around Ramsey. This girl could ruin me ten times worse than Lisa ever had. I needed to get away from her and out of this situation. Clearing my throat, I attempted the best response possible.

"Well,…I'm sorry things are complicated with me, Ramsey. Let's just forget the kiss happened. I don't think we need to discuss anything else tonight, it's late. I will see you Monday." I gave her a nod and started towards the door.

Ramsey moved behind me, and I caught a small hint of red on her face. I made it outside, and she still hadn't said anything, but she walked outside with me, in her pajamas and without the blanket. She stood there with her arms crossed over her chest, and her wet hair on top of her head. I hated that I was more worried about her getting sick than I was about getting the hell out of there. The weather had turned this last week, the temperature dropped by several degrees as soon as the sun went away. She looked like she was about ready to cry. Right as I reached my car door, I heard her say something. It was hard to catch because she was still by her door, but it sounded like, "Will you please come back inside?"

I had my hand on the door handle, looking at her, and waited. I wasn't sure that was in fact what she said, but I realized that even if it was, I wasn't sure I wanted to. I saw her move forward in her bare feet across the yard, then she said again, "Please, Jimmy, just come back inside. I was pissed, but I didn't mean what I said or how it came out. Just... let's start over... please?"

I wanted to start over. I wanted to wrap my arms around her and walk her back inside, and snuggle under that damn blanket with her while exploring more of our kissing abilities. But what I did instead was protect myself. I looked down at the ground and gently called back to her, "Good night, Ramsey."

I opened my car door and began to drive away. In my rearview mirror, I watched Ramsey stand there in the freezing cold, with hardly anything on, watching me leave.

Once I got home, I walked into the kitchen and threw my keys down, and slumped into the breakfast nook. I wondered what the hell just happened, and how I had just lost her before I even had her. I replayed the look on Ramsey's face tonight, and realized she was probably pissed at me to begin with, and we never did get to talk about her date with Jackson. Remembering that the asshole was probably on my couch, I walked into the living room and turned on the lights. Sure enough, he had passed out there. All previous signs of our theatre fort had been cleaned up earlier that day, so I had a clear view of Jackson.

I sat on the coffee table in front of him, tempted to punch him again, but seeing that he had a pack of frozen peas draped over his face, I decided to leave him alone. After a few seconds, my phone dinged.

·　·　·

RAMSEY: *PLEASE, JIMMY, I DON'T WANT THINGS TO END LIKE this with us. I didn't mean what I said. -Please give me another chance.*

I IGNORED IT AND PUT THE PHONE BACK IN MY POCKET.

Jackson slowly sat up and asked, "What happened with your girl, and why do you look so pissed?"

I rubbed my hands together while I looked around the room, trying to school my features. I didn't want to answer him, I had my own questions to ask.

"What happened with you two tonight at the restaurant?"

Jackson threw his head back against the couch and let out a sigh. "I figured she would have explained all this, Jimmy... I took her out to get to know her. For your sake, brother. I had a very frank conversation with her about how big of a deal it was that she not hurt you or the kids because of what you went through." He finished with a solemn look on his face, as though he was reliving some of the worst memories of my life with me again.

I spun the TV remote that was next to me on the coffee table, and looked at him. "Well, thanks for that." I didn't know what else to say.

"So, what happened over there? You look pissed," Jackson asked, while adjusting the peas to cover more of his face.

"We argued. We couldn't seem to get past what happened after our kiss, or why she left. She says she left to give me space and time with you. I think she left because she regretted kissing me, and wanted to back out of whatever it was we had started. She denied it, and we just kept spiraling, until she did say that she was starting to regret the kiss because everything with me is so damn complicated all the time." I let out a frustrated, shaky breath. I kind of felt like I was on the verge of tears, which was weird because I cried when my mom died, but I didn't cry when Lisa left. I was angry, hurt even...but I didn't cry.

"Shit, I'm sorry, man. Me showing up messed everything up." Jackson pulled his hand down over his face and let out another loud sigh. "You know, I came here because I got spooked in the city this week. I met someone through this business deal, and she and I couldn't stop arguing over a few stupid things. They were big deals to me because they had to do with my restaurant and my business portfolio, but like always, I screwed it up. But Jimmy, this girl chewed me up and spit me out, and it scared the hell out of me."

He said it with awe, like he revered this woman or something.

"Why did it bother you that she chewed you up and spit you out? That sounds like a normal occurrence for you, Jack," I said with a small laugh, trying to keep it light. This guy was my brother for all the reasons that mattered; we didn't share blood, but he was there for me when no one else was. However, Jackson had the tendency to be a jackass to the people who worked for him. So, if he got a tongue-lashing, he likely deserved it.

Jackson was staring straight forward now. "Man, I don't know, but I couldn't sleep, and I had to get out of the city. She saw through me, and no one has ever been able to see those parts of me. I have never felt more vulnerable. That's why I showed up on your doorstep so early, because some chick called me out on my behavior, and I got scared and wanted to hide," he said, sounding almost relieved to get it off his chest.

I looked behind me and then back at him. I knew he needed some reassurance that he didn't just ruin everything with Ramsey. I had done that on my own.

"Don't worry about it, man. Things with Ramsey are complicated, and she wasn't wrong. They are always complicated, and they were probably doomed from the start. I just keep pushing for something to be there when maybe it shouldn't be," I reassured him, and attempted to reassure myself.

Jackson leaned forward and put his right hand on my shoulder. "Look, Jimmy, I saw how you looked at her. Don't give up, and if she wants to make up for the comment she made, then you should let her. She's a good woman. She would be good for you, and for the kids."

I felt his words settle in my stomach. I knew he was right, but my pride was like a stiff outer shell penetrating any ideas of letting her back in or accepting her pleas to talk again. I knew that I would see her on Monday, and until then, I would figure out how to talk to her again. But for now, I was going to drink with my best friend and enjoy what was left of my weekend.

NINETEEN

I WAS MISERABLE. I was miserable for a few reasons. Partly because I was upset about what happened with Jimmy. Currently, however, I was miserable because I was sick. My head felt detached from my body, my nose was running nonstop, and had turned that awful shade of red, my body was aching, and my throat was throbbing.

It didn't help matters that my mom's immune system was practically nonexistent, so in order to protect her, I had been shut up in my room for two days. Thank the good Lord I had an attached bathroom, or else I might be urinating in a bucket. That's how serious my mom was about me staying put. She would leave food for me by my door, and then I would have to wait five minutes before opening it.

Sunday, I chatted with my mom, and did everything in my power to stay distracted from checking my phone to see if Jimmy had texted me back or called. He hadn't.

By Monday, I was half-alive and was faced with having to call in sick. Since I didn't want to talk to Jimmy's voicemail, I emailed him. Tuesday came around with little change, except that I wanted out of my room; it was stuffy and dirty and filled with Kleenex. I was tempted to rent a hotel room, just for a change of scenery, but I had no money.

It was now Tuesday afternoon, I think. I mostly had lost track of the time and it felt like an eternity had passed. I did notice that I had a few texts—one from Theo, five from Laney, and zero from Jimmy, and I broke a little more. It's not that I blamed him, what I said was terrible and hurtful, but I was emotional and angry, and people have always said hurtful, dumb things when they're angry. Jimmy himself had said hurtful and angry things to me, but I forgave him, I let it go. I was hurt because he wouldn't give me the same opportunity. He wasn't responding to my personal texts, but to my work emails he would respond, cordially and professional. To my email about being out sick, he responded with:

"Get well soon, thank you for keeping me posted- JS."

WHEN I GOT THAT EMAIL, I FELT A HOT SEARING PAIN HIT MY gut. He wasn't going to let this go and he wasn't going to give me another chance. I decided to write to him. Since he wasn't going to give me the time of day, he would have to settle for another email. I pulled up my laptop after a hearty dose of Nyquil—or was it Dayquil? I should probably have someone watching these kinds of things for me.

Nevertheless, I started the email, no longer caring about his feelings.

To: JSTENSON@GMAIL.COM
  From: rambam2800@gmail.com
  Subject: Moving on

JIMMY,

213

Since you won't give me the opportunity to apologize to you in the flesh, an email will have to do. I don't really want to see you, and that feeling gets stronger with each passing day. You played me and messed with my emotions with how you handled things with Jackson.

I wanted to let you know that I am done. You have made your position clear.

My mom's diagnosis gives her six months; if that is accurate, I will most likely be moving back to Chicago once she's gone. However, I would like to come and visit with Jasmine on some weekends. I made her a promise that I intend to keep.

- Ramsey

I ATTEMPTED TO REREAD THE EMAIL, BUT MY HEAD WAS pounding and every thought felt muddy and confusing. So, I just left the email there, figuring I should probably wait to send anything that serious until I could think clearly. Gently setting my laptop to the side, careful of the cord that was still plugged in, I laid my head back on the pillow and passed out.

TWENTY

JIMMY

It was Tuesday afternoon when I received a call from Carla. I was at work, desperate to keep myself busy with meetings, reviews, and checking out new vendors; basically anything to keep my mind off of Ramsey and the few unanswered text messages from her that were burning a hole in my pocket. My fingers ached from how many times I had held the phone, wanting to respond. I wanted to see her. But I didn't respond. Not being around her for three days was a new kind of hell that I had yet to experience.

Apparently, she had already befriended every single employee in the bar and every one of them wondered where she was, and each time that I had to reply that she was out sick, I felt a little surge of guilt. She was out sick because she was outside Saturday night with wet hair, bare feet, and wearing practically nothing; desperately trying to get me to come back inside and talk to her. I hated that she was sick because of me, but still, I hesitated to contact her, and I made sure to keep our emails professional.

I had to, otherwise I would fall apart and that would give Ramsey access to me again, where she could do some real damage. This was better. I had to believe it was better; eventually, we would move past this.

When Carla's number flashed on my screen, I felt a surge of panic. With Ramsey being sick and not knowing how she was doing, it felt like my only connection to her just reached out to me. I was in the middle of a big project, but I stepped away from it to answer.

"Hello, Carla?" I sounded worried, so I made a mental note to calm the hell down.

"Jimmy? Hello, sorry to bother you at work, are you busy?" She sounded a little breathless, like maybe she had been walking or moving too much. That didn't sit well with me.

"No, it's fine, Carla, what can I help you with?"

"Well, Jimmy, I was wondering if either you or your dad could come and help me with something? The pilot light went out and Ramsey usually lights it for me, but she can't come out of her room," she finished, in a tone that indicated that I should already know this. My mind was racing at this news, and why the hell Ramsey couldn't leave her room. Exactly how sick was she?

Dad wasn't doing anything, I should have him go over, but I had to know how bad Ramsey was. I needed to see her. I ended my call with Carla, telling her I'd be there soon. I let everyone know that I was leaving early, and I traveled those fifteen miles of highway to Belvidere to fix a pilot light and feed my Ramsey addiction.

I knocked on Carla's door and greeted her warmly. If she and Ramsey talked about what had happened over the weekend, Carla wasn't showing any sign of it. She was sweet, wearing a soft blue tracksuit and her head was wrapped in a blue bandana. She looked tired and that made me sad, like it usually did. She led me to where she kept her water heater, then handed me a long-necked lighter. I was wearing a rather expensive suit, but I was never one for caring about that sort of thing. It just happened to be a nice suit that happened to cost a lot of money, it didn't bother me that I was now lying on my stomach on the floor, lighting her pilot.

Once it was lit, I stood up and dusted myself off. Carla was standing with her hands on her hips, looking introspective. I handed her the lighter and slowly started making my way towards her kitchen. The house looked okay, which was good, but why was Ramsey not allowed out of her room? Placing my hands on my hips, I faced Carla.

"So, Carla, why exactly is Ramsey stuck in her room? Is she okay?"

Carla's eyebrows rose and scrunched together. "She's very sick, and my immune system is very weak, so she has to stay in there until she is symptom-free, which will probably be another three days, at least." Concern laced her voice, and she had her hands together as she shuffled her feet from side to side. I watched her with a curious glance until she looked up. She threw her arms out, yelling, "I make sure she gets food though!"

I held back a laugh. Of course, I didn't assume that she was starving Ramsey. I was hoping that Carla would let me see her; maybe she wouldn't care, maybe she would, but I had to try.

"So, you haven't been able to check in on her much because you can't be around her?" I asked with a bit of a quizzical look.

"No, not at all, and I feel terrible about it." She looked down at the carpet, as though she was trying to cover up for how ashamed she was about her declaration.

"Well, then I insist on checking on her while I'm here," I said, starting to walk towards Ramsey's bedroom. I wasn't sure what Ramsey looked like, if she was even dressed, but I guess I was about to find out.

Carla trailed behind me silently but didn't protest. Halfway to Ramsey's bedroom, she stopped and decided she would wait in the living room, probably remembering that she couldn't get too close.

I gently knocked on the door, but there was no answer, so I slowly opened it.

I noticed first that the room was dark and seemed depressing. She had one of those oil diffuser things in her room, her TV was playing episodes of *How I met your Mother*, and the volume was low. Ramsey laid face down on her bed, and she was covered in blankets, but I could see that she was at least wearing a shirt. She had her laptop resting on the pillow next to her head, and it looked uncomfortable because the cord was stretching from the wall across Ramsey's head.

I took a few steps into the room; it was messy and full of empty cups and tissues. I remembered how often my mom had taken care of me when I didn't feel well. I loved sunlight and a clean room when I was sick, with clean sheets and clean blankets. I felt bad that Ramsey couldn't have that. I went to reach for the laptop to move it, but stopped as soon as I saw the screen. It was still lit up, probably because it was plugged in. The screen had an email on it, and I wouldn't normally snoop, but it was an email addressed to me. I looked at Ramsey; she seemed thoroughly knocked out, so I felt okay to take a second to read it. I didn't remember this email coming through to my inbox and saw that it wasn't sent yet.

The email was sobering, it pinched and twisted my gut, as I read about how she didn't want to see me and how that was growing with each passing day. I slowly made my way down to the bed where I carefully sat and read the rest. The entire email was like a kick to the gut, but what really sealed the deal for me was the end, when she mentioned going back to Chicago once her mom passed.

I sat there on her bed, staring at this email that maybe I was never supposed to read. I realized that I could walk away and never look back. I could stay away from Ramsey, I could end it with her before it could really begin. I could stay away to protect myself, but I'd already done that. Which was why there was essentially a goodbye letter sitting on Ramsey's computer; I walked away, and she wasn't waiting around for me to pull my head out of my ass. That scared me more than the idea of being hurt by her.

Ramsey couldn't leave. She couldn't be reduced to some family friend that occasionally came and saw Jasmine on the weekends. Our relationship couldn't be reduced to some awkward hello here and there, until the day came that I heard through Jasmine that Ramsey was engaged or going to have a baby with someone else. That couldn't happen.

There was this thing happening inside of my chest that scared me. It was like this need just hit me. Like finding out I had another kid somewhere, or that my mother was still alive. It was a desperation, something I couldn't live without. And Ramsey was at the source of it.

I closed my eyes to try and move past the feeling. I looked over at Ramsey's crazy hair, her makeup-free face, her red nose, a tiny blue bruise on the corner of her eye from when Sammy hit her, and the tissues surrounding her, and knew what I was going to do.

I walked over to her closet and found a small duffle bag. I went to her dresser and invaded her privacy on way too many levels, but I packed her a bag with clean clothes, found her cell phone and charger, and threw them in. I walked into her bathroom and added her toothbrush, toothpaste, and shower stuff. I headed to the side of her bed and added in all of her cold remedies. I even unplugged her oil diffuser and grabbed the oils that were next to it and shoved it in the duffle. I turned off her TV, threw her duffel strap over my chest, and walked over and gently picked up Ramsey, along with her blanket, and walked out of her room. I walked down the hallway and yelled to Carla;

"I am going to take Ramsey to my house and take care of her there until she is symptom-free."

Carla appeared but kept her distance. She had a hopeful look on her face as she took in the duffel bag and her daughter in my arms, and a soft smile appeared on her face.

"Oh, Jimmy, you don't have to do that, but I appreciate it, and I think it's a great idea. Did you get her cold medicine?"

I smiled. "Yeah I got everything. I am sure she will call you when she wakes up, and let you know how she's feeling. Does she have any favorite soups that I can make her, or tea?"

Ramsey was still out, she must have taken something strong. She was surprisingly light in my arms for how tall she was, so I waited for Carla to think about the foods I should feed to Ramsey.

"She loves chicken noodle, but not the canned kind; only the real kind with veggies and chunks of chicken. She loves peppermint tea with a little milk. Here, take this tea with you, it is supposed to help with sore throats."

She started moving towards the kitchen, picking up a face mask on the way. She grabbed a box from the cupboard and gently placed it on Ramsey's stomach. I smiled and thanked her as I made my way towards the door. Carla moved to get ahead of me and opened the door, and then walked out to open the passenger side door of the Tahoe for me. I gently placed Ramsey in the car and put the seatbelt over her, then shut her in. I faced Carla again and thanked her for her help. I tried to reassure her about Ramsey being okay at my house, but she didn't seem to need much reassurance.

"Keep her as long as she's not a burden or inconvenience,"

she said, while placing her tiny hand on my arm, walking with me towards my side of the car. Right before I got in, she added, "She cares for you, Jimmy, she cares for you a great deal. You both deserve happiness. Just don't miss it when it stares you in the face."

She gave my arm a squeeze and turned to walk back into the house. I yelled after her, "Call if you need anything. I don't like the idea of you being alone. I can send my dad over in a matter of minutes if you need anything, okay?"

She smiled and waved her hand in acknowledgment.

I made my way home and pulled into the garage. I grabbed her duffel bag first, and ran ahead, opening all the doors I would need to have open in order to carry her in. I went back and gently grabbed Ramsey from the car. I made my way through the kitchen and into the living room, past my dad, who was on the couch watching some fishing show, and walked upstairs to my room, where I carefully placed her in my bed. I closed the shades, but left them open enough for the room to seem bright. I looked over at her in my bed and saw that she was starting to wake up. She opened one eye, took the palm of her hand and shoved it into her eye socket. With her other hand, she felt the sheets, and turned her head until she saw me, and froze.

She looked surprised more than anything. Confused, and a little embarrassed. All of which I could deal with, just as long as she wasn't mad that I had basically kidnapped her. She looked so tired, and sick, but strangely gorgeous. It was probably because I wanted to marry her. *What the hell?*

I shook my head at the craziness of it all and continued thinking, I knew if that fantasy were to ever become a reality, then I would be seeing a lot of moments in Ramsey's life where she didn't look her best. I wanted to be the only person in her life that was there to see her at her worst. I smiled at her, as I thought of becoming the man who got to love her in sickness and in health. She returned my smile, and then closed her eyes as she snuggled into my pillows and fell back asleep.

I needed to let her sleep, so I went downstairs and got her a glass of water and placed it next to the bed. I fished her cell phone out of the duffel that I had brought up, and put it next to her, so when she woke up, she wouldn't panic. I walked downstairs and filled my dad in on what was going on. He smiled and patted me on the back; it was his silent way of showing that he was proud of me, which was a medicine to old wounds that still festered every now and then.

While I waited for Ramsey to wake up, I decided I should probably respond to her text messages. Better late than never.

TWENTY-ONE

Ramsey

I WAS WAKING up from the most beautiful dream. In my dream, I was in Jimmy's bed and he was standing near me and looking at me like he cherished me, or loved me. I think if it's a dream, then you can make it whatever you want and I choose love. Yep, he definitely loved me. I was still sick in the dream, unfortunately, but I had this warm and cozy feeling that you only get from really good dreams. My eyes were still shut, but that was because my head still hurt, and my throat was still clogged with phlegm and all things disgusting. I was gross, and needed a shower and to brush my teeth. I also needed food and water; all the essential things to keep me alive.

I stretched my arms and began to turn my head. I barely opened my left eye—these things had to be taken in stages and opening my eyes while feeling like death was going to take several. My eye was blurry and gross, and all I could make out were colors and shapes. Odd shapes, but what I noticed immediately was sunlight, which was strange because I had blackout curtains in my room. I opened my right eye, so they were both open now, and began to lightly rub at them so I could clear away some of the crusty blockage that was impairing my vision. The light came into focus—it was definitely sunlight, coming from wooden slats that hung as blinds over a very large window. My eyes moved to the sheets that surrounded my pathetically weak body, and I saw white, so much white.

My breath caught as I took in the rest of the room; this was Jimmy's room. I didn't dream that look or being carried up a set of stairs or being gently placed into this massive bed of his. I froze, and panic began to gather in my throat, along with all that nasty phlegm. I started to cough, because I knew that I looked, smelled, and probably sounded like death, and death was not a particular look I wanted to have when seeing Jimmy Stenson.

Also, he was freezing me out, ignoring me, and infuriating me, the last time I checked. So why was I lying in his bed? The thought was making my head hurt more than it already was. This whole thing was making me freak out, and I hated freaking out because it usually involved crying and snot and an ugly face. *Okay, stop it, Ramsey!*

I slowly sat up and looked around. The good news was that the house seemed silent, which meant that I was likely all alone. That made me feel instantly better. I started to throw the covers back, and saw that I was still in my nightshirt and sweats; again, that brought me comfort, that meant that no one had to awkwardly change me.

As I moved my legs over to the edge of the bed, I stopped and noticed that my cell phone was plugged in, charging, and sitting on the bedside table. Relief flooded me. I grabbed it and pressed the screen, immediately I noticed several notifications. A few were from Laney and some from my mom, and a few from Jimmy. I wanted those first. I touched Jimmy's name in my list of messages and read the oldest one first, it was dated yesterday.

6:35 p.m.- Ramsey, please don't freak out when you wake

up. I will explain everything, but your mom knows you are here and helped me.

8:00 p.m.- Whenever you wake up, feel free to shower, there are fresh towels in the bathroom and your duffel bag is in there, with fresh clothes.

LASTLY, I FOUND ONE FROM THIS MORNING.

8:15 A.M.- GOOD MORNING, RAMSEY, I AM NOT SURE WHEN you will wake up, but I am heading to work then I will be back around lunchtime to check on you. My dad is at Sip N Sides if you need anything. I have my phone just call or text if you need something.

I CHECKED THE CURRENT TIME AND SAW THAT IT WAS A quarter to twelve. Which meant that it was lunchtime. My foggy brain clicked into gear just in time to realize that Jimmy was going to be home any minute, and I still looked, smelled, and sounded like death. I jumped up, then slumped back down because: death.

I considered giving up and getting back into bed; if I threw the blankets over me, Jimmy wouldn't be able to see me or smell me, unless I did actually end up dying. I decided against that plan and slowly got up and shuffled towards his bathroom.

I headed for the toilet first. After sleeping as long as I did, I was surprised that I hadn't peed my pants already. While I sat there, I looked around and found the bathroom in pristine shape, just like last time. It was immaculately clean, glowing even. Not a single loose hair in sight. No streaks on his mirror, or splatter from toothpaste. *Who lived like this?*

I stripped out of my disgusting clothes, found my toiletries in my duffel, and headed into his walk-in shower. The stones were cold under my feet as I admired the dark tones on the wall of the shower. I looked up towards the chrome shower-head, and then looked at the one on the opposite wall. Neither wall had any lever or knob, and there was nothing to indicate what would turn on the shower. A little confused, I pushed in on the stone wall, thinking maybe it was like a trick shower wall thing. Nothing happened. So, I stood on my tiptoes and touched the showerheads, one by one, and again, nothing. Damn it!

I was standing there about to cry. I just wanted to get clean. I tried the wall again, pushing, punching, but nothing happened. I considered this was all a big fat practical joke, and Jimmy was trying to get me back or something. I decided to give up on the shower and settled instead for the small swim-ming pool in the corner of Jimmy's bathroom.

I turned to face the huge, jetted bathtub, and of course, I wanted to use it, but not when I only had fifteen minutes until Jimmy would possibly be here. I sighed and walked over to it; thankfully the knobs were fairly straightforward. The jets had labels, as well as the knobs themselves, and I turned the one with the indicating -H- on it, then looked around for some bubbles. Typical man had no bubbles, which I couldn't fault him for. So, I decided to just add in some of my body wash because you absolutely cannot take a bath without bubbles.

I sat down in the tub while the water continued to fill around me, the aroma of lilac body wash filling the spacious room. I took what was left of my ponytail out, letting my crazy hair fall down around my shoulders, and leaned back against the cushioned headrest. Once the tub was practically full, I turned the knob off and just soaked.

The hot water was like some magical elixir, healing my aching body and clearing my head. I melted further into the luxurious tub, the bubbles moving and shifting in the water the only sound in the empty room. I dipped my head and scrubbed my hair, washing all the grease and germs from it. I'm sure there weren't actually germs in my hair, but I was one of those people who felt like everything was infected when sickness hit.

Once I was clean, I felt like a new person and had lost all concept of time. Honestly, I couldn't care about where I was or what I was doing, I just wanted clean clothes and a fresh bed. I got out and wrapped a large towel around myself, loving the feel of the soft, fluffy cotton against my skin. Just as I had secured it around my body, the bedroom door opened, and Jimmy walked in.

I was standing in the doorway of his bathroom, my hair soaking wet around my shoulders because my head hurt so badly that just the idea of piling it up with a towel made me wince. I also was delayed in my response by a few seconds, but just as my brain processed that Jimmy was seeing me in just a towel, I grabbed for the bathroom door to slam it shut. Instead, I just ended up groping around the frame like I was blind. Jimmy had no bathroom door. *Who the heck didn't have a bathroom door?!*

I placed my arms back over my chest to hold the towel secure and stared at Jimmy who was still just standing, frozen in the doorway of his bedroom. He was dressed nicely, which made sense, coming from work. Neither of us said anything and maybe I should have asked him to leave or told him to look away, but I let him look and as muddy as my brain was, I still caught him devouring me with hungry interest as his wide, green eyes roamed over my body. As much as I wanted to break the awkward silence, my throat still hurt and I didn't want to talk.

He finally blinked and looked down at the carpet. Awkwardly, he shuffled backward and kept his head low, "Sorry, um... I'll just go make you some soup and come back in a few minutes."

He turned completely and stepped into the hallway, shutting the door behind him. I felt the heat of his stare still lingering on my skin, as if it had branded me somehow. My movements were clumsy as I reached for my clothes. I wanted to be dressed before he came back, so we didn't do any more hot and heavy staring contests. I struggled to pull on my sweats, nearly falling over. I needed to slow down because my head felt like it had turned into a big fat balloon.

Once I conquered the sweats, I pulled on a sports bra and t-shirt. I gently combed my hair and braided it, then brushed the heck out of my teeth. I rounded the corner from the bathroom to the bedroom, just as Jimmy gently opened the door with a food tray in his hands. There was a bowl of soup, bread, water, medicine, and a small vase with flowers in it. How was I supposed to be mad at him when he brought me food on a tray with freaking flowers? He set down the tray, stood up, and moved over to his dresser, where a set of sheets were. He glanced at me as he moved towards the bed.

"Would you like to sit?"

I connected the words slowly in my brain, like there was a batch of pancake syrup that each letter had to move through before it made sense. Once it did, I nodded my head, indicating that yes, I would like to sit.

He carefully moved towards me, placed a gentle hand on my shoulder, and directed me to the chair in the corner of his room. He then stripped the covers off the bed and began putting new ones on. He put the down comforter back on, then replaced the pillowcases, and fluffed them. I watched, too sluggish to even talk to him, or tell him that he didn't need to change the sheets. I still felt like I was dreaming a little bit. I mean, how could I go from Jimmy ignoring my calls and texts, to him changing his bedsheets for me?

When he finished, he helped me back into his massive bed. He adjusted the pillows behind me so that I was sitting up, then he placed the food tray on my lap. I stared at the food and looked at him. I couldn't form coherent words, but I managed a quiet, "Thank you."

He sat near my feet, at the end of the bed, and looked at the food. "Eat up."

Just the smell of the soup was starting to make my head a little clearer, so I replied, "I'll eat if you explain to me why I'm here."

He smiled. It was one of those beautiful smiles that reached his eyes and probably made women swoon. I'd be lying if I wasn't feeling a little swoony at the sight of it. I decided to ignore his smile and focus on my soup. It was chicken noodle, with the fat chunks of chicken and the veggies—my favorite kind.

He cleared his throat. "Well, your mom called me yesterday to help fix her pilot light and when I got there, she made it sound like you were dying. I could tell she was miserable not being able to take care of you, so I offered to do it."

I scooped up another spoonful of broth as I thought about his response. It made sense; my mom must have laid it on pretty thick.

"Look I'm sorry if my mom manipulated you into this, but I am fine. Really, I will be back to work tomorrow and completely better. You didn't need to do all this."

I let my gaze settle on his face and linger on his eyes as I finished my sentence. His eyebrows drew together in confusion. He looked down and shook his head.

"No, that's not it at all. I wanted to check on you, so I went into your room and saw that you would probably be more comfortable if you had someone taking care of you... and I..." He started to trail off, letting out a loud sigh. He pulled his hand through his hair as he continued, "I wanted to take care of you."

Now I felt dumbfounded and really confused. "But why? I

was under the impression that you were angry with me, since you wouldn't return a single text since Saturday."

I could feel the anger seep out of my words. I clenched the spoon in my hand and had to release a breath to calm down. The hurt from his rejection ran deeper than I realized. I hated that he had shut me out, and that he got to decide when and where we were allowed to be friends. Even though I secretly wanted to be his wife didn't mean that I was okay with not being his friend. He frowned and dropped his gaze. He waited a few silent seconds before I saw his Adam's apple move.

"I'm sorry that I shut you out. I was hurt, and I didn't know how to be your friend. I didn't do it right and I wanted to be better, do better, for you... So I scooped you up and walked you out of your house. I'm sorry. If you want me to take you home, I will."

His downcast eyes only looked worse as he finished talking. I could see fear and regret on his face like an ugly mask. I let out a deep, loud breath and put my spoon down. I was getting really tired of this back and forth with him.

Jimmy tracked my movements with a hurt gaze, as I moved the tray off my lap, probably assuming that I wanted to leave. He helped me set the tray aside and offered me his hand to get up. I took it, but not to get up. I took his hand to help me gain leverage towards his body because as soon as I had the momentum I needed, I basically threw myself at him and put my arms around his neck. I hugged him. I hugged him as tight as my frail, body would let me. He waited for only a second or two before he wrapped his big arms around me and pulled me in until I was flush with his body.

We stayed like that for a while, until he whispered in my ear, "I want this."

I didn't want to read too much into it; he could have meant that he wanted friendship, but a warmth started spreading through my body at the thought that he just wanted me, in his arms. I started to let go, but as I did, he stuck his nose into my neck and inhaled. I pulled away and looked at him. He looked like he was in pain, and somehow with that look, although it did wonderful things to my heart, I had to stop it. He acted like he was going to say something, but before he could, I started.

"Jimmy, thank you for taking care of me. Thank you for being my friend." I said this while squeezing his hand, hoping he would get the hint. He looked at my hand and a sadness came over his face as he stared at it.

He quietly said, "Ramsey, I don't want to be your friend, you have to know that. I—"

"Jimmy, we barely know each other," I cut him off because I had to.

He kept going, "But we do know each other. I feel it, and I know you do too." He was staring so intensely at me, I was finding it difficult to breathe. Still, I had to stay strong, even if my brain felt like radiator fluid from being so sick. I took both of his hands in mine and replied as gently as I could, "It doesn't matter if I feel it too. Of course I feel things, Jimmy. I feel things that I have never felt about anyone before with you. It's because of that, that we need a foundation between us. I need to know you, be around you, be around your kids. I need to be your friend first."

He looked towards the window with his jaw locked, and his eyes narrowed—he was frustrated, I could feel it. I mean, I was frustrated too, but doing the right thing was usually frustrating. He looked back down at our joined hands.

"So, you want to be friends?"

He said it with a hint of disdain, and I held back the urge to punch him in the shoulder.

"Yes, I want to be friends with you. Real, true friends. Friends that don't stop being friends, and friends that don't freeze each other out. I want to see your good sides and bad sides and funny sides, and I want your kids to get to know who

I am. Not as your date, or girlfriend, but as your friend. I have to know that I can trust you with my heart, Jimmy. So far, it hasn't felt very safe with you."

I knew that last part would hurt him, but I needed to be honest with him. I could feel him hesitate, but he pushed through, "And... if you..." He swallowed and glanced up at me as he kept going, "If you find someone else, while we're friends? Or you decide that your feelings have changed for me because we became friends?"

He looked like he was in so much pain, and I hated that I caused it. He had a good point though, and I knew he was concerned.

"I plan on waiting for you, Jimmy. I know we aren't dating, and you don't owe it to me, but I want to offer that to you. I won't pursue anyone or date anyone or look for anything while I am building my foundation of friendship with you."

He physically looked relieved as his eyes softened, and eyebrows evened out. He let out a breath, squeezed my hands once, then let go and placed them on the bed. "And what if your feelings change?"

I looked past him as I thought about his question. I wasn't sure how to promise him that I knew my feelings for him wouldn't change, especially if I was given the chance to be around him. Then I had an idea.

"Okay, you may think this is stupid, but hear me out." I took another breath and continued, "I want you to find something or write something that represents how you feel about me now, or what you want out of our relationship once our foundation is built. For example, you can talk about where you want to take me on our first date, or you can write me a poem describing how you feel about me and talk about what you want between us. It can be detailed if you want or general, like if you want to date or if you just want to have sex. Whatever it is you feel about me. I will do the same thing, we put them in envelopes and it has to be soon, then we mail them to each other.

I know that seems dumb, but that way, you have mine, and I will have yours. We won't open them until six weeks have gone by of us just being friends. At the end of six weeks, we meet up, you can choose when and where. We will open our envelopes and see if we each have a similar goal for the relationship in mind, and then discuss if that is how we still feel. What do you think?"

He was staring a hole into my face, and I was starting to get nervous. Then a small smile appeared across his lips, and he looked down, then back up at me. I smiled, because he looked hopeful.

"I think it's a great idea because it gives us something to look forward to. Not that there isn't in just being your friend, but it gives me hope that in six weeks, maybe we will be more. If not, at least I will get to keep something from you that represents how you feel now. Besides, you make a good point. The kids are already so attached to you, that I wouldn't want to mess that up with them. So, yes, let's do it, and thank you for thinking of them."

I smiled and felt relieved. I cared so deeply for him, and I wanted more with him obviously, but I had to do this. I had to have something between us because once I lost my mom, I couldn't put that on him unless he was my friend. I moved in to hug him again and thought of what I was going to put into my envelope. He grabbed at the top blanket and flipped it over as he asked, "So, are there rules in this friendship thing that I should know about?"

I thought about it and realized there should be rules, especially with Jimmy. "Yes, we can't blur the lines. No kissing or physical stuff, we can flirt, but no crossing any lines. No ignoring me because you are pissed. You need to keep communication open, and the same goes for me. You have to hang out with me and get to know me, but you can't get all sexy if we are hanging out."

He laughed, but I was dead serious, I had zero willpower against him, and I really hoped he wouldn't find that out. I straightened my back as much as I could as I continued, "Starting tonight, after you put the kids to bed, you have to come back up here and watch some TV with me, and not get weird. It will be your first friendship test."

He grinned, his eyes smoldering. "You mean me walking back out of the room when you were in just a towel wasn't my first test of friendship?"

My face warmed at his comment, and where his mind was at. I hit his arm with as much force as my weak little arm could.

He laughed and tried to scoot back to avoid any further hits. "Okay, okay. I promise I will come watch TV with you, in all your nasty sickness glory, okay?"

I smiled and said, "Thank you."

He squeezed my knee cap and stood up. I already missed the warmth in the bed and snuggled a little deeper under the covers. He grabbed his cell from his pocket and looked at the screen. "I have to head back to work. I think you should call your mom."

"Okay thanks, I will call her. Um, and Jimmy?"

He looked back down at me and smiled. "Yeah?"

"How do you work the shower?"

He threw his head back and laughed. "It's on the panel outside of the shower. I know it's weird, but you program how long you want the water, the pressure, everything, from the outside."

I felt my face flush, even though normal people would never have known that. I squeaked out another "Thank you" before he came over, kissed me on top of my head, then turned and walked out. It was going to be a long six weeks.

TWENTY-TWO

JIMMY

I ALREADY KNEW what I was going to put inside the envelope. I knew the second she told me her cute little idea about building a friendship and sharing our feelings after six weeks. I respected the hell out of her for pushing us to do this. I didn't want to, and every cell in my body was pissed at the idea originally, but when she mentioned how she wanted my kids to view her and know her, I conceded.

I secured what I wanted inside the envelope and texted Ramsey for her address, then sent it off. That evening had been fun with Ramsey. We watched *The Office* for what felt like hours, as she tried to be subtle, hinting at how good of friends Jim and Pam were before they dated. She was so cute, but to make her mad, I pretended not to know what she was talking about, until she tried to explain it again and again. Then she wasn't being subtle anymore, got angry, and kicked me.

Normally I would have used her little outburst as an opportunity to move my body closer to hers, or hold her, but I didn't. I stayed in the friend zone. We spent the evening, laughing and talking about our childhoods.

. . .

"TELL ME ABOUT YOUR MOM?" SHE ASKED, WHILE PUSHING SOME of that unruly hair behind her ear. It wasn't easy to talk about my mother, but I loved remembering her.

"My mom was funny. Always willing to play pranks on me or let me learn my lesson through experiencing a little humiliation." I laughed at the memory. Ramsey had turned towards me, her legs drawn up under her chin as she watched me.

"She was always quick to hug me, though. I remember, on my eighteenth birthday, she had crept into my room just before dawn and held a little cupcake in front of my face. It had a lit candle and everything. She told me that I was officially an adult, and the only way to properly start my life as an adult was with a little glimmer of light and a whole lot of sugar." I smiled, fighting back a surge of emotion that rose with it. "She wanted me to remember what I had to look forward to."

I wasn't sure why I picked that memory out of all the ones I had of my mother, but it hurt more than I realized it would.

Ramsey had tears in her eyes, but pushed through them to ask, "How did she...?" She trailed off, her voice getting low. I knew what she meant, and I wondered how I'd never said anything about how she'd died yet to Ramsey.

"Tumor. It was quick. One day, she was grocery shopping, laughing, throwing popcorn in the air, trying to catch it with her mouth. The next, she was complaining of nonstop headaches. Dad took her in, and they found out she had a tumor the size of a baseball in the back of her head. She lasted ten months."

Needing a conversation change, I stood up and walked to my closet. I wasn't even looking for anything, but I needed a second to gather myself before I went back to Ramsey. Thankfully, she didn't say that she was sorry for my loss or that my mom sounded like a good woman. Those words always seemed to cheapen my pain, or water it down to something superficial, when it was the most vivid thing I'd ever gone through. I carried the weight of missing my mother in my soul, which was why I didn't like talking about her very much.

Ramsey moved behind me, touching the leather vest that sat near the back of my closet. I watched as she ran her fingers over the patches. I didn't say anything as she explored my MC cut. I didn't want to apologize for having it; they were a part of my life at one point and technically, I was still a member of the chapter.

"I heard at the bar, that night you fired me, some guys talking about how you were in a motorcycle club. They seemed to be afraid of you," Ramsey said, while slowly turning toward me. She had an eyebrow raised, like she didn't believe the story. I laughed and leaned back against the closet wall.

"The Brass, in Chicago. I was a part of the chapter for a few years, but I left after Lisa did," I explained, dropping my eyes to the carpet, where Ramsey's purple painted toes rested.

"My mother hated that part of my life and wanted me to leave it long before I actually did, but once I became a single parent, it was like a light-bulb went off and I had to get out," I said, now moving my gaze up to meet Ramsey's. She was mirroring my stance, leaning against the wall. I wasn't sure what I expected to see when I talked about the Brass, but Ramsey's face only showed curiosity, not judgment and thankfully, not fear.

"So, they just let you leave? I thought it was kind of like a gang." Pink entered her cheeks as she asked her question. I smiled, so not to discourage her.

"It is. MC, or motorcycle club or biker gang...it's all the same thing. Blood ties me to it because my dad was in it, just like my blood ties my own kids to it. I think Davis, the leader, knew I needed to get away. Not to say he is a kind person." I looked up at the light in my walk in closet, as I considered the next thing I was going to say. "I'm still technically a part of it. He gave me a sabbatical."

"So, you'll have to go back?" Worry laced the inflection of her voice.

I didn't want Ramsey near this part of my life, didn't want to share that I had already a meeting scheduled this week with them. The less she knew, the better.

"They can ask, but I have assurances in place if they ever get pushy about it." I winked at her while turning back towards the room.

Later that evening, I wanted to ask her about going back to Chicago and what she planned to do if her mom passed, but I couldn't bring myself to do it. I wanted to hear her say that she would stay, but I realized that maybe this six weeks was what she needed to push her to do it. So, I stayed quiet and enjoyed hearing the sound of her laughter as we finished up another episode. I said goodnight to her with a high five, and walked back down to the extra room in the basement.

I WAS IN THE MIDDLE OF A CLIENT MEETING WITH A NEW champagne vendor. The guy was going to charge double my current vendor, but was trying to convince me it would be worth it. I took the meeting as a courtesy to Jackson, who had set up the contact, to begin with, but I wasn't going to switch. Once the meeting was over and I promised to think over the options, I dialed Jackson. I made my way back to the town car waiting for me.

Jackson picked up on the fourth ring, out of breath and frustrated.

"Yeah?" he practically yelled; he must not have looked at the caller ID.

"It's me…Jimmy. Everything okay?"

I could hear him let out a loud sigh, but he was still breathing hard. "Sorry man, I was just getting off the tread-mill, and I thought you were my assistant calling again for the fiftieth time today."

I knew Jackson couldn't stand his assistant—she was twenty-two, or something like that, and had a major crush on him. It was painfully obvious, and he had been trying to find ways to fire her ever since he figured out that her crush extended to almost obsession territory. Problem was, she had complained about him to his company's HR manager, twice, for reasons that didn't exist, and Jackson didn't need the poten-tial legal headache.

"Sorry man, is she getting worse?" I tried to empathize, but I had warned Jackson not to hire the girl in the first place. I told him he needed a fifty to seventy-year-old assistant, with cute grandkids, a tight bun, and graying hair. Anyone younger, male or female, would be trouble for him. Jackson just had that kind of effect on people.

Jackson's breathing had normalized, and I could hear him turning the water on. "She's getting worse. She knows that I'm interested or rather, spending time with someone, and she's entered full-on stalker mode. She showed up at my house with three suits that I am positive she stole out of my closet, saying she found them at the dry cleaners. She's totally crazy, and I am talking to a lawyer about how to handle her."

Poor guy. That sucked, but then again, so did sitting in the friend zone, with the girl of your dreams acting as your assistant and accountant.

"Sorry man, that sucks. You want me to call later?"

Jackson laughed. "No man, your call is a nice distraction. How's it going? How are things with Ramsey?"

I smiled, thinking of last night. "Things are good. We're becoming friends for six weeks, after which I get to declare my feelings for her," I said in all seriousness. I could hear Jackson spitting out water as he choked on a laugh.

"What the hell? Are you serious, man?"

I smiled again because I loved that Ramsey had thought of it. "Yeah, I'm serious. But it's perfect, I get to hang out with her and ask her anything I want, and basically just get to know her without things being weird, or moving too fast or too slow."

Jackson was quiet on the other end until I heard him sigh. "Well, I'm glad it's working out for you, brother, I was worried for a second. I saw how hard you were falling... and I just want to be sure you were being careful."

"I know, and thank you. She wants to do this to protect

both of us, so we know each other, and there aren't any surprises."

Jackson laughed. "Well, you might want to tell her about Lisa, and a few other ghosts that might come back to haunt you."

I frowned. "I told her about the Brass, but I am working on the Lisa thing."

He let out a little laugh that was meant to be joking. "Did you tell her what it would take to get out of the Brass, once and for all? Because don't think they don't know where you have been, Jimmy. They are just waiting until they need to call in a favor."

A sick feeling twisted in my gut at the reminder that I hadn't told Jackson about the meeting yet. "Listen, about that." I ran my hands through my hair as I watched the city of Rockford pass by. "Davis found Lisa, he wants a meeting. It's set up for tomorrow."

I waited. Jackson was silent for longer than I expected, but finally, he let out an exaggerated sigh.

"Jimmy was that smart?" he asked, sincerely. He didn't let me answer before he continued, "She isn't worth getting tied back up with them. Think about Ramsey, think about what they might do if you piss them off."

I knew he was right and I hated it. Jackson had never been a part of the MC, but he was there to witness its effect on me. He was there when I lost my temper and there when I went to jail. He knew all too well what kind of impact their presence would have on my life. This was all stuff I owed to Ramsey, to tell her, so she knew. She deserved to know about my past, my anger issues, and Lisa. I just didn't want to scare her away.

"It's probably not smart, but you know that it was just a matter of time."

Jackson swore under his breath. "I suppose you're right. Do you want me to call Gepsy?"

"Yeah." I rubbed my forehead as I saw the turn off for the bar approach. "Look, man, I called to tell you that your champagne vendor is shit, and I'm sticking with the one I have, but I played nice and sat through all his pretentious pleasantries."

Jackson laughed. "Well, I figured as much, but I had to try. Thank you for sitting through all that. I know how much you hate rich people and all their weird dishware."

He was right, of course, and I hated the three different-sized plates they served miniature-sized food that would have fed a mouse. I also think the jerk had diamonds hanging from his ceiling. "Yeah, that was never going to work out, man, and you know it."

"I know, I know, but again, I had to try. Their champagne is amazing, bro." Jackson laughed again.

"Well good luck, man, I gotta go. I'll talk to you later, okay?"

I ended the call and was just around the corner from work when I noticed a certain green SUV parked in front of the bar, and my pulse jumped. I didn't think Ramsey would be well enough to come back into work so soon. The car stopped in front of the bar and I hopped out. Once I headed inside, I heard Ramsey's light laughter resonate through the bar. She had a cute laugh that started soft but, depending on how funny something was, grew more intense and eventually ended with her sounding like a seal. I knew because she laughed like a seal through nearly every episode of *The Office* last night.

I walked a little further in and noticed that Rav, our chef, was leaning against the bar with Wilson, our shift supervisor, along with a few of our waitstaff, Jenny and Kim. They were talking about being sick, and Ramsey was being very animated, but very accurate about how sick she was, while describing how loud the sound of her cough was and using her nose to emphasize how red it had gotten in just a few days.

She was wearing another blazer jacket with dark jeans. For

her still being sick, she looked very put together, in high heels, and her hair wavy had a few braids woven in. Her back was to me, so she was the last to see me coming up behind the group. Once I was next to her, everyone stopped laughing and they all looked at us. She looked over, still smiling from her story, and I noticed that she still looked tired. I wrestled with wanting to demand she go back to my house and sleep, and telling her to stay here because I wanted to be around her. She smiled, crossed her arms, and was the first to respond out of the group with, "Hey, boss."

I hated when she called me boss because it felt like she was reminding me that I shouldn't want to date her. I stared at her before responding with, "Hey, employee." I was being sarcastic and a little bit of a jerk, so I nudged her arm and pointed at everyone. "What's going on, did we all suddenly decide we didn't have any work to do?"

They let out a bit of laughter and started milling around. Rav was looking at me a little weird, shifting his feet, and darting his eyes from me to the kitchen door. I walked with him back to the kitchen as Ramsey headed for our office. Once we were in the kitchen, Rav tied a new apron around his middle section and kept his eyes on the food in front of him. He started separating garnishes and grabbed some parsley and started chopping. I stood there, waiting for him to talk. He looked up from the counter, and his eyes darted around the room, almost to ensure that we were alone.

"I got another phone call today."

I stood soundlessly, allowing him to continue.

"It was Davis again. Told me to tell you not to come tomorrow, he has a different date in mind."

I waited a second, looking around the kitchen, confirming there wasn't anyone that would hear us.

"Did he say why? I was under the impression that he was in

a hurry." I ran my hand along the counter top. Rav shook his head back and forth.

"Just that he needed a week."

I wasn't sure what to make of this new development, but I knew Davis liked to play with people. I nodded my head in understanding and walked out of the kitchen to my office, remembering that Ramsey was already set up to work in there. She had her feet propped up on my desk, her laptop in her lap. As I rounded the desk, she smiled at me, then threw her legs down.

"Hey, sorry, I just figured I'd get comfy until you came back."

I waved her off as I started my computer up. "No, don't worry about that. You can sit however you want, it's your office too."

She smiled and turned a little pink, which reminded me of her nose.

"Hey, are you sure you're feeling better? You must be feeling pretty weak after the last few days."

Her smile faltered. "Honestly… yes, I'm exhausted, but I need to get back to work. I'm not contagious anymore." She said this matter-of-factly, like she was hoping to convince me.

"I'm not worried about that, Ramsey. I'm worried about you resting and getting better."

I hoped that she would agree to go home, or to my house and rest, but she didn't. I let out a sigh. "At least go work in Belvidere for a few hours, then go home, or to my house and rest, please?"

She gave me a quizzical look. "You want me to go back to your house to rest?"

I smiled while nodding, "I think you freak your mom out when you don't feel good. So yes, go to my house. No one is home, sleep as long as you want. But if you absolutely feel the need to work, then go over to Sip N Sides."

She bit down on her bottom lip and looked down at the desk. "How would I get in if I go to your house?"

I didn't know why, but the fact that she was willing to go back to my house did something to me. I pulled my key ring out and started taking the house key off. "Here take this, I am going to make you a copy sometime anyway, since you will be hanging out with me so much in the near future." I glanced at her with a smug grin.

She blushed. "Yes, friends do have keys to each other's houses, I guess."

She took the key and bent down to grab her laptop bag. When she sat back up, she looked at me and let out a sigh. "Fine, Jimmy, I will go back to your ridiculously comfortable bed and sleep all day. If I start to get some energy, I will head over to Theo's place, okay?"

I smiled and started typing away. "Okay, thank you for dedicating the day to improving your life." I winked at her as she stood to leave.

She threw me a small wave over her shoulder and walked out of the office. I hated that I felt relieved that she left, but I wanted some time to try and dig into why Davis might want the meeting moved. The thought of putting all the Brass business behind me, once and for all, teased me. I felt that hope inflate my lungs like artificial air, hoping the sinking feeling in my gut would go away once I had a plan in place.

TWENTY-THREE

I TOOK the rest of the day to rest at Jimmy's house, but after a few hours, I was feeling better and headed over to Sip N Sides. I walked through the doors and waited the few seconds it usually took for my eyes to adjust to the darker room.

Except things weren't as dark as they normally were.

I stopped between two poker tables, near the entrance, and took inventory of the room.

The pool tables were still the same old tattered relics they'd always been. The standing table tops were also the same, as well as the older pictures covering the walls, but instead of low-hanging, green-plated light fixtures, there was now recessed lighting throughout the entire building.

What the heck? Since it was still early, the lighting was brighter, causing everything to look clean and new. Or maybe it was because the new barstools had arrived, and— Where was the carpet? I looked down at my feet and turned in a circle. *How did I miss that?* Where old, gray, very stained carpet used to be was now shiny wood flooring. It ran throughout the entire room.

I counted back the days to when I had last been at Sip N

Sides, and wondered how all this took place so fast? Theo finally made his way out of the office and found me gaping at all the upgrades. He immediately turned bashful, scratching at his hair while turning to look at the room.

"You think I went overboard?" Theo asked, hesitantly. Still in shock, I circled the room once more before answering.

"Theo, this place looks so good. How did you get it all done so fast?" It was a like a math problem I needed to solve. Theo shrugged his shoulders while looking around the room again.

"I knew a flooring guy. We ordered these stools last week from a local place, and a friend of mine does electric work and helped me out on the lights." Theo's dark blue and black flannel moved as he shrugged again, as if it were that simple. My mind was working too hard; it didn't even really matter, but I had to have more information.

"But you have to let the wood adjust to the temperature of the room for at least a week before they lay it down. I saw that on an HGTV show once," I explained, matter-of-factly, like I actually knew something about installing wood floors. Theo laughed while bending down to the floor.

"Ain't that somethin'? These beauties were resting right under all that carpet." He stroked the wood floor with a smirk on his lips.

Theo had real wood floors laying under that disgusting carpet?! What else was this place hiding? I started to eye the older-than-dirt photos on the walls, as though underneath them might be a hidden vein of gold.

Shaking my head to rid it of the need for more details, I moved on to Theo's office.

"So, you need any help with balancing the receipts for any of that stuff?" I asked, while powering up my laptop. He came in right after me, and took a seat in his squeaky, old wooden desk chair.

"Sure, that'd be nice," he answered, while pulling out a

small envelope full of receipts. My eyes narrowed to slits at how unorganized his receipts were. I grabbed the envelope with enthusiasm, which may be the reason Theo ended up leaving for an hour or so, but no one can be sure. When he did return, he had two guests with him.

"So, how was school today, you guys?" I asked Jasmine and Sammy while taking a sip of a chocolate shake. Sammy turned his thumb up while still gulping his treat. Jasmine looked a little more introspective as she sat dragging her finger through the condensation on the cup, instead of drinking the shake.

"Jasmine, everything okay?" I asked, reaching over to squeeze her side.

She kept her gaze straight forward for a moment or two, until finally, she released a sigh and turned to face me.

"These kids made fun of me today at school."

An anger that I didn't know existed rose to the surface like a foreign object in the ocean. I didn't realize how protective I had become over her and Sammy. I wanted to tell her to cut their ponytails off with scissors, but I knew that wasn't parental type of advice. Then, like thunder in the middle of freaking winter, that thought hit me. Did I want to be parental with the kids? Did I want to be parent-like in any way?

I felt my cheeks get hot, and I sucked down some more of my chocolate milkshake as the idea of being parental towards the kids wiggled its way through my heart like a fat little worm. I ended up not giving her any advice; instead, I just told her, "Jasmine, whatever they said doesn't matter, because they're jealous of you. Jealousy only makes us say things we don't actually mean."

Jasmine sniffled and swiped at a few tears. "They said that Evan Michelson was only my friend because he felt sorry for me... because I don't have a mother."

Holy shit. Kids were mean.

"Jasmine, you listen to me. We don't get to choose what

kind of life we'll lead, or what happens to us in it. Life isn't fair, but it's the people who find the good in the bad, the beauty in the pain, and the heart in the heartbreak, that win in life. You can't let what those girls said make you upset. You do have a mother. She's out there somewhere, and for some reason, she needed to leave. I don't know why, but I do know that she left you with the best daddy on earth and because of that, you've already lived ten times the kind of life that they ever will." Jasmine sniffed and hugged me tighter.

I held her until she moved to get up, then I braided her hair and told her jokes.

I SHUT THE FRONT DOOR OF THE HOUSE AND KICKED OFF MY shoes while I greeted my mother. "Hey Mama, how are you feeling?" I bent down to hug her, but she held up her hand.

"Are you symptom-free? Because you sound like you're congested," my mother argued while watching me skeptically. I did still have a bit of a runny nose, and felt tired, so I stood up.

"I'm still a bit tired," I admitted, while moving towards the kitchen.

I heard movement in the living room as I pulled a glass from the cupboard.

"So, how did things go over at Jimmy's?" She had made her way towards me and was now leaning against the counter. I turned to look at her. She wore a light pink tracksuit and her thin hair was hidden by a hat. Her brown eyes seemed excited as she waited for me to reply.

"Things were good. Although I'm not sure how I feel about you pawning me off on him." I gave her the side eye as I filled my cup with water from the fridge.

"You could have infected me!" she argued. I laughed while sipping my water.

"I'm kidding, Mom. It was fine. Actually, better than fine." I turned to face her while reaching for a tea bag from above the counter. "Now, do not get your hopes up, okay?" I implored her while setting the kettle in place. I turned to see her gather her hands in front of her chest and a smile break out on her face.

"I won't, I promise!"

I lifted one shoulder, suddenly very aware of her scrutiny and suddenly very shy. "Jimmy and I…" I stopped and held my breath. I hadn't thought through all the problems with telling my mother about this; all the hope it might create.

"Yes?" she demanded, her body shifting, and her foot started tapping.

I let out the breath I was holding, and just decided to let it all out, consequences be damned. "We like each other."

When she didn't respond or say anything, I added, "Romantically."

Her eyes lit up and danced with excitement. "I knew it. God answers prayers, he always does. I was just telling Carolyn about how I was praying for the two of you, and—"

"*But!*" I cut her off while holding up my hand. Otherwise, that prayer chain conversation would have lasted a good fifteen minutes.

"We agreed to be friends for six weeks before either of us does anything about our feelings," I finished, feeling confident and proud of myself for being so sensible.

My mother deflated. Her shoulders slumped, and her smile fell away. "Why would you do something like that?"

The kettle went off, and I busied myself with preparing the tea. "Mom, we barely know each other," I tried to reason.

"So, what! When you know, you know," she argued back gaining some steam. She looked very much alive and not weak or worn at all, with her hands on her hips and her face set firmly.

I tried so hard not to roll my eyes or act like a petulant child, like I normally tended to act whenever my mother argued with me.

I placed my hands on the counter and looked at her. She'd moved to the counter to fix herself a cup of tea. Suddenly my heart ached, like usual, because the sight of seeing my mom do ordinary things always broke it in a weird and happy way. And because it felt like we were caught in a horrible nightmare, where some huge hourglass was losing sand faster than it should and there was nothing I could do to stop it. I bit the inside of my cheek to hold off the tears that always surfaced when I thought about how little time we had left together. I fixed my gaze back on my mother and cleared my throat. "I know that you don't totally agree with what Jimmy and I are doing, but can you just trust me?"

She turned to look at me. She had a small smile on her face, as she stirred her tea. "Of course I can." She lifted her cup to her mouth and took a sip. I was about to turn away when she added, "But more importantly, I trust God. He will fix this and the both of you."

With a flick of her wrist towards me, she sauntered back to the living room. I smiled at my mother's spunky behavior. Every day, that she made jokes about God fixing me was a good day.

I grabbed my duffel bag and headed for my room, but stopped just inside my doorway. My bed was freshly-made with a vase of flowers next to it. All the Kleenex and dishes were cleaned up and the carpet had been vacuumed. I spun in a small circle, taking in all the beautiful lines on the carpet and the dust-free TV. Someone had cleaned my room. I stuck my head back into the hall and yelled.

"Mom, did you ask Carolyn from down the street to clean my room?" I knew she couldn't have done it, so who? I heard my mother's muffled reply as I half-hung out my door.

"Jimmy called a service. The whole house is clean, you didn't notice until now?"

I glanced into the bathroom, a little way across from my room. Sure enough, it was sparkling clean, like "brand new house" kind of clean.

"I didn't notice, but that was really nice of him," I yelled back. You'd think it was implied that I hadn't noticed until now, but my mother always required an answer to any question she asked out loud.

The fact that Jimmy had called a service to clean my house and used his own money did something to me. I never knew what was physically going on with my heart because I couldn't see it, but if it were possible for a heart to lurch or jump, mine just had. I hated that it made me want to drive back to his house and kiss the heck out of him. Paying to have someone's house cleaned was the sweetest thing ever.

I knew he liked me, but I didn't know to what degree. Did he just want to date me, or want sex, or a fling? I knew that Jimmy had abandonment issues from his ex, and was probably one of those guys who never wanted to get married again. That thought made me want to punch his ex-wife in the boobs. The idea that Jimmy only wanted something temporary with me wasn't enough for me to stay put after Mom. I would need more than that. I would need Laney. I would need someone who loved me because I would be broken and shattered once I lost my mother. I let out a heavy sigh and decided that now was the moment I would put my feelings into an envelope and mail them to Jimmy.

I pulled the leather-bound journal out of the drawer next to me and flipped through the pages until I landed on an entry that I made on September twelfth—it was the night I came home from babysitting Jimmy's kids. I looked over the black ink that filled the page, and as I read the words, they filled my soul and mind like a mixture of concrete. I knew it when I had the idea to give each other the envelopes that this was what I would give him, because even if he couldn't give me what I wanted or what I hoped for, I would be going all-in, knowing I gave him a piece of me that summarized what I wanted. I tore the page out of the journal, careful to keep it intact. I folded it up and fished out an envelope. I placed the white envelope in the larger manila envelope and walked outside to place it in the mail. It felt good, final somehow, that no matter what, at the end of this, he would know.

As I was walking back up to the house, I heard brakes squeak behind me. I turned and saw a silver sports car pulling up to the curb of my house. I stood there, watching to see who was in the car, but the windows were so darkly-tinted that I couldn't make them out. Finally, the driver door opened and a short redhead popped up. I smiled as my best friend materialized in front of my eyes.

I started towards her, but when she caught sight of me, I heard her yell, "Oh no, you wipe that smile off your face right now! I'm here because I am pissed off."

Oh shit. I never called or texted her back! I started to panic as I watched her. This was going to be bad. She had a small bag that she had thrown over her shoulder, and a purse, with a big pillow under her arm. She made her way towards my house, but walked right past me and went inside.

So bad.

I walked into the house after Laney and shut the door. She was busy hugging my mom and telling her how good she looked. Then she stood up, glared at me, and walked to my bedroom. This was not going to be pleasant.

Laney had her arms crossed and she was facing the window. She wore a tight charcoal gray pencil skirt with white converse shoes, and her white button-up work shirt was wrinkled. She didn't look like herself at all. Laney wore high heels, even when she was running to the corner store to grab milk.

Her shaky voice filled the room. "Did you know that you are the only best friend that I have ever had?" She slowly turned to face me. "When you had to move, I understood why, but I don't think you understood what it did to me, Ramsey. I had no one. Sure, Megan and Kiera are there to hang out or go to dinner with, but I had no one to talk to about my family, or about my crazy father, or my insane mother, or the guy…" She broke off, looking down at the floor, and that's when I saw how red her face was getting. I hurt her, and I hated myself for it.

"I told you about him. Things changed between us, and I don't know? I'm just so confused, and I needed you, Ramsey. I needed to talk to you. I was there for you with the Jimmy stuff, I was there for you and you weren't there for me. I called you about a million times, over the past five days, and you haven't returned my calls *once*!"

She was yelling now, and I totally deserved it. I was holding back tears because she was right. I had just ignored her because I was sick, and exhausted, and busy with Jimmy.

"You can't do that to me, Ramsey. My biggest fear with you moving was that you would forget me eventually. That you would just stop returning my calls and we would slowly stop being friends. You are all I have! You can't do that to me," she half-sobbed. She had moved to the bed now and I sat down next to her. I wrapped my arms around her and held tight. We sat in silence for a while, both of us crying, then I finally found my voice, as shaky as it was. I had to explain this to her, but then it hit me. Laney and I had fought before, but this time, it was different. The way she looked, the sound of her voice, her anger…

"Laney, what's really going on?" I whispered.

It was quiet for a second or two, then she hung her head and whispered, "I think I'm in love. But I hate him, and it will never work, and I stole his car to come here, so I might go to jail."

She started crying all over again. I held her and rubbed her back. I didn't want to touch that one yet, so I started trying to mend my side of things.

"Laney, I am so sorry. I don't have an excuse. I was so sick, and my mom couldn't take care of me. Jimmy came and got me, and I was at his house recovering. Then I went back to work, and it's just been a crazy week. But that's no excuse, I shouldn't have done that to you." She was still half sobbing, so I knew this was going to take a while. I kissed her head and stood up. "I'll be right back."

"Get the ice cream, Rams. Okay?" Laney said, catching my arm before I got too far away.

"You got it," I assured her and left the room.

My arms were full of Kleenex, ice cream, and two water bottles when I heard my phone ringing. It was still on the kitchen table where I had left it. I peered over the bundle in my arms and saw that it was Jimmy and although I didn't want to ignore my best friend, I also didn't want to ignore my boss.

"Hello."

"Hey, just checking up on you, and I have something for you. Would it be okay if I stopped by real quick to drop it off?" Jimmy asked, sounding like he was on a speaker, or inside of one.

"I am doing better, feeling much better, but... um... my best friend Laney just got here from Chicago, so I don't know if it's a good idea to stop by," I replied, a little concerned. I bit my lip and shifted the ice cream in my arms, not sure what he wanted to give me, but trying to be the devoted best friend and not get excited about it.

· · ·

"Oh, is everything okay?" Jimmy asked with a hint of worry in his voice.

"Yeah, I mean, no. We have some things to work through, but she is okay," I assured him.

"Okay, I understand, I am actually on your street, though, so would it be okay if I just left it in the mailbox?"

I smiled at that. He just had a way of making me feel like a priority to him, like he would follow through with me, for me. "If you are already on my street, then just go ahead and swing by, Laney will understand. I'll even ask if she wants to meet you."

Just then, I saw his black Tahoe pull up. I walked back to my room to tell Laney what was going on, and to dump the ice cream and goodies. She didn't want to meet Jimmy right at that moment, but I didn't blame her. She had black lines running down her face from her makeup, so I told her to change into some PJs and get into my bed.

I walked back out to the living room and opened the door for Jimmy. He was so tall, he always seemed to fill up the door frame completely. He smiled at me and I had to remind myself that we were friends. Just friends.

"Hey, glad you are feeling better," he said, as he leaned in for a hug. A *hug*. Because that's what friends did; they hugged each other when they saw one another.

"Thanks" I muttered into his shoulder as he pulled me closer. He leaned back and pulled out a silver key attached to a keyring and handed it to me. "Here, this is your key to my house, for whenever you need it."

He must have grabbed his house key from Theo already, which is who I had left it with. "Thanks, you really don't need to give me a house key, Jimmy."

He smiled. "I know, but I think you should have one. Jackson has one too, so it's a friend's thing. Even though he didn't use it the last time he came over." I smiled at that and it made me feel better. Jimmy gave me a weird look as he looked over his shoulder at Laney's stolen car. "Uh, speaking of Jackson, why is his car here?"

I laughed. "Uh, no, wrong car. That is this guy that Laney likes, or hates. I'm still not totally sure about it, but that's not Jackson's."

He looked back at it again, and his face contorted. "Yes, it is. I was with him when he bought it and, trust me, that car right there was his first major purchase after he started making decent money; it's his baby. The love of his life. I know because the license plate reads 'MINE'."

I looked over his shoulder, back toward my bedroom, then back at Jimmy, who also looked confused. His phone dinged, causing him to drop his gaze. I could see from where I was standing that it was Jackson. He read the text out loud. "Man, I guess I have the crazies in spades. This girl I had over last night stole my fucking car."

TWENTY-FOUR

I TOLD Jimmy that I would handle this. I could handle this. The idea that our best friends might be interacting was weird, but the fact that Jackson might actually call the police on Laney was a problem. Jimmy left and said that he would handle Jackson, and I walked back to my bedroom, not totally sure how to handle Laney.

I opened the door and found Laney in her PJs, watching *Gilmore Girls*, eating ice cream from the tub. I walked over to my dresser and found some pajamas and went to change in the bathroom. I tried to remember all the things that Laney had told me about 'this guy' that she didn't like; she never said she might love him before. He was the guy she ripped in half, so I was really confused how that led to them possibly falling in love. I replayed dates and conversations in my head. That was just last weekend when Jackson came to visit, it was the same weekend she told me she had ripped some guy a new one, and she was embarrassed because she thought he liked her. And while she was upset, I was on a fake date with Jackson. Great.

This whole thing was weird. I walked back into the room and snuggled under the blankets with Laney. It felt so good to be with her again, to hear her laugh, even hear her breathing. She was the closest thing I had ever had to a sister, and I couldn't believe that she thought I would just move on from being her friend. I was watching the show with her when I asked, "So, how does one go from total hate to possible love?"

She didn't look at me, and I knew that Laney might not answer me—sometimes she was in the mood and sometimes she wasn't. I could understand that.

She let out a sigh. "Cereal."

And after a few minutes of silence, I realized that "Cereal" was all I was going to get from her. I knew Laney might need a few days, and maybe she didn't even want to tell me, I could understand that too.

Finally, after a few more minutes, I turned to her. "Laney, you don't have to tell me everything, but aren't you at least worried that he might press charges against you for stealing his car?"

She groaned and pulled the covers over her face, and answered from underneath them. "Maybe, but at least I know where we stand, right? If he wants me in jail, then I know he doesn't want me."

I rolled my eyes at her logic and that short temper. As long as I had known Laney, she was impulsive and could go from zero to sixty in less than one second flat. I pulled the covers back and glared at her. "That is not acceptable! You can't go to jail, that doesn't work for me."

She gave me a weak smile. "Ramsey, I don't know… I really don't think he will call the cops. I had to get out of there, and I needed to talk to you, but you weren't answering, so I just took his keys."

I LOOKED BACK AT THE TV AND ALLOWED HER TO SLOWLY

situate herself again amongst the pillows, when I asked, "Where were you that you had access to his keys?"

She was quiet again, and answered, "At his house."

This was just getting better and freaking better.

"And you had an overnight bag on hand, because…?"

I saw her throat move, like she'd swallowed water, but her gaze stayed on the TV. Finally, she whispered, "Because I was planning to stay at his house."

I felt like I was pulling her teeth to get this information out. "And where was he when you took the keys?"

She slid further down in the bed. "He was in the shower."

She was going to go to jail.

"Laney, please tell me that you didn't sleep with the poor man and then steal his car!" I practically yelled at her.

"No, no, no, I wasn't going to sleep with him, or maybe I was, I don't know. I was staying there because I had nowhere to go, and I couldn't afford a hotel, because of my stupid renter's insurance situation. Anyway, our relationship is confusing and some stuff happened and it just confused me, and I snapped. So, while he was in the shower, I just took the keys and left. I don't know why."

I waited and let the episode continue on while I thought of what she'd told me. Finally, once I'd gathered all the information in my head, I turned my head towards her and replied, "I think I know why."

She snapped her head in my direction, her green eyes wide with question.

"Why?" she asked accusingly.

"Laney, you want to know if he will chase after you."

She laughed. "Well, I have his car, so he doesn't have much of a choice there, does he?"

I smiled, and her words must have hit her because her face turned red. After a second or two, she quietly confessed, "I do want him to have a choice."

She trailed off, picking at the comforter on the bed. I waited, knowing she wasn't finished. Finally, she looked over at me and whispered, "I just want the choice to be me."

I felt like she had just punched me in the ribs with that confession.

I gently grabbed her hand and asked her, "Lane, you just met him. Why is it already this far between you two?" I knew I was being a hypocrite because things had gone just as fast between Jimmy and me, but I had to know.

She squeezed my hand while looking at our joined hands, and answered, "I can't explain it. I feel like I know him, deep down. Like the second he wasn't being a total jerk to me, I was able to see him. When I saw him, I saw us. Is that weird?" she asked, confused and out of sorts. Her bottom lip was pulled in and her eyebrows were drawn together as she watched our hands.

I shook my head because I couldn't say anything. Unlike my friend, who dove into everything headfirst, I was forcing friendship on the only guy I had ever seen like that. I decided to change the subject because I was starting to feel like an idiot.

I told her about Jimmy and what I had decided and how he took care of me, and how I am forcing us both to only be friends for six weeks.

She laughed, and then laughed some more. "Rams, are you a masochist? Do you like putting yourself through pain? Why would you do that to yourself?"

I smiled. I missed her so much. "He has kids!" I exclaimed.

"They wanted you to be their mommy from day one, so don't blame this on them," she said, like I was an idiot.

Because I was one.

"I know, but I can't just open my heart up to some hot guy and hope he loves me, and doesn't just want some fling, and then what? My mom dies and that's too much for him, so I get cut loose? No thanks. I would rather him put in the work to be my friend and earn it, then have that happen."

She gave me a sad smile, and I heard those words as I said them. Honesty was sometimes such a bitch. I guess Laney and I both were messed up in our expectations of relationships. We both decided that we'd had enough boy talk. So, the rest of the night we gossiped about work. I talked about Jimmy's kids and how freaking sweet they are, and afterward, we fell asleep.

I WOKE UP THE NEXT MORNING TO A TEXT FROM JIMMY.
Take the day and enjoy your friend. No need to come into work unless you'd like to show her the bar. You're more than welcome to come as guests this evening and enjoy whatever you'd like, on the house.

DANG IT, SIX FREAKING WEEKS! I SMILED AND TEXTED BACK: *Thanks, I think we will do that.*

HE RESPONDED ALMOST RIGHT AWAY. *WHAT TIME? I WILL HAVE a table reserved for you two. Friday nights can get pretty busy.*

I HADN'T TALKED TO LANEY YET, BUT I KNEW HER PRETTY well. *7 pm work?*

JIMMY: *SOUNDS GOOD, I WILL MAKE SURE YOU LADIES HAVE A spot.*

ONCE I TOLD LANEY ABOUT OUR EVENING PLANS, SHE JUMPED

up and down with excitement and demanded that we take "the car"... as in, the stolen car.

When I asked if she was worried about getting pulled over and going to jail, she responded with, "At least I'll know where he stands."

She still hadn't told me what happened between them, and I was fine with that, Laney wanted to take her time. I figured that she mostly just needed a distraction this weekend. We spent the day shopping and getting pampered, and I even splurged on a new dress for tonight. She agreed to dip into savings for one too. Her income level may be much higher than my own because she still had that Dyson and Reed kind of money, but she was over her head with student loans.

I really wanted her to meet Jimmy and the kids, but I didn't want to weird them out. Still, I thought maybe Jasmine would want to hang out with us at some point. I couldn't stop gushing about Jasmine and how cute Sammy was.

At one point, Laney just looked at me, hit me on the forehead hard, and yelled, "*Six weeks, Ramsey!*"

I needed that. The day went on in a timely fashion after that, and it was already nearing six in the evening when we started getting ready. My dress was just a plain black one, but it was short, with one arm that had a full sleeve, leaving the other side bare. I had paired it with a pair of black high heels. I curled my hair and braided a few strands towards the back. I had never told anyone, but braiding my hair was a nervous tick for me.

There was a time when I was a kid that I needed to do something with my hands. I would touch everything or mess with things until it drove my mother and teachers crazy. Finally, a friend of my mom's suggested teaching me how to braid or knit. She did both, and when I wasn't braiding parts of my hair, I was knitting squares. I never progressed past squares for some reason. Now, as an adult, I was just used to having at least one braid somewhere in my hair—it made me feel in control.

It felt good to get all dressed up; plus, I hadn't gone out with my best friend in ages. Laney was wearing a red dress that fit loosely on the top but hugged her tight around the hips, with black high heels. Her hair was down and curled, and the red in her hair looked divine against the red dress. We were about to leave when Laney stopped in the middle of the hallway and looked down at her shoes. I laughed, knowing that she probably just remembered what car we were taking. She took off her heels and grabbed her converse shoes and slipped them on. As I laughed, she just sent me a scathing glare, and said, "It's because of the stick shift!"

I laughed again.

We got into the car, which wasn't easy because it was a tight fit for my tall body. I hated small sports cars, but I guess it was classier than my beat-up SUV. We took off and as we pulled into the parking lot of Jimmy's I felt anxious. I had never been here as a customer, and I was excited to get to see the restaurant in action. We parked the car and walked up to the bar where several other people were waiting in line. I didn't know if Jimmy would be there or not, but I assumed he wouldn't because of the kids.

We made our way towards the front, and I saw Jenny the hostess. She was a younger college-aged student, who was handling the masses like a champion. I told her that we had a reservation. She checked the book and smiled at me, then handed us off to another member of the waitstaff, Jessica, who was a little older, but just as sweet. I honestly liked everyone that worked here. She walked us towards the back wall, while chewing gum and looking over her shoulder.

"It's good to see you here as a customer. You know, letting your hair down and all," she said while looking forward, then back at us as we maneuvered around a few tables. "You should come out with me and my friends sometime. It'd be so fun." We went up a few small steps until we were at a cozy table set for four.

"Thanks Jessica, I'd love to sometime," I lied, and kind of felt bad about it, but I had no intention of going out with her and her friends. Jessica was about seven years younger than me and I just wasn't ready for that kind of energy. I eyed the table and the four chairs around it curiously.

"Hey Jessica, are you sure this table shouldn't be used for a bigger party?" I pointed between Laney and myself. "We're good with a table for two."

Laney nodded her head in agreement.

Jessica smiled, her red lipstick shiny under the lights. "No, Jimmy said to put you both here tonight. It's one of our best tables. Also, just so you know, sometimes there is dancing out on the patio if either of you feels like it." She left, not even taking our drink orders. This felt weird.

Laney didn't notice that anything was off; she just put her purse down and took in the atmosphere. Every table was full, and there were several people milling around and hanging out at both bars. The back patio seemed to be where the most action was happening. Music was playing inside, but not too loud. Before we knew it, we were being served small appetizers and our glasses were being filled with champagne. The busboy who filled them smiled and said, "Mr. Jimmy sends his regards and says he will see you shortly."

Then he turned and left. That sent butterflies, kangaroos, eagles, the whole freaking animal kingdom, running through me. Laney must have noticed because she giggled and started to make fun of my swooning. We chatted for a few minutes about the physical anatomy of swooning and couldn't stop talking about how good the food was. I told her that I would introduce her to Rav before we left.

Two men in suits started walking towards us. They walked

like they owned the place, with total swagger and confidence. I bet if I got close enough, they'd smell like money and expensive choices. It took me a second to realize that it was actually Jackson and Jimmy. I noticed that Jackson gave Laney a smile that was almost comical, or suicidal, like the Joker. He slid into the chair next to her, and Jimmy claimed the one next to me. I was silent, because, *what the hell was going on?* Things could get really messy in about one second flat, which was how fast Laney went from normal to crazy.

It was quiet between the four of us, and I was still in shock as I looked at Laney, who was looking at Jackson who was looking at the table. I glanced over at Jimmy and saw he was already looking at me, and with a non-friendly kind of expression. No, it was most definitely a date night, "let's get it on" kind of look. That made me feel all warm and tingly, but then I remembered Laney and the fact that she might go to jail or murder Jackson. Before I could say or think of anything to keep the peace, Jackson spoke up.

"Ramsey, good to see you again." Laney's eyes cut to me and her face turned red. *Shit on a stick.* I never told her about Jackson. She's gonna kill me. She started to get up when Jackson's hand landed on hers and he gave her a serious look. "Stay won't you, Laney? Seems like we have a few things to discuss."

TWENTY-FIVE

JIMMY

THINGS WERE TENSE, really tense. Tense between Jackson and Laney, tense between Laney and Ramsey, and tense between Ramsey and me. It occurred to me, just a little too late, that this whole surprise dinner thing might actually be a terrible idea.

After I'd left Ramsey yesterday, I called Jackson. He was in hysterics, saying he was going to use the tracking feature in the car to find "her" and then went on about some nonsense regarding women and relationships. I stopped him mid-ramble and told him that his car was in front of Ramsey's house. That stunned him silent, so I continued to tell him that a woman named Laney had taken it. When he asked why it was at Ramsey's, I laughed and told him because she's Ramsey's best friend. Then he went silent, because what were the odds?

When Jackson arrived, I had to calm him down and talk him into waiting for my crazy dinner idea. Him accepting it, and not going to get his car, seeing Laney as soon as he got into town was a whole different story. The kids and I worked all day to keep him busy, and now we were finally here, where I tricked

Ramsey into coming with her best friend to confront the man she stole a car from.

Laney's face hadn't turned a different shade from red since we'd arrived, and she kept looking around the room, like she was searching for an exit. I turned my head slightly and saw Ramsey's eyes, big and round, silently pleading with Laney. I glanced back at my best friend, and noticed how calm and collected he appeared. I watched as he carelessly reached for Laney's glass and took a sip of her champagne. Finally, he broke the silence.

"First things first, Laney. I'm going to need my keys." He watched her carefully as he put a stuffed mushroom into his mouth.

Laney straightened her spine and opened the purse next to her, pulling out a small black fob for the keyless ignition to Jackson's car. She slid it over to him, but made an effort not to touch him.

"Thank you," Jackson told her as he cracked a smile. Laney crossed her arms and looked down at her small appetizer plate.

"Did you call the police?" Ramsey asked, a little panicked and rushed.

"Of course not, why would I?" Jackson answered with a slight look of confusion. He glanced at Ramsey, then back at Laney.

Ramsey waited to see if Laney would answer, but she didn't, so Ramsey continued, "Because she stole your car— your baby, as Jimmy put it."

Jackson took a sip of water, then looked at Laney. "I wouldn't have called the cops, Laney, if that's what you thought... I'd never do that to you." He said it gently, like he wanted to be careful with his words.

Laney's gaze cut back to Jackson. "Why not?"

Jackson gave her a small smile. "Because I wouldn't need

to. I'd just come get you. That doesn't change the fact that we need to talk."

Laney stared at Jackson and then at Ramsey, giving her an anxious look, like she wasn't sure what to say. A couple from the back patio opened the glass doors and a soft chorus of music filtered in, along with a small gust of wind. I wanted to take Ramsey out there and dance with her.

I looked back over at Laney and noticed that her face had taken on another hint of red. She pulled herself straight as she responded, "We don't need to talk, I'm sorry I took the car. I'll never touch it again. But I'm here with my friend, and I think maybe we should get going."

Ramsey locked eyes with Laney as they both started to stand. Loyalty and solidarity seemed to be the name of the game tonight for these two. Ramsey made a sound with her throat and cut in, "Yeah, I think that's a good idea."

She glared at me and continued, "Jimmy, I would have loved the opportunity to introduce you to my best friend, but looks like that ship has sailed. Laney, let's go."

They pushed their chairs back, grabbed their purses, and started to move away from the table. I thought I was getting better at being her friend, and a friend would probably just let her go, but with the way she looked tonight, I couldn't. I looked over at Jackson and saw the same panic in his eyes.

"I need to talk to you, Laney…" Jackson pleaded. He started to stand and reached for Laney's arm.

She stopped and turned towards him, looking down at his hand and then back up to him. "Jackson, no, we don't. We have nothing to discuss."

"You kissed me!" Jackson's voice grew louder, then he looked around and realized he was very close to making a scene. He lowered his voice and continued, "You fell asleep in my arms, on my couch, and the next morning, you left and stole my car. No note, no sorry, or thank you for allowing you to crash at my place, to begin with, nothing. I think you owe me a conversation, Laney…" Jackson's eyes were narrowed, his tone firm, but his grip on Laney's arms looked light. He looked over at me for just a brief moment, and I knew that was code for 'give us some privacy.' I stood up and gently pulled Ramsey towards me. She was suspended in time, her mouth wide open in shock as she stared at her best friend. Laney hadn't stopped staring daggers at Jackson, but she finally relented and sat down, spurring Ramsey back into the present.

Taking advantage of the moment, I tugged on Ramsey's arm and pulled her away from the table. Once we were walking down the steps and onto the main floor, I grabbed her hand and linked our fingers together, leading her out to the patio where there were several couples dancing. The cold air settled around us as we gathered in the middle of the floor. I wrapped my arms around her and pulled her close to me. The heating lamps and fire pits gave off bursts of warmth against the cold September air, and from the speakers, a slow, haunting song with banjos and guitars played.

It was beautiful. Ramsey seemed to be enjoying herself because when I looked down at her, I saw her smiling, which was a relief after the surprise dinner fiasco. We danced under a string of lights. The lights, along with the few fire pits, was giving off a soft glow that made Ramsey look otherworldly, as cheesy as it sounded—she looked like an angel.

I pulled her a little closer, enjoying the closeness between us. Just when I thought I was home free of any issues from the dinner, I looked down and saw Ramsey's face, and that smile was gone, her head slightly tilted back.

"Jimmy, why did you pull this stunt tonight? Do you have any idea what could have happened?"

That made me laugh, I couldn't help it. "What exactly do you mean? What was going to happen?"

She reared her head back even further, until she was nearly

out of my arms. "You don't know how crazy Laney is! She could shut down this entire establishment, and still walk out like a lady when she was done." I smiled, but had to hold back rolling my eyes. I doubted that her tiny friend had that much fire in her. Still, I owed Ramsey something for what I pulled tonight.

"I'm sorry, I didn't know what to do. Jackson was going to find out regardless because of the chip in his car, and I didn't want him to show up at your house and start yelling or anything, and creating issues for your mom. So, I convinced him to calm down and wait until tonight."

She stared at my neck, like she was considering it. "Well, I can understand that, but next time, just tell me. I would have gone along with it, but it would have been nice to be in the loop." I was surprised. I was expecting yelling, the silent treatment, something other than understanding and acceptance. I suddenly realized how much I hated this stupid six-week rule between us. We were dancing again, and she tucked her head under my chin, moving her hands to the back of my shoulders. I held her closer; we were basically one person at this point. It wasn't enough. It never was with her, but the fact that she looked the way she did tonight, and I had her here pressed against me, in my arms, and I couldn't do anything about it, was too much. I leaned down and spoke into her ear, "Are we allowed to break any of these friendship rules?"

She kept dancing, but lifted her head to look at me, the hint of a smile on her lips. "Why, what rules are you thinking of breaking?"

I waited for a breath before answering. "I want to kiss you."

She was looking at me but wasn't saying anything, like maybe she was thinking it over. I thought I would use the silence to choose for her, so I leaned in to claim her mouth. Just as our mouths almost connected, she placed both hands on my chest and pushed, abruptly ending the chance for a kiss.

I watched her face as a sheen of red colored her cheeks. Her eyes were darting around the patio and tears were welling in her eyes, then her voice cracked.

"Not here, Jimmy, are you kidding me? This is where we work. I can't believe you would almost kiss me, where everyone can see us. Can't you see how that looks for both of us? Especially since we aren't... you know?"

I had so many thoughts going through my head. I was irritated that she stopped our kiss for the sake of other people, but I had to look at it from her perspective. This was our place of work, and I knew that she was still new here. She didn't want people to look at her differently. I understood that, but what did she mean by the last part of her sentence?

"What do you mean, 'we aren't'... we aren't what?"

She crossed her arms around herself, and I noticed goosebumps breaking out on her skin. She was obviously cold, which was kind of ruining the moment—or non-moment—that we were having. So, I gently grabbed her elbow and led her to a nearby fire pit, off the dance floor. She put her hand towards the flame and I slipped my jacket over her shoulders. Once the large jacket settled on her, she turned to look at me. I don't think she understood how hard it was for me not to kiss her; she really would have way more respect for me, if she had any idea whatsoever.

She started to gently explain, "I mean, we aren't anything but friends, and the people who work with us might get confused if they see us do anything that looks nonfriend-like."

I looked away from her and watched the flames; the term "not anything but friends" was rubbing and grating against me. There really wasn't anything like having the girl that you were falling in love with reminding you that you haven't won yet, and that the two of you were still only friends. I realized that I might screw up any chances that I had with her choosing to be mine after the six weeks was up, so I put a smile on my face and apologized.

"I'm so stupid, please forgive me. I can't believe I almost did that. I won't let that happen again."

She gave me a weak smile. "It's okay, sorry I freaked out on you. I just don't want people to think that I got this job because of certain things that aren't going on between us."

I knew that if I told her that half the staff was already giving me a hard time about not making a move on her, she would only get more embarrassed, so I just agreed and nodded my head. I looked towards the doors that led back to the bar and decided that maybe I should let Ramsey have her night back.

"Should we head back in now?" I put my elbow out for her to grab, she held onto it and nodded. We walked back in and saw that Jackson and Laney were still talking, which was good. Laney was leaning closer towards Jackson, there was a coffee in front of each of them, and a pitcher of water at the table. I could see, as we got closer, that Laney had been crying and Jackson's face was red as well. As we approached, Laney stood up and grabbed her purse, and said she needed to go to the restroom, grabbing Ramsey's arm and pulling her away. I sat down and watched Jackson as he poured himself some more water and finished it off. He turned his head towards me and gave me a look, like he was pained and exasperated.

"What's going on between you two?" I asked.

Jackson let out an audible sigh. "Man, I don't even know. I keep screwing things up with her. I am trying to convince her to let me drive her back to the city tomorrow, but she's pushing back and being stubborn ..." He let his head hang. I reached out and gripped his shoulder until he looked at me.

"Don't worry man," I tried to encourage him. "If she stole your car, then she is definitely feeling something for you; give it time."

He gave me a small smile of gratitude. I turned my head just then, and noticed Ramsey coming back towards the table. Laney was with her, but I didn't really see her because when Ramsey was in the room, all I noticed was her. Jackson gripped my shoulder, like I had done to him and whispered, "Six weeks, man... Six weeks."

TWENTY-SIX

"Jimmy, could you please take us home?" Laney asked as soon as we got back to the table. I turned to look at her, a little confused because she had just told me during our bathroom break that she wanted Jackson to take her back to Chicago tonight. I smiled at Laney while giving her a look that said I was trying to keep up with her mood swings. I encouraged the idea of Jimmy taking us home, hoping he had brought the Tahoe.

"Of course," Jimmy responded with a smile, but kept his eyes on Jackson. He must have been looking for some sign that Jackson wanted to take Laney, not that he would have had much of a choice. Once Laney made up her mind, that was it… like when she set her mind to stealing a car. I swear, she would end up in jail one of these days. Jimmy stood up, and Jackson looked like someone just kicked him in the kidneys, but he followed us out of the restaurant. He hung back with Laney, trying to talk to her. I even saw him try to reach for her at one point. Laney hadn't said much about what happened between them, except that she couldn't believe that he came after her. Which was ironic because she took his car.

I walked to the passenger side door in the front of the Tahoe. Jimmy followed me and opened the door for me, then walked over and climbed into his side. He started the car, as I pulled back the large arms from Jimmy's jacket that were covering my hands and moved all the air vents towards me. I glanced over my shoulder, out the back window, and saw that Laney was still talking to Jackson. At this point, they looked like two high schoolers who were fighting. Jackson got points for taking off his jacket and placing it over Laney's shoulders. Jimmy and I both watched them, although we gave up on looking over our shoulders, and settled for moving the rearview mirror until we could see them comfortably. I was toying with the hem of Jimmy's jacket, thinking about whether or not I should give it back to him at the end of the night when Jimmy spoke up. "Do you think I should start moving? Maybe we should just leave and let them sort this out?"

He was laughing as he said it, but I still swung my head over to him in disbelief. "No, we can't leave her! She asked you to take her for a reason."

"I know, I'm kidding, but I think Jackson might be in love, and he might appreciate it if we just left her here with him," Jimmy joked again.

"I know, but trust me, you don't want to do that unless Laney says so, otherwise you will have made an enemy for life." I attempted to educate him on some of Laney's mannerisms because it mattered to me that Laney liked Jimmy and vice versa.

The back door opened, and Laney climbed in with Jackson's help, he gave her a longing look and said, "I'll see you tomorrow." He looked in the mirror at Jimmy's eyes and Jimmy nodded, then she shut the door and we were off.

Throughout the drive, we didn't really talk about anything specific, but Jimmy grabbed my hand a few times. When I looked at him, he shrugged his shoulders, saying, "What?

Friends hold hands, don't they?" He looked in the rearview mirror and implored Laney for help. "Don't they, Laney?"

I looked back at her and she gave me the most sardonic smile. She was still wrapped in Jackson's jacket and, looking smug, she laughed and loudly said, "Absolutely, Jimmy. I hold Ramsey's hand all the time."

That encouraged Jimmy to squeeze my hand and he didn't let go for the rest of the trip. Jimmy talked about Sammy's soccer tryouts that were coming up, and I asked for all the details. I wanted to know when and where. I wanted to know how exactly I could be the absolute biggest fan of little Sammy Stenson.

"Two weeks from now, he will do some preliminary tryouts, but they are just so that the coaches can get a glimpse of the players before spring."

"Well, I want to be there. Can I be there? Can I talk to the people judging? Can I help train Sammy?" I was practically begging at this point.

Jimmy laughed again and looked over at me for a second with a look that made my heart rate rise to a point of medical concern. Then he pulled my hand closer to him and said, "Of course. To all of it. Sammy would love the help, you can talk to whoever you want, and you better be there."

I was starting to feel guilty because Jimmy hadn't really done anything but act like he wanted me. Not temporarily or for selfish reasons, he just acted sweet and like he genuinely liked me. I still stood by my need for a foundation between us because there was so much at stake, but I knew that I wanted to give him something. I sat there, putting my little plan together secretly, and let Jimmy hold my hand until the car stopped. We were in front of my house.

I made my way out of the car as Jimmy got out and walked around to meet me. He even helped Laney get out before he made it to me. Laney walked past me and went inside without even looking back and once the front door shut, I planted my hands on the car behind me. Jimmy was about a foot away, watching me. I looked up at him and waited, hoping he would step closer. I didn't know why I was so nervous. I wanted to be firm on the friendship thing and not confuse him, but I also wanted to show him how much I appreciated his efforts with me. Thankfully, he stepped closer and I took advantage. Clutching onto what little courage I had, I grabbed the front of his shirt, stepped into him, and kissed him.

My lips met his in a rushed panic, like if I didn't do it, I never would. He slowed us down by gently grabbing my elbows and pulling me closer, adjusting us until our kiss was slow and perfect. It was quickly building momentum though and my arms, on their own accord went around his neck and that little bit of distance between us was erased. His arms went around me, his hands splayed flat on my back. There was so much building between us in that moment and I needed more. I pushed closer, but he gently pulled his head back until his lips were hovering next to mine, our foreheads touching. His hands were still on my back and mine were still around his neck when he whispered, "That was some odd behavior for a friend."

I looked into those green eyes and matched his smile, thankful that he stopped us before things went too far. We started to separate, and I straightened out my dress, all while he watched me. I wrapped my arms around my middle.

"Well, I just... uh, you mentioned back at the restaurant..." I was tripping over my words and sounded like an idiot. I knew he liked the kiss and wanted it, but I could feel my cheeks heating at his joke. He stepped forward and pulled his jacket closer around my body.

"Don't get me wrong, I would love it if this type of behavior was acceptable for just being friends, but something tells me it's not." He was looking at me like he was trying to figure out a puzzle because I *was* a freaking puzzle. A complicated, weird, billion-piece puzzle.

I looked up into his eyes as I answered him, "Sorry, I shouldn't have blurred the lines or made it confusing. I do want to just be friends and build that relationship up for six weeks. I shouldn't have done that…"

HE CUT ME OFF WITH A HUG. A SWEET AND SIMPLE HUG, THEN he burrowed his nose into my neck and whispered again, "It was perfect. I get it, don't worry about it. We will go back to being friends. Just friends, thank you for this."

He let me go and I gently stepped away. As I walked towards the house, I turned around and gave him one more smile. I didn't know if he could feel it or not, but I was feeling it deep in my bones. I knew that I could bypass friendship all together and just be his. I was falling for Jimmy Stenson, falling so ridiculously hard, and I could only pray that as I fell, I wouldn't break.

I walked into the dark house and found that Laney was back in my bedroom. My tv was on, with *Parks and Rec* playing. Laney was in an oversized t-shirt under my covers. She glanced up at me and smiled. She knew. Of course, she knew. Then she started in on me.

"You little hussy. You totally kissed your single dad friend, who is also your boss." I bent down, grabbed a pillow, and threw it at her. It was an awkward throw because my hands were still stuck inside Jimmy's large jacket, which I totally planned to never give back to him.

"Shut up. You suck for reminding me of all the reasons why I shouldn't have kissed him."

She fell over laughing, and covered her mouth, probably remembering that my poor, sick mother was sleeping.

"I'm sorry, okay. I just thought it was hilarious how you

both kept giving each other those 'come kiss me' eyes all night. I would be a rich woman if I didn't only have myself to bet with because I totally bet that you would kiss him tonight."

I slipped the jacket off from my shoulders and laid it across my chair like it was a fragile piece of glass. I grabbed some pajamas and headed into the bathroom, but didn't shut the door. I called out from there to continue our little conversation. "I only kissed him because he wanted to kiss me at the club, but I shut him down because I was worried about people seeing us."

I was pulling the flannel shorts up my legs as I heard Laney respond, "You were worried about people seeing you?" She asked it with a tone. A judgy one.

I turned a mean glare on her as I left the bathroom and crawled into bed next to her. "Of course I was worried about that. It's my place of work, and I don't want anyone worried about me getting that job for sleeping with the boss."

Laney let out a snort. "You are so ridiculous. Did you sleep with the boss?"

"Of course not!" I punched her in the arm because she already knew I hadn't.

She started rubbing the spot that I hit. "I'm just saying if you didn't, you have to assume that the people Jimmy has worked with know him. Know that he wouldn't do that either. I think you are overreacting, personally."

I rolled my eyes because of course she thought I was over-reacting. I decided to flip the subject on her. "Speaking of over-reacting and being ridiculous, what is happening with you and Jackson?"

She turned up the TV as if to dismiss me. After about a minute of watching Leslie Knope execute another brilliant plan, Laney pressed mute again. "So, the friend who showed up on Jimmy's doorstep after Jimmy kissed you, the friend who you thought was hitting on you... That was Jackson?" she asked with a hint of worry in her voice.

"Yeah, it was him. Someone had just majorly pissed him off and sent him running to his best friend. I wonder who that was?" I cut my eyes towards her and rolled them when I caught her gaze.

She stayed quiet, so I continued, "It was a fake date. He interrogated me while simultaneously feeding me free food."

I caught a small smile spread across her lips. She looked down at her fingers and started messing with her nails.

"You know he hasn't been in a relationship with anyone?" she quietly said to the room. I waited, knowing it was a rhetorical question, then she kept going, "He and I, we're so much alike it scares me. Everything about him scares me." She was so quiet, she was practically whispering.

I grabbed her hands and squeezed them. I noticed a tear travel down her cheek and I knew that whatever happened between them was too intense for us to talk about tonight, but I did want to know what her plans were for going home now that she had no car.

"So, what's the plan for getting back home?"

She wiped her cheek and smiled at me. "I am actually going to let him drive me back tomorrow morning. Just makes sense, you know?"

I looked back at the TV, not wanting to overstep any emotional landmines that she had set up. "Yep, that makes sense."

We sat in silence, watching Ron Swanson systematically try to take down the government. After about half an hour or so, we both had scooted our bodies down to fall asleep.

I whispered to my best friend in the darkness, "I think I love him."

The words left my chest, and I couldn't take them back. I hoped that they might fall on deaf ears or invoke some argument to talk me out of it. Now that they were spoken, it felt final, especially now that my best friend knew.

Still expecting her to fight with me or try to prove me wrong, I was surprised when I felt her fingers find mine and squeeze. I heard her whisper back, "I know."

I closed my eyes and let my body drift to sleep, hoping I would wake with more courage to face being in love with Jimmy Stenson—my boss, my friend, and the father to two beautiful kids.

TWENTY-SEVEN

JIMMY

I WALKED into the house in a daze. Ramsey kissed me, she leaned in and initiated a kiss and it was better than I imagined it would be. She was soft and perfect. I was in over my head and even though I promised her that we would go back to being friends, there was absolutely no way that I could wait six weeks to kiss her again. I would just have to get creative and persuasive, she had no idea what she just started. I was still running my fingers over my lips, feeling like a teenager when I rounded the corner to the kitchen and found Jackson leaning against the island, eating cookies.

He never ate sugar, so I took the fact that he had polished off an entire row of Chips Ahoy as a sign that things with Laney didn't go well. I leaned against the counter and stayed quiet, waiting for him to spill. He finished his last cookie and started dusting off the crumbs, then he took a big drink of milk and let out a loud sigh.

"I must have missed it," he said, while keeping his eyes trained on the countertop.

I looked where he was focusing and narrowed my eyebrows. "Missed what?"

He let out a laugh and brought his hand up to run over his buzzed head. "Missed the moment that we lost our man cards. We basically handed them over to those two. I saw how you looked at Ramsey, and it's only gotten worse since I was here last."

I put my hands in my pockets, mostly to prevent myself from touching my lips, as though I could summon the feel of her again. "Yeah, I guess we did."

It was all I could think to respond with. He wasn't wrong about how I looked at Ramsey; it was the same look he gave Laney. The look of surrender, and finality. Jackson shuffled his feet and turned around to lean his elbows on the counter as he looked off towards the opposite side of the room. I wouldn't push him to talk, he would do it when he was ready. "I'm taking Laney back to the city tomorrow morning..." He turned his head towards me and let out a sigh before continuing, "If she doesn't change her mind tonight."

I felt for the guy. I had no idea what had happened between them to make Laney so skittish around Jackson, but it must have been bad to make her this confused. I cleared my throat as I responded, "That's progress, right?"

He looked at me and seemed to laugh to himself. "Progress with Laney doesn't exist. We just keep running around the same circular room, trying to find the corners. That's how maddening she is." His face was drawn, his eyes tired, and his lips thin. He looked like he was in pain, or maybe just exhausted.

I gave him a weak smile. "I feel your pain." We both fell silent for a few seconds.

Jackson looked up at me with tired eyes. "So, tomorrow. That still happening with Davis?"

I shook my head. "He moved the meeting."

Jackson scoffed. "Of course he did." I watched as Jackson shook his head in frustration. I bent down to grab my shoes.

"It'll just give us more time to plan. It's fine." I started to head for the stairs, as Jackson let out a sigh.

As I walked away, I heard him say, "I hope you're right."

I hoped I was right too. There wasn't any other option, other than to trust that I was.

JACKSON LEFT EARLY THE NEXT MORNING, AROUND EIGHT, before the kids or Dad woke up. I took the moment to pull my calendar up and looked at Sammy's soccer times, and reviewed Dad's schedule. I noticed a few gaps where the kids might need rides or someone to help out with getting the kids from one place to another. I pulled out my phone, knowing it was early, but also knowing that Ramsey was probably up because Laney had left with Jackson. I punched her contact info and waited to hear her voice.

"Hello?" Her voice was raspy and sexy as hell and suddenly, I needed her lips again, needed her here with me, needed the next six weeks to fly by.

"Hey, sorry, did I wake you up?" I asked cautiously.

She let out a laugh. "No, I was up because of Laney and her crazy ass."

"Good, I know it's early, but I needed to ask you a question, and I had a feeling that you would be up."

I heard a few things in the background move around before she responded. "What's up?"

"Well, next week, I have an out-of-town meeting for business, and noticed there might be a few days that Dad needs help getting the kids. Would you be willing to help out and be added as an extra emergency person on the kids' school list?"

I held my breath for a second because the heaviness of this question was weighing on me. I had never had anyone besides my Dad and Jackson for the kids, and it made me want to laugh and cry that we might finally have someone who would be there for the kids, for me, for us.

"Of course, I will. Please add me, I would love to be there for them if they need me. Please tell them that too." She sounded excited and it about made my heart burst.

"Okay, thank you, I will get you added on Monday. So, what are you up to today?" I crossed my arms over my chest, hoping that she would want me included in her weekend. She let out a little chuckle, no doubt assuming exactly what I was getting at.

"My grandparents sent some money, so that I would specifically go and spoil my mom. So, I'm taking her shopping for some new clothes, and getting her nails done. You know, making her feel pretty. I promised her that I would watch some classic movies with her tonight while we eat some fish amok."

"What is fish amok?" I asked, a little judgment in my tone, because anything with fish was usually gross.

"It's a Cambodian favorite. There is a restaurant in Rockford that serves international dishes. I called and asked if they could fix us two plates of the fish amok, and they agreed. My mom is so excited, and I would be happy to save you some if you'd like," she finished with a giggle, because she probably knew that I was grossed out.

"That is so kind of you, I would love some." I wouldn't admit my total and complete hate for all things fish-related. She laughed, really laughed, from her belly, or her soul, and I loved it, I was smiling like an idiot.

"Okay, you got it, buddy. I will save you some, but it probably won't taste very good after too long, so what are you doing tomorrow?"

I couldn't keep the smile off my face and it probably came through in my voice, "Apparently trying fish amok. Practicing soccer with Sammy and probably some family movie with the kids. Would you like to join us?"

I wanted her to join us so badly that I was worried that I would start begging her at some point. I was so relieved when I heard her reply, "I would love to join you, what time would you like me over?" I realized in that moment that I had no dignity left with this woman.

"Is breakfast too early? I think the kids would love to make you some of their famous blueberry pancakes. I heard it was something they were hoping to make you that morning that Jackson rudely showed up and sent you running home."

She was silent for a moment and I worried that I pushed it too far, but she let out a sigh and responded with an obvious smile in her voice, "The kids make these famous pancakes, huh?"

I smiled. "Yep, they are legendary. Will you be there, 8:30? Or earlier, if you would like to platonically cuddle me." She was laughing again and I laughed with her. I couldn't help flirting with her, I had to get her to kiss me again.

"I will be there at 8:30, and I will bring some coffee and hot chocolate."

"Okay, have fun with your mom today, and if you get the urge to sneak away tonight and tell me about your day in person, I would like to remind you of the key to my house that you are in possession of." I was laying it on thick and I didn't care. I would give her six weeks, but I would make it as easy on her as it was going to be on me.

"Okay, bye, Mr. Stenson, I will see you tomorrow." She emphasized the tomorrow part of her goodbye, unfortunately.

"Bye, have a good day."

I hung the phone up. This was going to be a long day. Good thing I had a ton of work to go over with my Dad. I was finally going to go over the books from Sips N Sides with him, and Dad had no clue whatsoever.

It had been six hours. Six hours of arguing, fighting, talking, laughing, arguing again, until finally Dad agreed to go over the books with me. Six hours of my life that I will never get back, and at one point, I thought I was going to punch him in the face and demand his computer. It even got so bad that I almost called Ramsey, ready to ask that she forget her relaxing day with her mother and come over here to force my father to talk.

Thankfully, I didn't do any of those things. I just waited and there I was, looking at a computer screen, showing me that my father had already paid off the bar, started remodeling it at Ramsey's suggestion, and was sitting better financially than I was. I was shocked. I had always assumed that the bar was drowning in debt, and the reason my father wouldn't go into retirement, but I was wrong, so wrong. I sat there, staring at the screen, and all of the zeros, and wasn't sure what to say. Finally, I brought my fingers under my chin like a wall, and looked over at my dad.

"So, were you ever going to tell me about this?" I sounded petty, and I felt petty. I felt like my Dad was keeping secrets from me, and it rubbed me the wrong way. What was worse, was the feeling that Ramsey was in on the secret. I took in my father's face, his pale blue eyes, and his weathered skin. He still looked so strong, but I could tell he was tired.

"Of course, I was going to tell you, eventually, but I didn't want to burden you. You just started your bar, and I didn't want to add any stress to your plate. I'm doing fine and didn't need to mention anything to you about it."

He had already gone through almost an entire bag of chips, and two glasses of cream soda, so I could tell this conversation wasn't easy for him. Sugar and salt were always his comfort food when he got stressed out. I pushed away my concern for him and pressed on with my questions. "Where did you get this kind of money, Dad?"

I was worried that he had gone back to the MC, to that life. Maybe not the Brass, but a different club. I was starting to panic because he couldn't go back, not after everything, not after my dying mother made him promise. I had my fists clenched and my jaw was tight. The more I pictured my mother as she begged my father to never return to that life, the angrier I became.

Dad cut into my thoughts just in time. "Jimmy, it's nothing like what you're thinking. So, calm down. Your mother, she left me an inheritance. Aside from the life insurance, she left me the remaining money from a trust that her dead aunt had left her. She wanted it to go towards the bar. The will had strict stipulations that it was to be kept in Sip N Sides, for you, but you didn't want it," my dad finished with a defeated sigh. He sounded heartbroken and I could physically feel my mother's disappointment through the look on his face. He and my mother had started Sip N Sides together as a fresh start, Mom had a dream that it would stay in the family forever and be something that would bind us together and, more than anything, it would keep me and my father away from the biker life. I knew she wanted something substantial to keep me away from them, but was probably worried about giving me the money directly. I closed my eyes and pushed away the disappointment that my father and, most likely, my mother had in me. I knew that my mom just wanted me away from the MC life and would have been proud of what I started. Still, it stung that I rejected what she had left for me. I didn't know how to fix this, I knew my Dad was waiting to retire, and from the looks of it, it was now a game of who to leave the bar to since his selfish son didn't want it. Now that there were hundreds of thousands of dollars invested into it, who could he trust to take it?

"Dad, what if Jackson and I took the bar and turned it into..."

"No. Stop, just stop it," my dad interrupted me and started waving his hands around as if to dismiss me. "Your mother wanted a family establishment, not some fancy, souped-up business bar. No offense. But you are not taking this bar and flipping it into anything." He looked so endearing, but he was infuriating. Why was he being so stubborn about this?

"Is that in the will? Mom didn't want it to be turned for more profit? That is hard for me to believe, Dad. I think Mom would have wanted us to capitalize on this opportunity."

Dad looked out the window and a sadness passed over his face. I knew talking about Mom was difficult for him, so this conversation must be torture.

"Yes, it is in the will. She wanted it to stay as the Sip N Sides, a low-key bar, and restaurant. She fell in love with Belvidere and wanted our family roots to stay here."

I pulled my hands up and rubbed my face with them. "Then what are you going to do, Dad? Run it forever?" I practically shouted at him, and I hated myself for it, but he wasn't coming up with many options that made sense. He refused to let it out of the family, but didn't want me to run it because he knew that I would flip it. But he was getting older and needed to retire. This seemed like a lose-lose situation. I scrubbed at my face some more and stood up to grab some water. I took a moment to peek out the window at the kids, and saw they were still jumping on the trampoline. Dad was playing with the tag from a bag of bread in front of him. It was quiet in our kitchen, my question just hanging in the air, probably because there wasn't an answer. Finally, Dad spoke up.

"I want to leave it to Ramsey."

He turned his head to stare at me while I drank my water. A weird feeling wormed its way through me—a feeling of betrayal, or jealousy, like the two of them had planned this. I shook my head to get rid of it, I was overreacting. I placed my glass against the granite counter a little harder than necessary and asked, "What do you mean you want to leave it to Ramsey?" My tone was immature, even incredulous, against my attempts to quell the feelings.

He straightened his back and squared his jaw. "I mean, that I want to retire and have Ramsey take over. You can stay on as half-owner, as long you sign a legal document stating that you will never try to sell it or change the name, unless you are facing financial ruin or bankruptcy."

I was trying to stay calm and keep my feelings to myself. I knew I was overreacting to this whole thing and I needed time to process it, so I responded with something simple.

"Why Ramsey?"

His face softened as he answered. "She's been like a daughter to me, from the first moment she sat in my bar and poured her heart out to me. She has a good soul and I want her to have a reason to hang around once her mama passes on. I want her to have family, and I can't count on you not screwing that up for me."

He smiled at the end of that statement, trying to make a joke out of it. He knew how I felt about Ramsey. Even though we had never talked about it, I am sure that he knew. The thought of having her stay here with us, be with us, softened the blow a bit, and the more I thought of her as a business owner, the more sense this whole thing made. But the sting was still there—they had left me out.

"Well, when do you plan on asking her?" I finished off my water and headed back towards the table.

Dad was looking up at me, as he answered, "I think after the new year. As it is, I am letting her upgrade the entire place as much as she wants, but she hasn't figured out why yet. She's fair with the money, though; even though it's not her own, she's careful. That's how I know she's the right one, because once she knows it's hers, she will just make it even better."

I smiled at him. Just thinking of Ramsey made me smile. "Yeah, that sounds like her."

He suddenly got serious and reached for my hand. "Son, be careful with her and take your time. Please don't scare her off. She is important to me and the kids as much as she is to you."

I looked down at his hand and then looked at his eyes. I knew this was one of those big moments, one that I would remember a long time from now once he left this earth, but I couldn't help feeling irritated at his implication.

And before I knew what was happening, I opened my mouth and blurted, "Dad, I love her."

Even as the words left my mouth, I felt a settling in my gut, deep down inside where those words would fall like seeds and grow into something bigger than I could imagine. This was the first time that I had said the words out loud and I knew they were true, but it didn't change the fact that my brain was now taking off in fight-or-flight mode.

Loving Ramsey made me vulnerable, loving her made me scared, loving her made it possible for her to hurt me, or hurt my kids. My dad must have noticed my battle because he gripped my hand until I looked him in the eyes.

With a soft voice, he reassured me, "She's different, son, she isn't Lisa. Ramsey has been looking for where she belongs her entire life, and she found it here with us. I know it. Just be careful with her heart when she gives it to you."

I smiled and nodded at him, but my throat was closing up at the thought of being hurt again, and worse, by someone that had taken me so off guard like Ramsey. This whole Sip N Sides business information was at the forefront of my mind. She knew, and she kept it from me after I specifically asked her about it. Why did she hide it, what else was she hiding? My brain went on and on, in a vicious cycle until the only thought that I could think was—Ramsey was capable of lying to me.

That thought started to war with my feelings of love towards her. I had to get out of there.

I stood up and grabbed my jacket, looking over my shoulder, I threw out a quick question to Dad, but I knew he wasn't going anywhere, so it was mostly for respect, "I'm heading out Dad. Would you mind staying with the kids, and doing dinner? I won't be back for a while."

I didn't wait for him to respond. I opened the garage door, found my boots, and got on my bike. I needed to clear my head, or purge my heart, one or the other, but either way, I was not falling for someone who could lie to me. I couldn't do it again, I wouldn't survive.

TWENTY-EIGHT

THE BEAUTY DAY with Mom was a total success. We found her three new hats, some new shoes, some new outfits, we did our nails, and finished our night with the most delicious fish amok that either of us had ever tasted. I was watching her nod off while watching Doris Day in some classic movie that was on, when my phone dinged. I tried not to look at my phone much during the day, because it was all about Mom, and she deserved all of my attention. Sometimes I would get scared if we had a really good day, wondering if that night, I would lose her. As if God was saying, "I gave you a great last day, be grateful."

It was messed up, I knew that much, but still, I always felt the lingering effects of that or, if I paid attention to someone else, in a flash, she would be gone, and if I had just spent that last moment with her, I would have it, as a reminder. I was thankful for sleep, because I didn't feel bad when she slept; it wasn't my fault if I missed anything.

I ignored my phone and went to help Mom to her room. I kissed her forehead after I helped her into bed, like she had done with me so many times throughout my life, and held back the tears that burned to be released. I didn't want to lose her. I inhaled her citrus scent and tried to force it to memory, tried to remember how soft her hands were, how brown the irises of her eyes were. I wanted to remember everything.

I wanted to keep her, I wanted her to be my children's grandmother, and the over-involved mother-in-law to my husband. I wanted her to be there with me on my wedding day, and I wanted to call her in the middle of the night when my baby wouldn't sleep. I wanted so much more time with her. I stood in her room, watching her, and did something I hadn't done in a long time—I prayed.

All the Sunday School verses and songs went through my head for a second, taking me back to those days when I prayed at night with my mom. Back to when I sat and read the Bible with her, back to when she would sing songs through the house at the top of her lungs and ask me to join in. I reached for the shredded threads of my faith and dug in deep as I asked God to give me more time. I fell to my knees and asked him to let me be selfish, to leave her here on Earth for me to take care of.

I sobbed into the blanket as I knelt at her bed. She was already asleep and wouldn't hear me, wouldn't hear me begging or how much I needed her. I pleaded with him in the darkness of her room, while silent tears spilled down my face. I stayed in her room, crying and praying, until I decided to just crawl into her bed next to her. Ignoring my phone, the TV that was still on, and the world. In that moment, I just wanted my mom, and I wanted to hold her all night. I did just that; I grabbed her hand and held on until I fell asleep.

<hr />

THE NEXT MORNING, I WOKE UP IN MY MOTHER'S BED. SHE WAS

still asleep, and it was still dark outside. I slipped out of the bed, walked into the living room to turn off the lights and TV that had been left on all night. I searched for my phone on the couch, where I'd been sitting. Finally fishing it out of the deep crevice it had fallen into, I noticed that I had a blinking green light. I pressed the screen and punched in my code, then set it back down and turned on some coffee. Once I grabbed it again, I noticed that I had a few missed text messages and a few missed phone calls.

I opened the texts. All of them were from Jimmy. That made me smile until I started reading.

9:12 P.M. - *RAMSEY, I REALLY NEED TO TALK TO YOU TONIGHT. Call me when you get a chance.*

9:30 P.M.- *PLEASE CALL ME, CAN I COME OVER? I REALLY NEED TO talk to you before tomorrow.*

10:30 p.m.- *I'm coming over*

11:00 p.m.- *Ramsey, this is important Damn it! I need to talk to you. Open up!*

1:15 a.m.- *I'm not leaving until you open up*

THAT WAS THE LAST TEXT. MY HEART WAS IN MY THROAT, WHAT the hell was going on? I quickly pressed my voicemail icon and skipped to the last message, left after midnight.

"Ramsey, I don't know why you are ignoring me. I needed to talk to you! I guess you don't want to talk to me. Vwhatever, I wanted to hear you say it. Tell me with your voice, from your lipsss, but I guess I can't, can I? Just say it, Ram, say it. Say you lied to me, tell

me that you are a liar, so that I can stop feeling like this."

He was drunk. So clearly drunk, his voice was slurred and didn't make sense. My heart was thundering now as panic started to set in. I ran to my room and threw some clothes on, pulled my hair back, and grabbed my keys. I half-expected to see a passed-out Jimmy on my porch, but he wasn't there. No car, no bike, nothing. I ran to my car and started it. I looked at the clock briefly and saw that it was only seven in the morning. It was earlier than we planned on seeing each other, but he offered for me to let myself in. I had no idea what he was talking about, what had I lied about?

I drove over to his house, nothing seemed out of place. His green lawn was covered in a layer of frost, as was his pitched roof. His front door still had the fall wreath on it that Jasmine had bought for him from a school fundraiser, Theo's truck was in the driveway like normal. I parked along the curb and quietly walked up to the house. I pushed his house key into the top lock and turned, then did the same with the bottom lock and pushed the door open.

The house was warm and dark, I slid my shoes off by the door and crept through the house. Quietly, I tiptoed up to Jimmy's room. I knew in that moment that this was a dangerous idea. Early morning, pajamas, the fact that I had kissed him just the other night, but something was clearly muddled between us and needed to be cleared up, which could require some apologies. I knew this, and still I climbed the stairs. I had to know he was okay and find out what in the world was going on with him.

His door was shut. I gently turned the knob and pushed it open, only to find his bed empty. I walked all the way in. It looked like no one had slept in it the night before. I walked into the bathroom, and it was empty too, the towels dry, no water drops in the shower. Jimmy hadn't come home, or if he had, he hadn't been in his room or bathroom. Confused, I walked back out of the room and shut his door behind me.

I carefully opened Jasmine's door and peeked in. She was nestled in under a mound of pink covers, still sleeping. I did the same to Sammy's room, and he had a few limbs hanging over the edge of his bed, but he was still sleeping too. I crept back downstairs, and realized that Theo was there, and the kids were fine, but curiosity got the better of me. I opened the door that connects to the garage from the kitchen and peeked in. The Tahoe was parked, but Jimmy's bike was gone.

My gut clenched. He was driving his bike last night while he was drunk? Maybe he wasn't drunk and driving at the same time, but it still worried me. I stood there, not sure what to do. I didn't want to panic Theo if I didn't need to, so I pulled out my phone and called Jimmy. It rang a few times, then went to voicemail. Clearing my throat, I left him something, short and sweet. "Jimmy, it's Ramsey. I left my phone on the couch last night and didn't get any of your texts or calls until this morning. I am at your house and worried. Please call me ASAP. Thanks."

I hung up and fought the urge to dial him again until he picked up. I sent him a text, relaying the same info that I had in the voicemail, hoping he would respond, but he didn't. I just stood there in his garage for a few more minutes, waiting.

I decided to curl up on the couch until he came home. He was expecting me for breakfast anyway, so it wouldn't be weird. I sent off a text to my mom, so she didn't worry and knew where I was. I pulled a blanket over myself and prayed again that Jimmy was okay. My stomach was in knots at the idea that he was hurt, or something had happened to him. After about an hour of tossing and turning on the couch, I got up and paced the living room. No one had woken up yet, and I felt like I was going crazy with worry. I tried calling Jimmy again, and nothing. I called him again, and again, and again, and still nothing. I broke down and dialed Laney. I knew it was low, but I needed answers and she had Jackson's phone number.

Laney didn't answer, and I didn't blame her. It was Sunday morning and I had just seen her the day before. So, I called her again until she finally answered. She was groggy and pissed.

"Ramsey, someone better be dead!" she shouted into the phone.

"Laney..." I croaked, and couldn't help the tears that started to fall.

I heard her clear her throat and shift in her bed. "Ramsey, what's wrong? Is your mom okay... oh God. I'm so sorry, Ramsey, I can't believe I said that..."

"No, it's okay, it's not my mom. I need Jackson's number... I think something happened to Jimmy... I don't know..."

I trailed off, hating the sound of my own voice. Laney was silent for a second, and then let out a sigh. "I heard Jackson talking to him on the phone last night, they were yelling. I couldn't make out their conversation, except for the words, 'knock this shit off, and go home,' but Jackson didn't say anything when he came back inside, he just looked pissed."

I didn't want to speak, I was scared and worried, and just wanted Jackson's phone number. "Laney, are you at Jackson's house? I need to talk to him, so give me his number or wake him up. I don't really care what the thing is between you two, just get him."

She let out a sigh. "Okay, he's in his room. I'm in the guest room for the record, and what you think is happening between us isn't happening."

I heard her open a door and I heard walking, then the phone was muffled. I heard a very raspy, manly, "Hello?"

"Jackson?" My voice was weak, and I hated it, "Jackson, where is Jimmy? I'm worried about him. He left me all these texts and calls last night, and he isn't home."

Jackson was quiet, then let out a breath. "Yeah, I know he

isn't. I'm sorry you got pulled into this, Ramsey. He's safe, but you should just go home. Theo is there with the kids, right?"

My stomach was tight, and I wanted to puke. "What do you mean, he's safe? Do you know where he is?"

Silence, then another sigh. I was getting tired of the exasperated sighs.

"Yes, Ramsey, I know where he is. He's safe. Please trust me. Go home."

It took a second, but it finally registered—Jimmy was with someone. He had spent the night with someone and that was why Jackson wasn't telling me. I started to cry, and I hated myself for it.

"Oh, he's... okay, he's with someone. I get it, it's just, we had plans today, and he left all these messages. Thanks, Jackson, I just wanted to be sure he wasn't spread across the highway somewhere." My voice was cracking all over the place, and I was crying, and I couldn't keep it out of my voice, as hard as I tried.

Jackson practically yelled at me to stop. "No, Ramsey, listen to me. It's not what you think, but Jimmy needs to get his head on straight. Let him explain all this to you when he gets a chance. He will be home later today. Go home and wait for him to call you. Okay? Just don't go there with your mind. I swear, it's not what you think."

I laughed. "Jackson, he called me drunk, I think it might be exactly what I think. But it's fine, he doesn't owe me anything, we're just friends." I straightened my spine and tried to steel my voice.

"Ramsey, I think we both know that you two are more than friends. Jimmy knows that too. Trust him, give him a chance to explain himself."

I nodded and realized that he couldn't see me, so I ignored my clogged throat and responded, "Okay, thank you, sorry for waking you up. Tell Laney I will talk to her later." I hung up.

I shut my eyes and let out a strained sigh. Returning to my car and heading home I decided that I would get lost in my work and focus on my mother; exactly where my focus should have been from the start. At least that was the plan. I told myself the plan over and over, even as the tears fell down my face and I felt like a giant hole had just opened up in my heart.

TWENTY-NINE

JIMMY

I woke up in a dark room. There was a red sheet covering the window, giving the room a creepy, dark glow. My head was pounding, and I wanted to puke. My whole body ached and pleaded with me to stay still, but I knew that I needed water and some aspirin.

I felt my chest and was surprised to find that I wasn't wearing a shirt. I looked down and found a dark blue sheet over my body. Thankfully I had my jeans on and my socks, but no shirt and no shoes.

I looked around the room again, trying to adjust my eyes to the surroundings. It felt like a mobile home—the fake wood paneling on the walls gave it away—and the thin windows. There was a small dresser in the corner and huge, flat-screen TV on a table in front of the bed. It felt wrong.

Dread gripped me, and fear clogged my throat. What had I done? I heard a flush and looked over towards the other end of the room, sure enough there was another small door in the room. A blonde-haired woman, in a tank top and underwear, walked out while brushing her teeth. I'd never seen her before.

This wasn't happening. I slammed my eyes shut, trying to escape what was going on. She looked over at me and stopped brushing, then walked back into the bathroom, and I took the moment alone to sit up and find my shirt. I had to get out of there. The woman returned a few seconds later, she had on a pair of shorts and a sweater now. She had her arms crossed and looked irritated.

"Glad you're finally awake. Your damn phone hasn't stopped buzzing since early this morning."

I looked around the room again, my head throbbing. I licked my dry lips and managed to ask, "Do you know what time it is?"

She still looked pissed as she moved to the dresser and picked up a phone, tossing it at me. "It's ten, Shutter fly."

I wasn't ready to look at it, I knew who was calling. Instead, I tried to focus on what damage was done here. "Shutter fly… Why'd you call me that?"

She was messing with her own phone now but looked up for a second. "You were too shy to do anything last night. That, or you're married. Not even a kiss! I brought you back to my place, thinking you'd get more comfortable and maybe, you know… want something after a little sleep, but nope. You just slept, and now you're looking at me like I have a third eye."

Thank God. I was so relieved that I actually might kiss her, but I wouldn't cross that line and confuse the poor girl. I stood, looking for my boots.

"So, what happened? How'd you get me to agree to come back here?"

She laughed and tossed my shirt at me. "Your phone was dying, and you kept saying you needed to talk to the liar of your heart and needed to charge it. I offered you a charger, you got in my car and came here with me." She trailed off.

I coughed and tried to clear my throat. "I'm so sorry, I

appreciate you giving me a place to stay. Anything I can do to repay you?"

She scoffed, "Yeah, tell Davis to leave me and my sister the hell alone. You seemed to be pretty buddy-buddy with his guys last night."

Shit.

How could I have been so reckless? I pulled on my boots and started to stand, when a knock came from her bedroom door. I looked at her and she glanced at me, then the door, and a man's voice yelled out, "Jimmy boy, come on out here if you're done with Jill. I know she's fun, but I need to talk to you."

Davis. That was Davis, the fucking leader of the Brass. I had just run right back into the belly of the beast.

I stood and grabbed my jacket. Jill, I guess, looked terrified. She grabbed my hand before I reached for the door and whispered, "Be careful," before I slipped out.

I walked down a short hallway until it opened into a living room, with carpet that might have once been white, but was now covered in stains. Old, black leather couches framed the small room, a large screen television sat against the wall, and Charles Davis sat with a baseball bat in his hands at the center of the room. Two guys were in the kitchen, arguing over food or something, and Davis watched me as I came closer. I put on the mask I used to wear when I walked around the Brass, let anger roll off me, and stood my ground.

"What the hell do you want, Davis? Weren't we scheduled to meet next week?" I practically spat at him.

He smiled and started running his hands over the bat. I wondered if that was a new thing for him, he never used to carry one.

"Jimmy boy, you don't remember much from last night, do you?"

I grappled with my dehydrated brain and body and tried to remember something, anything, but nothing came. What did I do? The fear of what I might have done was overwhelming, so I stayed quiet and waited for him to continue.

He let out a low laugh. "Figures. You're so much like your old man sometimes, always offering the farm without thinking it through first." He let out a sigh and continued. "We had a deal, Jimmy. You wanted a sabbatical, I gave it to you, and I found your whore of an ex-wife, on top of it. You should be thanking me, happy to see my beautiful face."

He leered and paused for a second. "It's time to get back to work for our beloved chapter. I have a job for you; I need a licensed, business truck to deliver some delicate inventory."

He paused and waited for his words to register. They slowly trickled into my brain and I had to hide the look of dread on my face. I still didn't speak, so he kept going.

"I was going to wait until next week to handle this, but you showed up last night and I figured you were eager to set up the deal. So you start today, Jimmy boy." He slapped my shoulder as he walked past me.

I swallowed the thick, disgusting bile that was threatening to come up. "How long will you need the truck for?"

Davis walked towards the kitchen, where the other guys were. He stopped at the sink and got a glass from the cupboard, filling it with water. He turned and handed me the cup. "Two weeks."

Shit. I was such a fucking idiot. I had driven to the Brass to confront Davis on why he moved our meeting. I was paranoid and drunk as hell. I should have just driven to Jackson's. Now I was launched back into the Lion's Den, and without setting up anything back home to prepare for it. I was out of options and backed against the wall, so I did the only thing I could do—I stuck out my hand and he grabbed it in a shake. Davis took a step back and looked at the two guys in the kitchen.

"Now, Jones and Adams here, are going to go with you and hang out for a bit, to make sure you're not going to flake out on us or do anything stupid. You know, because of genetics. Wouldn't want a repeat of dealing with the Ripper." Davis winked at me.

I knew that it wasn't up for debate, so I just nodded to them. I knew I wouldn't have any time to call Ramsey, or my Dad, for that matter, before I got on the bike and rode back to Rockford to get the truck set up for them. It had to be today, when most of the staff was off. The only one I would have to deal with was Rav. I moved towards the front door when I heard Davis click his tongue behind me. "Did you forget our protocol?"

I turned back to face him. He held his hand out, waiting. Shit, this was so fucking bad. I tried to hide the fear that had crawled its way up my neck, but I wasn't doing a great job of it. I dug for my cell phone and handed it over to Davis. He handed it to Jones, who flipped it over, opened the back cover and placed something small and black inside. A fucking tracking chip. This would give them total access to my phone calls and text messages going forward. Great. Jones closed up my phone and handed it back to me. Davis winked again.

"Just being cautious, you know the drill. This deal can't go south." He sauntered back into the kitchen. I didn't want to spend any more time there, so I pushed open the flimsy door and headed for my bike. I needed to get back before the two idiots.

As I rode down the freeway, I considered the cost of doing this, of setting up this meeting with Davis, with coming out of hiding. They would know where I lived, they would know about my kids, they would find out about Ramsey. *Shit,*

Ramsey. Shame and grief spread through me at the thought of what I had texted her, and what I had left her on her phone. She must be worried sick about me or pissed as hell. I completely harassed her all night and then disappeared and ditched out on the plans we had made for the day.

Sure, I was hurt that she lied, but I still wanted her. That desire to have her, a future with her, and no strings from my past was what made me decide that I could do this last job for the Brass. Because this would be my last job, my way out. While these guys followed me around, I would need to stay away from Ramsey. I didn't want her mixed up in this, and I definitely didn't want Charles Davis to know about her.

I ARRIVED AT THE BAR SOONER THAN ADAMS AND JONES, SO I pulled out my phone and texted Jackson.

Me: *Take out the porterhouse rib, and don't forget to shut the meat locker.*

It was a simple code between us and since Davis had access to my phone and everything else, I had to be careful. Jackson knew what the text meant, and I hoped it would be as simple as that, like it was once before when I split away from the MC. I called my dad and made sure he knew I would be home in a few hours. Then, the dreaded call. I pulled up Ramsey's information and dialed. A myriad of emotions swam through me. I was pissed and hurt, embarrassed and afraid, but more than anything, I missed her. I wanted to hear her voice to calm down the storm that had started brewing in me. She answered on the fifth ring.

"Hello."

I panicked for a second, and was tempted to hang up, but I found some nerve and started talking. "Ramsey, it's good to hear your voice."

She waited, and I heard her shut a door, but she didn't talk, and it scared me. Finally, she let out a breath and said, "Jimmy, I'm glad to hear you're okay."

I looked down at the ground, so badly wanting to clear the air, and come clean and invite her into all of this. "Yeah, I'm fine…"

She was quiet and then slowly replied, masking some emotion, but I heard her voice crack. "You seemed like things were pretty urgent last night. I guess you figured out something to do until you spoke to me today."

That didn't sound good. Did she assume that I slept with someone? I mean, she wasn't that far off, but I didn't think hearing the hurt in her voice, carrying that pain, would tear through me like this. "No, Ramsey, I didn't do anything like you might think. I did get drunk, and I ended up in Chicago. I am back in Rockford now, and we do need to talk about what I did last night, but…" Just then, I saw Jones and Adams pull onto the main road leading to the club. I had to get off the phone.

"Look, Ramsey, I want to talk this through, but not this week. I will be gone and in and out of work all week. I just wanted to touch base with you before I go radio silent."

There was silence, and then, "So that's it?" Her voice was high, like she was holding in emotion or trying not to cry.

I was silent. I didn't want to hurt her, but I also needed her to stay away from me this week. I didn't want Davis anywhere near her. I waited too long, and she spoke again.

"Okay, Jimmy." Her response was plain, flat, and with no emotion before hanging up.

I grabbed my chest as the phantom pains surged through me. I hated this. All I wanted was to drive to Ramsey's house with dinner, take her by the hand, and have a date with her. To kiss her again, to tell her that I had fallen in love with her, to share with her how much she meant to me, but I couldn't. This had to come first, I had to do this job, see Lisa and put this behind me. Then I would go to Ramsey.

Hopefully, by then, it wouldn't be too late.

THIRTY

In college, I took a course on understanding the different types of pain. While most pain was classified by the damage it left to the body, and was referenced to be a physical thing, there was a lot to be said about psychogenic pain. Psychogenic pain had to do with psychological factors but could also stem from tissue damage that affected the psychosis of a person more than the physical well-being of a person. I often wondered if that was how people could die of a broken heart.

I mean, I wasn't on the verge of death from my heart being broken, but I was pissed as hell, and it hurt. I wasn't too big of a person to admit that I was in pain over Jimmy, which just added to the pain that radiated through me, regarding my mom. The damn clock seemed to be at odds, once again, with me.

"Sammy, you can't kick it out of bounds and keep going, buddy. You need to stop and come back in once you kick it out," I yelled while lifting myself up onto my elbow, covering my eyes, to block the sun. Jasmine sat behind me, my hair laying in her lap, while she braided it. Sammy corrected his position on the field, heading closer to the center. I laid back down on the grass and closed my eyes, letting Jasmine continue with my hair. It was an unusually warm day for the end of September, but I liked it. The sun felt fresh and clean, like it was somehow consoling me, like it knew that I was angry. It was Friday, and I had yet to see Jimmy the entire week.

I was supposed to be working at Sip N Sides, finishing up the financial report for the end of the month, but instead I was here, at the park with the kids. Theo didn't seem to care that I took off and I doubted that Jimmy would ever know. I had gone into Jimmy's every single day this week, partially expecting to see him walk in or to find him talking to Rav in the kitchen, but I never did. Rav tried to encourage me with jokes and scones, I tried to keep my face expressionless. No other employee seemed to be affected by Jimmy's absence, so why should I?

I was mad that it bothered me, angry that I wasn't being professional about it, but the fact that Jimmy just left my life overnight was too much.

He mentioned work, that it was a busy time, but things seemed normal at the bar. Nothing seemed out of place but then again, I had just started there, so maybe this was normal for Jimmy. But it didn't feel normal, something felt off about all of it. It felt strange, but it wasn't my place to say anything or push for more information than Jimmy was willing to give.

"Ramsey?" Jasmine's voice brought me out of my thoughts and back to the field I was laying in.

"Yeah, honey?" I kept my eyes closed as I talked to her. I wasn't ready to embrace the power of the sun yet.

"When are you coming over to our house again? I like it when you come over." She sounded so sweet, so innocent, and she still had no idea that I liked her dad romantically. I had no idea how to answer her, so I went with vague.

"Not sure, sweetie, but it's up to your dad and grandpa too, and I know things are crazy right now for them." Jasmine pulled a few strands of my hair back.

"Daddy had two of his friends over the other night. He told me and Sammy to stay in the backyard, and not to go in the house until his friends were gone. But I had to go to the bathroom, so I went inside. They didn't seem very mean or scary, they just have lots of stuff on their arms like my daddy, but they had long beards and smelled kind of bad."

I laughed. I didn't mean to, but picturing little Jasmine creeping around her house, trying not to smell the two guys, had painted a hilarious picture in my head. Jasmine started laughing with me. Sammy ran over and sat next to us, just to be included in the laughter. I realized that things were going to be fine; they'd be just fine as long as I had laughter in my life.

Once I got home, I turned my phone off. I turned it on once my mom went to sleep; she needed to be my priority and my sole focus when I wasn't working. Tuesday and Wednesday, I actually expected to see a text or call from Jimmy, once I would turn my phone back on. I never did. So, by Friday, I stopped expecting it. I only heard from Laney or on the rare occasion, Theo, if he needed something work-related. It hurt, and I was angry that Jimmy wasn't talking to me. Whatever he was mad about must be pretty bad for him to just drop me the way he did.

There were several nights that I wanted to just drive over to Jimmy's house and confront him. I knew that he came home every night, according to the kids, and that he too seemed sad. Whatever, he can eat a bucket of rusty nails. Except that I didn't want him to get hurt, because I still loved him. That was the worst part of all this; this separation from him only confirmed that I didn't want to keep doing this friendship thing, I wanted to be his, in every possible way. I still had the last voice messages saved on my phone that Jimmy had left that night, and all of his texts. I reread them over and over again, I listened to each message. I felt helpless and deranged, and I knew that I was bordering crazy town, but I didn't know what else to do. I missed him and was mad at him, I wanted to punch him and kiss him all at the same time.

It had been about two hours since I changed into pajamas and crawled into bed on a Friday night. I would be embarrassed, if I hadn't been hoarding drunk calls and texts like a maniac. I tapped the screen of my phone and saw that it was eleven thirty. I couldn't sleep and the warmth in the air from earlier in the day still lingered. I threw the covers off of me, and got out of bed. I pulled on some jeans, a sweatshirt, and tennis shoes. I braided my hair, grabbed my keys and my phone, and walked out of the house. I didn't get in the car, I just walked past it.

The night air was soothing and calm, the full moon above me assisted the streetlights with brightening the dark night.

I pulled my hood up and pushed my hands into the pockets of my sweater while I walked. I didn't plan on it but after a few minutes, I was heading down Jimmy's street. *Crazy town, here I come.* I noticed that Theo's truck was gone, which meant he was probably at his bar, but more importantly, it meant that Jimmy was home. I stood in front of his door for a few minutes, thinking. I could knock, but I'd wake the kids. I pulled out the silver key on my keyring and stuck it into the top lock—it was exhilarating and intoxicating being in crazy town, I might just decide to move here.

I started to turn the key, except it wouldn't turn. It was frozen. I pulled the key out and tried the bottom lock, only to find the same conclusion. I would wonder if it was me, but I had easily unlocked this door only five days ago. I stood there, confused, until it hit me.

Holy shit, did he change the locks? He wouldn't. Would he? I kept telling myself that he wouldn't come into my life, offer me a key as a friend, and then be a coward and change the locks. I tried the key again, in both locks, and still nothing. I stood there, just staring at the door, and the key. There weren't any lights on, and I couldn't hear anything, which at least helped with my mortification.

I turned away from the door as tears started to form in my eyes. In case he was watching, I didn't want him to see this. My eyes stung as the air hit the tears running down my face. Heat was clawing its way up my throat. I very slowly and carefully unhooked his house key from my keyring. Tears were still falling down my face as I carefully turned back around and placed his key on his welcome mat, then I turned and walked away.

Why did I feel like I had been dumped, when all we had between us were a few sparks? Okay, for me, it was like a freaking forest fire, but I was careful. I waited. I pushed for friendship! I was yelling at myself internally, in crazy town. I needed to snap out of it, and soon. I was acting like a lovesick, rejected sixteen-year-old, who was in love with her teacher.

I shrugged my shoulders, as if I could somehow shrug away the pain of rejection or loosen the tension of shame. I felt desperate and utterly pathetic. No, this wasn't me. I wasn't this girl. This sad, and very low moment, was the final nail in the coffin for Jimmy Stenson. His kids, I would die for, his father was still my hero, but my relationship with Jimmy Stenson was over. It wasn't even that he changed the locks, it was that he didn't even have the decency to tell me that he wanted to change the locks. I didn't want that stupid house key to begin with, it wasn't like I asked for it. I walked up the steps to my house and decided that the weekend had just started, and I needed to get rid of this rejection that had started growing, like a poisonous weed inside my gut.

For the record, I ran this whole thing past my best friend, who was smart and educated and made really good choices. She saw my blind spots. So, when I told her what happened with Jimmy, she used some very colorful language to tell me to get my butt out of the house and go find something to do. I decided that I would take up my coworker Jessica on her offer to hang out. It was Saturday afternoon when I called her and with a very high-pitched scream, Jessica gave me several, "Oh My God's," and a few, "Hell Yes's." So, our plan was to hit up a bar called Infinity in Rockford, with a few of her girlfriends, and drink.

I didn't really care about anything she said, except that I didn't have to drink alone, so I said yes to everything else. I wasn't going to drive, so I planned ahead and found an Uber willing to drive out to my house. The guy was really nice, he told me that he would be giving rides all night, but that he wouldn't mind giving me a ride back to Belvidere when I was ready. It was nine at night, I felt old and tired. I wasn't used to being out so late, but Jessica promised that it wasn't even worth leaving the house until nine, that was when the whole town came alive. The Uber pulled up to the curb of the nightclub and I carefully got out after paying my fare. I waved goodbye to Steve, the Uber driver, and headed towards the winding line around the brick building.

I wasn't sure where Jessica was yet, so I pulled out my phone to text her, but I stopped as soon as I heard her squeal. I wasn't sure what else to call it, but Jessica was twenty-one and perky as hell. She squealed and screamed any chance she got. She headed towards me, with two girls flanking her. One was a tall brunette, and the other was blonde, like Jessica, but shorter and curvier. They both looked to be about the same age as Jessica, and they both wore barely enough clothes to cover their lady parts, which made me wildly uncomfortable for them. I waved hello to the girls, and Jessica did a quick introduction of everyone. When she was done, I shifted in my high heels, and pulled Jessica away from her friends. I was nervous and self-conscious, and nearly thirty years old. "Hey, Jess, am I dressed okay?"

Her beady blue eyes about fell out of their sockets. She slapped my arm and I winced, "Girl, you are effing hot! Are you kidding me? Don't downplay your hotness, it is going to be work for us other girls to get any guy's attention with you around. So shut up and follow us, we are so using you to get in tonight."

I looked down at my black dress, it was pretty modest compared to what everyone else seemed to be wearing. It was almost knee-length, and strapless, but I wasn't busty or anything, so I didn't have an issue of my boobs falling out. My hair was straightened, level ten difficulty, and I had on some darker eye makeup. I finished my look off with some red lipstick.

Suddenly, I was feeling a bit better. The four of us walked past everyone, and I kept my head low to avoid attention as we cut everybody in line. Jessica pushed me until I was in front of our little group, facing a large bouncer. I smiled at the bald-headed man full of muscle and tattoos, and thankfully, he smiled back and waved us forward after looking at our IDs. We didn't even have to pay the cover charge. I felt bad for the long line of people waiting to get in, but suddenly my insecurity about being rejected by Jimmy Stenson started to melt away.

We walked into the club, and I couldn't help but feel a little giddy. We all grabbed each other's arms and headed towards the edge of the room. Jessica yelled into our faces, so we could hear her as we huddled around a tall table.

"Okay ladies, the goal is to not pay for a single drink. Let's take this two at a time, so that our odds are better. Lindsey and Jen, you two stick together. Ramsey and I will team up."

I thought I saw Lindsey, the tall brunette, roll her eyes, but I could have been wrong. I took a second to really look around at the place, to get my bearings.

There were neon lights flashing in all different directions. The floors were hardwood, the tall tables along the edge of the room were white, and the bar was white. There was an upper level that had black ropes blocking it off, and a silver sign that said 'VIP' hanging from the drooping center of the ropes. I couldn't see anything above the rope from where I was sitting though, so I let my gaze wander around the room. The bartenders were not only insanely handsome, but they all wore black shirts with white ties. The waitresses, equally as gorgeous, all wore white dresses with one thin black strip down the middle. The music was so loud that I could feel the bass in my bones; it was deafening and alluring. I was excited to try this drink challenge out. Jen and Lindsey headed towards some of the booths in the back, where there were a few groups of guys huddled up. Jessica and I headed towards the bar.

There were already several people standing around the bar, yelling out their drink orders. Jessica spotted two guys alone, and headed their way. I was nervous; I wasn't a flirt, and I didn't mind paying for my own drinks. More than anything, I really didn't want any more rejection. The two guys watched as we approached, and both of them unleashed megawatt smiles. They weren't too terrible looking, so I dug deep and put on a smile for them. Jessica headed for the shorter blond-haired guy, who was sporting a good amount of scruff and had on a nice suit. The other guy was taller, with dark hair and a strong jaw. He wasn't bad-looking, but there weren't any sparks either. His eyes were brown, not lake green. My heart ached a little at that, but I pushed it away. The taller guy leaned in towards me, so I could hear him.

"Hi! I'm Clark."

I didn't try to lean back to see him, I just shouted back, "I'm Ramsey!"

He leaned back to catch my eye. "Funny name. Good thing you're hot."

Oh, hell no.

Was this guy for real?

"Can I buy you a drink, Ramsey?" he yelled, and started gently rubbing circles on my bare arm. If I had to use someone, I guess this chump would do. I nodded and asked for a martini, making sure he requested the good vodka. Once I had my drink in hand, I smiled my thanks and walked away.

Jessica caught on and followed after me with her drink. She grabbed my arm and laughed into it. "I can't believe you did that, Ramsey!"

I kept walking and shouted over my shoulder to her, "Well, he was a jerk, and no one told him to buy me a twelve-dollar drink. I sure as hell didn't say I'd be sticking around."

Jessica laughed again. "Oh my God, you're the best!"

I smiled as I finished my drink. Jessica pulled me towards the dance floor as a new song started. "Come on, let's go fishing for more free drinks on the dance floor."

I followed after her, our arms up high above the crowd as we blended in with all the bodies. Jessica made her way over to a guy who was standing on the side, watching. She pulled his arms around her and they started moving to the music. That same feeling of panic or insecurity started flaring up again. Maybe it was just melancholy because I'd rather be in my sweats watching a princess movie with Jasmine right now. I wasn't spotting any guys that were alone, and I wasn't brave enough to cut into a couple that was already dancing, so I just moved to the music on my own.

Suddenly, there were arms around my waist and someone's nose next to my ear. Their big hands were moving all over my front as they grinded into me from behind. I tried to turn and look, but the hands held me forward.

He rasped in my ear, "When I buy someone a drink, it's usually followed with some gratitude. If you want to act like a bitch, then I'll treat you like one."

Clark the asshat had found me. *Great.*

Clark's hands gripped my sides so hard that I cried out in pain, but with the music, no one could hear me. I tried to find Jessica, but she was facing away from me, and halfway across the dance floor. I couldn't move. Clark's hands pulled my waist back and shoved my butt into his groin, where he held it while he moved. I could feel him getting hard, and I wanted to puke.

I pulled away again, and tried to turn around, but he held me firm and yelled again, "I'm getting my money's worth, baby, whether you like it or not. Just be thankful you walked away after one drink, or else I would be hauling your ass up to one of those rooms in the VIP area right now." Then he licked my ear, and tears started to burn at the edges of my eyes.

I didn't know what to do. His grip was anchored at my waist, which left my torso freer to move, so I leaned forward as much as I could and threw my head back as hard as I could, right into Clark's nose. He let go of me instantly, which was the in that I needed. My head hurt, but I'd suffered worse on the soccer field. I turned my body quickly and kneed Clark in the groin, just in case he had any thoughts about grabbing me again. I was breathing heavily, while I slowly backed away from him. Clark's nose was bleeding everywhere, and he was pitched forward, holding onto his junk. There was a huge hole where we had been, and around it, there were several couples huddled together, watching.

I looked up and noticed a few bouncers on their way over. I scanned the room for a brief second before my eyes went towards the VIP area, my mind going back to what Clark said about there being rooms in this club to take women to. Was it possible for guys like Clark to drag girls up to a private room and rape them? My heart was in my throat at that thought, and I vowed to make sure that was looked into. As I scanned the VIP area for those rooms, my eyes caught on a familiar face.

Jimmy was standing there in the VIP area, watching me with a murderous look.

He was near a booth that had a few guys, who each had a woman on their lap. A few seconds passed between us before a leggy blonde in a tiny silver dress walk forward and laid her hand on Jimmy's chest to pull him back towards the booth. I turned away and pushed through the crowd. I knew the police would be called and that I would have to deal with that, but I had to get out of there. First, I needed a mirror and a second to compose myself. Jimmy couldn't see me fall apart; I *wouldn't* let him see me fall apart. Not after he just witnessed me head-butting some guy, and not after I witnessed him being here with someone else after ignoring me for an entire week.

THIRTY-ONE

JIMMY

I HAD SLOWLY BEEN LOSING it all week. I'd check my phone and see that Ramsey hadn't texted and every single time, I'd breathe in relief. If she texted me, Davis would see it. I missed her, but I didn't want her to reach out. I'd drive by the restaurant and see her car, and my stomach would pitch. I'd drive by her street in my dad's truck, just to see that she was home. I was starting to crack. The fissure was evident for certain today.

I walked into the kitchen to talk to Rav about the menu for the weekend. Just as I got close to him, I smelled Ramsey's perfume, and all my buried anger came to the surface in an instant, and I lost my temper. I stalked towards Rav until I was in his face, and grabbed a fistful of his shirt.

"Why the hell do you smell like Ramsey?" I snapped at him. I had no idea what was happening to me, but jealousy was running the show and it wanted blood.

Rav put up his hands in surrender, and then gently took my hands off his shirt. He took two big steps back. My brain registered that Rav was built like a dump truck and could easily hurt me if he wanted to. Even as I stood there, not sure what I was even doing, but ready for a fight, I saw Rav soften.

His big eyebrows drew down, his shoulders slumped, and he looked worried. Rav would never hurt me, he was too good of a friend for that. *Shit.* What was I doing? I stepped back and turned away from him, still breathing hard and fighting for control.

Silence surrounded us and after a few seconds I heard him say, "Jimmy, calm down, man."

He waited for me to take a few breaths before continuing. I turned towards him and hated myself for the dark expression on his face and the fear in his eyes. He wasn't afraid of me, he was afraid of what I would do to myself. What damage I could do to my reputation, to our friendship, how much I'd hate myself for it. I looked down and focused on who was in front of me—my friend, someone I would never hurt. Rav must have seen the change in my face because he chose that moment to continue.

"She was really sad today, so I baked her those scones that she loves. I walked into the office right as Jessica was testing some of Ramsey's perfume out or whatever. The two of them were talking and Jessica said she wanted to try some on. Anyway, the stupid shit hit me right as I walked through the door."

I looked back down at the floor, shame stinging my face. I pulled my hand through my hair and let the air out of my lungs.

"I'm sorry, Rav, I just…" I trailed off, not sure how to even explain this. Rav didn't even know that there was something going on between Ramsey and me, but after this, it probably wouldn't take much work to know there was.

"I just… it's hard to be away from her right now, and she thinks that I hate her," I croaked in a low voice.

Rav crossed his arms over his chest, his bald head shining under the lights. There was no one else in the kitchen; the three other kitchen staff were in a different area. Which was good, I didn't need rumors to start that I was manhandling my employees.

"She said you were mad at her, that you showed up at her house drunk, then disappeared, then…nothing… Is that what happened?" Rav asked, his eyebrows drawn together, and his jaw was tight. He was pissed and I didn't blame him. I knew that he and Ramsey were friends, and he had his own relationship with her.

"It's complicated, but yes. She lied to me about something or didn't tell me the entire truth about it. I freaked out because it brought back some fears I have about Lisa, or whatever." I waved my hand, trying to brush off the topic. I didn't want to dig up my entire life right now and Rav didn't need to know every detail. "Anyway, I haven't even been able to talk to her about any of it yet," I explained in a rush, trying to get it all out. Rav let go of his arms and turned away from me, grabbing a white rag, and started wiping down the counters.

After a few swipes, he looked back over at me from over his shoulder, and replied, "Well, that sucks, Jimmy. A little advice, my man? Find some way to explain things to her before it's too late."

He turned his head back around and kept wiping. I stared at the floor, letting his words sink in. I knew he was right, but I didn't know how to go to her without putting her on Davis' radar. I didn't want to explain any of this to her. She would be disappointed in me and may even consider not giving us a shot if she knew that I had taken up a job for the Brass. No, I just needed to let the dust settle and trust that Ramsey would still be there when it was all done.

THAT NIGHT, I HAD TURNED DOWN THE TWO MC IDIOTS AND their offer to "go out."

Bored, they abandoned me, and went somewhere else while I stayed home. At least, I hoped that's what they did. I had no idea where they stayed or went; that was a part of the "watching me," game they played. Sometimes they would disappear, and I wouldn't see them for an entire day, other times they would show up in front of my house at five in the morning, acting like they had been there all night, sending the very clear and direct message that they were always watching me. Which explained my near heart attack when Ramsey came by that night.

I had a security camera set up to go off if my perimeter was breached. I was on my laptop in bed, trying to stay distracted with work, when the footage came up and I saw her hooded body walking up to my front door. My heart was in my throat in an instant.

I grabbed the computer and rushed downstairs, trying not to make a sound. Thankfully, the computer screen was dark and wasn't giving off any glow. She was so close to me. All I had to do was open the door, pull her inside, hug her and kiss her, and explain why I had been so distant.

At this point, my anger over the whole lie was completely gone. I just missed the hell out of her and wanted her back in my life. I didn't open the door, though. It killed me, and when I heard her try to use her key, I actually started choking up. I knew how confused she would be, and how much it would devastate her. I had to do it, though, and I just needed a moment to explain myself, but right then, Jones or Adams might be watching, and it would be a lot easier to explain away a tweaker on meth, than it would explaining the woman I loved, coming in at midnight. No, she'd be leverage delivered to them on a silver platter. Who knew what they might do to her?

So, I stood there, with my back against the door, shattering and breaking, while the woman that I was in love with walked away, heartbroken and hurt. I slid down to the floor, fighting tears, fighting anger, and rage; all the emotions rolling through me were so intense. I was terrified of losing Ramsey, but I couldn't bear to have her mixed up in this shit. I kept sitting against the door, on the floor, until I fell asleep.

The next morning, I woke up to someone's silhouette blocking the sun. I heard a loud, "Get up, son."

"What's going on, Dad?" Confusion tainted my words and probably my face. It had to be early, and he never woke up before ten after a late shift.

"What's going on is my son fell asleep in front of the door, like a damn dog. What in the hell is going on with you?"

I still hadn't come clean with him. Dad just thought I was avoiding Ramsey because of the lie she told about Sip N Sides. He didn't know that I was working with the Brass again. I started to stand up, slowly, feeling every awkward moment from the night before in my muscles and joints.

"Sorry, Dad. There was someone on our property last night, and I was trying to make sure they left. I must've fallen asleep while I was waiting."

He looked down at me with his weathered face, in his checkered pajama pants, and sighed.

"Who was it? Did they try to break in?" he asked, alarmed. *Shit.*

"No, just some teenagers walking, but one of them walked in our grass by the curb, so it tripped the alarm," I explained while keeping a straight face, so he wouldn't sense my lie. He waited a second, watching me with a curious look on his face. His eyes drilled into me until he finally gave up and turned away while yelling over his shoulder. "Make your kids break-fast, and son, I think you should get out of the house tonight, go do something with your friends. You need some fresh perspective."

I stood, trying to rub circles into my back and ease out the discomfort. "Okay," was all I could manage as a reply. I didn't want to leave, but I was just going crazy by staying home and doing weird things, like sleeping in front of the door because it was the closest thing that Ramsey had been near.

I decided that I would take the two idiots out, and away from Belvidere, away from Ramsey, and get some of that fresh perspective.

I SHOULD HAVE KNOWN THAT BY OFFERING TO TAKE JONES AND Adams to one of the nicest clubs in Rockford, that they would act like total assholes and demand the entire VIP treatment; including the women. Where they found these ridiculous women, I didn't know, but they all looked fake and plastic. They had "one" for me too. A tall blonde with drawn-on eyebrows, a fake tan, and low self-respect, based on the way she was pawing at me with absolutely no returned interest or given any physical encouragement. I was miserable, and while all the other women sat on the men's laps, poor Christy was left sitting next to me. I wouldn't pay her any attention and when she tried to rub my thigh, I pushed her hand away. I ignored the group's laughter and conversation, since I had no interest in being a part of it. Instead, I busied myself with watching the lower floor.

After a while, I caught sight of a tall woman with straight hair that was Ramsey's color, in a black dress. She reminded me so much of Ramsey that it hurt. I followed her with my eyes all the way to the bar, and watched her as she whispered in some guy's ear. I tried to watch other people and get my mind off of Ramsey and how much that woman looked like her, but my eyes kept finding her. It wasn't until she got her drink and she stalked off with a shorter blonde that I noticed the woman's face.

Ramsey. No, it couldn't be her. My mind was just playing tricks on me. Still, I stood up, walked away from the booth, and tried to follow her through the crowd with my eyes. What if it was her? What was she doing here? Why was she talking to that guy? Emotions were swirling through me as I locked my gaze onto the back of the woman's head and tried to watch her as she joined the other people dancing. I lost her in the crowd a few times, but then the guy from the bar stalked forward and stopped in the middle, putting his arms around someone.

No. This wasn't happening, he wasn't dancing with her. The crowd shifted and moved, I did too, so I had a better view. I could see that he had a hold of her by the hips, and that dead and buried anger was resurrecting itself again. Heat hit my face. I could feel it moving to the tips of my ears. I looked down, I couldn't watch someone who might be Ramsey dance with some guy who was pulling her ass into his crotch. There wasn't enough willpower on the planet that would allow me to.

I watched the floor for a few moments, swallowing the lump that had lodged itself there. I glanced back up, heat still stinging my face, I shoved my hands into my pockets, so that I wouldn't use them to shove forward and down to her. I noticed she kept trying to look back, and I wished I could see her face so badly. The guy was too close to her. I realized that if that really was Ramsey, she would never let a stranger hold her like that, unless she was wasted, or he wasn't a stranger. I didn't have a chance to draw a full conclusion on that thought, because suddenly the woman threw her head back and hit the guy's nose. Blood was everywhere and an instant later, she turned to knee him in the balls.

Oh shit.

I could see her, perfectly, and my breath caught. It was Ramsey, it was really her. Every single bone in my body, every drop of blood running in my veins, screamed at me to rush down there and finish what Ramsey had started, but then she saw me. I wanted to murder that guy, so I could only imagine what my face reflected. Christy chose that moment to walk up and put her fake manicured hand on my chest, like she fucking knew me, and tried to pull me back to the booth. I couldn't see Ramsey's face very well, with the lights and the darkness, but from where I stood, I could make out that she looked pissed. Then she was gone, pushing her way towards the back part of the club where the restrooms were. I couldn't stand it anymore. I turned to the guys.

"Hey I need to go see what all the commotion is down there. I see one of my employee's talking to the bouncer, I'll be right back."

Jessica was talking to a bouncer, so I wasn't lying, but I walked past her and headed for where Ramsey disappeared to. The hallway was darker, with just a few lights in the ceiling. This was a fancier club, so they had the nice pampering rooms with sofas, and couches in each restroom before the actual stalls and sinks. I waited for the hall to clear and headed into the women's restroom. Thankfully, it was empty, which was an oddity for a club this size, but maybe it was just a divine moment from the big guy upstairs. I didn't care, I just cared that Ramsey was somewhere in there. I walked forward on the hardwood floors, past the white couches, and floor to ceiling mirrors, towards one of the private stalls. I knocked and heard sniffling. I waited and knocked again.

Then I heard Ramsey say, "Jessica, I just need a second, okay?" I stayed quiet, then I knocked again. I heard the door handle move, then Ramsey say with exasperation, "Look, I just need a second... Can—" She opened the door a crack, and I pushed my way in.

I shut the door quickly behind me and locked it. The private stall was a complete shut in room with a toilet and sink. It was lined with white brick and wood floors, and floor to ceiling mirrors that Ramsey had just walked back up against.

She crossed her arms, her face was red, and her eyebrows shot up in surprise. Once she seemed to accept that it was, in fact, me standing in front of her , she looked down at the ground. I kept staring at her. I wanted her focus on me, selfishly.

I took two steps forward and Ramsey looked up, expressionless. I took a few smaller steps towards her, until I was directly in front of her. I could hear her breathing, see her chest rising and falling. She was looking at my chin, not my eyes. I carefully raised my hands until they were almost touching the sides of her face and kept them there. I knew if I touched her, it would be too much.

"Did he hurt you?" I whispered, as I let my hands fall a fraction closer to her face. She looked up at me, latching onto my eyes, and she shifted, taking some of the weight off her feet.

"Yes…" She took a small breath and closed her eyes. Then, getting some of her confidence back, she continued, "But it was nothing compared to what you're doing to me."

That knocked the air out of my chest. I took a step back, because her words physically hurt me. "Ramsey, I am not trying to hurt you," I choked out. Tears started to fall from her eyes, and she looked away,

"That's why you've ignored me all week? Why you disappeared Sunday night after drunk texting and calling me, and why you were upstairs with some blonde? Why you changed your locks! You aren't trying to hurt me?" She was pointing at her chest and waving her hand between us. I ran my hand over my face.

"Ramsey there is so much going on, and I wish I could tell you…"

Ramsey took a step forward, then cut me off by yelling, "Then tell me, Jimmy!"

Ramsey's face was red and blotchy, and she had a huge red

mark on her forehead. I wanted to touch it, feel her face, touch her so that I knew she was still here with me.

I took another step back and pleaded with her. "Look, I want to, and I would. I was hurt Sunday because I finally found out what is going on with Sip N Sides. It hurt that you lied to me, hurt that you kept it from me, it felt like—" My voice broke and I trailed off, realizing how much I didn't want to have this conversation in the bathroom of a club, but Ramsey finished for me.

"Like when Lisa left?"

I stared at her and nodded my head. "I spiraled out of control with all these fears about my feelings for you, and the possibility of you hurting me like she did, and I made some poor decisions because of it."

Ramsey's head drew back quickly, as though she'd been slapped. She took a step closer to the wall, retreating from me. I stepped forward, reaching for her.

"No, I didn't...nothing happened with anyone. That blonde up there is with the guys I'm with, not me."

Ramsey rolled her eyes. "Yeah, she really looked like she was with the other guys when she grabbed your chest, like she owned you."

I pulled at my hair. "Ramsey, I want you to believe me. I am doing something I can't bring you into, but I am not trying to get with other women right now. You're the only one I want, and I can't even have you!

"You want friendship, Ramsey? Then let's be friends, be my friend through this. I need support, I need understanding, I need you to trust that I want you and that I am not shutting you out!" I yelled at her.

She flinched and leaned back. Tears were still streaming down her face, and she was quiet, we both were. I took in her looks for a second, her hair was glossy and straight, and absolutely gorgeous. I had never seen it this straight before, and my fingers itched to run through it to find her braid. She was watching me intently as she took a few shuffled steps closer.

"You're right, Jimmy. I'm sorry, I haven't been your friend, and that is all I asked from you for six weeks. I haven't been fair, but part of being friends is opening up to each other, trusting each other with burdens, and that isn't something you have done with me. I don't know what you are into, but it doesn't take a genius to figure out that it's probably related to something you were associated with in the past. I want to be your friend. When you are ready to be mine, let me know..." she finished firmly, like that was it. I was about to speak up and say something when a loud knock sounded at the door.

"Ramsey, are you in there? Open up, girl, are you okay?!" It was Jessica, and her timing was horrible.

Ramsey walked past me, not even hugging me, looking at me, or anything. She unlocked the door and slipped out.

I waited a second, then left as well, ignoring the weird looks from the women lounging on couches. I headed back towards the VIP area, everything in the club had gone back to normal. My anger had subsided now that I knew Ramsey was okay, but my gut was in a hard knot. I hated how we left things, that she didn't think I was being a friend to her. I guess she was right, but it wasn't that simple. She would decide that she couldn't have anything real with me if she knew I went back to the vomit that used to be my life; I'd lose her for sure. I was on the steps towards the upper floor of the VIP area when I felt my phone vibrate in my pocket. I looked down and noticed a text from Jackson.

Meat is ready for pick up.

Finally, some good news. This would bring me one step closer to being finished with all this bullshit, so that I could start putting things back together with Ramsey.

THIRTY-TWO

I<small>T WAS</small> T<small>UESDAY</small> <small>AFTERNOON</small>, and I was bored. The events from the weekend had caught up to me on Sunday, and I ended up sleeping most of the day. I wanted to shut my mind off, and not process or think about what Jimmy had said in the club. Although, hearing him say that he wanted me, and seeing the look on his face, I knew he wasn't lying.

I was just struggling with the part that he *was* lying about. The part he wouldn't share with me, the part he was purposely leaving me out of. That part sucked. I tried to take a step back and really be his friend. I tried texting him and got no response, I tried calling him and got no answer.

So, I let it go and just let him work through whatever the hell it was that he was doing. So now, it was Tuesday, and I was at work, and there was hardly anyone here. It was October, and the air was cold, but the city was beautiful. I had wrapped myself into a large necked sweater with skinny jeans and tall boots. My hair was up in a ponytail with small braids trailing down the length of it. I didn't put much effort into getting dressed these days because I knew that I wouldn't see Jimmy. I realized that I shouldn't be putting forth effort for Jimmy or any other man, I should just be me and be happy. Always, easier said than done, though.

I was going over the facts that Jimmy had given me again, in my head for the billionth time. Telling myself that he did want me, and that there wasn't anyone else until I completely believed him. It made me feel better, like I was on his side again. I was just about to pack things up and head to Sip N Sides, when I got a knock on the office door. I yelled for whoever it was to come in.

I was stunned when a woman with white-blonde hair poked her head in a second later. She was thin and lean, and taller than me. She had a huge smile with gorgeous white teeth, her hair was long and curled down her back, and she wore a tight white t-shirt that left little to the imagination. She had black leather pants on that would probably need to be surgically removed in order to get them off, and the cutest ankle boots that I'd ever seen. I wanted to grow up to be this woman, she was that beautiful and well put together. She smiled at me, then looked around the office.

"Uh… can I help you with something?" I asked, while smoothing down my sweater and jeans.

The woman crossed her arms, turned her head to the door, and then looked back at me. "I'm looking for Jimmy."

I looked down at the desk, trying to school my features, because of course this gorgeous woman was looking for him. "He's not in the office today, can I leave a message for him?"

She smiled and grabbed the door handle as if she was about to leave. "Yeah, could you tell him that his wife stopped by? He's been calling me nonstop for weeks. Now it's just a matter of us getting in the same place at the same time, do you know what I mean?"

She laughed like this whole thing was hilarious and not tearing my heart into pieces. Then she flipped her hair over her shoulder, gave me one last smile, and headed out the door as she said over her shoulder, "Thanks."

I sat down, because my damn legs wouldn't hold me anymore. What the hell had just happened? His wife?

I was going to kill him.

He was dead.

MY MIND WAS TRAVELING A BILLION MILES A MINUTE. OF course he was still married to that woman, she was a freaking model. Why wouldn't he stay married to her? Insecurity and anger gripped my heart. I wanted to puke, run away, and curl up into a ball at the same time.

I couldn't believe that he would lie to me like that. I gathered my laptop and my purse, and started for the door. Tears were threatening to fall, but I wouldn't let them. I walked out the front door and climbed into my car and started to drive. I had no music, nothing, just the silence and the sound of my heart shattering into a million pieces. I may be able to make excuses in my head for what Jimmy was doing, and there was a lot I would put up with from men but being married wasn't one of them. I would not, and could not, pretend to be Mrs. Jimmy Stenson when there was already one out there somewhere. How could he stay married to her when she left them? My mind was reeling so badly, I didn't even notice that I had bypassed Sip N Sides. Instead, I drove straight to the duck park, where a little pond sat, with several ducks waddling around it. I parked my car in front of the water and watched the ducks move around. I watched and stared, not crying, not anything, until it was too dark to see the water. Finally, I turned the car back on and drove home.

I walked into the house and found my mom working on some soup in the kitchen. She was in high spirits, and I felt like a jerk for being in such a crappy mood.

"My sweet daughter, you're home! Good, I am making some soup, and it's nearly ready," she said in her beautiful Cambodian accent, that was still strong after almost thirty years of living here.

I smiled at her as she grabbed my face in between her small hands and kissed my cheek. "Okay, Mom, let me go shower really quick, and I will be right out."

She released me, and I padded off to my room. I stripped out of my clothes and stepped into the steaming hot shower. I wanted to spend a fun evening with my mom. I didn't want to cry or mope, so I didn't let a single tear fall in the shower, I would wait. I dressed into warm sweats, a sports bra, and a hoodie. When I walked out, I fully planned to put the day behind me. As final as it felt to be done with Jimmy and as much as it hurt, I wouldn't allow it to impact my time with my mom.

My smile was almost complete as I headed back into the kitchen. I heard the soup bubbling and the house smelled good, so I thought I would start there. "Mom, the soup smells delici—"

I stopped mid-sentence because my mother was lying on the floor of the kitchen. She was on her side and her arms were splayed out in front of her. Everything moved in slow motion; it was like one of those bad dreams where you know that you need to run fast to escape danger, but your legs wouldn't move. I tried to run to her side but felt like my feet were in cement. I started feeling for a pulse, while I grabbed my cell from the counter and dialed 911.

I heard the operator ask, "911, what's your emergency?"

I couldn't breathe, couldn't get the words out fast enough. "My mother fell, she's sick, I need help." My words were choppy and rushed.

"Okay, ma'am, a unit is on their way. I need you to tell me your address."

"2244 Northeast Cherry Loop, Belvidere," I choked out through tears, "okay, ma'am, can you tell me if your mom is breathing, can you feel a pulse?"

"I don't..." I cried and tried again. "I don't know if she is breathing, but she has a pulse. How do I know if she's breathing?!" I practically yelled at the woman, because I hadn't even thought of that, and my brain wasn't working at the moment.

"It's okay, ma'am, just watch her chest and see if it's moving."

I watched her chest, and laid my head on it, feeling her warmth against my cold, tear-stained face. "Yes, she's breathing," I whispered into the phone.

"Okay, that's good. Now, is she bleeding anywhere? Does she have any contusions, or bruising?"

I was getting frustrated. I just wanted to be alone with my mom before the paramedics got to our house, but this lady kept asking questions.

"No, I don't see any bleeding, no bruising either."

"Okay, that's really good."

"Excuse me, can I get off the phone now? Please? I just want to be with my mom and hold her with both hands until they get here," I sobbed.

"No, ma'am, I'm sorry, I need to stay on the phone with you, and I need you to leave the body exactly where it is."

The words, "the body" ran through my head. I flipped the words over and over in my mind. She was just a body, she was going to leave me, and I would have no one. Just then, a swift knock came on the door, followed by someone opening it, and two paramedics, dressed in navy blue uniforms, walked through my door and rushed over to my mother.

I moved away so they could access her. They touched, poked, and prodded her body, then one of them ran out and grabbed a long, stiff board and started loading my mother onto it. They weren't talking to me.

"Can I ride with her?" I asked one of them, I wasn't even sure which one.

The female with brown stiff hair responded, "Of course."

I double-checked that the stove was off, grabbed my purse, and followed them out the door. I climbed into the ambulance after them, they shut us in, and we traveled to the hospital. "Does she have any complications that we need to know about? Any medications?" the male paramedic asked, while attending to my mother.

"She has liver cancer." I swiped at my eyes and rattled off the meds that I knew she was on.

"Anything else we should know?" The paramedics brown eyes bore into mine. I blinked and tried to think. I could forget something that could save her life or end it. I felt foggy and muddled. This wasn't really happening, was it? I felt more tears fall and shook my head.

The hospital in Belvidere was small and old. I stared at the white tiles in the small room they'd given her in the ER. Nurse after nurse came in, did tests, took blood, and left. I paced the room, held my mom's hand, but she never woke up.

After a few hours, the doctor came in. He had white hair and wore blue medical scrubs with a name tag that said Dr. Fry.

"Your mother's prognosis will require a more advanced team to evaluate her. We are moving her to Rockford via helicopter. You won't be able to go with her on the transport, unfortunately, but I will give you all the info that you'll need to see her once you get to Rockford yourself."

Dr. Fry gave me a piece of paper, letting me know the details of her transfer and location and turned to leave. At least he didn't apologize. Although, some apology for why it took them hours to figure out that she needed transported would have been nice. I walked out of the ER and towards the main entrance of the hospital and checked the time. It was nearly midnight, and I had no way to get back home to grab my car.

I didn't know who to call, except for Theo. I hated that the wife thing was stopping me from wanting to call him. But the longer I waited, the longer my mom was alone. So, I pulled out my phone and punched in Theo's information.

It rang a few times, and then I heard a scratchy, "Hello?"

I swallowed any pride that I might have left. "Theo? I need you to come pick me up, it's an emergency."

Silence, then some shuffling, "Where are you?"

"The hospital in Belvidere. I just need a ride to my house, please, so that I can get my car."

He was quiet again, but I heard keys jingling, and a muffled, "Be back soon, it's an emergency" to someone. My throat closed up. That was probably Jimmy. Then I heard, "What's going on?" muffled in the background, before Theo came back on.

"I'll be right there." Then the call ended.

I waited exactly eight minutes for Theo. His dark green pickup pulled up to the covered pick up and drop off area in front of the hospital. I watched through the window inside the hospital, and as soon as he came to a complete stop, I hurried outside and jumped into his truck. He was in one of his signature flannel shirts and checkered pajama pants, his hair all messy. Clearly, I had just woke him up. As soon as I got in, his eyes were trained on me, and his face was soft with concern.

I looked over at him, swallowed the lump that was lodged in my throat, and said, "Thanks for this, Theo. I didn't know who else to call."

He gave me a soft smile, then turned his eyes towards the road. He shifted into gear and pulled the truck forward, softly grumbling, "No problem, you can always call me."

Then he was quiet. I knew I owed him an explanation, I just couldn't bring myself to say any words. I watched out the window as street lights lit up our little city. My mind wandered to Chicago, and whether or not I'd move back there, since my plan to marry Jimmy had come to an abrupt stop. I slammed my eyes shut, but kept my body positioned towards the door.

Soon we were on my street, and I still hadn't said anything. As we were nearing my house, I saw Theo periodically looking over at me. He cleared his throat and asked, "Your Mama okay?"

I looked out the window, and quietly responded, "No. She's being flown to Rockford." Once he pulled in behind my car, he put his truck in park, and unbuckled his seat belt. I turned to look at him.

"Thanks again, Theo. Sorry for how late it is."

He waved his hand and grunted. "Stop it, you're family to me, so don't worry about it." The reminder of Jimmy's wife slammed into me with force, again.

"Right…" I quietly responded, because there was already another girl out there who called Theo family by way of a father-in-law. I opened the truck and slipped out. I heard Theo's door open too, and he walked around until he was in front of me, then he pulled me into a tight hug. I tried to keep it together, but I hated being alone. I had no dad, no siblings, no one to help shoulder this burden with me, and I hated it.

I heard Theo whisper into my ear as he squeezed me, "It's going to be okay, sweet girl, it's going to be okay."

I nodded into his shoulder that I heard him and believed him, even though I had a bad feeling about this one. I had a feeling that my mom was leaving me, and I would be totally and completely alone. I pulled away from his shoulder and started to walk towards the house, and decided I better cover my bases. "Hey, Theo?"

He looked up at me through his gray lashes. "Yeah?"

"Know how I omitted information about your financial status from Jimmy?"

He shifted his stance a little and faced me more fully. "Yeah," he drew out.

"Well, you owe me one, and I'd like to collect."

He let out a light chuckle and looked at the ground. "Okay, darlin', what do you want?"

I stood tall and spoke clearly. "Don't mention this to Jimmy."

Theo just stood there for a second, hands on his hips. It was cold outside, I only had my hoodie, and was starting to shiver, so I didn't wait for him to respond. I turned around and headed inside. A minute later, I heard Theo's truck leaving.

Once I was inside, I focused on getting out of there.

I went into Mom's room and stared. Her room was exactly how it always was; a double bed with a dark blue comforter with white lilies on it. Very nineties, but she never cared. She had two white side tables with big, obnoxious lamps that you might find inside of a cheap motel. She had a long dresser with a full vanity mirror along the opposite wall of her bed. The room smelled like her. I reminded myself that she wasn't gone yet and pulled myself together; at least enough to pack her a bag.

The trip to Rockford was uneventful; a nearly empty highway, and a silent car. I couldn't bring myself to allow a soundtrack to accompany this part of my life. Not with losing Jimmy and possibly losing my mom. I'd take silence over being reminded of this horrible, sickly feeling in my gut.

The hospital in Rockford was much larger, with several more stories to it, and an entire parking garage dedicated to its patrons. I found an open spot on the second floor and headed inside.

I walked onto the bleached white floor and found my way to the reception desk and inquired about my mom. A petite woman in her late fifties checked her computer, then with a sympathetic look, told me that they had put her into the ICU, but wouldn't reveal why. At least she was helpful enough to call ahead and let them know I was coming, so they could buzz me in.

I made my way to the elevator and punched in the fifth floor, then waited. Everything seemed to move in slow motion when there was a loved one hanging in the balance: the motions of the elevator seemed to take longer, people walked slower, phone calls rang longer. It all just took longer. It felt like forever for the doors to open, but once they did, I was surprised at how empty and eerie the hospital was.

A carpeted waiting room welcomed me, there were large floor to ceiling windows with large green plants near them. Televisions were propped up in the corners of the rooms and there was a kid area, comfortable couches, snack machines, and a coffee bar. I was the only one there. I walked further into the room until I saw a small alcove with a large door. It had a button panel on the outside and a white telephone on the wall next to it, with a sign that read, "Lift receiver to check in." I did as the sign said, and as soon as I lifted the receiver, it rang three times, and then was answered by a female. I told her my name and who I was here to see, then I heard the door click.

I walked past three rooms, until I found the white board that read, 'Bennington, Carla Room 8, F5, 1 Dennis.'

I gently pulled the curtain aside and walked into the room. Mom was hooked up to several monitors, she had an IV tube in her arm, and a white monitor band around her head. She was alive, that was all that mattered. We could face whatever it was, if she just kept breathing. That's what I told myself, over and over again, as I waited for someone to come in and tell me what was happening to her.

It took about five minutes before a blonde-haired nurse came in. She pulled Mom's chart up from the bottom of her bed, scanned it, and moved over to one of the computers and started typing. She didn't even acknowledge me. I stood up and cleared my throat, hoping that would do it. She looked over at me and smiled. "Hey there, I'm Kate."

I smiled and walked over to shake her hand. "Ramsey, I'm her daughter," I said, as I gestured towards Mom. Kate smiled and looked back towards her computer,

"I'm sure you have lots of questions. I will answer what I can for you, but some things may have to wait for the doctor."

"Okay, when will he or she be here?"

She stopped typing and instead, stood near my mom to take her pulse with her fingers while watching her wristwatch.

After a minute, she responded, "Tomorrow morning, around eight. You should pull that couch out all the way and make yourself comfortable."

I guess so, since nothing was going to happen tonight.

I looked around the room, and all I could feel was sleep tugging at my eyes to give in.

I made the couch bed as best as I could, piled the pillow into a big fat mound and laid down, pulling the covers up and over my head, and prayed for sleep.

THIRTY-THREE

JIMMY

I⊤ WAS Thursday and things were looking up. When Davis said he had found my whore of an ex-wife, he wasn't exaggerating. I had paid a Private Investigator to look into her whereabouts when I tried to serve her with divorce papers six months after she left, and nothing turned up. This last year, I reached out to a different firm who had a slightly bigger pool of connections, that might have slightly better luck at finding her. Meaning, they were MC and had connections to the Brass through a few sorted affiliations.

I didn't want it to leak back to Davis, but I wasn't surprised that it did. I guess he took it upon himself to negotiate with Lisa to physically take this meeting with me. I received a text Tuesday morning from an unknown number, telling me when and where to meet her. I knew better than to question who'd set it up or waste my time getting upset over Davis meddling in my affairs. Because when you're a part of the chapter, your business is Davis' business.

I was about to walk into a lunch meeting and see, for the first time in five years, the woman who'd abandoned us. I wasn't nervous, I wasn't even angry, I was just ready to put this part of my life behind me. Jackson walked next to me. Since he and Rav were the only two people who knew about my meeting with Lisa, I decided I would rather have my pit bull friend versus my terrier. Rav was most definitely a terrier when it came to women; he was soft and sweet. Regardless of what they had done in the past, he had a soft spot for the ladies.

Jackson wore a crisp, black suit, similar to mine, and we walked the few porcelain steps of the Hotel Grand, down in midtown Rockford. It was a nice place, we were scheduled to meet in their restaurant, and my lawyer would be coming in about fifteen minutes.

I wanted to watch the look on Lisa's face when Rake Haverford walked through those doors. Rake was someone she had once had a fling with, then dumped for me. He was never in the chapter, just a hopeful, but he cleaned his life up and became a lawyer. I looked him up and hired him for all my business dealings, and now personal things. We shared a mutual dislike for Lisa, and a mutual desire to stay on the straight and narrow.

Jackson looked over at me as we stepped into the lobby, his eyebrows raised, likely looking for confirmation that I was ready for this. I nodded my head at him in reply. We veered past the check-in desk and headed into the restaurant. There was a large piano in the corner, being played lightly, and a large water fountain off to the side. I gazed at the several tables set up with white cloth and flowers, and spotted Lisa in the middle of the room.

Her blonde hair was over-styled and probably stiff as hell from hairspray. I wasn't sure what I would feel if I saw her again, but I was surprised at the complete indifference I felt towards her. Almost like she was a complete stranger.

We got closer, and when she saw me, she stood up and smiled, like she was some lovestruck idiot who'd just won the dating lottery. Was she fucking serious? She leaned in for a hug, and I almost laughed. I walked past her, and sat down, leaving her in the lurch, just like she had done to me. I unbuttoned my jacket and took the seat across from her.

She had no one with her, just her glossy, over-styled hair, thick makeup, and designer clothes to keep her company. Jackson took the seat directly to my left, and she looked over at him and smiled again. It was a "come over here and kiss me" smile, if I had ever seen one, and she was using it on both of us. My guess was, she was eager to bag one of us, now that we both had made ourselves some money.

Lisa had been raised in the Brass; she'd seen the ugly side of having a father in the club business and the lonely side of having a mother who'd married someone in the club business. Before we had the kids, she was happy about my involvement with the chapter, felt I owed it to them. But the more I turned away good-paying, illegal jobs, the more she withdrew from me. Lisa needed someone who could financially keep her comfortable, not like her daddy, who could barely rub two pennies together. Lisa grew up broke, ignored, and alone. I thought marrying her and giving her a family would be enough, but I think, deep down, money was the only safety net she'd trust.

"Hey, Jimmy, baby, it's good to see you." She sounded like she was out of breath.

Baby? So, this was how it was going to be.

"Lisa, I'm glad you finally got my calls, and reached out. We have a lot to discuss."

She moved around in her seat, most likely trying to adjust her cleavage to look more appealing. *Fat chance, honey.*

"Well, I thought your assistant would have told you that I came by the office on Tuesday. She said she would leave you a message, didn't you get it?"

My assistant…? What the hell? Did she mean Ramsey? She had seen Ramsey?

I took a drink from the glass of water that was already filled up in front of me, then exhaled while trying to rein in the anger that was bubbling up inside my chest. "What exactly was the message you left with my assistant?"

She leaned forward, again with the attempts of cleavage. She was trying so hard.

"I knew that girl wouldn't give you the message, she looked so incapable." Lisa let out an exaggerated sigh. "I told her to tell you that your wife was looking for you, that you had been trying to contact me for weeks, and I was trying to track you down. I told her to tell you to call me. But then I didn't hear from you until yesterday evening."

Wife? My wife...... My fucking wife!? *What had she done?* I lowered my head into my hands and tried to breathe. Jackson took the hint and started talking.

"Lisa, you aren't his fucking wife, why would you say that?"

I couldn't see her face, but I heard a little scoffing sound. "I am his wife. I never signed any divorce papers."

She finished with a happy little sound as she gulped the wine in front of her. What the hell was going on? I looked up, and Jackson was smiling. I would be too if I wasn't thinking about Ramsey right now. This was such a mess.

I regarded my ex-wife, "I sent you divorce papers six months after you left us. You couldn't be found. I tried to get in touch with you for two years, Lisa. The judge finally granted me the divorce because we didn't know if you were dead or alive. So yes, we are divorced."

Her face paled, with a little bit of red coloring her cheeks.

"But... but the kids?" she started stammering.

I was glad she said "kids" instead of their names, if she could even remember them.

I looked up and noticed that Rake was headed towards us.

"Yes, Lisa. Let's chat about the kids."

I stood up to greet Rake with a hug, because after him

helping me with the divorce and me putting his name out there with my business contacts, we had become friends.

Rake took a seat, and I wish I could have taken a picture of Lisa's expression. Her face was pinched, her lips thin, and her eyes wide. She looked confused or constipated, maybe angry and alone; I wasn't sure, but it was priceless.

"Rake, what the hell are you doing here?" she whispered, as her face continued to turn red.

He took out a briefcase and opened it, pulling out two sets of papers. Rake was always a bit thinner, not much muscle mass. His hair was a thick dusty-blonde color, shaved on the sides, longer on the top, and he had a softer face, but his blue eyes were like glaciers. He smiled at Lisa as he organized his piles,

"Hello Lisa, it's nice to see you again." A moment later, he went into lawyer mode. "I am here, representing Mr. Stenson and his children."

Lisa sat back, looking angry, "*Our* children!" she seethed, and pointed at her chest. "What the hell is going on, Jimmy?"

She threw daggers at me with her eyes, like I would actually care.

I stayed quiet, which was what my lawyer suggested, so he spoke up and answered for me. "We are here today, Ms. Stenson, to have you sign over all your parental rights of the children."

Rake said it while setting a pen in front of Lisa, like he wasn't worried about her backlash in any way. "I have here for you a few papers to sign and make this official."

He started to set a paper in front of her, but she grabbed it and ripped it in half.

She sat taller in her chair and then addressed us. "If you think I am going to give up my rights, then you all are out of your fucking minds. Don't do this, Jimmy. Let's just talk for a bit. Please," she begged.

I stayed quiet, knowing my lawyer had this well in hand, and I would just make things more difficult for him if I spoke.

But Rake didn't continue, he watched me with hesitation. I shifted in my chair and leaned back. "No. I don't want to talk. There's nothing to discuss. Please sign the papers." I sounded like a robot, but I didn't want to lose my temper and start name calling or throwing chairs.

Lisa paled and placed her face in her hands. "Do you know how hard it was for me to leave you?" She looked up at me, tears streaming down her face. Her makeup was a mess and her entire body was shaking.

"God, Jimmy. It wasn't easy for me to leave, just like it wasn't easy for me to stay. I had to make a decision, and I went with the best one that I could think of to keep our children safe. I knew that if I left, you'd stay, and you'd be the best option out of the two of us."

I broke.

"Why?!" I slammed my hand on the table. "Why did you think I was the better fucking choice, and what kind of mother thinks that and mentally processes that shit?"

Lisa looked as though I'd slapped her across the face, but her retort was just as quick.

"The kind that grew up without a mother. The kind that grew up poor and pathetic. The kind that wasn't fucking strong enough to parent them alone," she sobbed. Tears and snot were mingling together on her face like a glistening fountain, and I shook my head in frustration. I didn't want to fight with her or argue why she'd left. If she had come back a year, even two years later, I would have heard her out, but not five years later, and only at the demand of Charles Davis.

"Lisa, I'm not doing this. What we had is over. What you did to the kids is inexcusable," I confirmed with a quiet tone, to hopefully get us back on track. Lisa wiped at her face with her napkin and blinked furiously.

"I'm not signing anything. I'm stronger now, I'm going to fight for them. They're still young, they'll forgive me." She crossed her arms, looking defiant and proud.

Rake took the opportunity to pull out another paper from the pile, but kept it in front of him, then pulled out another, with some things highlighted, and set it in front of her.

"Lisa, I think you will agree to sign over your rights, and here is why. The PI looked into your finances, and it looks like you have done all right for yourself as a dancer over the last few years.

"If you look at the highlighted portions of this page, you can see exactly how much we will be suing you for if you do not sign over your rights."

Lisa looked pissed, her face was red and blotchy. She grabbed the paper and looked it over. Rake grimaced and quietly said, "Back child support for five years."

I continued to keep quiet, as did Jackson, both just watching her. She carefully set the paper down in front of her and cleared her throat. "If I do this, then I can never see them again?" She looked to me for an answer, and I nodded my head.

"Correct. This is for good."

She flinched when I said that and looked down at her hands.

The silence was thick, and Jackson looked uncomfortable with the way he kept loosening his tie. Lisa had silent tears running down her face.

"Jimmy," she whispered. "I couldn't be strong for you, but you're strong now and you don't need me to be. Please give me one last chance. I'm begging you."

I watched her eyes and hated seeing Jasmine in them. Hated that I was tied to her at all. Hated how gutted she left me all those years ago. I leaned forward and placed my hands out in front of me, like a prayer.

"Lisa, you don't get to walk with someone when they're strong, when you refused to crawl with them while they were weak. At least not in my life. Sign the papers."

Rake maneuvered the pen so it faced her. She looked murderous now, but she took the cap off the black pen and began signing every highlighted section that Rake pointed out. Once she was done, she leaned forward and fastened me with a glare. "I'm curious, Jimmy. Why not just file for this on your own, without me? I'm sure the court would have allowed it. Why go through all this to contact me?"

She was right, I could have gone through this process without her, I could have filed for a few different things without her. I sat up straight and made sure she was looking at me when I responded.

"I wanted to be sure you understood that you can never come back. Never. You can never come around my children again. It was an assurance that I needed for myself and for the kids."

Her eyes darted around the table as she inhaled through her nose, then slowly exhaled as she handed the papers back to Rake. "So, this is it? After this, you won't try to come after me for child support or anything else?"

"No, we don't want anything else from you," I stated calmly.

Finally, this part was over. Now she could leave, and I could move on with my life. She sighed again, pulled her purse up from the floor, then scooted her chair back and stood to walk away. Just as she was about to leave, she stopped and then looked back at me and said, "For the record, I'm sorry."

I looked up at her and agreed. "Me too."

She turned away from me and sauntered out of the restaurant, and out of my life, once and for all.

Rake shuffled his papers, then placed them all back in his briefcase. He let out a long breath that he must have been holding in. "Man, I am glad that went okay. I was worried that she was going to get crazy." Rake was always worried about a scene.

Jackson laughed, and then stood up. "Yeah, I wasn't sure how that would go down, but I am glad it's over. I feel like we should get some victory drinks or something, man," he said, looking over at me. I was standing and buttoning my jacket.

"No thanks, guys, I have to try and repair what damage was done by Lisa with Ramsey. I will catch up with you later. Rake, do you need anything from me?"

He smiled and stood with us. "Not right now. I will get this filed and let you know what comes next."

I shook his hand and left.

I KNEW, FIVE YEARS AGO, THAT IF I HAD THE OPPORTUNITY TO end things with the Brass once and for all, that I would take it. So, after I left, I went to a detective named Franklin Gepsy, who'd been working on taking down Davis and the chapter for a while, offering him intel. I sat with him for hours, identifying key players for him, illegal drug runs they were a part of, weapons and arms dealings they were involved with, and helped with as much of his case as I could.

I told him that if I was ever approached by Davis again, or I went back, that I would contact him so that he could put together an undercover operation. I brought Jackson in on everything with me from the start, and since Gepsy encouraged our contact regarding the Brass to be anonymous, we developed a code: Meat delivery.

Jackson sent the necessary information to Gepsy, since my phone was hacked. Monday morning, I saw Franklin Gepsy at my bar blending in as a server. Gepsy was a tall bulky man who looked like he might have retired from those old wrestling shows. So, the fact that he had already set up and monitored the entire truck smuggling situation without any suspicion was impressive. He knew that I needed to have my meeting with Lisa first, before he moved in on the evidence he had on the Brass, just in case they decided to pull something over on me and hide her again. So, after the meeting with Lisa, I headed back to the bar to let him know he could end this whenever he was ready. I still couldn't text or call Ramsey, but I planned on finding her and figuring out how to see her, now that Gepsy could move.

I walked through the kitchen doors of my bar and found Rav dicing onions. Rav didn't dice onions, he always had someone else do it because he hated the texture of them. I eyed him suspiciously while moving a little further into the kitchen. His eyes darted up and around the room, like he was nervous. Once he caught sight of me, his shoulders relaxed, and he physically looked relieved. Like he was expecting someone else, but glad I wasn't whoever it was. He stopped his chopping and wiped his blade while watching the room. I looked around as well before I asked, "Rav, what's up?"

Rav glanced at me, then back at the door. He leaned in closer. "Jimmy, Davis assumed you'd pull something after your meeting with Lisa," he admitted in a near whisper.

"And?" I asked, with a gesture for Rav to continue, not totally sure why he stopped.

"And, I don't know. Just be careful," Rav finished with a little red in his round cheeks. He swiped a few trays off the counter in front of him and headed into the pantry. Something was wrong. Rav was nervous, but why was he keeping it from me? I needed to see Ramsey and get out of there.

I made my way out of the kitchen and saw Gepsy walking through the restaurant with an apron tied around his waist. He blended in so well that I even momentarily forgot that he was here undercover. I walked towards him and waved him over, we stood in plain sight of everyone. Using his cover name, I explained the situation.

"Adam, make sure you check the meat freezer when you get a chance, that order is finally in."

Gepsy's posture was slack. He was a big guy, so I felt awkward giving him any orders, even if they were coded. He didn't smile, he just nodded his head and was about to take off, but I held up my hand to stop him. I looked around, then focused on him, ensuring he understood my warning about Davis.

"And Adam, will you check to make sure the meat isn't spoiled? I have heard a few rumors about other restaurants getting spoiled meat on accident. I wouldn't want us to accidentally serve something that could hurt someone because we didn't take precautions."

Franklin watched my eyes, and slowly nodded his head in understanding. "Absolutely, boss. I will make sure and be careful with the order."

I patted his shoulder as I walked away, hoping it would be that simple. I knew he wouldn't be careless as he proceeded, but I just wasn't sure what kind of plans Davis had up his sleeve if he was worried that I would do something. I continued walking to my office, giving a slow look around the restaurant that confirmed for me again Ramsey was nowhere to be seen. I hadn't seen her or heard anything from her in a few days, even though I had my suspicions about my dad getting a late call the other night.

Now that I knew what Lisa had said to her, I needed to make sure she was okay. My pulse raced at the idea of things going back to normal with Ramsey, now that this was all behind us. Now that Lisa and the MC would be out of the picture for good, I could give Ramsey the friendship she wanted and when she was ready, a relationship. There wouldn't be any demons from my past that would come to hurt her.

The office was silent, and clean. Clean, like no one had been in it for a week, which was odd, because I knew Ramsey was coming in every day for a few hours before we opened. I looked at the books, which showed she had accessed them last just yesterday. She was probably staying in Belvidere at Sip N Sides to be closer to her mom, and further from me. That thought hurt. I knew she still didn't fully know what was going on with me; she had her assumptions but not the entire picture. I just hoped that I would have enough time to explain every-thing to her.

I didn't want to be around as Gepsy did his job, and some part of me had this deep need to pull everyone who mattered close to me, just to ensure that Davis couldn't hurt anyone. I grabbed my phone from my pocket and dialed the kids' school. The perky receptionist picked up on the third ring.

"Hello, Belvidere Elementary, this is Cindy, how may I help you?"

"Hi Cindy, this is Jimmy Stenson. I am planning on pulling my two kids out for the day in about thirty minutes."

"Okay, Mr. Stenson, I can send their teachers messages, and have them ready for... oh." Cindy stopped mid-sentence and I waited, assuming that she saw something on her screen or was reading a note on my kids' account.

When she didn't continue, I cleared my throat. "Everything okay?"

"Oh, sorry. Yes, it's fine, it's just that your daughter was already pulled out of school. It looks like the other authorized person on her file pulled her out earlier today."

"Oh, okay, I will give my dad a call then."

She hesitated. "Uh, no, Mr. Stenson, it was the person on the file by the name of Ramsey Bennington who pulled her out."

Ramsey had pulled Jasmine out of school? That was strange.

"Did she write in a reason for taking Jasmine out?"

"Um, let me check the clipboard." She paused for a moment before continuing again, "She wrote 'Ice Cream Date' under her reason for checking Jasmine out... I'm sorry, Mr. Stenson, did you want to edit the people who are allowed to check your children out?"

Of course, I didn't, but I did want to know what Ramsey was up to.

"Uh no, that's okay. Thank you, could you just have Sammy ready then?"

"Of course."

"Thank you." I hung up the phone. I wasn't sure what my feelings were about Ramsey pulling Jasmine out. I wasn't upset, I was just confused, but somewhere in the deep part of my stomach, it ached with worry. Ramsey would have called me... wouldn't she? That small kernel of fear began to wind around my heart, tightly. I needed to find Ramsey.

THIRTY-FOUR

I WAS ready for this stupid week to be over with already. Tuesday, my mother scared the hell out of me by going into a mini-coma. Or at least, that's what I called it. The doctor had a different explanation of what happened.

"Your mother's body is a complex issue," Doctor Stephens said, while adjusting his glasses. He was a thin man, with dark hair, tinted with streaks of silver. "The failure in her liver is systematically affecting other parts of her body. So, your mother blacked out because there wasn't enough blood flow to her brain."

His hands were splayed open, like he was showing me a book. My mother had woken up early that morning, and was groggy. So, it was left to me to ask questions.

"So, are you saying this will happen again?" I asked, exhausted and emotionally spent.

He looked around the room and lifted his shoulders. "It's hard to say. We just aren't sure what could happen at this point. She's stable for now, so we are sending her home. We aren't recommending hospice, but we do recommend having a nurse come every few days just to check her levels."

We drove home later that day, and I made a call to Mom's regular doctor, who suggested we check with a colleague of his in Chicago. It was a center for specialized cancer treatments. I didn't want to get my hopes up because she wasn't even a candidate for chemo, but he said that as a last resort, we should at least see what other options they might have.

I talked to my grandmother on the phone and told her about the situation. They wanted to pay for Mom to try the treatment center in Chicago, and for a nurse to be at our house daily until we left. I helped set up all the arrangements, and with her trip to Chicago came my own decision to move back there permanently. I knew, at this point, all the treatment she needed would be better coming from the specialists there. I knew Mom wouldn't want to go, but she needed the best shot she could get at survival and staying there only meant the possibility of better help for a longer period of time. She'd eventually agree with me. Besides, Jimmy was married, so nothing was holding me here, except my job, Theo, and the kids, but with their mom back, I would only complicate things.

Thursday, I decided I would break the news to Jasmine first. I had texted Theo earlier that morning, asking if I could take Jasmine for a bit, and he said it was fine. I didn't ask Jimmy. I couldn't ask him, or even face him right now. I went around two in the afternoon to pick up Jasmine. I used a silly excuse, but an honest one. We were going on an ice cream date. I waited in the attendance office for five long minutes, all while the school secretary and school nurse gave me the stink eye. I didn't care, they could disagree with my reason for taking her out being 'ice cream,' all they wanted. Once Jasmine finally made her way to the office and saw me, she beamed.

"Ramsey!" she squealed and ran into my arms.

"Hey kid, let's get out of here for a bit."

I grabbed her hand and we walked out of the school, headed towards my mom's old SUV. The day was bright but cold, and the sky was a beautiful blue against the orange and red trees that scattered the property of the school. Jasmine climbed in and threw her backpack behind her, into the rear seat. She buckled herself and then turned to me and smiled. "So, where are we going?"

My heart broke at the thought of telling her the news, and I had to gently breathe through my nose. Maybe this wasn't such a good idea... I swallowed the lump in my throat and responded, "I thought ice cream might be fun."

She clasped her hands together and bounced up and down in her seat. "That sounds perfect!"

We drove the few miles to the ice cream shop, with Jasmine picking different music on my phone. She'd find something with a good beat, and then move her whole body in the seat like she had worms. It was hilarious, and it made the ache in my chest worse.

I parked and we went inside, where we planted ourselves in front of the glass case of ice cream flavors. Once we both decided and were served our cones, we found a small booth in the back.

Jasmine was busy drowning in sugary bliss, when I cleared my throat. "So, Jas, you remember when we had that talk about how, even if we didn't live close to each other, we'd still see each other?"

She stopped eating her ice cream and cautiously eyed me when she answered, "Yes, why?"

Setting my cone in the Styrofoam bowl they gave us, I pushed it aside and laid my hands flat on the table. I didn't want to do this.

"Well, my mom is getting worse. She had something happen this last week, and her doctors think she should try a facility that specializes in her growing issues."

Jasmine slowly kept at her cone but stayed quiet so I could keep going. Except, I couldn't. There was an awkward silence that fell between us until Jasmine spoke up again.

"That's good, right?"

I exhaled slowly, thinking of a way to deliver this news without crushing her. The thought of having this conversation with Sammy and Theo had my throat feeling tight.

"It's good, yes, but the facility is in Chicago. We'd have to move there for treatment."

I talked to her like I would an adult, hoping some of the harshness would go over her head.

It didn't.

She stopped eating her ice cream, her eyes glassing over, and a red flush had crept into her cheeks. I hated myself for trying to commit her look into memory, but I loved her so much and I didn't want to forget anything.

Her bottom lip started to tremble, then she looked away from me, pushed her blonde hair back and practically whispered, "You're moving away?"

I wanted to pull her into my arms and explain everything to her. Explain that I wanted to marry her dad, that I wanted her as my own, that I thought I'd be here forever, and that when my mom passed, I pictured myself staying. I wanted to give her a piece of myself, something, anything, but all I managed was a small nod.

She looked around, seemingly fighting emotions that were starting to surface with how she kept biting her lip and shifting in her seat. I imagined how this was coming across to her— another abandonment. I held my stomach as a wave of nausea hit. I reached forward and grabbed her small hand to try and keep her with me.

"Jasmine, if there was any other way..."

"I know," she said somberly, while looking down at the floor. She grabbed her elbows and physically looked smaller, like she was shutting down. I waited, not sure what to say next, when she stood and threw her half-eaten cone in the garbage can.

Her face was void of any emotion, which scared me. She

started heading toward the exit and I scrambled to catch up to her. Once I was behind her, she pushed the door open and stormed off in the direction of my car. I felt empty. Jasmine had her arms crossed and tried to keep her face away from me; she even climbed into the back when I unlocked the doors.

I started the car and headed towards Sip N Sides. It was after three now, and the bus would be dropping Sammy anytime now. I watched her in my rearview mirror and gave it one last attempt.

"Jasmine, we talked about still being friends, even if I moved. We said that I'd still come see you on the weekends, and maybe even get to take you to stay with me in Chicago. I'm not going anywhere, I'm still going to be in your life."

She tightened her arms and set her jaw, and she looked so much like her dad right then. It was quiet again, and I felt like I could hear her heart breaking. We rode in silence, I wanted her to shout at me, yell, scream, something. Just not be silent. Tears were running down my face as I looked back at her, the second we pulled up to Sip N Sides, she grabbed her bag and got out of the car without saying goodbye. I couldn't face Theo yet, or Sammy; I was barely breathing after that. I watched her head inside, saw Theo greet her and hold the door for her. He tried to catch my eye to figure out what was going on, but I turned my face and started backing the SUV up. I needed to get out of there. I quickly pulled away and drove home.

The tears made driving rather dangerous, but thankfully, my house wasn't too far. I wondered if I should have just kept my mouth shut about moving, since I hadn't even convinced my mom yet. Still, I knew she would cave once I explained about Jimmy, she had to. She needed the best care possible, and she no longer had any reason to stay here, or to hope for something to happen between Jimmy and me.

I pulled into my gravel driveway, my face still wet with tears and my eyes blurry from crying, which is probably the reason I didn't notice someone walking toward me as I headed for the porch. All I knew was that I was walking one second and the next, I was falling. A sharp pain pricked my neck, and my eyes darted toward the sky. I saw blue, and I thought of walking out of the school with Jasmine, of how badly I wanted to redo this afternoon and have another chance to walk out of the school with her. I would wait to tell her until after she'd eaten her ice cream cone. I watched the blue fade into black, and then there was nothing.

I WOKE UP, BUT EVERYTHING WAS STILL DARK, AND IT FELT LIKE I was dreaming. The only proof that I wasn't was the excruciating pain in my arms and hands. They were tied behind my back. A wave of intense nausea hit me and made me feel like I was physically falling. My head was pounding, and the right side of my neck was on fire, or felt that way at least. I hated not being able to see; I didn't know who was with me, or who would hurt me. It was dark, but there wasn't anything firm around my eyes or mouth, just something light that was touching, I figured it must have been some type of hood that had been put over my head.

I kept trying to stay still, but the need to get the damned hood off my face won out, and I started to move. I threw my aching head forward in an attempt to loosen the hood, or flip part of it up so that I could see. It didn't do anything but cause more of a headache and the pain in my arms and hands to throb. I tested my hands, moving them around, but something cut into them and held them in place. Just as I was about to test out my lungs and make good use of not having a gag or duct tape over my mouth, the hood flew off my face.

It took a second for my eyes to adjust to the light. Once it did, I saw three men in front of me. The closest one to me was tall. He had long, dirty-blond hair, intense blue eyes, and a strong jaw. He wore a leather vest like I saw in Jimmy's closet. In fact, all three men wore vests like that.

The other two men stood further back. One held a baseball bat, and he had graying short hair, slicked back, with a few pieces falling forward. The last one was shorter than the rest. He had shaved his head, and ran his hand over his head as he watched me. They all looked at each other, seemingly communicating without talking. The sight of them sent a thread of fear so deep in my bones that I wasn't sure I wasn't already dead. My whole body was trembling; this was some mob movie junk, not real-life stuff. This couldn't be really happening, I blinked and tested my eyes again. Still too afraid to talk or move, I just sat there and watched the men. I noticed that the guy closest to me and the one with the shaved head kept looking at the guy with the bat, which meant he must be the leader.

Great.

I suppressed a groan as I felt the ache in my back grow; my arms being tied back was killing me. I stayed quiet, until the one with the baseball bat moved forward, stopping directly in front of me. I looked down at his black biker boots and suppressed a shudder; he was standing on concrete. That was the first time I noticed anything about my surroundings, which wasn't good. I had to come to terms with the fact that I had been abducted, and if I ever made it out, then the cops would ask me details about where I was. I mentally scolded myself and tried to be more vigilant.

The feel of cold wood being used to tip my chin upwards brought my thoughts back to who was in front of me. He used the bat to tip my head up so he could see me. The man had gray eyes, he wore a dirty white shirt under his vest, and dirty blue jeans. He smiled at me without showing his teeth, which somehow made him more menacing. I stayed quiet.

He finally looked over at the other two men and said, "My, my, I can see why Jimmy boy tried to keep her a secret."

The other guys started laughing. I was still trembling; my body was going cold. My arms ached, and I wondered how long I was out for from the drug they must have given me to get me here. I also wondered what in the hell he was talking about regarding Jimmy keeping me a secret, but I didn't want to let anything show.

The leader crouched before me, so that we were eye level. He took my face into his hands and whispered to me, "Did you know that he plans on betraying me?" He tilted my face to the left, like he was inspecting me. "Did you know that he thinks I don't know?"

He tilted it to the right, then stroked the side of my face.

"He has no idea what I am going to do to you, to teach him that no one double-crosses me."

He stroked my face again, and I let out a small breath that came out shaky. I closed my eyes, not knowing what was coming next, if the worst thing would be affection or torture. Then it came, another stroke of affection on my skin, followed by a hard slap across my face. The slap was so hard it made my teeth vibrate.

My face stung. I moved my jaw around and slowly opened my eyes. Tears were building in the corners just from the sting of the slap. Then it came again, another slap across my other cheek. That one hurt worse, much worse. I felt warm liquid and noticed two rings on the hand he just used to slap me.

I shut my eyes again. I decided to try and speak because this shit was getting old. "Look, I don't know why I'm here, but Jimmy and I aren't together. He's married. I'm just his employee." I tried to put some emphasis to my words, but they felt dead on my tongue. Lifeless and horrible.

Everyone was quiet for a moment, and then all three of

them laughed. I opened my eyes, not understanding what they were laughing at.

The one with the long hair shoved his golden mass to the side of his face, and then the leader spoke again. "That slut isn't his wife anymore. He divorced her years ago, after she left him. See, we've kept tabs on our little Jimmy. He needed a break to be a dad, so I gave it to him, and this is how he fucking repays me." Saliva flew from his mouth as he pinned me with a feral look. I thought he might hit me again but instead, he stood up.

He walked toward the wall; it was split into several opaque glass squares. It let in sunlight, but you couldn't see through it or out of it. The clouded windows lined the room I was in. There was a cement floor, in a room that was about as large as my kitchen, and a solid-looking white door was behind the men. Nothing else was in the room that I could see, but light poured in on all sides from the walls, and it was unnerving not being able to see through them.

The leader started to swing the bat around and around, and my heart was in my throat at the idea of him using it on me. I was so focused on the upcoming pain that I didn't give much merit to the words that he spoke about Jimmy. The bat swung around some more, then the leader faced me again. I was straining my neck to look up at him, but I didn't want to be surprised by a hit to the head. I would rather know it's coming. He stopped again near one of the windows and pulled out a cigarette, lighting it. He took a few drags, then continued talking about Jimmy.

"You're lying to me about Jimmy." He took another drag and exhaled the smoke in my face. On instinct, I turned my face away. The leader invaded my space. "I don't like liars, he said, with obvious distaste.

He put his cigarette out on my leg. I'd planned to be brave in front of them, but when he pushed the butt in with force, I let out a cry of pain. It singed and stung like nothing I had ever felt before. He stood and turned away from me before he bellowed. "You want to know how I know that you're lying, Ms. Bennington?" He quirked a gray eyebrow at me. I didn't move, just sat there watching him with the wooden bat.

"He was so careful, we almost missed it. We knew he was planning something, but couldn't figure out what it was or who it was with. Then one of our guys noticed a fresh face show up at the bar, posing as a waiter. We needed to know if he'd been there before our deal with Jimmy, so we went back through the security footage." He stopped and half-crouched to catch my eye, then pointed his bat at me.

"Imagine all of our surprise when we found footage of the two of you sharing a table, looking cozy, and then dancing. It didn't take us long to figure out that the two of you have something going on. We dug further, and found out just how close of a family friend you are, my dear. Trust me when I say, that us having you here will greatly upset Mr. Stenson." He gave me a sick smile, like this whole thing was bringing him the most joy.

"I am looking forward to seeing the look on his face when he sees you here," he said, shaking his head back and forth, a smile playing on his lips.

I let out a little laugh, the absurdity of all of it was hitting me. Was that why Jimmy had been so distant, why he changed the locks? I felt so stupid. He had been trying to keep me safe. But why not just tell me? Anger ripped through me, that I was in that stupid chair, and anger at the assholes in front of me. I was furious that I might die without having time with Jimmy, without having time with my mom. A laugh bubbled up out of me, and then I couldn't keep back the sobs. I sounded like a lunatic, but this was really crazy. All of it was.

The leader walked over to me, and pulled my hair back in order to see my face. "What's so funny?" he seethed.

I tried to form words, but only a few would come in between my laughter and sobs. "You, and Jimmy, and all of this... I'm an accountant... My mom has cancer... He doesn't want me, and I'm still going to die."

More laughs, more sobs. I couldn't control the wave of emotion that was hitting me. The week of thinking Jimmy had a wife slammed into me, the emotions from my mom almost dying on me. The irony of her slowly dying on me but still leaving me regardless. All of it hit me.

It must have been too much for them. He gripped my hair tighter, then said, "Oh, he wants you. I'm banking on it."

Then his hand formed a fist and landed in my face, and everything went dark again.

THIRTY-FIVE

JIMMY

I PICKED Sammy up from school a little before three, when we headed over to Sip N Sides. I needed my family together until I knew what Davis had planned. Sammy was looking through the window in the back seat as I pulled into the deteriorating parking lot of Dad's bar.

I planned on contacting Ramsey once I was on the road with Dad and Sammy; I didn't want to be anywhere that Davis might look. He knew where I lived and knew where my dad's bar was. I was so thankful he didn't know about Carla or Ramsey, and I knew my distance from her was going to pay off. I parked and helped Sammy out of the car, then we both headed into the bar. Once I walked in, I noticed Dad leaning over the counter, watching Jasmine as she cried, pushing away a basket of fries. *Why was she here? Where was Ramsey?* I silently wondered, as worry slid in between my ribs. I walked up to Jasmine and put my arm around her.

"Hey Jas, what's going on? Why are you crying?" I asked, while looking over at my dad. His face was solemn, and he shook his head back and forth, like he didn't know what was going on.

Jasmine pushed out of my arms and stood from the stool she was sitting on. She wiped her tears away and then ran off to the bathroom. I let her go, and looked back over at my dad, "What's going on with her?"

Dad gave me a look, then pushed off the counter and began pouring a glass of water for Sammy, who had climbed up in Jasmine's chair and started eating her fries.

"She came in like that. Right after Ramsey dropped her off, about twenty minutes ago. She hasn't stopped crying, but she won't tell me what's going on," Dad said with a shrug.

I pulled my hand through my hair and walked towards the bathroom. Before I turned the corner, I yelled back at my dad, "We need to leave. Do what you need to, either close up or put someone else in charge for the rest of the night."

Then, without looking back, I pushed towards the girls' bathroom. I pushed the door open and found Jasmine washing her face, but it didn't help get rid of the pink streaks on her forehead and down her cheeks. I crouched in front of her until I was at her eye level. She sniffed, then threw her arms around me and started crying into my shoulder. I let her cry until she whispered with a shaky breath, "Ramsey is moving."

Her silent sobs started back up again. I hugged her tight, swallowing the pain that was trying to make its way up my throat. I didn't know all the details, but I needed to get them from Ramsey. She couldn't leave. Half my brain said it was okay, it's not what it sounds like; the other half screamed at me that it was too late and that I was losing her.

I took the corner to Ramsey's street a little faster than I probably needed to, the realization that Ramsey was told I was still married hit me again and I pushed harder on the gas. I had so much to clear up with her, to make right. I pulled up to the curb in front of the house and saw Ramsey's car was parked in the driveway, which meant she was home. I noticed a small blue car on the curb ahead of me; it was slightly close to their house and I wondered if they had company. Relieved that she was here, I let out a small sigh and helped the kids out of the car. Dad pulled my arm gently until I was facing him. His eyes were drawn together, and his lips were thin—he looked concerned.

"You going to tell me what's going on yet? I know something's up, something has been up, but I've just been waiting for you to talk to me."

I put my hand on his shoulder. "Yeah, Dad, I will clear things up with both you and Ramsey at the same time. Let's get the kids inside."

I grabbed Jasmine again and Dad held Sammy's, and we started walking to the door when I noticed Ramsey's purse on the ground in front of her house. I bent to pick it up and noticed her wallet and cell phone was all still intact. My heart rate surged as panic filled my lungs. I wasn't ready to admit that this meant anything. Nothing was wrong, she was fine. She just dropped it and I needed to get inside. I knocked and, after a few moments, an older lady wearing pink medical scrubs answered the door. My gut twisted as the reminder of missing out on Ramsey's life and Carla's hit full-force. I realized the nurse was waiting for someone to explain why we were on the doorstep.

"Hi, we are looking for Ramsey, is she here?" I asked.

The nurse's face changed to a relaxed expression. "Not yet. We saw her car in the driveway, but she hasn't come in yet."

I looked down, and quietly responded to the nurse, "Well, I'm Jimmy. A family friend, as is my Dad, Theo. Can we come inside?" The nurse looked back towards the living room and with a panicked look. She probably wasn't supposed to let me in. Shit.

"I'm not supposed to let you in unless Carla says so, but..." She trailed off, looking back towards the living room again, then down at her watch.

"Her daughter was supposed to be here and relieve me from my shift. I have to go and pick up my granddaughter from dance lessons," she finished in a rush while moving aside to grant us access. I smiled at her in thanks as we went in. My eyes darted around the room, trying to think, to get a plan.

I was on autopilot as I turned to look back at Dad, and asked, "When did you say she dropped Jasmine off?"

Dad looked at his watch and then back at me. "She dropped her right before three, then left. She was driving the SUV."

We walked in, and I noticed a variety of medical machines set up in the living room, all hooked up to a sleeping Carla. Dad walked over to where Carla lay and knelt down next to her. I ignored him, and kept heading towards Ramsey's room. Her door was open, her bed was still made, her room picked up and tidy, but it was empty. I walked further in and checked her bathroom too, then walked through the rest of the house and checked the back-yard. She wasn't anywhere. Something was wrong, I could feel it.

I told the nurse to go home, and assured her that we would stay with Carla until Ramsey showed up. I showed her a few pictures of Ramsey with the kids to help her feel better about leaving. She could lose her job and was reluctant to leave, but I could tell by the look on her face that she was panicked and needed to go. I had ordered pizza, knowing the kids needed fed, but my mind was still on overdrive about where Ramsey was. My only thought kept circling back to it having something to with Davis.

Dad was at Carla's side, feeling her head and watching the monitors that she was hooked up to. Sammy didn't seem fazed by what was going on, but Jasmine looked worried. She finished her bite and drank some of her soda. "Do you think Ramsey's okay, Dad?"

I smiled at her but had to get past the lump of worry in my throat. "I sure hope so, sis."

She looked down at her pizza. "Do you think, because I was so upset, that she ran away or something?"

Her words were like ice water thrown in my face; she felt like it was her fault. Again.

I turned toward her and wrapped her in a hug. "No, baby. Ramsey wouldn't just leave. I think if she could be here, then she would be. We might need to call the police to be sure she's okay, but it's not your fault, sis. Ramsey loves you, she'd never do anything to hurt you."

Jasmine nodded her head and continued eating her pizza.

Knowing the police wouldn't do anything until after twenty-four hours, I was hesitant to call them. Until I had any proof that Davis was involved, I didn't want to distract Gepsy from his case. I just needed a second or two to form a plan on what to do. I walked over to my dad, noticing that he had made himself comfortable on the couch next to Carla, and was flipping through channels. I knew it was time for me to come clean about what was going on, and why we came here instead of our house. I ran a hand over my face.

"Dad, I think we need to talk," I said quietly as he settled on some football. He looked over at me, and just nodded his head for me to continue. I sat back and started at the beginning.

"I haven't been totally honest with you. I have been trying to find Lisa for a few years, with a PI." Dad turned towards me, his face scrunched with disapproval.

"Why would you try to find her?" I could tell that he was trying to control his anger.

I let out a tight breath. "It's something I had to do. I needed closure and assurance that she wouldn't try to come back."

Dad watched me, his face set, and his arms crossed. "Okay. I understand, what does that have to do with this?"

"My PI couldn't find her. I reached out to the Mazzarati's." Dad's head flung in my direction, his face lethal.

"Son, you didn't?" He breathed the question out.

I looked down at my hands, trying to hide my shame. I slammed my eyes shut and kept going. "I didn't think they'd leak it back to Davis. As far as I knew, they weren't exactly in contact anymore. Besides, it wasn't anyone directly, just a PI that was a member." I watched my Dad breathe slowly, but his face was turning red. I hoped he didn't make a scene in front of Carla. She was sleeping, which I was grateful for, but once she woke up, she would be asking questions about Ramsey.

Dad asked quietly, "So, let me guess. Suddenly Davis reached out and said your time was up?"

I swallowed down the embarrassment and just decided to answer straight-on, no excuses.

"Yeah... demanded a meeting."

Dad nodded his head in understanding. "And what exactly was his first job for you?"

I looked down at the carpet, not wanting to face this truth. Face that I was back in the viper's nest. "The use of my company truck to move product for two weeks."

We were both quiet. "Did you finish things with Lisa?" he asked solemnly.

"Yes, she signed papers, and knows that she can never come back."

Dad shook his head in agreement. "So, is Davis the reason why I couldn't stay at the bar, and why we can't go home?"

I nodded my head again. "Rav warned me that Davis thought I might have tried something after my meeting with Lisa."

Dad slowly turned his head towards me, his eyes wide. In a firm and very slow tone, he pinned me with a glare and said,

"Son, if that's the case, then he knows about Ramsey, and likely has her."

My heart rate shot through the roof, anger lacing my words, "Why?"

I hated that he was jumping to the worst possible conclusion, but his history with Davis had me worried. Dad stood up and started pacing the living room then yelled, "Get Gepsy on the phone now, Jimmy!"

"Dad, you need to tell me why you think that!" I stood and yelled back. I winced a bit at my volume and glanced over at Carla. I saw that she was still out thanks to the meds.

Dad hung his head and, in a softer tone, continued, "Jimmy, several years ago, we had an informant try to rat us out to the cops. We were real clever about catching him and then exploiting him. We used our tech guys to scan through security footage for all the places the guy went for weeks. Grocery stores, church, gym, work, favorite food spots. We combed through everything to find the informant he had met with." He looked at Carla then back at the kids and continued, "We uncovered more than the face of his informant. We found out he was married and had kids. Davis took his wife, killed her, and sent back her wedding finger as a reminder to never double-cross him again."

He trailed off, letting me connect the dots. The dots of this pathetic situation that clearly painted that it wouldn't take much digging for Davis to find Ramsey. All my stupid effort to keep her safe was undone, and now I may lose her. I grabbed my phone, and just as I was about to dial Gepsy, I had an incoming call from Rav.

"Hello?" I answered, a bit more frantic than I would have liked.

Rav responded in a quiet tone. "Boss, we have a problem…" Then, with a rushed breath, he said, "It's Ramsey."

THIRTY-SIX

THERE WAS a buzzing sound near my head.

It was like falling asleep on a summer afternoon but having that one fly that wouldn't leave you in peace. Except I knew it wasn't summer, and I knew I wasn't taking a relaxing nap.

I slowly opened my eyes to find the source of the buzzing. Everything was blurry, and pain sliced through my head as I tried to move it. My body hurt, everywhere.

I blinked, trying to recall the last time I was awake. The memory of a man with a leather vest and baseball bat came back like a nightmare. I looked around and noticed a small light in the corner of the room, sitting without a lamp shade. It was on the floor, like me. Then a little black fly buzzed past my head—source of buzzing noise found and confirmed. At least it was proof of something living in this cold, miserable place.

I looked down and saw a ratty mattress with bloodstains on it, and I held back the urge to vomit. I tried to get up, but all my attempts resulted in more pain. My body was cold. I managed to feel my left arm with my right hand, and it was freezing. I slowly moved my hand up to my face, and let my fingers discover what condition it was in. As soon as I touched the surface, I winced. I could feel that my bottom lip was larger than it should be, there was a large cut in it, and what felt like dried blood on my chin. My fingers moved up to my nose, and my eyes began to water as I gently touched it. I moved on to my eyes; my left eye wasn't opening as much as my right one, and I could feel swelling, but I couldn't apply enough pressure to really discover anything else. My conclusion was that my face was a hot mess.

I knew all my fingers were in place on my right hand, and I slowly moved to feel my left hand, which was numb. Lowering my face or moving my neck resulted in waves of pain that I wasn't brave enough to endure, so I used my fingers to feel the rest of the way. There were cuts on my left hand, and swelling in my fingers; they were all there, but any pressure at all from that hand resulted in blinding pain. Just that small movement had exhausted me. I was thirsty and hungry, freezing, and my whole body was aching.

I couldn't remember much after I was knocked out, and I didn't know how long I had been in this place, or if anything else happened. Horrified at the idea of what else could happen to me, I tried to look down at my legs. I moved my hips; they didn't hurt, and I could feel my pants and underwear still in place, nothing hurt down there. Relief flooded me.

I knew that I needed to take care of my body, I just didn't know how to. I laid there and thought of my mom, and wondered if she was okay. I wondered what her nurse did once she knew that I wasn't coming. Surely, she wouldn't just leave my mom. I tried to exhale, I knew that the service wouldn't let my mom be alone, someone would be called. Hoping that my mother was too drugged to notice that I hadn't returned was a sad reality I found myself in. I didn't want her to worry, and since I knew that she would, the only thing I could hope for were that the drugs would last and be effective.

I closed my eyes and tried to control my breathing, focusing on getting out. I tried to gather what information I could from what I remembered.

I knew that I had been kidnapped with something like a needle to my neck. I knew that it was most likely a motorcycle gang that was holding me. I knew that they were violent, and somehow had a bone to pick with Jimmy. They assumed Jimmy and I were close, and that by taking me, it would get back at him. That was all I had to go on for now. I didn't know what I would do with it but having some kind of information felt like a form of armor.

I was going through the details of what physical attributes I could remember about the men when I heard a door open somewhere in the room. I froze. I wanted to shut my eyes, but I didn't want to miss what was going to happen next. I needed food, and some kind of blanket, and more than anything, some water, so my eyes stayed open, just in case whoever entered wasn't there to further hurt me. I saw a shadow move across the room, and then a shape come into focus. A tall man with a bald head was coming towards me, but in measured, small steps, like he was trying to be quiet. As the man got closer to me, I recognized him. It was Rav. I was so happy that I started to cry, which hurt like a mother, and I immediately tried to stop. I moved as much as I could to sit up, which ended up just being an elbow propped up behind me. Rav came close, and started to whisper to me, "Ramsey, don't say anything."

He looked over his shoulder, then back down at my face. He gently cradled my head to the side and made a face at what he saw. Rav looked like he just ate a bunch of spoiled grapes, and from what I felt with my fingers, I assumed what he saw wasn't good.

"Ramsey, I'm so sorry." He gently brushed my hair off my face with warm fingers. I leaned into his touch, responding to the warmth more than anything else. I stayed quiet like he said, but he needed to start talking, and soon.

As if he read my mind, he began to explain in a light whisper, "Ramsey, I want to get you out, but we have to wait for help to get here. I called Jimmy. He will know who to call. I can't just call the local cops, a number of them are in Davis' pocket. But the guy Jimmy is working with isn't, and I know he's building a case against these guys."

I didn't want to wait. I wanted out, I needed to get out. I tried to speak, and tell Rav this, but my voice wouldn't work. I grabbed on to Rav's shirt with my good hand, to try and get him to feel my urgency.

"Please," I whispered.

Rav's eyes glossed over, then he turned his head away. I had to try again.

"Rav, you can do it. You can get me out. We can't wait. I can't..." I sobbed, needing him to try, but he shook his head. I suppressed the tears that threatened to fall. It hurt, and I didn't want to hurt anymore. He wasn't going to get me out, and it wasn't worth it to waste my energy trying to convince him. I didn't have any fight left in me.

He pulled a blanket from behind his back and laid it over me, then pulled out a clear, plastic water bottle. He opened the top and helped me lean up to drink. It was awkward and painful, but I managed to get a few gulps down. I hurt, but I also felt better. I pulled the blanket up closer to my chin. I had so many questions, but I was so tired. Rav had a pained look on his face, and he was gently stroking my hair again,

"Ramsey, I would give you food, but your lips and mouth were busted up pretty badly. I think we should wait for you to get medical help."

He looked away, and I could be wrong, but his eyes looked watery. I heard him swear and then he turned back to me. "I don't want to know the person Jimmy will become after he sees what they did to you," he whispered quietly, while carefully touching one of the cuts on my face.

I considered his words and winced in a completely different kind of pain. I didn't want Jimmy to hate himself, or to change. I knew why he did it now—stayed away from me, everything; it was to protect me from this. I felt so little, so exposed, and so angry that his attempts had failed. I was angry that I had been hurt and abused, angry that people like these men existed and were allowed to be a part of society. Then, like a gentle pebble settling into the rough ocean, I realized that Jimmy used to be one of them. It was like looking in the mirror and seeing for the first time, what everyone else saw. Jimmy's past—there was so much I didn't know about it, so much I didn't know about him. I felt like a fool for allowing myself to get so emotionally dependent and involved with someone I barely knew. Sure, I pushed for friendship, I did try, but by then, I was long gone. Jimmy already had my heart.

Now, I didn't know if I could ever get that part of me back.

"Rav, can you tell me a story or something and distract me? I'm terrified, and if you aren't going to help get me out, then I need something to distract me from this pain." I pulled the blanket higher. I was cold, and my body was shaking.

Rav situated his body, his face clouded. Rav had pretty brown eyes and right now, they were focused on me as he seemed to fight some internal battle. Like he didn't know how to help me, or what to do. Finally, he leaned closer to me.

"Did I ever tell you how I met Jimmy?" he asked in a whimsical tone.

I shook my head while staring at the blank wall. Rav smiled and his brown eyes lit up.

"Jimmy was working with my brother, Evan. Evan was a prick. Jimmy was supposed to rig a fight that the Brass put together. Instead of just beating the guy, he was supposed to kill him. It was going to start this war between clubs, but Jimmy wouldn't do it. I respected him for telling Davis no. Evan planned to break Jimmy's ribs before he entered the fighting ring, to teach him a lesson. I didn't know Jimmy, but I found him and warned him. After the fight, Jimmy found me and told me that I saved his life and that because of me, he would get to go home and see his new baby."

Rav rubbed his bald head and let out a breath. "Jasmine had just been born."

I wanted to kiss the top of Rav's head. I was glad that Jimmy had someone in his life as good as Rav.

"Ramsey, I've known him for a long time. He cares about you. But after this..." He looked away and trailed off. I watched his face, trying to decode all the emotions playing there. He turned his head back, his eyes downcast and worried.

"Hold on tight to who he was, Ramsey. Don't let him go, no matter how hard he pushes you away after this." Rav stood and walked back towards the exit. I heard a door close, and then I was alone again. I considered Rav's words, and thought about getting back to Jimmy, back to Theo, to the kids. My heart tightened at the idea of Jimmy changing or pushing me away. I couldn't go through that again. I hoped Rav was wrong. I relaxed into the nasty mattress and clung tighter to the blanket and did my best to wait.

It was probably just minutes later, but it felt like hours when I heard the door open again. I smiled, thinking Rav had figured out a way to get me out. That, or he was just going to stay with me. Either way, I wouldn't be alone. I watched the wall for Rav's shadow to emerge, but it wasn't his shadow that I saw. It was someone much thinner but still as tall. They came closer and I saw unwashed jeans, gray, slicked back hair, and that damn black vest. He didn't have a bat this time, thank God, but he did have a look on his face that made me want to shrivel up and die. He had clear gray eyes that seemed to look right through me, and I swear he saw exactly the place he'd deliver his last punch or hit, ending me.

He walked to the edge of the mattress, and then crouched

low, coming eye level with me. He went to wipe the hair from my face, then grabbed the back of my neck, pulling me towards him. Pain exploded throughout my body as it resisted being pulled and forced forward. He was spitting in my face as he said in a low, shaky voice, "You think you'll get away from this? That Jimmy will get away with betraying me? He won't."

He stood up, still holding my hair, and kicked me in the stomach. I couldn't breathe. I kept trying to reach where his hand was on my neck, just out of instinct, but then he kicked me again.

I heard someone shouting and a loud *boom* at the door. Davis watched the door, frozen for a second, before another loud, *boom* echoed through the room. His grip on me tightened as someone forced their way through.

"Get on the ground!" someone screamed in our direction. I couldn't see anything but the black dots swimming before my eyes from how hard Davis gripped my hair.

"Get on the ground now!" someone repeated with more force. Davis let me go, and I fell back on the mattress. I saw Davis' feet in front of me, but I was too afraid to look up, to hope that this was real. That people were here, ending this nightmare for me. I closed my eyes and waited for someone to confirm that this was over. I heard a scuffle, then handcuffs being used, and Miranda rights being read. I opened my eyes, and watched as a burly man in a thick, bulletproof vest hand-cuffed my abuser and walked him out of the room.

An officer with a gentle face approached me while holstering his gun. He bent down to examine me and started yelling for an EMT. He stayed with me until they got there. A tall, skinny man with blond hair, and a fit-looking woman with brown hair in blue uniforms hustled toward me. They started poking and prodding around my body, asking questions and shining lights in my eyes.

Moments later, I was being lifted onto a medical bed. On

my way out of the building, I saw Rav giving a statement to a cop. I noticed some police dogs, who were sniffing around one of the offices. I wasn't in a warehouse, but an auto body garage, which was actually pretty nice. It was clean and organized, and higher end cars were being worked on by the looks of it. I must have been somewhere in the back, behind the employee area.

Near the entrance of the garage, I saw people moving about, officers walking in and out, but in the midst of all the chaos, standing in a wrinkled suit with no tie, was Jimmy. His hair was a mess, and he had dark circles under his eyes and a panicked look on his face, until he saw me—then it was just pain. I attempted a smile, but Jimmy didn't return it. He stared at me, the pain intensifying, tears building up in his eyes. He looked down at his feet as I got closer, his jaw worked back and forth as he asked questions of the EMTs. They asked if he wanted to ride along with me to the hospital, but he hesitated and my heart broke. I tried not to cry, not to make more of a mess of my face than it already was, but I just wanted him, and he was already pushing me away.

I was slid into the truck, and one of the EMTs shut the first door, then they asked Jimmy one last time if he was coming. I couldn't see him, I just heard the EMT ask. I heard someone climb into the truck, and then Jimmy was on the bench next to me. He wouldn't look at me, he stared at his hands, as tears streamed down his face. Rav's words came echoing back to me. I wanted to reach for Jimmy's hand, but I couldn't even feel it to move it towards him. I suddenly regretted Jimmy being in the ambulance with me. I would have preferred to face him once I was patched up, like maybe that way, it would make this easier somehow. Maybe it wouldn't feel like I was losing Jimmy one stitch and suture at a time.

THIRTY-SEVEN

JIMMY

I HATED the sounds in the ambulance. I hated how bright it was, and how it smelled. I hated how it looked, and everything about it. I shouldn't even be in here with Ramsey, I should have stayed back. It was selfish of me to jump in at the last second. I should have just stuck with my original decision to stay behind, but I needed to be close to her and to see with my own eyes that she was alive. Now I hated myself for it, more than I hated myself when they pulled Ramsey out of that room and I saw her face.

My heart constricted at the memory of it, of seeing her, white as a ghost, with dark bruises and blood on her face. With cuts so severe that it rearranged her face to the point where if I didn't know her so perfectly and spend so much damn time staring at her, I wouldn't have known it was her at all. It looked like he used her face as a punching bag. One of her eyes was almost swollen shut, and she had cuts on her cheeks from where she must have been slapped. Her beautiful lips were swollen and cut up, she had a deep gash near her hairline, and her right hand looked like something had hit it, repeatedly. I tried not to look at her while we rode in the ambulance. I tried, but every few seconds, I would hear a new sound from one of the machines, and I would panic and look at her to make sure she was still with me.

Then I would take in all of her injuries again, and the process of self-loathing would begin all over. I didn't deserve to be next to her, or here with her at all. I knew the second she was wheeled out of that room that I would never forgive myself for this.

I heard the EMT rattle off vitals and talk about her being stable. I heard them mention a concussion and talk about the bruising, and the hairline fracture in her hand. I tried to push the rest of the words out and away from me. I had to get some distance. I was toxic for her, I ruined her, just like I knew I would. Just like Lisa knew I was toxic; it was why she left me, left the kids. Because I was a mess-up, a screw-up, someone not worthy of love. I swallowed the lump in my throat and tried to clear it.

Davis had taken Ramsey to fucking Chicago, so getting to her, and getting her back home, was going to be difficult. I let my head fall into my hands and tried to wipe away the tears that had fallen down my face. I glanced at Ramsey again, she was watching me. I gently reached for her hand and brought it to my lips. I kissed it as gently as I could, and then I kept her hand in mine for the duration of the ride. I knew I was being selfish again, but I needed to feel her, to know that she was really safe, and okay. The ride to the nearest hospital wasn't long, and before I knew it, we were being rushed into the ER, and Ramsey was being rolled into a room. Nurses were on her and plugging her into machines. A few were yelling about getting a cat scan ordered, while others were saying things I didn't understand. I stood there, amidst the chaos, just watching my beautiful Ramsey as she lay there. Right then, a dark-haired nurse in a pair of purple medical scrubs, with a name tag that read "Amy" came up to me and placed her hand on my arm.

"Sir, are you okay?"

I knew she was asking in the medical sense, but I wasn't sure how to answer. I swallowed my uncertainty and responded the best way I knew how.

"I think so, I just..." I gestured toward Ramsey, hoping that she would understand my struggle. She looked over at her patient, understanding dawning in her brown eyes.

"Of course, let me show you where the waiting area is. Someone will be out soon to let you know where we put her once we have made her a little more comfortable. Okay?"

She kept her hand on my arm and started herding me toward a pair of double doors that was obviously the exit. Beyond the doors, was an L-shaped hallway with several chairs, a vending machine, and a few TVs in the upper corners of the ceiling. I headed to a chair and sat down. The nurse looked empathetic; she crouched down and leveled with me.

"Is she your wife?"

I laughed and held back tears. "No, I was hoping to get there eventually." The tears won, and slid down my face freely, I stopped fighting them.

The nurse looked sad, like she was sharing in this pain with me, yet she didn't even know me. "Well, we will do everything we can to make sure your girl is okay, all right." She smiled at me, then stood and pointed down the hall. "Coffee machine is down the hall to the right."

She headed back through the doors we came from, and with a swipe of her badge, she left me to my thoughts, and my misery. I laid my head back against the wall and played the evening back through my mind. I thought about the phone call I had got from Rav...

"Jimmy, we have a problem. It's Ramsey."

"What the hell do you mean, Rav?"

"Jimmy, I came over to the garage, the one on Larch Street. I walked in, looking for Davis, and I found him beating someone up. I walked a little further in and noticed it was a woman, with dark hair and brown tinted skin. When he pulled her head back and I saw who it was… Jimmy, it was Ramsey. He has her, I don't know how he does or why, but he has her, and he's hurting her. What do I do? What can I do, Jimmy?"

"Do you know who else is there? How many guys are there? I need all the details you can give me."

"Dev is here, and Reuben, and I think, Mark, but I only saw his jacket, I haven't seen him. Then, of course, Davis is here."

"Okay, watch her, and when you see a moment to go to her, to comfort her, do it. I will call Gepsy, and we will be there as soon as we can. Don't, for any reason, leave the garage, Rav. Do you understand me?!"

"Yeah, Jimmy, I won't leave her."

That call felt like a lifetime ago, but that was only around seven. I thought back on the panicked call I made to Gepsy right after I talked to Rav, how I moved outside so the kids wouldn't be scared of what they were hearing. Gepsy had picked up on the third ring, and I was already on edge.

"Jimmy? What happened? What's wrong?"

"It's about Ramsey, the girl I told you about, the one I was trying to protect. Rav called me just now, they're in Chicago, at an auto garage off of Larch Street. He has her, and the son of bitch is hurting her. Gepsy, I need you to call your team or whoever, and get over there."

"Jimmy, okay, I hear you, buddy. I will get her… I can't stress how important it is that you stay put. You have to stay away from this entire thing. You can't be implicated at all, or have it appear, in any way, that you were aware of Davis' actions or what he was up to. That's how this works."

I stayed silent, processing what he just told me.

"Jimmy? Did you hear me?"

"Yeah, I heard you. I won't go, but you have to. Get to her, Gepsy, I can't lose her. Please get her and take that son of a bitch down."

"Consider it done. Stay available, we will call for building specs."

I had hung up the phone and within seconds, decided I was going. I thought about the look on my Dad's face when he realized I was leaving. Carla was still out, she had no idea that her daughter was being tortured by a sadistic monster—and over a stupid man, who didn't even deserve her. The thought made me sick, and brought me back to this moment of sitting, waiting to talk to the woman who held and owned my heart, but needed to be liberated of it. She deserved better than me, deserved better than small-town Belvidere, and stupid demons from my past chasing her around. And with me, there would always be demons.

I ran my hand through my hair a few times, and dialed Dad. I knew it was close to midnight, but I knew that he would be up until I called to update him. I dialed and waited for his rough voice to pick up. A few rings in, and I heard his voice, keeping me grounded like an anchor in the storm.

"Jimmy? She okay? You okay, son?"

After a few seconds of letting his voice hit me and wash over me, I responded.

"Dad, yeah, she's in the hospital. She is… she's alive. I'm here, I'm all right."

I didn't know how to answer him. Ramsey was far from okay, and I wasn't really either, but I knew he couldn't do much from Belvidere.

"What do you mean, she's alive, son? Is she okay or not?"

"Dad, she's been hurt really bad. He hurt her." I started choking on my words, unable to give him any more details.

"Son, she'll get through this. She's strong."

I was holding back sobs now. "Dad, she looks so bad. How could I let this happen to her?"

"Jimmy, did you tell those bastards about Ramsey?"

"No."

"Did you bring her around them at all, or even call her

while they were around?" I knew what he was doing, but it still felt like this was all on me.

"No, Dad."

"Then this isn't on you, so don't start this shit."

I knew he was right, but I couldn't get past it. It was like a dark cloud that I took everywhere with me; this stupid past of mine. I hated it, and I hated how it affected the people in my life. I wanted to cry and shout and hit something. Gepsy knew that too, when I showed up at the garage. His eyes went wide, and his nose flared in anger. He knew that I wanted a piece of Davis, that I wanted to use my fists to end his worthless, fucking life. Gepsy set an officer on me and told me that I wasn't allowed into the garage, I wasn't allowed to move, and if I tried, that I would be arrested for obstruction of justice. I believed him.

So, I'd stayed put, pacing like a madman, knowing the man who hurt the woman I loved was inside that building. I wanted blood. I still did, and I needed an outlet for my anger. I knew where I was in the city, and where a few bars were that would be easy enough to start up a fight in. An image of my fists slamming into flesh ran through my mind; it was so tempting. I let out a slow, controlled breath and finished my conversation with my Dad. "Dad, I know. It's just hard."

"Daddy?" Sammy's voice came over the phone, sleepy but anxious.

"Sammy, what are you doing up, buddy?"

"I miss you, and I'm worried about Ramsey. I just wanted to talk to you and know if you're okay."

All the anger left me in an instant. Dad probably did that on purpose, knowing my tendencies when I felt worthless. My kids always brought me back.

"I'm good, buddy, and I just saw Ramsey, she's okay. Don't worry and get some sleep, all right?"

"Okay, Daddy. Love you."

"Love you too, buddy."

I hung up the phone and leaned back in the chair. I was struggling to stay focused and to stay awake. At the same time, there was no way that I could sleep. I got up and walked to the coffee machine and after a few seconds, my cup was full. I was sipping the scalding liquid as I made my way back to my chair. The same nurse from earlier came out of the double doors a few minutes later, and walked over to me.

"Okay, we have her comfortable in Room 404. Go ahead and head up when you want. I talked to the charge nurse, and it's okay if you stay in the room with her tonight, even though visiting hours are over. You look like you could use a little rest on the pull-out chair." She laid a hand on my shoulder and I smiled up at her. She was kind, and I really needed a little kindness.

"Thank you, could you show me...?" I responded, a hint of exhaustion leaking into my tone.

I stood up and followed her to the elevators, glad for the company. She was a little older than me, and carried some weight on her figure, but it didn't take away from the obvious beauty that she had inside of her. She was one of those women that truly shined more because of what dwelled on the inside, it made her eyes sparkle and her skin glow. I must have been tired, because crazy ideas, like this lady being an angel, were going through my head. We rode up to the fourth floor in silence and I still had my crappy cup of coffee. She smiled at it and then looked down at her phone. "I can't tell you anything medical about her. Family only, but I can get you in the room."

I was thankful and figured as much. "That's more than fair, thank you so much for the help."

She smiled as we exited the elevator. We walked down the hallway, passing doors with charts and clipboards outside of them. Once we were in front of 404, we stopped.

"This is where I leave you. There's a pull-out bench near the window, and a blanket and pillow in the medical cabinet."

I gave her a weak smile. "Thank you."

I turned to enter Ramsey's room. She was covered in a white blanket, a small IV tube was hooked up to her hand, and something plastic was under her nose. She had several bandages and small stitches on her face. Her right hand was in a cast, otherwise she looked intact. I took off my suit jacket and my shoes, then my collared shirt, leaving me in just my undershirt and pants.

Laying there on the pull-out bench, I watched her sleep. Watched the screen next to her head, watched everything. I tried to sleep, but my eyes kept finding her, watching to make sure she was with me, safe and alive. After about an hour, I gave up, picked up my blanket, and quietly walked over to Ramsey's bed, gently sliding in next to her. I carefully made sure her hand wasn't bothered, then curled around her as much as I could and nuzzled her neck. I knew I would probably get in trouble for it, but at least I might get some sleep. I closed my eyes, and fell into a peaceful sleep, thinking of all the reasons why I should keep Ramsey, even though I didn't deserve her. They were good thoughts to end the day on. Especially knowing that come tomorrow, I'd let her go because in this, I would lay down my selfish desires and let her have what she deserved—a life free of me.

THIRTY-EIGHT

I woke up to a full bladder that was nearly ready to explode. I lifted my head and looked down towards my legs, trying to see if there was a catheter line put in. I mean, I thought I wouldn't feel the pressure on my bladder with that thing in. I couldn't see anything, and it was still slightly dark outside, so I pressed the red button on my TV remote, requesting a nurse. She came in seconds later, and must have known what I needed because she moved my guard rail on the bed into the correct position and helped me get up. The nurse seemed nice; she grabbed my IV stand and followed me to the bathroom that was attached to my room. As I got situated, I dared ask her, "So, no catheter then?"

Her blue eyes seemed to light up at my question, and she may have even held back a smile. "No honey, your legs work fine, so we left that out."

She shut the door and left me to do my business. As I did said business, I wondered what had happened to my snuggly bedmate.

I had woken up in the middle of the morning, or night, whatever it was, and felt a body next to mine. I couldn't look up, but from the angle down and the smell, I knew it was Jimmy. The safety and comfort, and probably drugs, helped me fall back asleep, but now he wasn't around. It made that sickly feeling come back, that he might pull away or leave me alone. I didn't want Jimmy to leave me, I wanted him to help me get through this. I washed my hands, careful to avoid the IV line, and then looked up at the mirror and stared at my reflection. I didn't recognize myself. There were tiny cuts and large bruises all over my face. My nose was bandaged, my lips were cut and swollen, and my whole face was puffy and gross. I gently touched parts of my face and held back tears. I tried to focus on my hair instead of my face. I also really wanted a shower but figured I might need to wait until they took out the IV line. I pulled my fingers through my hair as best as I could, and tried to braid part of it back, but without a hair tie, I couldn't keep it in. For now, it would have to do. I finished the braid and headed back into my room.

The nurse was typing on a laptop that was attached to a large machine. When she saw me, she smiled. "Everything okay?"

As in, did I pee? Oy, the vulnerability of this place. I gave her a quick look and headed to the bed. "Yes, all good, thanks."

I got back in as comfortably as one can with an IV hooked up to their hand. The nurse kept typing, so I took inventory of the room. There was no extra pillow on the pull-out bench by the window, no extra blanket, and it looked like no one had been here at all. I wondered for a second if maybe I had imagined Jimmy being with me last night. He felt so real, though; that, or I wasn't ready to admit delirium yet.

"So, hon, we have the doctor coming in to go over things with you in a bit. Anything I can get for you until then?" the nurse asked, while finishing up some notes on the whiteboard that was by the entrance to my room. I realized how ravenous I was, and definitely required some food.

"Uh, there is room service or something like it, right?"

She looked over at me from the whiteboard. "Yeah, something like it, they open at 6:15." I looked at the big wall clock and wanted to cry—still another forty-five minutes to go.

"Are you sure they can't open any sooner? I haven't eaten in a long time, and I think I might be starving."

She gave me a funny look when I said that, sure she probably didn't believe me. I wanted to point to my face and hand as proof, but what good would that do? She put the lid on the whiteboard marker and turned to me with an empathetic smile.

"Sorry hon, I can't force the warden who runs that kitchen to do anything. Don't you have someone here that can run to a fast food joint or something for a breakfast sandwich? I thought I saw a guy curled up next to you last night?"

A-ha! I knew it.

If my face would cooperate, then I would smile like the devil himself. I knew Jimmy had snuggled me last night, but where the heck was he now? I looked down at my hands, and then out the window. "Uh, yeah, I think he had to go into work early. I'm not sure."

Pathetic. So, pathetic.

She gave me another sad smile and then looked at the clock. "Hang in there, hon, it's almost time." The nurse looked at her wristwatch and then left me, starved and alone. I was being a little dramatic, but in that moment, it felt very justified. I didn't have my cell, or any way to call someone. I wouldn't call my mom and I didn't know Laney's cell by heart since she changed it.

Damn you, digital age!

I rested my head back against the bed, and closed my eyes, hoping to fall back asleep, when I heard a light knock on the door. A second later, it opened and in came another nurse holding a white paper bag that smelled like sausage and cheese and right at that moment, heaven itself. My mouth watered as the nurse made her way towards me. She had dark hair and looked a little older than me. She wore purple medical scrubs and the closer she got, I caught her name tag said: Amy. She came up to my bed and helped turn the table next to me into an actual food tray over my lap.

"Hey there, sweetie, someone thought you might be hungry when you woke up and asked that we bring this in for you."

Jimmy strikes again. That man was worrying me, feeding me, and melting my heart, but also pissing me off all at the same time.

I tried to put some hair behind my ears as I sat up straighter. "Thanks, I'm starving." She opened the bag and placed the breakfast bagel out in front of me, then pulled a plastic cup from the bathroom and filled it with water, setting it in front of me.

"It might not be my place, so I apologize if I overstep, but that man sure seems to care a lot about you," she said with a dreamy smile on her face. She was so pretty when she smiled, it was like she glowed or something.

I took the cup of water and sipped, then replied gently, "Maybe, but then why isn't he here?" I tried to sound funny, or joking, but it came out with a little edge to it. Amy the nurse straightened and threw away the extra bag and napkins.

"He was worried all night about you. He knows he isn't exactly allowed in here until official visiting hours because he's not family."

Oh. Duh, Ramsey, always so dramatic.

I tried to hide my embarrassment over assuming that he had just ditched me. "Oh, that makes sense. Thank you so much for bringing this in."

Hopefully giving her the hint, she needed to vacate my

room, so I could stop turning fifteen shades of red and also eat my food like a ravenous wolf.

She smiled again and looked like she wanted to say something else, but turned and walked out the door. I would feel bad, but I remembered that I had just survived abduction and abuse, so I deserved a little slack.

As hungry as I was, I had to gently and tentatively bite into my bagel, as I worked past my wounds. I slowly, and painfully, began to devour it. The juices from the sausage and cheese blended with the egg, and all morphed into a magical tonic for my aching body. Once I finished, I felt full and happy. I leaned back in my bed and closed my eyes, thinking about Jimmy, the food, and the fact that he took care of me. It made me smile. As awkward as it felt to smile with my mouth all jacked up, I did it anyway because Jimmy wasn't pulling away from me—I hadn't lost him.

A LITTLE AFTER SEVEN IN THE MORNING, THERE WAS A LOT more activity in the room. The doctor had stopped by. He informed me that last night, when I was brought in, I was given a variety of tests to ensure there wasn't any brain damage. The cat scan had shown some concerns, in addition to the bruising on the face, which earned me my overnight observation. I had a hairline fracture in my right hand, and several small cuts that needed sutures that would dissolve on their own, in time. But mostly, I was fine.

I wanted to tell them that part of my care should have been food, and a warmer blanket, but this wasn't some good Samaritan who had found me, it was the fine folks of Mercy Hospital. My doctor and nurses assured me that I would be released that afternoon, as long as someone was there to pick me up. The doctor did send in someone from the psych ward to talk to me about PTSD, encouraging me to talk with someone about what happened. I took their printout of suggested therapists and grunted my agreement. I just wanted to go home, but my head injury and body aches required some heavy pain meds that would prevent me from driving. I wasn't exactly sure what to do about leaving, since I wasn't able to contact anyone. I still had no way of contacting Laney, who was the only person I would call, since Jimmy still hadn't shown up after visiting hours started again.

I decided that I would call my old place of work and get Laney's desk phone. It was Friday, so she should be working.

Just as I started calling, I heard a commotion outside my door. I watched to see if someone would come in, hoping and even praying a little that it was Jimmy. I wanted to see him, talk to him, and process everything that had happened with him. The door started to open and a short, redhead came storming through with a shopping bag, and a large purse. I stared at my best friend as she made her way to me, and I noticed my strong and independent Laney had tears running down her face.

I reached out to grab her hand. She took it and held it gently, as she took in my face and bandaged hand. Her eyes had turned glossy from the tears, and her mouth was turned down. We stood like that for a second, and I tried to see myself through her eyes. If my best friend was hurt and damaged, I would be furious. I could see that Laney was battling some anger as she wiped at her tears and walked over to the bench by the window. She cleared her throat, still facing the window.

"I brought you some yoga pants, a sports bra, and a t-shirt. You're so tall, all I could think of was yoga pants, or some shorts. Since it's so cold outside, I thought yoga pants would be good. The bra will be tight, because you're bigger than me, but it will better than walking around with those things on the loose."

"Laney." I tried to get her attention because she was

rambling, and she only did that when she was scared and trying to deflect some deep emotions.

"I didn't think about shoes, though. I think I figured you would have shoes. Do you have shoes? I can go find some slippers, this place is a hospital, I'm sure they have slippers somewhere."

"Laney..."

"Do you have socks?" She started rummaging through the bag and pulling things out of it.

"Laney, stop, look at me." She had to stop, I needed her to stop.

She kept rummaging, refusing to look at me. "Damn socks, I always forget about socks. I blame the summer and flip flop season. It just barely ended, you know? I miss summer, I could have just grabbed you a t-shirt and shorts, and you could have walked out of here barefoot. But no, we live in Chicago and it's freezing..."

"*Laney!*" I yelled, and she turned around, dropping the bag. She looked like she had just come out of some mind trance or something.

"Stop, please. Come sit and talk to me." I held out my hand out, but Laney started shaking her head back and forth.

"No, Ram, I can't stop. Because if I stop, and we sit down, and we talk about the fact that you were kidnapped, and tortured, and almost killed, I will lose it. Do you understand me? I will lose it!"

She yelled the last part before she turned back around and started to gently fold the clothes she had taken out. Once she was done, she turned to face me again.

"What do you need? What can I get you? They told me you can go home today, so maybe I can help you get in the shower?"

I wanted to respect and understand why she didn't want to talk about it, but I needed to talk about it. But maybe talking about it outside of the hospital would work, so I let it go for now.

"Yes, a shower would be great. They took out the IV line earlier, so I just need to wrap my hand and be careful of my face, and it will be fine. I don't have anything, though…"

Laney cut me off by holding up a finger, then leaned down to pick up her big black bag. She pulled out two bottles of what looked like shampoo and conditioner, face wash, a toothbrush and toothpaste.

"All here. I knew you wouldn't have anything."

I tried to smile at her, and it only made her frown and turn away from me. She grabbed my clothes and headed into the bathroom, then came back for me.

Once I was all done with the shower, she brushed my hair and put my hair in a pretty braid. I was sitting cross-legged on the floor in front of her, while she sat on the bench by the window. Once she tied my hair off, she leaned down to hug me. She held me and after a few seconds, I felt hot tears hit my neck. I let her cry, let her feel broken with me. I cried too, hoping it would somehow cleanse the evil that infected me. I thought the shower would help, but I still felt their hands on me, their mouths, even their words. I was broken, and I wasn't sure if I'd ever be whole again. Laney held me for a while, until a chime came from her phone.

She sat up and started wiping at her tears. I slowly got up and walked back over to the bed. I didn't want to climb back in it, because there's something about returning to a bed that held you while you were broken and hurt. Once you feel healed, you don't want any part of the brokenness ever again.

I looked over at Laney and saw that she was looking at a text with frustration as her face scrunched together. We hadn't talked about her knowing that I was in the hospital. I assumed Jimmy told her, because he still hadn't shown his face. I also assumed he told her, so that I would have a ride home. Not that I didn't want and need my best friend, but I really did need to go over some things with him. I needed to talk and to vent, I needed to feel his arms around me, and for us to finally put an end to the distance that had been between us.

Laney typed a few things, then set her phone down and looked over at me. I was still awkwardly standing.

"Everything okay?" I asked, while trying to fold one of the white blankets on the bed, there were a few drops of blood on it. I scrunched my face and tossed the thing away. Laney let out a long sigh before she responded.

"Yes, it's okay. I just thought...I thought maybe Jimmy wanted to take you home. Not that I don't want to. Please understand, I do. I just know you pretty well, and I know you would want him to take you home."

I walked toward her, near the bench.

"Yeah, I was kind of hoping he would want to take me. What did he say?" I asked gently, hoping her response would be equally as gentle, and I wouldn't be crushed.

"He just said that he had to get back to the kids and wondered if I could take you home. He said he'd pay for our cab ride and mine back home."

I looked down at my bare toes, not wanting to discuss if Jimmy thought of me as a responsibility or not. I knew he felt responsible for what happened. I also knew that Rav was right, and Jimmy was pushing me away. Laney must've caught on to my mood, because she didn't push me after that. She sat down and wrapped an arm around me. "Men. What in the world are we going to do with them?"

She laughed, and I couldn't help but laugh with her.

I checked out of the hospital around one in the afternoon. Laney asked our cab to stop by a pharmacy and get my pain meds, then we headed to a sandwich shop for lunch. The way home was full of conversation but void of anything I needed to say. Laney finally turned to me and said,

"Okay, spill it. What in the heck happened, and why is Jimmy acting weird?"

I told her about the distance between him and I. I told her about Lisa's visit and my decision to move to Chicago with my mom. I told her about ice cream with Jasmine and then the room I woke up in. I slowly and gently walked through as much detail as I could, while still holding some things back, because although someone loves you and may want to know of your trauma, they usually aren't prepared for the gore of it. Once I got to the part where Rav told me that Jimmy would push me away, Laney made a sound, like it was all clicking together for her.

Once I was done telling her everything, she was quiet. She seemed like she was holding something back, the way she kept opening her mouth and closing it. Her gaze was fixed on the road in front of us, but her mind seemed like it was somewhere else.

"So, you are moving back to Chicago now?"

Her avoidance about the abduction stung a bit, but I couldn't hold it against her. She would rather not ask me anything than risk asking me the wrong thing. I looked out the window and tried to answer her question as best as I could.

"I honestly don't know. I don't want to leave Jimmy or the kids, or Theo, but at the same time, if it's the best shot for Mom, then I'll take it. Besides, if Jimmy is going to push me away, then maybe it would be better if I wasn't around for that. I barely survived the first round of it."

I saw Laney nod her head in agreement, then she looked over and smiled.

"It's going to be okay, Ram. I know it. Just hang in there. I finally have my place back, so if you need to come visit me, or stay with me, do it."

That actually helped, because if I could stay with Laney, then I could be close to Mom. Last night, I was considering going to Chicago temporarily and making sure Jimmy knew that I would be back because all I wanted was to have another shot with him. Seems he had another idea in mind.

"I think I will see if Jimmy wants to talk about it, or to talk to me, even to check up on how I am… you know?"

Laney nodded her head again, then asked, "If he doesn't?"

I looked out the window and tried to push away the pain that was starting to grow in my chest. "Then I'll have my answer. I will take Mom to Chicago, permanently."

That was the end of our heavy talk. The rest of the drive revolved around Laney's work drama, and a few stories of her latest saga with Jackson. As usual, her conversation revolving around Jimmy's best friend was short-lived and sparse. I didn't mind, I knew she would eventually want to talk about it, but it was no use trying for more when I knew she wasn't ready.

When the cab pulled up to my house, I had this haunted feeling come over me, like a monster was lurking in the bushes. I slowly got out, looked around, and started walking the steps I took just days ago. I had to remind myself that they got him, they caught the bastard. It was safe now. Saying a quick hello to my mother's caretaker, I rounded the furniture enough for my mom to see me. Once I was in front of her, her whole face lit up. She couldn't get up on her own, so I bent down to her and put my head in her lap. She stroked my hair and started crying, praising God in Cambodian. Mom always got really spiritual in her native tongue.

She released me, and I looked up at her, swiping at my own tears. Laney hugged my mom too. After a while, Laney mentioned she needed to head back to the city, and Mom's caretaker finished her shift as well, so it was just me and Mom. I sat next to her recliner and went over the details as much as I could with her. I didn't want to upset her, so I was gentle and skipped a few parts, jumping to the end, where the police came in with guns and an ambulance nearby.

She cried, and I cried. She told me how Theo was here when she woke up, and the kids. She said Theo very sweetly explained what was going on, but that Jimmy had gone to get me. The kids worked on distracting her with games of checkers, and Jasmine was asking to knit. Then, this morning, they all left once her caretaker showed up, but they promised that I would be there in the afternoon, so she just waited.

Around eight, I helped Mom get ready for bed. Once she was tucked away, the whole day hit me at once. I was exhausted, but before I could go to sleep, I remembered my cell and wondered if it was in the house somewhere. Getting up, I headed into my bedroom. I saw my bed, and noticed my purse, then turned and sure enough, on my dresser was my cell, plugged into the charger. I knew it was Jimmy. I had no idea why the man was so thoughtful and sweet, but so determined to push me away.

I touched the phone and sifted through a few emails and texts, but there was nothing from Jimmy, or anyone else, for that matter. It was weird; after an earth-shattering experience like that, I kind of expected there to be more people who cared. Except that no one knew what had happened to me. Really, I wanted to hear from Jimmy, just something. I was tired of waiting.

I decided to call him. I had played his game of distance and being away from him. Now there was no reason we had to play that anymore.

The phone rang a few times. It was still only a little after nine, so I knew he would be up.

It rang until his voicemail picked up. I tried not to acknowledge how much that stung, but it did. So, I left him a voicemail and decided that would be that. I heard the beep and left my message.

. . .

"Jimmy, it's Ramsey. I was really hoping to talk to you tonight. I think we have a lot of catching up to do, a lot of things to talk about. I understand you have had a busy day, so I won't bother you, but please call me tomorrow."

I hung up, then walked back into my mom's room and curled up under the covers. I placed my phone next to me, and for about thirty minutes, I waited, but no call or text ever came. My mind wandered all over the place, and as much as I didn't want it to, it drifted to the idea of leaving. I couldn't be here if Jimmy didn't want me, not after everything. Somewhere in the back of my mind, I saw Rav's face, in that room again, and I kept hearing him say, *"Remember who he was, don't let him push you away."*

I dreamt of Jimmy pushing me through a door while trying to shut it, but I wouldn't budge... eventually he walked away entirely.

THIRTY-NINE

JIMMY

"SAMMY, use the outside part of your foot to kick the ball, it will help direct it." I had been shouting the same thing at Sammy for an hour, and he still wasn't getting it. Jasmine had jumped in a few times to try and show him, but he wasn't catching on. I was about ready to grab a mitt and a baseball and call this whole soccer thing quits. I let out a frustrated sigh, and ran my hands through my hair, "Okay, buddy, let's try the drill from the top."

"Dad, can't we call Ramsey?" Sammy asked with a whine. He had been asking for the past hour. I had been avoiding his question for the hour, replacing his question with directions on how to position his feet. I think he was finally fed up.

"Buddy, Ramsey is still recovering, and I want to give her some space."

I had been saying that so much to the kids that I was actually starting to believe it. I still played Ramsey's voicemail from over a week ago, over and over at night, when no one else was awake, just to hear her voice. I hated this distance, but I was serious when I decided to let her go, and to keep her away from anything else that could cause her harm because of me.

Like a jerk, I didn't call her back, and I have been playing the avoidance game ever since. It didn't take much effort; Ramsey and I just fell back into that same horrible routine. She hadn't tried to call me again, and I knew she was tired of it. I swallowed the same damn lump in my throat that always surfaced when I pictured losing Ramsey.

Sammy's strong kick of the ball brought me back to what I was doing, and where I was. My kids, soccer practice, and the rest of my lonely life. Sammy had kicked it halfway across the field where it rolled to the side, close to where the fence opened. Sammy took off running towards the ball, just as someone started walking to the opening in the fence. I started to call Sammy back, when I noticed who it was.

Ramsey came strolling in through the opening, her right hand still in a small cast, but her face looked significantly better. Her hair was down, and straight, and she wore a pair of jeans and an oversized sweater that somehow transformed her into this gorgeous woman who would put anyone in a magazine to shame. I loved her. Seeing her walk toward us with her hand shoved into her pocket, her face determined and strong —I couldn't breathe.

Sammy ran to her and jumped into her arms. She wrapped her arms around him, awkwardly because of the cast, then kept walking toward us. So much for my recovery speech. I noticed that Jasmine, although beaming, was hesitant to walk toward Ramsey. I forgot about their little ice cream date, and the pain that Jasmine had endured after hearing about Ramsey's plans. I had to refer to them as plans, because I wasn't strong enough to confront what her plans really were, or what it would officially mean for us. Ramsey walked closer, and I could hear Sammy talking to her about how I had told them she was recovering. She shot me a quick look, then set Sammy down.

"Sammy, go grab me the soccer ball. I am much better now, buddy."

Sammy took off for the abandoned ball by the fence. Ramsey stood there and found my eyes; she looked hopeful but reluctant. I looked at the ground. Like a fucking coward.

She ignored me and moved over to Jasmine. She kneeled in front of her, then, with her good hand, pushed some of Jasmine's hair away from her face. Jasmine started to cry, then threw her arms around Ramsey's neck. Ramsey stood with Jasmine, rubbing her back and soothing her with words too quiet for me to hear. Seeing her hug my daughter, the daughter that had no mother, that had been abandoned and left; God, it opened me up and made me want to kick my own ass for what I was doing to Ramsey, and to me.

Ramsey gently set Jasmine back down and then kissed her on the forehead. Sammy had run back and handed the ball to Ramsey. She spun it in her hands a few times, then bounced it from knee to knee, dropped it on the ground, and started to demonstrate the same kick to Sammy that I had been attempting for an hour.

"See my toes? Sammy, watch what I do with my foot. See how it forces the ball to go where I want?"

Sammy was watching her feet intently, while I couldn't stop watching her face.

"Yeah, I see. I just don't know how to make the ball go that way," Sammy replied, a little confused.

"Look ahead and see where you want the ball to go." Sammy watched her and moved his feet, until they mirrored hers. Ramsey nodded her head.

"Exactly like that, but with your eyes, and the edge of your toes."

Sammy brightened up as understanding seemed to sink in.

"Now go practice, superstar." She patted his head lightly as Sammy took off toward the field. Jasmine joined him, so he would have some competition while he worked on the drill.

That just left the two of us, and I was so cowardly, I was ready to fake a phone call to get out of having to face her. She must have seen what I might do, because she turned to me with her arms crossed and her face set.

"I just came to see the kids, Jimmy. I don't want to make this awkward for you, but I wanted to say goodbye to them before I leave tomorrow."

Her tone was sharp, and I hated it. She was mad at me, and some part of me that was still alive and breathing wanted to caress her hair and rub her back, and do everything to make her happy again.

My heartrate had spiked, and breathing was difficult. It felt like a lifeforce had claimed my body and refused to cooperate with what I wanted, which was Ramsey. I didn't trust my voice, but I had to say something to her.

"How long will you be gone for?" I kept my eyes on the kids.

She shuffled her feet and watched the kids as well.

"Three weeks. Mom has a chance at surgery, and some other methods that might help…"

She stopped talking and watched the circle she had drawn in the dirt with her foot. My fear had become a reality—I had pushed her too far and now she wanted to leave. I didn't realize that I had stopped watching the kids and started watching the ground by my feet until I heard her speak again.

"After that, we might stay there. It will all just depend on a few things and how they go. I will work remotely for you, and for Sip N Sides, if that's okay?"

I finally turned to look into her beautiful clear blue eyes. I nodded my head, because my words wouldn't be enough. She looked like she wanted to say something else. I waited and prayed it was anything but goodbye.

"Jimmy, I..." she tried again. God, I wanted to kiss her, to take her and never let her go. I hated this, hated me, hated everything.

She looked like she was holding back some tears as she finally said her peace. "Goodbye, Jimmy."

The air left my lungs, my stomach cramped. Goodbye. There it was, the word that would finish us. All I had to do was say something to stop her, grab her arm, pull her in, hug her. Something. Anything.

Instead, I stood there, allowing the weight of departure, and the finality of her getting free from me, hang between us. I reminded myself that she was better off. She needed better, deserved better, and eventually would get better. I watched her walk away from me. Watched her cross the field. Watched her kick the ball several times with the kids, and then she knelt down in front of both of them and hugged them tightly. She stood, and without a single glance back at me, she walked back through the gate.

I WAS FOLDING CLOTHES IN THE LIVING ROOM WHEN DAD CAME home. He wore one of his flannel shirts, with his dark navy-blue coat, and a black snow hat. We didn't have snow yet, but the weather had turned colder over this last week. As if I needed proof, I felt a shiver run up my arms as the cold air crept in with him when the door opened. He had red in his cheeks from the cold, and his expression was happy as he made his way from the entryway into the living room. He started to shrug out of his coat and hat, then turned and with one look at me, his whole face changed. I finished folding the pair of Spiderman pajama bottoms and turned away from him. I wasn't in the mood to discuss Ramsey, or her leaving. I knew he wanted her to stay, and he knew that I would somehow manage to screw it up. I placed Sammy's clothes back into the basket and started up the stairs until Dad's voice stopped me.

"So, that's it? You give up, and she leaves, and that's how this story ends?"

His voice was gruff and laced with anger.

"Dad, this isn't a story. She's going to Chicago for treatment for her mom for a few weeks. She might come back... might not," I replied, while holding the basket against my hip and leaning against the wall.

Dad looked at the ground, then placed his hands on his hips. "I see."

He sounded sad. I hated that I had ruined this for him, and for the kids, but eventually they would understand that love wasn't selfish. Selfish would be to keep her, knowing that I was the reason she was kidnapped and hurt. I was the reason she wore a cast on her hand.

Seeing that my dad wasn't making any moves to continue the conversation, I turned and headed up towards the kid's bedrooms to put their clothes away.

I took my time with the clothes, and then with the dishes, then with the dusting. I didn't stop moving until well after midnight. I didn't want to stop and think or remember the look in Ramsey's eyes as she said goodbye to me. I was about to head out into the garage to work on my bike when I heard my Dad making his way upstairs.

"Jimmy, you up, son?" he called as he drew closer to the top of the stairs.

"Yeah, Dad. I'm right here."

He came to a stop at the sight of me. He carefully made his way up the last three steps, then stood in front of me. Looking down, then hesitantly lifted his right hand that held a book...

"Look, son, I found this, and I think..." He trailed off, sounding as if he was reconsidering his decision.

Putting the small leather-bound book in my palm, he looked me square in the face as he finished his thought.

"I think you should read this. I don't share it lightly, and would never betray her thoughts, but I can't shake this feeling, like maybe you need to read it."

I looked down at the small book and noticed a dried flower holding the place of a page. I ran my hands gently over the pages and carefully opened one of them. Black, cursive ink jumped out at me, and the top of the page was dated 1978. My eyes shot up to my dad's, whose were worried, and misty.

"Is this her journal?" I asked, a little out of breath, because the idea that my father had this the entire time made me feel confused and angry.

"Why did you keep this from me? I would have wanted to read her thoughts... you knew how much I missed her."

The words were choppy and strained. How much more of my mother was my father hiding from me?

"Son, I understand your hurt, but these were private thoughts from before her and I married, before you entered our lives. There's things in there that I didn't want...." Dad trailed off with a hint of sadness. He gripped his neck and looked at the ceiling.

"There's things in there that I didn't want you to read about me. To know about me," he finished with a gruff finality to his voice.

I saw his point, but it still was painful. Mostly because I just missed her and would love her advice right now. I pushed aside the hurt that was now making its way through my chest and closed the book. I carefully ran my hands over it and gave my father a small nod of thanks, then turned around heading to my room.

I shut the door behind me and placed the journal next to my bed on the nightstand. I sat down and looked at the tiny book as emotions rolled through me. There was something precious about getting to read someone's rumination after they had left this earth, and it wasn't something that I was going to take lightly.

I laid back against my headboard and reached for the journal. Cradling it in my hands, I opened to the page marked by the flower, dated April 14th, 1978.

APRIL 14TH,

TODAY WAS A PAINFUL DAY AND HONESTLY, I AM SHOCKED RIGHT now that I am up at this hour writing. My mind can't seem to shut off, or stop playing what happened over and over, like some horrible movie.

I WENT TO PIKEY'S BAR TONIGHT. I MET THEO THERE BECAUSE he wanted me to. God, I love that man, so he knew that I would come, even though I hate biker bars, and I hate that part of his life. He had called me while I was at work and agreed to meet for dinner at the bar around six. I went straight there after work, walked in, and found him playing pool, drunk as a skunk. Again. If this was the first time he'd called me to meet him, only to end up getting hammered before our date, I might be surprised. Sadly, it was a regular occurrence for him. I knew before he even turned toward me that he was hammered, and probably high. When he called me earlier, he wasn't stoned or drunk, so he must have gotten busy between now and then. Tonight, was supposed to be a fresh start for us. He promised me that he was pulling out of the biker life, pulling out of illegal things, pulling out of all of it. Silly me, I actually believed him and the rest of my shift at work, I smiled and even felt excited about seeing him tonight.

I stood there in the bar with my arms crossed, waiting for him to see me, or recognize that he'd done it again—called me, made plans, only to end up too hammered to follow through. I waited for ten minutes before I walked over to him. I was so embarrassed that I was the one who had to

409

physically pull him away from the pool table he was at. Once I did, he laughed, then tried to kiss me. I slapped him and walked away. He didn't follow.

I came home and showered off the smell of that place and washed away all the tears that I cried over this man that held my heart and continually crushed it. I didn't know how to be free of him, I loved him so much it hurt. Because when he isn't drunk or stoned, he's amazing. He's funny, and charming, thoughtful and kind, and the type of man that I could see being a father to my children, and a husband to me. Later that night, Theo came by the house. Stacey let him in, knowing that it was important for me to see him.

Theo followed me into my room, but he didn't move to touch me. He was sober, or nearly there; sober enough to talk at least. He sat across from me, in my vanity chair. He looked sad, and tired, his black hair was greasy and looked unwashed; staring me down, he told me that he couldn't keep doing this to me. That he wasn't any good for me, that I could do better, and deserved better than him. He told me that he was sorry, but he loved me too much to keep putting me through it, and thought that if he let me go, I would find some good man who could give me everything I wanted and needed.

Once he was done, I stood up, walked over to him, and slapped him across the face, then asked him to leave.

I'm angry. I'm angry that he would take the coward's way out, that he would sink so low as to assume what's best for me, without even asking me. Only a coward would do that. That's not love, it's fear.

I know what I want. I know who I want. I know what I'm worth, and I know exactly what I am willing to wait for and put up with. No one bullied me into loving Theo Stenson, no one tricked me. I knew exactly who I was falling in love with from the beginning. I said yes to falling in love, with every scar, bruise, injury, and demon in mind. I knew the broken mess that Theo is, and I still said yes, and I still wanted him. Sure, it's hard to see him like that, it guts me when I find him drunk after he already made plans with me, but it should be my choice to push him away, not his. He took away my choice in the relationship, I feel tricked. I should have a say

in how the love of my life leaves, I should get a chance to stay or go. I
should be worth more than just a man making a decision to end everything,
when we haven't both agreed on what to do. I am so angry and hurt, but
Theo won't get rid of me that easily. I will haunt his life until I get a say
in this relationship, until I get a proper make-up or break-up, but no way
am I sitting here while he calls all the shots.

I WAS COLD FROM THE INSIDE OUT. HOW CLOSE OUR LIVES HAD
become, my father's and my own. How close he had come to
losing my mother, the best thing that ever happened to him.
The woman who hung the moon and stars, according to him,
the woman who he could never replace because he said she
took his whole heart, and now there was nothing left to give to
anyone else. He was entirely content to live his life alone,
without her, because she had completed him so entirely. Their
love was legendary to me as a child, and as a teen growing up.

Reading about my father's actions angered me and realizing how worked up I had gotten over the idea of him walking
away without her having a say in it, was sobering. I understood
now why Dad had given this to me. Dad tried the same move
on Mom all those years ago. I had a feeling if I kept reading, I
would see the only reason my parents had me, would be
because of Mom's persistence. I smiled at that, then immediately frowned. Ramsey had tried to be persistent with me, but I
pushed her away, every chance I got. She was now leaving
because I pulled this stupid stunt on her, and I didn't know
what to do to fix it.

I could feel the crater in my heart start to heal over at the
words from my mother, it gave me a glimpse into Ramsey's
mind. If women were anything alike, then I had a pretty good
idea at how I should play this one out. Either way, I had to try.
It wasn't fair for me to just walk away without even giving her a
choice in it. I had to figure out a way to fix it. The idea of

keeping Ramsey was like breathing again; it felt right. I closed the journal, placed it back on the nightstand, and started thinking over my plan. I had made a lot of mistakes with Ramsey, so I couldn't downplay this. I had to get it right. Somehow, someway, I just had to.

FORTY

MOM HAD BEEN CHECKED into the Chicago Center for Medicine for two weeks now. The first week was hard on her, she didn't want to be there, and even refused a visit from me, stating that I forced this on her. I answered that with a fat eye roll and a large glass of wine at Laney's apartment, where I had been crashing while Mom did her treatments. The second week was easier, and so far, she hadn't refused to see me. Although, I did receive a lecture nearly every single day about leaving Belvidere, and Jimmy.

I wouldn't even have to deal with the lectures if the idiot hadn't shown up right before we were going to leave. Suddenly he wanted me to stay, suddenly he wanted to talk, suddenly he wanted to apologize. I walked past him, loaded my mother into the medical van, then walked to my own SUV and drove off. I had to put the idea of Jimmy wanting me, or wanting something to work between us, out of my mind before I left Belvidere. I had to, otherwise, I would never allow myself to heal.

I watched my distorted reflection in the shining elevator doors and waited for the *ding* of the tenth floor. I glanced down at my bare hand and smiled. I went and saw a doctor here about the cast, and he said it could be removed as long as I wore a brace at night. Once the elevator lightly arrived and the doors opened, I headed to my mother's room with my head down and my hand wrapped around my coffee cup. I came every day, and stayed all day, except for three times a week, when I visited my therapist for an hour. I started seeing someone for the PTSD I was struggling with after the abduction. I found someone here in Chicago, whom I was really connecting with. The therapy seemed to be helping which, after the last few weeks, was huge.

I pushed down the handle to Mom's door and went in. The rooms here were lightly furnished, so the residents didn't feel like they were in a hospital. I padded to Mom's small kitchen and set my coffee cup down. I started yelling to her from where I was, knowing she was awake, and most likely in the living room.

"Mom, what do you want to do for lunch today? I know it's early, but I thought if we planned ahead, maybe we could get an order in to that soup place that you like."

I was still looking through her small fridge when I heard muffled voices. I stood up and shut the fridge door. I heard a male voice that was distinctly not from a television. I headed into the living room and stopped short when I saw Theo sitting on my mother's couch. He was drinking coffee, like it was the most normal thing in the world. I must have been in shock, because it took me awhile to register that he had started talking to me. After a few seconds, it hit me and I heard him.

"Hello, Ramsey, how are you doing, hon?"

I stared, wide-eyed, as I neared the chair opposite of him, "I'm doing good, how are you?"

I didn't let him answer before I started in on my other question. "What are you doing here, Theo?"

He gave me that smile, the one that I pegged as a Dad

smile. One I thought I might get from my own dad a time or two, if he hadn't left us. He set his coffee down on the coffee table and leaned forward.

"I came to visit your Mom... and to see you about a few things."

I looked over at Mom, who smiled sweetly. She had one of her knitted hats on, and a pink tracksuit, her feet covered in slipper socks. I was honestly glad to see Theo, and glad that he had come to visit with Mom, she loved visitors. I smiled at the man sitting across from me, unable to resist moving toward him for a hug. I missed him. He wrapped me in his big arms and closed me in his fatherly embrace, then kissed the top of my head. A few tears gathered in my eyes and were threatening to fall.

I heard him holding back his own emotions as he said, "I've missed you, kid. Place isn't the same without you there."

The tears fell, and I let them. After a few minutes of just laying against him, I sat up and wiped at my face.

"I've missed you too, Theo."

He stroked my hair and gave me that Dad smile again,

"Well, I'm glad you're here. I have a little business to go over with you, at some point today, but I want to finish visiting with your mom before she has to go in for her rounds."

He patted my knee and I moved to stand, while smiling at him. I was glad he made my mother a priority. I chose to take the opportunity to go finish my coffee at the kitchen counter, and to catch up on emails. I leaned against the counter, while cradling my cup and holding my phone in front of my face. I hadn't checked the phone since I had left Laney's house this morning. I took the train and then walked two blocks but chose to read a finance magazine on the trip here, keeping my phone snug in my purse. I had started doing that last week, after I couldn't handle seeing the texts anymore.

At some point, I had to read them, but each day, I worked

to put it off longer and longer. Today would have been the longest I had gone before checking them, but seeing Theo here reminded me of emails that needed to be caught up on for his business. I pressed the password in for my phone and saw the little notification at the top of the screen telling me that yes, Jimmy had texted again this morning, like he had every morning since I left. Every single day, it was the same thing.

7:02 A.M.: *GOOD MORNING, RAMSEY*

8:02 A.M.: *I MISS YOU, RAMSEY. I MISS YOUR SMILE, I MISS YOUR eyes, I miss your braids, and I miss your smell.*

9:02 A.M.: *THINGS I HAVE NEVER TOLD YOU #14... THE FIRST day of your interview, I secretly wanted to give you the job, but it would have been for the wrong reasons. I can tell you those reasons if you want. Or I can show you.*

9:30 A.M.: *I WAS SO STUPID, AND I HOPE YOU CAN FORGIVE ME*

EVERY DAY, HE STARTED OUT TELLING ME GOOD MORNING AND that he missed different things about me. He then would give me some fact or thing he never told me before, then he would ask for forgiveness. The first week was all about the different things he went through and missed about me during the time he was doing the deal with Davis. This week had been a little bit of everything, but I didn't mind.

Every day, I looked forward to them and every day, he whittled away at this barrier between us. I missed him. I still

416

loved him, but not once had I responded to a single text message of his. Although I wasn't replying to him, it didn't stop me from rereading his messages late at night, every night, as well as stalking all his social media platforms, and replaying old voicemails. It was pathetic. Still, I had to remember that it was my turn to put distance between us. Not because I wanted to punish him, or because I was being petty, but because I hated the girl I had become. I hated how weak I was while I waited for Jimmy to make all the rules. I needed to remind both of us that I couldn't be that person ever again. Not to mention, all the things I was working through with my therapist regarding the abduction, and my mom. I just needed some space from the drama that consumed me.

I moved to my email folder and started going through the calendar for Jimmy's restaurant. We were coming up on November, and I wanted to get a look at the Thanksgiving work schedule and what timecards would look like. I noticed that the first week of November had an entire Friday evening blocked out for a private event, but no one was staffed for it. I wrinkled my forehead as I swiped my finger back through October's notes, just to see if there was anything about it.

Why would there be an entire evening blocked out, during one of the busiest days of the week? It didn't make any sense and the more I dug into it, the more confused I became. I had managed to handle business for two weeks without contacting Jimmy, and I planned to somehow keep it that way. Someone must have information on the staff shortage, so I decided that I would shoot an email to Jimmy's manager. Surely, he would know, especially with the date a little over a week away.

HEY JOSH,

. . .

I WAS LOOKING THROUGH THE CALENDAR FOR NOVEMBER AND noticed a Friday night on November 6th, where the whole restaurant is closed for a private party, but no staff is booked for the event. Do you know what that's for, and how we can fix it? Thanks for any help you might have regarding the issue.

RAMSEY BENNINGTON

I SENT THE EMAIL OFF TO JOSH, AND THEN CLOSED OUT OF MY business email account. I was about to pull my laptop out when my phone chimed again. It was Josh with a reply. *That was quick.*

HEY RAMSEY,

I SEE THE DATE YOU ARE REFERRING TO, BUT THE ONLY NOTES I have on it are: 'boss override: see Jimmy for any questions.' Hope that helps, he will know what's going on.

JOSH JAKOBS

I LAID MY HEAD DOWN ON THE COUNTER AND STARTED LIGHTLY banging it on the surface because I *really* didn't want to talk to Jimmy. I wouldn't even care about someone's stupid mix-up, except that I needed to plan ahead for payroll. I decided that I could put it off for a few more days; maybe Josh would say something, and Jimmy would fix it. I pulled out my laptop and started working on Theo's books, so I would be prepared for the business talk he wanted to have later. Everything seemed fine, he had made a few other big purchases, but it was all to improve the interior of Sip N Sides. His business was steady.

I heard a small knock at the door and then saw Alice, Mom's nurse, come in. I liked Alice. She was in her late forties, and grew up on a farm, like Laney. She was tough as nails, while being as caring and protective as a Mama Bear. Mom loved her too, probably because they both liked discipline and an older, more archaic, way of life.

"Good morning, time to start your rounds, Carla," Alice said in a sing-song voice, while walking further into the room. It didn't take her long to spot Theo.

"Oh my. Who do we have here? I didn't know you had a gentleman caller, dear."

I moved around until I could see Mom's face. She always got embarrassed too easily. Sure enough, she had a red face and waved Alice off with a huff.

"Oh, stop that. This is Theo Stenson, a very good friend of mine. He just came to visit with me and go over some business with my daughter."

Alice turned to me and smiled. "Gee-whiz, does he have a son?"

She winked at me, then Theo's eyes slowly met mine. My eyes were dry and irritated from tears that I refused to shed for his son. Just the mention of him had me breathing harder, and my face blushing. I hated my reaction to this whole situation, so I turned away and headed back to my laptop. Alice seemed to notice my awkward reaction.

"Must have stepped in some messy horse poo with that comment."

She went to help Mom up and together, they made their way out of the room, into the hall. I waved at Mom and told her I would be here waiting when she came back.

Once they were gone, the room was too quiet, and too

stuffy. I didn't want to talk about Theo's son, or me leaving, or the fact that his son had been sending me text messages all day, every day, since I had been gone. I packed up my laptop and threw away my coffee cup as Theo made his way to the door.

"Let's get some air and talk business, hon."

I WATCHED THE WATER FOUNTAIN SPLASH, THE WATER LAPPING from stone to stone as Theo situated in his seat. The indoor fountain was supposed to be serene and therapeutic to everyone who was here for treatment. Although we were both here to see someone we cared about, I couldn't help but feel like an imposter, taking the serenity from the room that the fountain offered, that was reserved for the hurting and broken. I guess I could argue that we're all hurting and broken in our own way.

I looked around the room and took in the large open seating area. There were floor to ceiling windows and solid hardwood floors. Comfortable white armchairs and couches were neatly placed, and a large piano sat in the corner. It was peaceful and calm, like a beautiful bubble, to contain all the pain and agony that went on in here. I watched the spraying water a few moments longer, getting lost in the sounds of the flowing water, then focused on the graying man in front of me.

Theo had a silver laptop open in front of him, a pair of small black glasses perched on his nose, and his eyebrows drew together in a look that could only be described as frustrated or utterly confused. He was determined to start up the laptop and get it ready for me without any help. Whatever "it" was. A few moments later, he held up his fingers and snapped while letting out a sound that I could only compare to The Fonz from *Happy Days*. I smiled at him and tried to lean forward to see his

420

screen, which was dumb because there was no way that I could see it from where I was sitting.

I sat back in my chair, trying to be patient as Theo watched the screen load, only to find another screen that needed to load. I knew this because he kept letting out exaggerated sighs while saying, "Come on, how many screens need to load in order to use this thing?"

I stifled a laugh and pulled out my cell phone, so I didn't rush him.

It was a mistake because I saw a text message come through from Jimmy. It was a picture of him and the kids. Sammy was dressed in his soccer uniform, Jasmine's hair was in a sloppy braid, and Jimmy was kneeling next to Sammy wearing dark jeans and a black hoodie. Sammy had both hands raised, like he was celebrating, and his smile could put the earth and moon to shame. I choked back a laugh and a cry at the same time, because seeing them all together opened the locked-away hurt and rejection that I had been holding in. The caption with the photo read, *"Sammy won his game yesterday. His coach complimented his footwork..."*

I TURNED MY PHONE OFF, SO THAT I WOULDN'T CRY, OR respond, because if there was one way for Jimmy to get me to respond, it would be with the kids.

Theo finally let out a relieved sigh and turned the computer toward me. I sat up straight, put my phone in my purse, and looked at the screen in front of me. It looked like a document of some kind, that Theo had pulled up from an email attachment. I skimmed over it, but from what I could see, it looked like a legal form of some kind, with verbiage like "As the current owner, I beseech..." and "In the event of..." typed everywhere.

I glanced at him. "Theo, what am I looking at here?"

He leaned forward and took his glasses off. "Ramsey, I want to shoot straight with you. From the first night you walked into my bar and told me that awful story about my son, of all people, you became like a daughter to me."

I gave him a sly smile and reminded him of that night. "You mean, the son you let me complain about for over an hour, but refused to tell me was actually your son?"

He gave me a look of exasperation. "Yes, that one. Now listen. I thought long and hard about this, and you might say no right now, but I want you to think it over and let me know *after* you have had a chance to read through it and talk to your lawyer friend about it."

Confused, I glanced over what was in front of me again. "Theo, what are you saying? What is this exactly?"

Theo sighed and sat back in his chair, then pitched his fingers under his chin. "Loretta always wanted the bar to go to someone who knew the pain of going through somethin' to build it. Not just flashy cash and real estate. She wanted someone with salt, with blood on their hands and fire in their heart, to take it over, and then continue to pass it along to the same type of strong individuals.

"The bar was never a good fit for Jimmy because he's beyond it. He sees money and a future in the flashy things. The bar needs someone more down-to-earth, someone with a heart," he finished saying while staring at the fountain, no doubt drawing from its powers like I was earlier.

I glanced at the computer screen again, not brave enough to scroll down on the page. "So, this is about you retiring, and leaving the bar to someone?"

He smiled and nodded. "Yes, I'm ready to retire."

I smiled at the idea of that—of him relaxing, spending time fishing, and with his grandkids.

"Okay, I am glad to hear that you're retiring, but who are you handing it off to?" I was a little sad. I loved Sip N Sides. It was old, but it had grown on me, like an old sweater or an old dog that's faithful and that you can't imagine your life without. My mind started to wander to who would take it over. What if they were terrible, what if it was a bank? What about everything we pinned on Pinterest? I felt like I was about to come out of my skin as I waited for him to answer.

Theo smiled, then gestured at me with his hand. "You, honey. I want you to have it. To own it. The only request I have is that you leave the name alone, and keep some of the theme the same, so it will always feel open to the everyday person. Not the suited men and women of America, but the flannel shirts, the waitresses, and dock workers. I want it to be a place for people to gather after a long day, where they find rest and comfort. That was always Loretta's dream."

I couldn't find words. Loretta sounded like my kind of woman the more I heard about her. I loved her dream, and something warm started to take root in my heart at the idea of owning Sip N Sides, of keeping a place for people to gather.

Before I could reply, Theo started in again. "Did I ever tell you why Loretta originally wanted to open Sip N Sides? It's not about the dream I just told you." He waved a hand at me, like he was trying to dismiss my train of thought.

I shook my head at him and stayed quiet.

"I couldn't stay away from the biker bars. I can't tell you how many times I would call her up and ask her to meet me at one, knowing she hated them, but needing her anyway. She'd show up, and I was always either fighting, gambling, or doing something illegal. When I *was* sober, I would see the look of disgust on her face. She hated those bars. One day, during one of our uglier fights, she was screaming at me, wondering why I kept going back to them. Wondering why I couldn't just leave them behind. I finally told her, because it was a place to gather, a community, a home away from home. As messed up as it sounded, it was the truth. The only truth I had."

Theo's eyes were sad and had this far-off look in them. He stared at the table, not looking at me as he kept talking.

"Anyway, after that fight, she came up with this idea to create our own place, our own bar. She knew giving up the liquor wouldn't be that difficult if I changed the environment and became the person making money from it. It would force me to stay sober. She wanted to give me what I couldn't find—the strength to leave the biker bars for good. So, she did. We opened Sip N Sides, I left the biker bars, the whole biker life behind, as much as possible. I still went back from time to time because they owned me, but it wasn't my regular hangout.

"We started a life here in Belvidere. Loretta poured her heart and soul into that place, and it was all so that I would have a place to go that wouldn't tear us apart and wouldn't end up killing me or getting me arrested. It did something to us, her and I. It forged this fire between us, it bonded and sealed what we had, so that it would never again be shaken. I could never thank that woman enough for creating that place for me."

I was crying, because it was a beautiful story of love and sacrifice. Loretta clearly loved Theo, she loved him so much that she created something just for him, so she wouldn't lose him. My lungs felt heavy as I considered the similarities between Theo and Loretta, compared to the dysfunction that painted the connection between Jimmy and me. She had dealt with the ugly world of biker life, the Brass, and probably Davis at one point. She fought through it, survived, and won her happily ever after. I wanted very much to carry that on. I just didn't want to hurt Jimmy over accepting it. This was his mother's dream; he must be crushed that it was being offered to someone else.

"Theo, I am so honored to be asked to continue something so important. Every part of my soul is shouting, yes! But my mind is worried about how Jimmy would take this? Won't he be angry that it's being offered to me?"

Theo leaned forward and smiled. "Jimmy wouldn't stop harassing me these last few weeks about when I was going to ask you. He wants very much for you to say yes."

So that I would stay. So that I would give him another chance.

I gripped the edge of the table with my good hand and with my still healing one, I searched for a date on the screen while asking Theo, "When did you draw these up? Is this just some ploy to get me to come back, for Jimmy's sake? Because I—"

"No, No, No. Stop right there," Theo cut in, his face stern.

"I have watched you two ping-pong back and forth too many times to keep up. This has nothing to do with whatever is happening between you. I had these drawn up after the first time I let you build a Pinetree board for the bar."

I couldn't keep in my laughter at that. "You mean a Pinterest board?"

His face flushed, and he waved a hand at me. "Oh, whatever it's called. When you started decorating it, I knew then. When you were careful with my money, even after you saw how much extra I had. You treated it like it was yours."

I was smiling like a fool. "Theo, I do want to look it over with Laney, only because she can usually tell me if the food is too big for my mouth or not, if you know what I mean. She knows me better than anyone else, and if she thinks I can do it, then I know I can. Thank you for believing in me, and for asking me."

I moved to stand up and he met me halfway, wrapping me into a big hug. Theo hugged me tight, then gently said in my ear. "On a side note, the kids, and I sure miss you, honey."

That made me feel like crap. Was I punishing them for what was going on between Jimmy? I stood back and straightened my shirt.

"Theo, the doctors have no idea what is going on with

Mom. She's responding to the treatments, which hasn't happened since she was diagnosed. They originally gave her six months, but now she's doing so well, that they want to send us home. Which is great, I mean, amazing, but what I mean is, we will be going back to Belvidere. Please don't say anything to Jimmy yet, we will figure out our friendship once I'm back, but as far as you and the kids go, I will set up a date to see you and the kids as soon as I'm home."

He hugged me again. "That's great news, honey. I can't wait."

THAT NIGHT, I HAD LANEY GO OVER ALL THE LEGAL STUFF. SHE smiled big, with her million-dollar pearly-whites. Okay, maybe a million is stretching it, but those suckers cost a pretty penny. She jumped up and down, like she had just won the lottery, and threw her arms around me. Her two-bedroom, fifth floor apartment wasn't very big, but it was homey. But with her jumping, I was sure the surly Italians that lived below her were going to give us a piece of their mind. And they scared the hell out of me.

"Please say you're going to do it!" she squealed.

"That depends, Laney, does it all check out? What do you think?"

"This is beyond perfect for you, Ramsey. *Beyond!*"

"So, I should take it. You don't think it would be a bad idea?" I asked again.

She looked at me after calming down a bit, then turned her head to the side, like an inquisitive dog. "You know the books already. Is it a money pit?"

"No, not at all. It's solid, and even without the reserve, it does well enough."

"It's like a lighthouse in the storm for people. I love that."

Laney's voice trailed off as she made her way to her bedroom. Probably finding the good liquor, no doubt.

She came back with a bottle of something stupid expensive and began to pour it in two tumblers.

"Who broke up?" I asked, a little curious. She usually pulled that stuff out for bad days, or when she found out about a celebrity divorce. That breakup between Ben Affleck and Jennifer Garner was an ugly binge. She could not come to terms, no matter how much we talked it through.

"We are drinking to celebrate, duh! And to loosen you up for that phone call."

I was going to play this one off for as long as I could...

"What phone call?" I asked, acting truly ignorant.

She smiled at me. "Oh, don't play dumb. You are going to call Jimmy and ask him about that work thing, since you refuse to answer any of his personal calls or texts. You owe him some communication, and this work thing is a perfect starting place."

Shit, with a capital S. I knew I shouldn't have told her about that annoying date on the work calendar. I looked at the clock on the oven, it was only a little past seven, still completely acceptable to call about work. I panicked and looked around the room for anything else that I could use as an excuse to get out of this moment, but she was faster than me. She shoved the tumbler in my face, I drank it, then she dialed with my phone and put it on speaker. My heart was in my throat for the three very loud rings that pierced the air. Then I heard his voice.

"Hello?"

It was calm, perfect, like he was writing in a journal before he picked up. I cleared my throat from the burning alcohol as best as I could.

"Jimmy? Hey." My face was on fire. I gripped my cell phone so hard, I thought it might break.

"Ramsey?" The hope in his voice sliced through me.

"Yeah, uh…it's me. Um, sorry to bother you at home, but I have a work concern that I feel needs your attention."

Nice, businesslike. I could totally do this, like the professional I was.

"Uh… okay, what business concern do you have?" He emphasized business like it was code for something.

It wasn't! It was just business, I wanted to yell into the phone.

"There is a Friday night in November on the calendar that is booked out, but no one is staffed to accommodate the party. I need to know who all will be staffed to make payroll projections for the month."

I could hear Jimmy clicking around on his keyboard. Then he spoke up, like he had just solved the issue.

"Oh, yes, sorry about that. I just fixed it. There is one staff member I will need there. Beyond that, I won't need anyone. I just emailed you the details. Thanks for checking in about them. Did you need anything else?" he asked, with a light finality. He was being nice, but I could tell he was also being sneaky.

"No, I don't think so…" I drew out.

"Okay, have a good evening, Ramsey."

Then he hung up. I stared at my phone for a full minute before Laney pulled the phone away from me. *What just happened?* I didn't want Jimmy to hang up. In fact, I was struggling not to be angry that he didn't push to talk about us. I was a total backwards idiot, because I *didn't* want him to talk about us, but *because* he didn't, I was mad. He was sending all those texts and the picture message from earlier. Suddenly, I felt even worse because I didn't even respond to him about Sammy's big accomplishment. I sat down on Laney's big, white couch, and it swallowed me up. I drew my knees up to my chest and wanted to cry.

Laney didn't have to talk to know what was going on with

me. She tried to distract me by bringing the work thing back up. "So, what was the thing he forwarded then?"

Remembering that he was forwarding me the details, I pulled up my work email and loaded the one from Jimmy.

It was a meeting request for the Friday night mentioned... I drew my brows together as I read the rest of the email...

MEETING REQUEST FOR NOVEMBER 6TH @ 7 PM
Location: Jimmy's—Courtyard

WE WILL BE EXCHANGING OUR ENVELOPS AS PROMISED, AT THE end of six weeks. Please arrive promptly, so we can go over our findings. This is a non-negotiable meeting—You promised.

I STARED AT THE WORDS ON MY PHONE SCREEN OVER AND OVER. I read them out loud, I read them in my head, I even had Laney triple-check it to be sure I wasn't misreading or misinterpreting things. There was no accept or decline option on his email. The sneaky bastard. I guess I *had* promised, and the honorable thing to do would be to show up—it was what I would want him to do. Guess it was time to decide how exactly I would respond to what he was going to open. Was I going to say I still felt that way, or was I going to say goodbye?

"Laney!" I yelled.

She poked her tiny head out from the small kitchen. "Yes?"

"We are going to need more alcohol."

She gave me a questioning look, then looked at my phone, and grabbed two bottles of wine, and headed towards me, where I was seated on the couch. It was time I fess up to her about Jimmy and my little envelope game.

FORTY-ONE

JIMMY

"WE APPRECIATE all your help with this matter, Mr. Stenson. We understand that you have been trying to part ways with the Brass for some time. I'm sure you were as surprised to hear of Charles Davis' death as we were. Still, I can only imagine how stressful this whole thing has been for you."

The police department had assigned someone in PR to contact me. I wasn't sure where Gepsy was, or why he hadn't contacted me since the bust, but I had heard nothing until this phone call from Leslie, the PR officer.

"It's my pleasure to help however I can," I explained with a sigh, then the PR cop hung up. I felt relieved to get this over with, but hearing that Davis was found dead in his jail cell, was a surprise. Apparently, he'd hung himself with his bedsheets. Unfortunately, for anyone still loyal to Davis and the Brass, everyone in the club knew that Davis would rather go down, taking out half the country, before he took his own life. So, anyone who knew him, knew this was a murder, not a suicide. Still, I struggled with wanting to kill him myself for what he did to Ramsey, and now I was struggling with the idea that death was too good for him.

I was supposed to testify against Davis in court, but I guess that wouldn't be happening now. His death would save Ramsey from an ugly round of testifying too, but the other men who helped abduct her, would still need to be testified against.

I leaned back in my office chair and threw my phone onto the pile of papers I had been going through before I got that phone call. It was still pretty early, so I decided to go for a run before I had to get ready for work. I stood up and looked over at the bulletin board that hung over my desk. It usually held bills, and important school notices for the kids, but right in the center was a small piece of paper torn from a journal. I lightly pulled at the pin that was holding the white paper and ran my thumb over the purple lilacs that swirled along the edges of the page. As usual, I began to read it line by line, all the way through, letting the words serve as a memory and a guide for the rest of my day. This was how it was every day now, and quite possibly how it will be every day going forward.

The day Ramsey left for Chicago was a difficult one. I knew she was leaving that morning, so I got up, drove over to her house, and told her I wanted her to stay. I told her that I needed to explain, that I needed her. That we needed to talk this through, but she just walked past me, got in her car, and drove away. I sat in her yard and waited, thinking she might come back. That she might change her mind and finally give us the shot we deserved. She never did. So, I got on my bike, and rode it until it was time for Dad to go in to work.

I drank, and texted Ramsey a variety of incoherent things about how much I missed her. I repeated that disgusting pattern for three days, until I couldn't stand myself anymore. Slowly, a thought seeped in through the alcohol and the various kids' movies that narrated every night. I realized that what I was feeling was exactly what I had put Ramsey through during the Davis deal. She had endured weeks of silence from me. She had endured rejection, and now I knew how horrible those weeks were, and I wanted to kick my own ass because of it. I decided to do better. I started writing her coherent texts, instead of crazy things about how desperate I was for her. I started thinking of her and trying to be the Jimmy she deserved. Then one night, the weakness hit again. The first week with no communication from Ramsey ended with me pulling out her manila envelope.

I caved and read it without her. I had to read something from her, anything, just some words or thoughts besides the old voicemails and texts that I still had on my phone.

So now the letter stayed pinned to my bulletin board and every day I read her words, and let them wash over me, refresh me, and revive me.

I pinned the paper back in place, then headed out for my run. I needed to clear my head and get my plan together for next week.

It was a few days after the second week that Ramsey was gone that I had the idea to block out a date on the restaurant's calendar to schedule our six-week talk.

I knew the blocked-out Friday night would catch her attention, but I didn't know it would catch it as soon as it did. I was only slightly prepared for her phone call because Josh, my manager, had informed me that Ramsey had contacted him about the lack of staffing. I still didn't totally expect to see her name come across my phone that night. I smiled at the memory of our conversation about that specific night, how her voice wavered when she talked to me.

I quickly typed out the meeting request and sent it to her, knowing she wouldn't read it until we got off the phone.

It wasn't easy, but just getting to hear her voice, and getting to talk to her was more than I thought I would get.

I ran two miles, then headed home. Still thinking back about the phone call from last night, I couldn't get her voice out of my head. The run was good, it got rid of some of the excess adrenaline I had building up. I knew from what Dad had told me, that Ramsey and Carla would be coming back to Belvidere by next Wednesday, which gave me a week before I would get to see her. I decided that I would use the time to set things up for her, because if I had my way after our little meeting, she would be sticking around for a while.

I showered and dressed, then woke the kids. While they made their way down the stairs, I grabbed my phone and sent off the usual texts to Ramsey that I did every morning.

Me: *Good Morning, Ramsey.*

I always waited, just to see if she would respond to me or not. Usually after twenty minutes or so, I would send off another.

Me: *I miss you. I miss your laugh. I miss your hair. I miss getting to talk to you.*

I made the kids eggs and toast, and we talked about the big project that we were working on in the garage. The kids had found some old wooden signs and decided to paint them and write some 'Welcome Home' messages for Ramsey on them. I checked my phone, while Sammy shoveled the rest of his eggs into his mouth and Jasmine drank her orange juice.

Still nothing from her. I wasn't sure why I thought that talking to her last night would remind her that talking to me wouldn't be a bad thing, or a painful thing. I thought maybe it would remind her to be my friend.

I ran upstairs to make sure the kids had brushed their teeth, they had shoes on that matched, and had all their stuff. I attempted Jasmine's hair, although nowadays, she was getting better at doing it herself. Then I dropped them at school and headed to work. I hated those fifteen miles, because no matter how loud the music or how interesting the podcast, my thoughts always went back to Ramsey. What was she doing right now? How was she handling her dreams after the abduction? Did her body still hurt, was she okay, was she going out with Laney at night? Over and over, the questions would come and go, and by the time I parked the car at the restaurant, I felt like I had an ulcer.

Before I walked into work, I shot off another text.

ME: *THINGS I HAVE NEVER TOLD YOU #15: THAT DAY THAT YOU showed up to babysit my kids and you were so angry at me, I stayed longer than I needed to. I made it seem like I needed to show you more things about the kids, but really, I just didn't want to leave. I ended my date early, all because the entire date, I compared her to you, and all I wanted was to be around you again.*

I PUT MY PHONE AWAY, KNOWING THAT IT WOULD DRIVE ME crazy waiting to see if she responded or not. A few hours into the shift, I walked into the kitchen, and came face-to-face with Rav. Things between us were strained since the incident. He was interviewed and held for a few days in jail, then released when I vouched that he was in on our deal, and that Gepsy knew of his involvement from the beginning. It, of course, helped that Gepsy confirmed this as well on his own. After that, Rav wouldn't look at me or talk to me, except to ask about Ramsey. I put up with it for a while, until one day, I'd had enough. It was a Thursday, and the restaurant was dead. Rav was acting like he had been, and I slammed my hand down on the counter to get his attention.

His eyes jumped to mine as I quietly asked him, "Why? Why are you acting like this? I lost her, I can't lose you too, buddy."

Rav looked apologetic, then angry. He grabbed the back of his thick neck as he answered, "How can you even *want* to look at me, Jimmy? We both know that I was there that night, working for the Brass. I was working for that sick fuck who almost killed Ramsey!"

He shouted at me, then looked down and to the side, shame taking over his features.

I calmly and quietly responded to him, "So was I. He trapped both of us, Rav, let it go. I love you like a brother. So please stop acting like this. If you weren't there that night, I wouldn't have gotten to her as fast."

He looked up, red tinting his firm face. Then he gave me a simple nod. I nodded back and then left the kitchen. That was last week, and I was hoping this week, we would get back to normal.

Rav was making scones when I walked in—Ramsey's favorites. The smell of them was making my heart do little flips and dips at that memory of her.

"Smells good in here," I said, trying to sound encouraging and not heartsick.

"Yeah, just getting some of the baking out of the way," Rav said, without turning around. At least he was responding to me now. I walked forward a bit, until I was leaning against the counter opposite of him.

"So, next Friday… you don't have to come in, but I was wondering if you could make something Thursday night that I could easily reheat?"

Rav turned to look at me with a confused look. "You have a date or something?" he asked, concern obvious in his tone.

I smirked at him. "Kind of, but it's more of a business meeting," I joked. He didn't seem to think it was funny, because he turned away and started kneading the scone dough with more force than necessary.

"I can't believe you're already moving on," he grumbled under his breath.

I couldn't help but laugh. "Rav, the meeting is with Ramsey."

He turned towards me quickly, making me wonder if he'd planned to attack me. Instead, his face was soft, and his words were gentle. "She's coming back?"

I smiled. "Yeah, she's coming back...for now, at least." I hated that I still wasn't sure what her long-term plans were, or if she'd forgive me for shutting her out.

Rav stepped forward and wrapped me in a bear hug, then stepped away like nothing ever happened. I'll take that as progress. He replied firmly, "I'll make you the food."

I smiled again and walked out of the kitchen, back towards my office.

The rest of the day went by slowly, like it did every other day. I had checked my phone an insane amount of times too, just like I did every other day. Still nothing. No replies.

THERE WAS ALWAYS A TIGHTNESS IN MY CHEST AT THE END OF the day, after texting and reaching out to Ramsey and getting nothing. Today was no different. The tightness was there, making it difficult to breathe, difficult to live. I was in the pickup line at school when I saw Sammy walking out of the building with a huge bundle of blue, shiny balloons in his little fist. There had to be at least ten or fifteen balloons tied together. It made it difficult for kids to move around him, and for adults to see over him. I got out of the car, not worrying that people behind me were honking. I ran towards Sammy, who was standing next to an irritated Jasmine, I knelt in front of him.

"Hey buddy, what's going on with all this?" I gestured toward the balloons floating above his head.

He looked down at his fist, where the ends of the ribbon were tied around a red anchor. His face brightened, as he faced me. "Dad, these are from Ramsey!!" he squealed. My heart was beating rapidly, and the tightness was gone.

"What do you mean, they're from Ramsey? Is she here?" I started looking around for her like an idiot. Sammy started laughing as we started walking back towards the car.

"No, Dad, silly. She sent them to me, with a balloon man or something, but she sent this note too." He reached into his pocket with his free hand and pulled out a white piece of paper. I unfolded it and read the message,

"Sammy, I am so proud of you for winning your game. Sorry I am a little late, but when I get back, I am taking you out for ice cream, bud. - Love, Ramsey."

I refolded the paper and handed it back to Sammy, then opened the back hatch of the car to put the balloons in. Sammy and Jasmine climbed into the car and I tried to calm my emotions. I knew it was obviously sweet that she did this for Sammy, but she also wanted to avoid going through me, which left me feeling empty. I climbed back into the car and took off. As we drove, I noticed that Sammy was holding my cell phone in the back seat. I was about to ask him about it when I heard a ringing coming from the Bluetooth speaker, and saw on the navigation screen that Sammy had dialed Ramsey's number. I held my breath while it rang. Just when I thought it would go to her voicemail, I heard her beautiful voice answer...

"Hello?"

I kept quiet while Sammy yelled into the phone, not realizing it was the Bluetooth speaker that was working now.

"Ramsey, I got the balloons! I love them, and everyone was so jealous. Thank you so much!"

"You're welcome, buddy," Ramsey said with a little giggle.

Jasmine was giggling next to me in the front seat. Ramsey must have heard her because she mentioned her next.

"Jasmine, is that you? Who else is on this call?" she asked with a curious tone.

Jasmine laughed into her hand. "Yes, I'm here, so is Dad. It's just us."

Ramsey was quiet again, then spoke up. "Well, I sure miss you guys. I get back next week, what do you think if we—"

"Wait! You have to come over to our house and let Dad cook for you. He keeps saying he's cooking up a surprise for you, so you'll have to come see it!" Sammy cut in.

My face was burning. Leave it to the kids to replay words that weren't for Ramsey to hear yet, since he was, of course, referencing the night at Jimmy's that I was planning. It had nothing to do with actual food.

She was quiet, probably being pushed too far, again.

I decided to say something. "Sorry, they misunderstood a project that I was working on… That's all."

"It's no problem. Well kids, I have to run along. Thank you for calling me…"

"When can we talk to you again?" Jasmine asked softly.

Ramsey made a sound, like she was thinking, and then laughed while she responded, "Anytime you want."

Jasmine smiled. "Okay, can I call you tonight around dinner?"

Ramsey genuinely sounded happy when she said, "I'd like that."

It was after dinner, and after the kids had gone to bed, when I was washing dishes and Dad came in from Spin N Sides. My mind kept replaying the conversation that Ramsey had with Jasmine. Wondering what they talked about, Ramsey called, and Jasmine answered, then ran up to her room talking for half an hour. When she came back down, she was all smiles and giggly. It made me happy that she was reaching out to the kids, that they were connecting, even though Ramsey and I were not. Still, the tightness in my chest was there, and hadn't eased up since her name came across the screen of my phone tonight. Dad shook me from my thoughts with his hands on my shoulders as he passed me on his way to the fridge. I looked over at him and smiled, he looked happy. A lot happier than he had been in a really long time.

"Why are you so happy tonight?" I asked with a little laugh, because seeing my dad happy made me happy, but I loved to give him hell for it.

He laughed as he grabbed a bottle of water from the fridge,

"Well, I just may have gotten a phone call from a pretty girl who accepted to take over my business."

He finished with a little body sway and goofy smile. Dad had been putting off asking Ramsey ever since she left. I didn't know if he was worried about me, or her, so I finally confronted him on it and told him to track her down and talk to her about it. I may have had my issues about it in the past, but I knew beyond a shadow of a doubt that Ramsey needed Sip N Sides as much as Sip N Sides needed her. I smiled at Dad and gripped his shoulder. "She said yes?"

Dad gave me that goofy grin again. "Yep, she called me this evening and told me that she would officially like to accept the offer to take over as owner. She agreed to start training when she gets back," he said, taking a sip of his water and still grinning like an idiot.

I was happy, and this meant that she was staying here, but starting so soon meant that she might try to quit working for Jimmy's. Part of me knew that this was another weird way for her to get distance from me. I smiled for Dad anyway and patted him on the back. He made his way down to his room and I stood in the kitchen, wondering when the tightness in my chest would let up. Everyone in the house was talking to Ramsey, everyone but me. After everything I had tried, every day, it still wasn't enough. The ache in my chest grew and felt like it was consuming me. I rubbed at my chest, turned off the water, and headed upstairs to take a long hot shower and then hopefully get some sleep.

———

THE SHOWER HELPED, BUT EVERYTHING STILL ACHED. IT WAS just after ten, and I was about to turn off my lamp when I heard my phone ding. I let the lamp stay on as I grabbed the phone, and my heart was in my throat as I saw who it was from.

RAMSEY: *"THERE ARE THINGS I NEED TO KNOW. THINGS I NEED answers to… I think we should start there. I don't want to talk, because if I talk to you, I won't be strong enough to ask what I want to know or say what I need to say. Do you accept?"*

THIS WOMAN. DID I ACCEPT? OF COURSE, I ACCEPTED, DID SHE even have any idea?

ME: *OF COURSE.*

RAMSEY: *WHY WAS THERE A BEAUTIFUL, BLONDE-HAIRED WOMAN who came into Jimmy's saying that she was your wife?*

THE REALIZATION THAT RAMSEY AND I HAD NEVER SPOKE about this felt like acid in my stomach. It was all twisted and horrible. I hated that texting was the format in which we were talking about it now.

ME: *THAT IS A BIT OF A LONG STORY. FIRSTLY, IF YOU THINK she's beautiful then you should know, she has nothing on you...*

...SHE THOUGHT SHE WAS STILL MARRIED TO ME. TWO MONTHS after she left, I started the divorce process, but I couldn't find her for two years. Finally, a judge took pity on me and absolved my marriage once he saw what lengths I went through to find her with no success.

She never received any documentation, but it was legalized years ago.

RAMSEY: *WHAT WAS SHE HERE FOR THEN?*

ME: *I SOUGHT HER OUT WITH A PI—DAVIS FOUND HER INSTEAD and set up a meeting for us.*

Ramsey: *Did it go the way you hoped?*

I WAS SMILING. RAMSEY COULDN'T HELP BUT BE CARING AND I loved it. This entire exchange was proving she still cared.

ME: *YES. SHE SIGNED AWAY HER RIGHT TO THE KIDS permanently and won't be a future concern for them or for me.*

IT TOOK A FEW MINUTES FOR ANOTHER RESPONSE FROM HER.

. . .

RAMSEY: *WHY WERE YOU SO ANGRY WITH ME THAT NIGHT THAT you called and then got drunk and disappeared? I mean, beyond the little pieces that you said in the bathroom that one night…*

ME: *I FELT LIKE YOU WERE LYING TO ME ON PURPOSE, EVEN though I know that wasn't true, I couldn't separate what I once walked through with Lisa, and what it felt like you were capable of doing to me. I wanted to talk to you, so you could help me see that what I was fearing was ridiculous. I needed to see you that night because fears from my past were wreaking havoc on my heart and mind. I'm so sorry how I handled it, how I made you worry.*

MY STOMACH HURT, AND I OFFICIALLY FELT LIKE THE BIGGEST idiot in the world. The more she asked, the more I realized how poorly she was treated through this entire thing, and it brought back the old sensation to just let her go because she deserved so much better than me.

RAMSEY: *DID YOU…*

RAMSEY: ………

Her texting dots kept starting and stopping, I knew she wanted to ask me something, she was just struggling. Which meant that it was probably not going to be a good thing.

RAMSEY: *DID YOU SLEEP WITH SOMEONE THAT NIGHT?*

· · ·

How to answer this one? And how to answer to where she would believe me and wouldn't shut me out...

Me: *Not in the way you might think. I didn't have sex with anyone, I didn't kiss anyone. But I did end up in a girl's bed. She let me crash there after drinking way too much and lent me a charger for my phone. I'll admit that it doesn't sound good, and I can only imagine what you are thinking, but I'm telling the truth.*

Ramsey: *So, you went to her house fully conscious then?*

Shit, I knew where she was going with this.

Me: *Yes, I was conscious, but I wasn't sober.*

Ramsey: *Then how do you know that nothing happened?*

Me: *The girl that was in the room when I woke up... she told me that I was a loser, that she thought if she brought me back to her house, then I would cave and do something with her, but she said that I didn't, not even a kiss.*

Ramsey: *I think that's enough for one night. Thank you for answering my questions.*

I needed her to keep talking to me, I needed to know

how she was taking what I told her. I didn't want to push her further away. But I couldn't force her to keep talking to me.

ME: OK... I UNDERSTAND. I AM HERE IF YOU NEED ANYTHING else. And for the record, Ramsey, I'm so sorry.

RAMSEY: GOODNIGHT JIMMY.

ME: GOODNIGHT RAMSEY.

FORTY-TWO

IT WAS the last weekend before Mom and I were going to head back home to Belvidere, and I promised Laney that I would go out with her. Mom was doing so well that it made leaving her a little easier than normal. I usually hated leaving her. Every night that I headed to Laney's, I felt a panic attack trying to take me down over the idea of something happening to her. I would always imagine Mom dying right after I got into those elevators, and I would have to live with that forever; that I left her to die alone in a hospital room.

I pushed my eyes closed to get the image out of my head and focused on the fact that my mother wanted me to live my life, that's what brought her joy.

I applied some mascara and added a little more blush before turning off Laney's bathroom light. I headed back towards the guest room that had become my home away from home these last few weeks and stood in front of the mirror that hung on the back of the door. I looked tired, with the dark circles that laid under my eyes and the pale complexion of my face. Sure, I looked appropriate to go out for the night, in a borrowed black dress from Laney, the 'longest' dress she owned. It still came up pretty short on me. I also had to borrow her black, strappy heels, because I didn't pack any outfits to "go out" in, because going out was the last thing on my mind. I didn't mind the dress. Laney called it her funeral dress, so it was more modest. Which I preferred, because although I was going out with her, attracting attention was not on my list of things I wanted to do tonight. Laney came around the door and peeked at me. She was wearing a small, white dress, that made her reddish hair look amazing. She paired the dress with some red lipstick and now she was slipping into a pair of red stilettos that made her almost as tall as me. *Look out world, here comes Laney Thompson.*

She looked at me, her head tilted to the side and her lips pinched together. She wore an expression that said she knew I didn't want to go out, so I gave her a weak smile. I really did want to spend time with her, but I would have been happy wearing jeans and sweatshirt, while catching a movie and eating some tacos.

But this was Laney's life, the Chicago life, the life I left behind. My heart splintered a little at the idea that my idea of fun had transformed so much since moving to Belvidere, since meeting Jimmy and his kids. My idea of having fun would be one of their annual pizza and movie nights, complete with a blanket fort. I wanted to cry, because as I looked in the mirror and saw my reflection, I realized how badly I wanted that life. I didn't want to go out as a single girl into the Chicago night scene with my best friend. If I had to go out at all, I wanted to go out as a woman who was taken, off the market, unavailable, preferably married to Jimmy Stenson.

I breathed through my nose a few times to clear my head, and then grabbed my small leather jacket, and flipped off the switch.

Laney had called an Uber, so we could drink and just let

loose tonight. She didn't understand that I would never be able to let loose as long as my mom might need me. It wasn't long before a silver SUV pulled up to the curb. Laney confirmed it was our driver with her phone, and his. He punched the address into his navigation screen, and we were off. The car had some light music playing, but not so much that the driver couldn't hear us, or we couldn't hear each other.

Laney looked over at me and smiled. "So, how are things going with Jimmy?"

I gave her a questioning look, because I didn't tell her that I had been texting him, or that I had talked to the kids. I started texting Jimmy a few nights ago, but after I received the text about how he had ended up in some girl's bed, I couldn't bring myself to text him again. I knew that he was just being honest, that nothing happened, but the fact that he was in her room, in her bed, just made me sick.

Every night, I would toss and turn, and start a text with another question, just so that I could talk to him. Then I would picture him waking up in some girl's bed, who was in the room when he woke up, and I would stop. I hated this. I wish I hadn't asked him that, I wish I could have seen his face or felt his arms around me after he told me, but with that and the bomb about his wife—or, ex-wife—it was just too much at once. For days, I wanted to ask him why he didn't think to tell me, or to warn me about Lisa, or what he was doing? Why all the secrecy, why didn't he feel like he could trust me with it?

I imagined the girl he woke up with was someone he knew in his past. I even went as far as imagining that she touched him while he was unconscious, or that something did happen and she just told him that it didn't. I mean, how would he know? I felt nauseous all over again. My face must have reflected it, because Laney put her hand to my forehead, pulling me back to our recent conversation.

"You feel okay? You look like you're going to puke."

The Uber driver angled his rearview mirror until he saw us. "No puking in here, please. Let me know and I will pull over if you need to, but please, please, do *not* puke in here."

I moved her hand away from my face and looked at the driver's eyes in the mirror. "I am *not* going to puke. So, relax."

Then I turned towards Laney to answer her previous question. "Things with Jimmy are… I don't know." I put my face in my hands. I felt her hand on my back, rubbing it gently,

"What happened?" I could hear the worry in her voice, and I hated that, right off the bat, I had ruined our evening.

I sat up and smiled at her. "Nothing, just the same old stuff between us. I asked him some questions, that I never got answered since everything…" I waved my hand around as a way to demonstrate everything. She looked at me with a worried expression.

"What kind of questions?"

I took a deep breath and answered as firmly as I could, "Remember that early morning I called you while you were at Jackson's, and I had to talk to him because I didn't know where Jimmy was?"

Her face was turning red, something that happened whenever Jackson was brought up. "Yeah I remember…" She trailed off.

"Well, I asked Jimmy about that night, if he… you know… if he…"

I couldn't even finish the sentence, tears were already threatening to fall at just saying the words.

"Ramsey, you didn't? Why would you put yourself through that, honey?" she asked, grabbing my hands.

"I had to know, Laney, it was burning me up inside, not knowing all this stuff from him. He's so secretive," I said, justifying myself and my questions.

"What did he say?" Laney asked, her eyes zoned in on mine as her eyebrows drew together.

"He said he woke up in some girl's bed, but she told him that they didn't do anything, not even kiss." I said it without crying, then let out a little sigh of relief.

"Then that's a good thing, right? Why are you so upset about it?" Laney asked, giving me the most confused look, I have ever seen on her dumb, beautiful face.

"Laney, he woke up in another girl's *bed*, in her *room*, she was there when he woke up! What do most girls who are looking to have sex with a guy look like when they wake up in the morning?" I said with a sharper tone, because Laney wasn't getting it.

She winced and looked down. "Yeah, I guess when you put it that way... but were you guys even...?" She trailed off. I knew what she wanted to say but I was going to let her say it, because she should already know the answer to this.

"Were you guys exclusive? I mean, I thought you agreed to just be friends..."

She wasn't wrong, so I dialed my tantrum down a bit with my reply. "It's complicated. Yes, we agreed to be friends, but we both agreed that we weren't dating during that six weeks of us building a foundation between us, because after the six weeks, the whole goal was to date each other," I said with a little flick of my wrist.

"Okay... but the whole thing confuses the hell out of me. I think you shouldn't hold this against him, because from what I hear, the guy is miserable."

She said it without much thought, which showed in her expression when she finally looked at me and saw my face.

"Oh, Ramsey, wait don't get pissed," she said, leaning back a bit and raising her voice.

"What do you mean then, Laney? You better explain what you mean by, 'from what you hear,'" I said, holding her in place with my stone-like, bitch face.

"Okay, okay, it's just that Jackson and I still text from time to time, and he asked what I was doing this weekend, and I told him that you were here, and mentioned that we might go out, because I felt like you needed a night out after everything with Jimmy…" She took a deep breath; my face hadn't changed at all yet.

"Anyway, when I mentioned Jimmy's name, Jackson sent an emoji that was rolling his eyes, and said it was more like Jimmy needed a night out after what you were putting him through, then he said that Jimmy was trying everything to apologize to you, but you weren't even talking to him…" she finished with a light blush.

I moved my eyes away from her and looked out the window, trying to get my temper under control. How on earth did I get made into the bad guy here? Jimmy and I kiss, then we make a date, he finds something out, doesn't clear the air with me, so he shacks up with some girl for the night. He freezes me out for a few weeks, at the end of which I end up getting abducted. He then pushes me away for God knows what reasons, and I finally muster up the courage to leave and get healing from him, and *I'm* dubbed the bad guy? After everything?

The memory of being tied to that chair, with *him* in front of me, surfaced, and I started to gag. I could feel the tightness in my throat start to grow. No, Jimmy didn't get to be the victim here. I would say all this to Laney, but it would come out much harsher and louder than acceptable in our little Uber car. So, I bit my tongue and watched the street lights until we stopped in front of a nightclub. It was a large brick building, with lettering on the side that said, "Lit Republic."

There was a long line of people that trailed down the side of the building and a roped off area at the front, complete with a large bouncer guarding the entrance. I got out of the car without even looking at Laney. She knew my temper and she knew that I just needed some space for a second. I didn't wait for Laney, as I made my way to the front of the line, not because I expected to get in, but because I needed a bathroom and some privacy, as tears were likely expected to start soon.

I was hoping the bouncer would take pity on me, one big smile in his direction and he did. I walked right through the rope, showed my ID, and made my way through the throngs of people towards the back of the room where I knew a bathroom would be. Of course, there was a long line of glitzed-up women waiting outside the bathroom door. I moved to the front of the line, and said to the women that I was just getting tissue and that I didn't need to pee. That seemed to satisfy them.

The bathroom was spacious, it had at least ten stalls, and a long counter with three or four sink spaces. It was lit enough to apply makeup but not awkwardly fluorescent. I found some paper towels because all the stalls were full. I dabbed under my eyes, and stared at the faucet, wishing I could wash my face. In real life, that never worked. I took a few breaths in and out and tried to think back to a few of my therapy sessions. I focused on gaining control of the situation that I felt was making me feel powerless. Rage was forming in my throat, and it threatened to come out in the form of screaming. I wanted to hit something. This was my new normal.

When I remembered being in that room, tied to that chair, something inside me snapped. Like releasing a caged beast that had been imprisoned too long. I felt so, powerless, and afraid, like something was taking over my body. I wasn't strong enough in that room. I couldn't stop them, I wanted to stop them. They violated my body with their hands, their mouths, and the bat. They hurt me, they were going to kill me. Suddenly it was too much, and I ran into a stall that just vacated before the next girl in line could go in. I slammed the door shut against her pounding, and yelling, and vomited into the toilet. I hated how connected those feelings were to Jimmy, how I hadn't told Laney about my therapy or about that night in that room, about what they did to me.

I couldn't tell anyone, not my mother, not Laney, not even my therapist knew everything that happened in that room. The person I wanted to tell was Jimmy, because he was my connection to the piece of shit who touched me and hurt me. After the hospital, he just cut me out of his life, knowing that I was fucking abducted.

He hadn't asked about the nightmares that kept me up at night, about the vomiting I did anytime I thought of the tall man who smelled of mildew and smoke. Or how I still felt the zip ties on my hands, his hot tongue on the side of my face, licking the cuts he just opened with his fists. I pushed my eyes shut to try and force the look in *his* eyes out of my mind. It hurt that Jimmy hadn't asked me about any of it, and yet they said he was going through a hard time? A rage that was unlike anything I'd ever experienced started to take over. I left the stall and walked through the bathroom, pushed open the door, and joined the mass of moving bodies.

EMOTIONS WERE FLOWING OUT OF ME AS I DANCED, AND danced, and danced. I didn't look for Laney, I didn't care about her right now. No one needed or wanted a villain, which was what I had become. I let men buy me drinks. I gave them all a good time on the dance floor, let them use my body however they wanted. I didn't care, rage and anger were calling the shots.

I was gone but so was the pain, the anger, the rage. They let me be. I just danced and danced and danced, until I couldn't anymore. The darkness claimed me; where it was quiet and peaceful. There were no walls to keep me in, there was no chair, there was no face. No hands to hit me, there was no dirty mattress with my blood to coat it, there was no bat.

There was no one. Just the darkness and me, and I welcomed it with open arms.

I HEARD MUFFLED VOICES. I COULDN'T OPEN MY EYES, IT HURT too much. My whole body felt numb and cold. I didn't know where I was, but I didn't really care. I felt weightless, like I could float away. I wanted the darkness again, I wanted the rage and anger, I wished I could summon them like a super-power. I wished that I could...

"No, she just needs to rest, Laney. Just let her rest... she'll be okay..." a man's voice whispered in a hushed tone. I knew that voice. It was so far away, though. Images of sunlight and grass, a soccer ball, and smiles with missing teeth. Sammy. Jasmine. *Jimmy...*

Why was Jimmy here? He wasn't there when....

No. I didn't want to think about that room without anger and rage as a defense. They fought my battles for me, and right now, they weren't here.

I heard someone crying, sobbing, it sounded like a woman, I knew that voice too. "I don't know what happened, she's never done this be-before. Sh-she just snapped and left, and th-the next thing I know, she's dancing and drinking, and ...God, it was so bad, I didn't even recognize her. Is she having a breakdown? I just want her to be okay."

I could hardly hear Laney through her choked sobs and stuttering. Was she talking about me? I still couldn't open my eyes.

"Just get some sleep, I'm going to stay in here again, to make sure she's okay."

Jimmy again. What did he mean by, 'stay here again'? I didn't know, I didn't care, I was weightless, and there was the darkness I loved. It came to claim me again.

Here I am, I said to it, as it took me away.

FORTY-THREE

JIMMY

I CLOSED the door to Jackson's guest room where I was staying for the weekend and turned off the light. It was quiet now, without Laney's sobs, and cries. Ramsey was still asleep, like she was yesterday. I knew it wasn't a good idea that she had literally slept for an entire day, but I knew she was okay... I knew that she just needed rest. I knew, because I had come down from a few bad highs in my time.

I sat in the chair by the large bay window and watched the rain pelt the glass with its heavy drops. I laid my face in my hands and then looked up to see Ramsey's sleeping body from across the room. I thought about the night before, when Jackson and I were playing a hand of poker in his game room with a few of his friends. He had called me on Friday, and told me to come for the weekend, to get my mind off of Ramsey and off the fact that she hadn't texted me once since I answered her questions, the last one about not sleeping but waking up with someone else.

I had texted her every day, like usual. I apologized, even tried calling her, left her a few voicemails, but still nothing. So, Jackson and Dad insisted that I get away for the weekend. I pointed out that being in the same city as the woman who was putting my heart through the blender was probably not the best idea, but Jackson simply replied by saying it was a big city.

So, I came Friday, and we planned a big poker game, no women allowed. It was going great, until Jackson got a phone call around ten p.m. from Laney. I didn't know what was wrong, but I saw the worry etched into Jackson's face, and when he stood from the table and found my eyes, I knew it had to do with Ramsey.

I stood up with him, he headed upstairs and found his coat, and he kept telling Laney to calm down, that we were coming and to keep Ramsey there. My heart was pounding so hard, I thought it might stop working entirely. I was fumbling for shoes, and my coat, worrying, hurting, scared to death that something had happened. Finally, he hung up and ran out of his house, I was close on his tail. Once we were in his Jeep and driving, he filled me in as much as he could.

"It's Ramsey…she's trying to leave with two guys… Laney said that Ramsey…" He trailed off, gripped the steering wheel and glanced at me, then continued, "Ramsey, has been acting weird all night. Laney said she tried to keep an eye on her, but every time Laney would walk up to her, Ramsey would go and drink more with different guys, and then dance and she said she was dancing like…"

He trailed off again, I didn't need him to finish, my imagination worked just fine. My fists were clenched so tight, I could feel the blood loss from it. I knew it was going to take every ounce of willpower not to punch one of those guys' faces in, just for touching Ramsey. Jackson must have known where my mind was at, because he pressed a button on his steering wheel, then said, "Call Theo."

Dad came on over the speaker, and Jackson only had to say, "Put one of the kids on," for Dad to know what was going on. I was still clenching and unclenching my fists and grinding my teeth; my jaw ached from how hard it was set. I was battling those demons pretty hard, and I was so glad that I had Jackson, because I would more than likely end up in jail tonight without him. A few muffled seconds later, I heard a sleepy Jasmine start to talk, "Uncle Jax? What's going on?"

Immediately, my heart rate lowered and my fists relaxed, as I breathed in and out. Jackson took over the call, so I could focus on breathing.

"Hey sweetheart, sorry to wake you. I was wondering if you could help me with something? Could you tell me who your favorite person in the whole world is? Your dad seems to think it's him, but I am positive that it's me," Jackson said with a smile, because my kids could make anyone smile.

I was breathing in and out slowly when Jasmine's sleepy voice, spoke up again, "Well, I do love you so much, Uncle Jax, but Daddy is my favorite."

I could feel that same old, thud, thud in my heart that happened when my kids took over and changed my atmosphere, changed my mood, changed my world. Jackson looked over at me and gave me a half-smile. "Oh yeah? Why is he your favorite?"

Jasmine giggled. "Daddy builds stuff for us, he makes us breakfasts and dinners, he goes to work to make money, he builds forts with us, he just loves us. He's funny and makes us laugh. He's just Daddy," she finished with a little laugh. I was thankful for my beautiful little girl, her words like water on the flames that were raging through me. Jackson told her goodnight and ended the call. I looked over at him.

"Thanks man. I'll keep it together tonight."

Jackson kept his gaze straight forward, then let out a long breath. "You deserve happiness, Jimmy. Remember that tonight when you see your girl. Remember that when you see the men she's with, remember that she needs you tonight. Nothing else matters. Okay?"

I nodded, because words wouldn't be sufficient. Minutes later, he was pulling into a free spot near some club. We were making our way towards the entrance when I heard raised voices. Near the entrance, Laney was standing with her arms crossed in a way that made her look like a small mountain. She had black streaks running down her face, and it was clear she was upset. Next to her was a bouncer, who also had his arms crossed, and they were facing down two tall men in suits, who each had an arm around Ramsey.

My breath caught when I saw her. Her hair was curly, cascading down her back, and there was a small crown of braided hair on the top of her head, making her look like a princess. She couldn't hold herself up, her mascara was running, she had her head tilted back, and she was laughing. We got closer, and I could hear her. "Laaaney, …stop being a spuch up bitch…" She laughed again. "I want to lo have some smfun."

She was trying to stand and slurring her words. I could tell just by looking at her, that she wasn't just drunk. God, I had never seen her like this, and my heart was shattering at the sight of her. This strong, defiant woman, who loved my children like her own, who took care of her dying mother. There was a thick lump in my throat, as tears threatened to fall in front of all these strangers. I stepped forward towards the two men, who were trying to leave with Ramsey, and stared them down.

"First, take your hands off of her and step back," I snapped, while trying to control the anger that was rolling through me.

They stood there for a second, then the one with dark hair laughed and said, "Fuck off, she's with us."

Big mistake.

I grabbed his chin, squeezing his cheeks, forcing his lips to pucker out. He only had one hand free to get me off of him, and it wasn't enough.

"Let her, the fuck, go." I seethed in his face. The bouncer spoke into his walkie and started looking around. I knew he'd probably throw all of us out any second, which was fine, but I needed to get Ramsey away from the assholes first. One of the men watched the bouncer's movement as well.

Finally, they loosened their hold on her, and I stepped in and scooped her into my arms. She immediately snuggled into my chest, putting her head under my chin.

I adjusted her in my arms and eyed the two men again, then quietly asked, "What did she take?"

Both men looked at each other, then me, and the one with short blond hair answered, "Nothing, she's just wasted."

"Bullshit," I spat, "now tell me, what the hell is she on?!"

I was yelling now and could feel Jackson stand behind me. The one with darker hair loosened his tie, like he was nervous, but still they didn't answer. I stared them down again, this time, Jackson came to stand right next to me. "Last time. What did she take?"

The blond looked down, then said, "Just a little X, man," barely loud enough for us to hear him.

My fists itched to hit these fucking idiots, but I had Ramsey in my arms, safe, and that's all that mattered. Besides, now that they confirmed slipping her drugs, the bouncer would report it. I turned around and left the club. Laney followed me out, I walked so her little legs could keep up. Ramsey didn't even seem to notice what happened, she was still trying to convince Laney to let her go, and then she was laughing. She kept laughing. Each time, it was like a barb in my heart.

I opened the back-passenger door, and gently laid Ramsey inside, while Laney climbed in the other side. I wanted to be next to Ramsey, but I could tell by the look on Laney's face that she needed it more. Jackson was there a moment later, getting in and starting up the car, and driving off. Laney held onto Ramsey's hand like she was worried she might lose her. Ramsey was still laughing, strapped into her seatbelt, but leaning forward, fighting the restraint. Then she started to talk, and I wanted to die.

"Didge you know that Jimmy won't lask me about the chair, Laney-bainy?" she asked softly, still slurring her words a bit. I held my breath; not sure what Ramsey was talking about.

"He won't ask me what the monster didge to me. He doesn't want to know about the chair, about the hitting or the spitting or the licking." She was laughing again.

"He won't ask me, Laney-bainy. I can't tell anyone how much it hurts. I want him to ask me, to hold me, but he pushed me away."

She laughed, but this time there wasn't much behind it, like she was losing steam. "He used a baseball bat on my hand, Laney. Did you know that?" Her words were clear and concise this time. I wanted to throw up. Laney held her hand up to her mouth, and a sob escaped from her, as tears streamed down her face. We were all silent.

Another laugh. "He kissed me after that. Then he hit me again. He let the other one lick my face after it was cut open by his fists, then he'd slap it. Then they would do it again," she said in a sing-song voice, like it was *funny. Then there were no more laughs, she was so quiet now. Tears were streaming down my own face, as I fought the bile rising in my throat. I didn't want to hear anymore.*

"They wanted to vrape me, but they thought... they um... they thought that Jimmy and me, that we were... vyou know... together." Another laugh. "So they said, that I was used trash, that they would never touch someone that had been with Jimmy Fucking Stenson... Small blessings... right?"

She was laughing hard now, but then she hung her head forward, and she was quiet. The silence was thick, and Jackson cleared his throat a few times. I didn't want to look at him; I knew that sound, he made it when Jasmine used to talk about how it was her fault that her mom left. He was fighting tears. I was fighting everything.

I wanted to leave, I wanted to stay, she deserved better than me, but I knew she needed me. I hated myself. Minutes later, we pulled into Jackson's driveway, and I walked with Ramsey in my arms up the stairs into his three-story townhouse. I carried her into the guest room where I was staying and laid her on the mattress. I pulled an extra shirt and sweats from my duffle bag and laid them on the bed, then looked at Laney who'd gone pale. The lamp next to the bed offered a soft glow to the room.

"Will you need help changing her?" I asked hesitantly. Laney kept her focus on Ramsey's unconscious body and nodded her head. I leaned forward and gently pulled Ramsey into my arms, so Laney could undo the zipper at her back. I had imagined a million different times what it would be like to have this woman in my arms, getting her out of her dress after an evening out. It made this so much worse. I pushed the pain away and laid Ramsey back down. Laney started to remove the dress until Ramsey was in just her bra and underwear. She was so beautiful, but it wasn't lust that I felt at the moment, it was pure agony. How did we get here? I wanted to punch something until this made sense to me. Until the pain of this moment subsided. Seeing her like this wasn't something I wanted to remember and that made this hurt worse. I made quick work of holding Ramsey up, so that Laney could slip the shirt over her head, then I did the same for her with the sweats. I tucked her into the bed and then we waited.

Ramsey slept all day and Laney was a mess. She couldn't stop crying. I shut the door, to keep her brokenness out; there was enough in this room. The words Ramsey said in the car were running on a loop in my head. I threw up after I pictured what Ramsey went through, after the image of Davis hitting her with the bat seared itself into my memory.

Laney came back today with fresh clothes for Ramsey, so she must have gone home at some point. It was night again, and she wanted to stay close in case Ramsey woke up. I told Laney no and to give Ramsey some space, mostly because Laney couldn't stop crying.

I walked out onto Jackson's third story balcony to make the call to Carla, to fill her in. The sun beat down on me but the chill in the air made it feel like it wasn't there. I dialed Carla and waited. A few rings in, she finally picked up with a soft and concerned voice.

"Jimmy?"

I fought the urge to hang up, I didn't want to tell her this news. "Carla, hi. How are you feeling?"

She let out a sigh. "I'm fine, dear, but I haven't heard from Ramsey since she left last night. Is everything okay?"

It was my turn to let out a sigh. "Not exactly, no." I took a seat on the patio furniture and Carla waited for me to continue. "We aren't exactly sure what happened, but Ramsey had some kind of breakdown while she was out with Laney. She got a little wasted and tried to go home with two men that she didn't know. Laney was scared, so she called Jackson. I was with him, so we picked her up and she's still sleeping."

Carla was silent, then she started speaking in a different language. I assumed it was Cambodian. "She has PTSD, Jimmy, and takes medication for it. I'm assuming she had one of her episodes. I'm not sure why she didn't have her meds with her, that seems unlike her."

That added up, according to her behavior, but I also wondered why she'd go into a stressful environment without her meds.

"Her therapist is Glenda Stanza, let me find her number. Maybe she can tell you how to help her. Please have Ramsey call me when she feels up to it," Carla said, just as someone told her it was time for her rounds in the background.

"Okay, I will."

She gave me the number and ended the call. I jotted down the number she had rattled off. I called Glenda that afternoon, but she couldn't really talk to me about anything, she just told me to make sure Ramsey called her as soon as she woke up.

I WATCHED THE RAIN AS IT HIT THE WINDOW. MY TEARS FELL again as I thought of Ramsey, waiting for me to talk to her about what she went through. Waiting for me to hold her, to help her, and I never did. I was broken, I was aching, because I knew, deep down, that Ramsey and I wouldn't recover from this. How could we? I started to wipe at my face, just as I saw movement on the bed. Ramsey was starting to stir.

FORTY-FOUR

It was dark, and I was really warm, and comfortable. All good signs. Then I moved my head, and I wanted to die. My stomach was cramping, and my throat was on fire. The material of the blanket that was on me was different than what's at Laney's house, and I smelled...I smelled Jimmy. Which meant I was probably dreaming, and I needed to wake up. I tried to sit up, then a large hand landed on my shoulder, and someone was shushing me, telling me to take it easy.

I opened my eyes, and found it dark, but I could make the shape of a person, and feel a body press down onto the mattress.

"Hey, it's okay. It's just me."

Just me? What was going on? Then, like the time I learned my mother had cancer, a series of images came flooding back, reminding me that, yes, last night did happen. Drinking, dancing, the men... God, the men. I was going to be sick. I tried to get up and throw the covers off, so I could run to the bathroom, but my body wouldn't cooperate. Suddenly there was something round in front of my face, and a warm hand was grabbing my hand and placing it around the object. After a second or two, I made out that it was a garbage can.

"I'm going to turn on the light, is that okay?" Jimmy asked. His voice was gentle and caressed my aching heart.

I nodded, but realized he couldn't see me, so with a rasp I responded, "Yes, it's okay."

I could see him move closer to me, then I heard a click and I was assaulted by the blinding glow of the lamp next to me. I slammed my eyes shut, then slowly tried to reopen them a few times, until my eyes were adjusted. Jimmy was sitting on the bed next to me; his face looked tired, he had dark circles under his eyes, and his eyes weren't that lake green that I loved, they were watery and red. I remembered being angry at him, at Laney, at Jackson, because they'd turned me into the villain. I turned my head away from him and looked out the large window in the room.

After a few seconds of silence, I found my voice, "Where am I? Where's Laney?"

Jimmy let out a slow breath, then quietly answered, "Jackson's. Laney is here."

I was so embarrassed. I didn't want to know what happened, or why I was in this bed, wearing clothes that weren't mine, with Jimmy sitting with me. But as much as I didn't want to know, I knew that I needed to. I needed to face up to whatever it was that I said or did that might have hurt my relationships.

"What happened?" I whispered, hoping Jimmy heard, so I wouldn't have to say it again.

Jimmy stayed where he was, but gently touched my chin to turn my face back to him. He was so handsome, even looking as tired and worn as he did. My heart was beating fast, just at the sight of him, at his mere proximity to me, after all these days and weeks away. The last time we were even this close was in my hospital room, but that didn't count because he left me.

He bit his lip, and quietly answered without looking away from me.

"I was here visiting Jackson for the weekend. Laney called him because she was worried about you. You were…"

He looked at me with pain in his eyes. I knew this must be hard because I remembered a few bits and pieces of the night before. I knew what my intentions were when I left that bathroom. To let loose, to forget…

"You had been drinking some and wanted to leave with two guys that Laney didn't know. She was worried about you, so we came to get you both," Jimmy said with soft concern in his voice.

God, it was worse than I thought. How stupid could I be? I set the can next to me and pulled my knees up to my chin, resting my face on the tops of my knees and cried.

"How long have I been here? I heard voices, and I heard you say that you were staying with me again," I asked through the steady stream of tears running down my face. Which only added to my splitting headache.

"It's Sunday morning, around two a.m.," he answered.

Panic shot through me; I hadn't checked with my mom, she was probably worried sick. I sat up and started looking around for my phone. Jimmy's hands landed back on my knees to calm me. "We called your mom, she knows that you're safe, and she told us to call Glenda. She would like you to call her later this morning," he said with that gentle tone again, like he was talking me down from the ledge. Maybe he was.

Shame and embarrassment flushed through my body at the sound of my therapist's name. How much did my mom reveal? Jimmy must have noticed, because he spoke up, "Your mom didn't tell us anything, neither did Glenda… but…" He trailed off, then ran his fingers through his messy hair. I missed his hair, I missed him. My body ached, and my heart hurt, and regardless of what was going on between us, I just wanted his arms around me. I was crying again, but I was also leaning forward, until I was close enough for Jimmy to catch the hint.

He looked surprised as I scooted closer to him, but he caught on, and wrapped his arms around me, pulling me into his chest. He rocked me and kissed the top of my head as I cried into his chest. I realized he had said the word 'but' at the end of his last sentence, like he was going to say more.

With my raspy, phlegm-filled voice, I asked him about it. "What were you going to say, Jimmy? After you said Glenda didn't say anything, you said, 'but'..."

He stopped rocking. I leaned back and looked at him, he was crying and not just little tears, but big ones.

He choked on his words as he answered my question. "God, Ramsey, I'm so sorry I didn't ask you. I didn't think..." He was almost sobbing now. I had never seen this side of him, it was wreaking havoc on my heart. He wiped at his face. "I didn't think you would want to talk about it, or for me to... I stayed away because I thought if you saw me, it would remind you of what happened. I pushed you away. I hated that because of me, you got hurt. I'm so, so sorry," he said again, while crushing me to his chest, harder than before, like he didn't want there to be any chance of losing me.

I didn't know what to say, I didn't know how much he knew...maybe I should start there.

"How much do you know... I mean... did I..."

I couldn't even say it, because it was literally one of my worst fears, that I would accidentally tell someone every evil thing that happened to me in that room. Jimmy knew, he must've, because he didn't make me finish,

"You said a few things in the car, things that happened to you... how you wanted me to talk to you about it, how much I failed you... Ramsey, you deserve so much better than me, I'm so sorry. This is why I tried to push you away, because what kind of person doesn't ask about this stuff?" He was crying into my hair, crushing me tighter and tighter into him. I leaned back to look at him.

"Jimmy, yes it hurt, that's why I haven't talked to you in so long. You pushed me away and I can see why, but you didn't give me a choice in the matter, and all I wanted was you. All I still want is you... to help... get through it." I felt like I was choking on my own sobs. "Just, please don't leave me again, Jimmy. We have things to work on, but don't leave me. Promise me, please."

I was begging him, shamelessly begging, but I didn't care. After last night, I needed him in my life. I was done with this space and distance between us.

I heard him breathing in and out of his nose, slowly, before he answered, "If you'll have me, then that's where I'll be. That's all I want, Ramsey... I'm so sorry about what we last texted about. I didn't hear from you, so I know it upset you."

I shook my head back and forth at his admission, because that couldn't even be an issue between us anymore. "No, Jimmy, don't. I mean...yeah, I struggled, and I'm sorry that I did, we weren't even..."

He hugged me tighter and cut me off. "Yes, we were together. In my heart, we were, we still are. But nothing happened, I swear. I wasn't that out of it. If someone would have woke me up, I would have known what was going on."

I tried to clear my throat but failed as it clogged with my own admission. "I can't even be angry now. After last night, after what I did... I don't even know what I did..." I said through a stream of tears. The shame was worse than the physical aches and pains that I had, something I realized I should remedy sooner rather than later.

Jimmy was running his hand down the length of my hair, stroking it, then he said in my ear, "Let's forget about last night. I mean, I want to talk it through with you and know what made you want to go that far, but I don't want you to hang on to anything that you don't need to."

I nodded into his chest and then pushed back away from him. "I want to tell you, I just need some water, and a shower. Maybe some food, and a toothbrush first," I said, wiping at my face and trying to untangle my hair with my fingers.

Jimmy started to stand and held his hand out to me. "Yeah, of course, sorry. I should have thought of that first."

I took his hand and tried to stand, but I was alarmed at how sore I was. I tried to think of why I was so sore, was it just from just laying down for an entire day? Then I thought of all the dancing. Which made me wince.

Jimmy turned away from me and grabbed a small black bag and then handed it to me. I peeked inside and saw my clothes and toiletries. *Hallelujah*! I had never been as happy at seeing my own face wash as I was right then. He turned to open the door and led me to the third door down the hall, walked in, and turned the light on. It was sweet, I could tell he didn't want to be away from me. Once he realized that he was still standing in the bathroom with me, and I was clutching the bag to my chest, his face turned red and he headed towards the door. "Sorry, I'll go make you a sandwich."

Then I was alone.

I peeled off the clothes that I assumed were Jimmy's and headed for the shower. I let the hot steam wash over me, wishing it could do more than rinse my skin. Wishing it could somehow rinse my soul, or my mind, and get rid of my memories.

Once done, I changed back into my own sweats and t-shirt, then brushed my teeth, twice, because my breath was horrible. I brushed out my hair and pulled it into a loose braid.

I made my way out of the bathroom and started heading towards what I figured was the kitchen. Jackson's house was impressive. The whole house seemed to be made of huge, floor-to-ceiling windows, and he had large, wooden slat-like curtains that covered some of the windows, the rest were left exposed. He had hardwood floors with thick, warm rugs that seemed to run everywhere.

I came around a wall and found the only other light on in the house, or on the floor, and saw Jimmy standing at a large, marble island, making two sandwiches. The kitchen was massive. All granite, chrome, and dark grays, it looked really manly. I leaned against the wall, watching the sandwich making. Jimmy looked up and smiled. In the light, it was easier to see him; he had on a pair of dark shorts and a white T-shirt that hugged him tightly. I noticed one of his tattoos peeking out from the top of his shirt. I wasn't sure why, with all his other tattoos on his arms, that one stood out to me, but it did.

I walked into the kitchen a little further, after Jimmy put his attention back on the sandwich, and sat on a barstool.

"What does your tattoo mean?" I asked quietly, pointing towards his neck.

He slid a plate with a large, fully-loaded, turkey and avocado sandwich towards me.

"I'll show you once you eat something and take some aspirin," he replied with a little smile, while taking a big chunk out of his own sandwich. He watched me as I slowly took a few bites of the food. We stayed like that, in silence, until I had finished half the sandwich. Then I drank some of the bottle of water down, followed by two aspirin. Jimmy dusted off his hands before walking around the island towards me. Once he was standing just a foot or two away from me, he started pulling at the hem of his shirt until he pulled it completely off.

I stopped drinking, because it should be noted that Jimmy Stenson was a kind of magnificent that belonged in an exhibit. Trying not to gawk, I finished off the bottle of water, allowing him the chance to explain his ink.

"These," he said, pointing towards two black wings that

looked like they were laying over each shoulder, "are for my kids. They give me flight, make me soar. Anything I do, I do with them in mind."

"This…" He pointed towards his heart, where a tattoo of an actual heart, as in the organ, was outlined in black. From it, there were words wrapping around it and trailing up his torso, all the way to his neck. I tried to read the words, but they were written in a different language. He saw me trying to read them and took my hand, placing it over his heart. He looked into my eyes and said, "Though it's dark, let there be light. Let it be unwavering and unrelenting, one that leads me home." He said it in a whisper that I could feel settle deep, deep in my soul, like they were written just for me.

I didn't realize that I'd shut my eyes until I felt the pads of his thumbs brush over my eyelids. Without thinking, I kept my eyes closed and took my hand from his heart and placed it on his jaw and pulled him towards me. I opened my eyes and saw him watching me, with a pained, but hungry expression. Determined, I pulled his face closer towards mine until his lips were inches from my own. Then I let him take over.

He closed the gap between us and pressed his lips to mine. He stayed there for a second, just gently kissing me, before he grabbed just behind my ear, holding my head in place as his kisses turned impatient. His tongue licked my bottom lip, gently but urgently, requesting access, which I gladly gave to him. I moved my face to the side to get a better angle, then wrapped my arms around his neck. Lifting my body just a little, he wrapped his arm around my back and with his other arm, he lifted me until he was cradling me. All the while, he didn't break the kiss and it was perfect. Beyond perfect. Then he turned and started heading towards the bedroom.

JIMMY SLOWLY SET ME DOWN ON THE BED, LIKE HE WAS

worried that if he moved too fast, then the moment would break. Once he knew that I wasn't going to stop him, he turned the lamp off. He kissed me, thoroughly and deeply. He would pull back and then gently place kisses on my eyelids, my eyebrows, and then move to my ears, and my neck. It was the sweetest, most intimate, thing anyone had ever done to me. We knew that nothing was going to happen here, tonight in Jackson's house, but having him near me, close to me, making up for lost time—it was everything. It was exactly what I needed and wanted; slow kisses in the dark, his arms around me, holding me, warding off the memories of what I had done, of what had been done to me. I knew that if I hadn't slept for an entire day that I might actually get some sleep in his arms. I knew the nightmares would stay away while he held me. He kissed me until we were lying down, under the blankets. Until we broke apart, needing to stop before anything else happened.

In the dark, he traced the lines of my face as I lay facing him.

All we could hear was the rain, until he softly spoke up and asked, "What triggered you?"

I was watching his lips, still so focused on what it felt like to have them on me. My eyes shot to his. "How did you know I was triggered?"

He smiled, but didn't stop tracing my face, "I know a thing or two about working through them, getting over them... I have spent a few years in therapy to get through my past."

His admission was so soft, delicate, like it was just the two of us confessing sins to each other, begging for absolution.

"Laney mentioned something that Jackson texted her, about how I was being hard on you, that you had tried to apologize, and I wasn't giving you a chance." I took a breath, then continued, ready to let this go, once and for all. "It made me feel like I was putting you through something, like I was the bad guy.

"What triggered me was thinking about how unfair it was that I was being seen that way after what I went through. It brought up all these unresolved things about how you handled it… how you pushed me away. Before I knew it, I was gone, past the point of no return. The images were coming, I didn't have my meds, I was just angry. Then I just decided to become the villain you guys saw me as."

I finished with a small sob, still ashamed of how I handled it all. Still ashamed of this dark place, that had so much control over me.

Jimmy shifted closer, until my head was under his chin, then he wrapped his arms around me. I cried into his bare chest, embarrassed by the fact that I was crying again, and the fact that I was getting snot on his chest.

He rubbed my back gently, then began to talk in a low, soothing tone. "Ramsey, I am so sorry. I did complain to Jackson, but it wasn't how he made it sound. I deserve the distance you put between us, because I put it there first. I'm sorry how this all came across to you, but mostly, I am just sorry I stayed away from you. I went through hell to not talk to you, see you, be around you in any way, just so they wouldn't know that you were the way to hurt me."

"If that was the case, why didn't you keep your kids away? The kids mentioned being around those guys a few times," I asked, a little confused.

Jimmy kept rubbing circles into my back. "The MC is complicated. Each chapter has their own rules, their own bylaws and values. Davis was a sick prick, but he had a thing about not hurting kids. No one was ever allowed to take revenge out on kids, not until they were at least sixteen, that was his age limit. I don't know why sixteen, but it has to do with the Brass legacy law," he said, like I should know what that meant or something.

"What is the Brass legacy law?" I asked with a light tone, hoping he didn't stop.

He continued without hesitation, which felt wonderful after so many secrets between us. "The legacy law is confusing, but basically, if you are a part of the Brass, which takes a lot to get into, then your family is the Chapter by default, it doesn't matter if they want to or not. Once you say yes, you say yes for your future kids, and theirs, and so on. My dad was the one to initiate into the Brass when he was nineteen. His involvement complicated things when he met my mom, who wasn't a part of it. Usually, guys try to stick with club wives, because it makes their lives easier. I was initiated when I was sixteen, whether my mom was okay with it or not. She didn't have a choice."

"Why not? I mean, I understand what you're saying about legacy, but can't you challenge it some way?" I asked, a little defensively for his sixteen-year-old self. Sixteen was still so young, still such a huge burden to take on.

Jimmy let out a quiet laugh at my defensiveness. "The only way to escape from being in the Brass, is to fight your way out or outsmart them."

I nodded my understanding into his chest as he continued, "Dad fought his way out after my mom died. He was on a rampage and just wanted to be free, for the sake of my mother's dying wish. He was hunted down and had to make some tough choices but ultimately, in the end, he won his freedom. I did not. I stayed in for a few more years, wanting to get out, but not sure how. Once Lisa left, I had to get out of there. I knew they'd take advantage of the fact that I needed money, they'd want my kids around, they'd be the supportive family I needed. Only it wasn't support, it was manipulation and control. So, I met with Davis and asked for a sabbatical, time to sort my shit, away from the city."

"And he said yes?" I asked in disbelief.

"He didn't like it, but I reminded him that he'd made

special arrangements in the past for other club members. One of which was my dad. He allowed my dad to travel back and forth for club business to Belvidere, back when mom wanted to move. Eventually, Davis agreed and said I could go, as long as I remembered that I wasn't done," Jimmy finished with an easy tone, like this was something simple or a fond memory.

I stayed quiet, hoping he would keep going, but some of these questions got the better of me.

"So, these guys who were tracking you, wouldn't they know about your dad's bar then? Wouldn't they go after him for revenge?"

Jimmy gently shook his head. "No. My dad was basically untouchable after what he did to the Brass when they attacked him. The only way they'd attack was if he entered their territory, which was southern Chicago. Although, if they knew dad was in the city at all, I'm sure they would have gone after him. The guys who followed me knew this and knew better than to go into his bar."

It made me wonder what Theo did to defend himself all those years ago, but I also didn't want that kind of knowledge in my brain.

"Davis found Lisa for me, even though I didn't ask him to. He used her meeting as an excuse to pull me back into 'work.' Told me he needed to use my company trucks to move product. I agreed because I didn't have a choice. I got to finalize things with Lisa and finish things once and for all with Davis, all in one deal. I just had to be careful, and since my phone was bugged by Davis, I couldn't contact you, in any way."

It made sense, but it still bugged me that he kept me in the dark.

"Why didn't you explain this to me? I would have understood and stayed away from you. But you just left me, Jimmy. It hurt so badly, I thought... I thought you just changed your mind about us."

I was holding back tears again; the memory of being left out of his world still ached.

He pulled me tighter against him, then placed a kiss on top of my head. "It all got so messed up, baby. I wanted to, I planned to, Davis had a date that he wanted to meet. I wanted to tell you before, but then Dad told me about his plans and that you hadn't told me, it just hit too fast. I ended up going to Davis that night. When I got drunk, I talked with him and ended up starting that next day. So, when I talked to you on the phone that morning, I didn't have time to explain because his guys were already with me. I screwed up. I'm so sorry."

"Okay, but why not figure out a way to contact me, where they couldn't see. Why not sneak a message to me, or something. I mean, there were ways to do it, Jimmy," I said, a little flushed, and irritated.

"I wanted to, so many times. I sat in front of my door and cried like a damn baby when I saw you come and try to get into my house that night. I hated myself, but I knew you would hate me too, if you knew that I had gone back to the MC. I kept trying to picture that conversation and since you were already so hesitant to be with me, I felt like the MC thing would push you further away from me than you already were."

Tears were running down my damn cheeks again. I felt horrible, because he was right. I would have been pissed, and it would have complicated our very fragile and confusing relationship. I asked for friendship, but I would have responded like a girlfriend, and gone all crazy protective over him. He must have felt my tears, because he pulled away and looked at me. I wiped at them, desperate not to repeat the snot on the chest situation. "Jimmy, never do that again, please. I know, you probably made the right call, but I don't want that anymore. I want you to be honest with me and include me. Let me stand by you, help you, be with you."

I stopped because I was very close to admitting that I loved him, and that was an admission I did not want to make right then. I needed him to say it first, because I was still so insecure about how he felt.

He dipped his head and kissed my lips, softly, then pulled me back to his chest. "We never have to worry about it again. Davis is dead, Ramsey."

I pulled away and stared at him; shock and nausea were at war in my body.

Jimmy gently and carefully pulled me back to him as he continued, "I found out a few days ago. He's dead, Ramsey, and I wasn't sure if they would call you or tell you, I didn't know how to. But it's one less thing you have to worry about."

I had gotten calls, but I just ignored them all. I knew I had a court date coming up, everything else could wait. I didn't want to talk to reporters, or to anyone else. I was afraid that if I took the calls, then I would somehow be found by him again. It was crazy, but crazy kind of described my life at the moment and that's why I was seeing Glenda two times a week. She told me not to worry about the calls until I was ready. I wasn't ready.

I rested against Jimmy again, letting the news settle between us. I didn't really believe it, but at least there was a part of me that wanted to. It felt like progress.

RAIN WAS STILL PELTING AGAINST THE LARGE WINDOW IN THE room. It was bright enough outside now that I could see the rain, drop for drop, as it attacked the window. Jimmy's arms caged me in against his chest, as we lay snuggled under a mass of blankets. He was slowly breathing in and out, hopefully sleeping. I had no idea what time it was. I wasn't tired, but I knew he was and I wanted him to rest.

I closed my eyes, trying to memorize the feel of his warm

chest behind me, of his arms around me, the feel of his skin. I started rubbing the hair on his arms, to memorize the feel of it —*because I was that weird*—when he started to move behind me. His hand slipped under my shirt and splayed flat on my stomach. His mouth moved to my neck as he started to slowly kiss behind my ear.

I was breathing hard, because his hot breath on my skin set me on fire and I'd wanted this, I wanted him. I could feel that he felt the same by the way his body responded behind me. I started to turn towards him, to catch his lips with my own, when the door flew open. We both turned our heads back towards the door and saw Laney standing there, looking exhausted, and angry. I moved to get up but Jimmy held me firmly in place. I started to laugh, as I lay back against him. He pulled the covers up over our heads, as though he was trying to hide us from Laney. It was funny, and I would have enjoyed this moment more, but I knew Laney was not in the mood. I turned towards Jimmy under the covers and kissed him, and that's when we heard Laney yell.

"Ramsey Bennington, you will come out from under those covers right now and talk to me!"

Jimmy laughed, kissed me again, then released me. I pulled the blankets back and carefully stood up.

Laney was wearing an oversized blue shirt that was definitely not hers, and definitely a man's. I decided that I would ignore that, and her hair, for the moment.

She stepped forward and grabbed my hand, then pulled me out of the room towards the kitchen but bypassed it and headed for the stairs that went up to the third floor. We went up to a floor that was all white, with plush carpet, and floor-to-ceiling bookshelves. The walls were a soft, light blue, and the shelves were a dark stained wood. She headed towards a large window seat that was overlooking the water. I didn't even know that Jackson lived near the water, but then again, I wasn't exactly lucid when I arrived.

Laney curled up on the cushioned bench, pulled a blanket over her, and sat against the wall. I copied her movements until we sat looking at each other. I started to talk until she put a finger up, as if to stop me. A few seconds later, I heard foot-steps running up the stairs, and Jackson appeared. He was wearing black running shorts, a beanie, and a gray sweatshirt that had the same logo on it as Laney's shirt had.

Interesting.

He was carrying two coffees in his hands, while walking towards us. He handed one to Laney and gave her a secretive smile, then he turned to hand me mine, but before he handed it to me, I saw his eyes. They were full of pain as they took me in. I tried to ignore it and took the coffee from him, giving him a quiet, "Thank you."

He nodded, then hesitated a second before leaning in and kissing the top of my head. Then he turned back around and jogged back downstairs.

I gave Laney a look and asked, "What in the world was that about?"

She sipped her coffee and looked out the window, before responding. "You said some things in the car, about what happened to you..." She looked down and swallowed before continuing, "None of us knew, Ramsey... Jackson, well...he took what happened to you pretty hard. He cares about you, you know. It just was hard to hear that stuff, is all."

I looked down at my coffee, fighting the red that was stinging my cheeks. I hated that it embarrassed me; it was something my therapist and I were working through, but I haven't gained victory over yet. I didn't know what to say, so I stayed quiet.

Laney sipped her coffee again, then looked at me. "Ramsey, I'm so sorry about the other night. I didn't know that what

I said would upset you like it did..." She stopped because tears were running down her face, and her words were starting to get stuck and a high-pitched sound started coming out of her throat. Laney hated crying. Hated it. She got red and blotchy, and she could never talk through her tears, so the conversations always took a long time to get through. I always thought it was funny, but it's the reason I never pushed her on things she wasn't ready to talk about.

I leaned forward until I was touching Laney's hand. "Stop, it's not your fault." I sat back a little, looking down at my cup, realizing it was time to come clean about my 'episodes' to my best friend.

Laney wiped her face and sniffed. "Then what happened last..." She stopped again, her throat making that awful sound again.

Saving her from having to push through the tears, I explained, "Anytime I think about what happened, during... the... uh..." I looked out the window, cleared my throat, and took a breath. "Anytime I think about the abduction... I have, what my therapist calls, an 'episode.' Basically, I lose control, and essentially have a break down. I usually take meds for it, but I didn't have them with me." I watched the rain drizzle onto the cars below us, there were several parked on the street that ran along the waterfront.

Laney sniffed again, then asked, "Then what triggered it? We never talked..."

I started shaking my head, cutting her off. "It wasn't your fault, and no, we didn't talk about it. It was when you mentioned that Jackson said Jimmy was going through a hard time... it just triggered all this stuff about how I actually went through something, and somehow I was still coming out as the villain to you guys."

Laney leaned forward and grabbed my free hand. "God, Ramsey, no, never. I would never think that about you." There was an urgency in her tone, and I knew she was telling the truth, but it didn't change how it made me feel.

I squeezed her hand. "I know... I just, it didn't change anything for me when I started to spiral. I just wanted to let go and forget the memories of that night and being in that room." I took a few breaths in and out, trying to be as brave as I was last night when I went over this with Jimmy.

I sipped my coffee again. "Jimmy told me Davis died... in jail, I guess. But he's gone," I said in a rush, hoping to gloss over this particular subject.

Laney nodded her head as a few more tears fell, then softly said, "Good... I know I shouldn't be glad, but I am. I am so sorry that happened to you, and that I didn't let you talk about it in the hospital."

I smiled at my friend, grateful for her big heart. "I'm sorry for what I put you through, Laney. I'm so embarrassed that you had to call Jackson and get everyone involved," I said while shaking my head, trying to shake the shame.

Laney gave me a mischievous smile. "Looks like it did some good with you and Jimmy, from what I saw this morning." She raised her eyebrows up and down. I laughed and then kicked her.

"You should talk... I love that shirt, by the way... Would you mind showing me where you slept last night? I'd love to see your guest room."

Laney flushed a deep red, then mumbled, "Jackson only has one guest room in this freakishly large mansion."

I laughed and finished my coffee off, then I reached forward and grabbed my best friend in a hug. She held me tight, and whispered into my ear, "Please don't ever do that to me again, Ram. I honestly thought I lost you that night."

I shook my head against her shoulder. "I'm getting help, Lane. I'll get there, I just need time. But yes, let's avoid places with men and alcohol for a while."

We separated and wiped at our faces, then looked around the room.

"How come you've never told me how loaded Jackson is?" I asked, lightly hitting her arm.

"What difference would it make? It's not like it matters to me," she said shyly, playing with the fibers on her blanket.

"Why did he bring us coffees this morning?" I asked, hoping we could move on from my life for a second.

She let out a loud breath, then grabbed a fistful of blanket, and scrunched her face up before answering. "Okay... so, Jackson and I kind of hooked up last night, because I was going out of my mind about you and he was pretty messed up too over the whole thing, and we just kind of were there for each other. I left him this morning, so I could go talk to you... I guess he just assumed about the coffees... pretty sweet of him, I guess."

I smiled and covered my mouth to hold back a laugh. "So, are you guys together then?" I asked.

She rolled her eyes and started drawing things on the window with the condensation that had built up. "No, I don't think so. It's complicated. I mean, there is some drama in the mix and sure, we like each other, but a relationship? Jackson doesn't do relationships. Or so I have heard," she responded then trailed off, probably thinking she was too quiet for me. My heart hurt for her, but I knew now wasn't the time to try and push this.

Before I could respond, I heard Jimmy calling me from the lower level. Laney and I stood, and I hugged her tight again, then we headed downstairs.

Jackson was making breakfast and Jimmy was dressed, his duffel bag by the door. I knew we couldn't stay in this bubble forever, but my heart sank at the idea of us being apart again.

I tried not to let my disappointment show as he grabbed my hand and led me into the kitchen. Jackson made us eggs and toast, then gave us each a yogurt cup. Jimmy ate with us, then handed me my fully-charged cell phone and told me that Glenda was waiting for my call. I grabbed my phone, then followed Jimmy to the entryway.

I looked at his bag, then him, he wrapped me in a tight hug, saying against my hair, "I will be waiting in Belvidere for you. Will you be okay the next few days?"

I nodded into his chest. "Yeah, Laney will take me to her house, then I will go see Mom and tomorrow, I will see Glenda. It will be okay."

He leaned back and looked at me and said, "I know *it* will be okay, but will *you* be?"

I leaned forward and kissed him, then stepped back. "I'm getting there, boss," I stated, winking at him. He rolled his eyes at my 'boss' comment, then attacked me with another kiss.

FORTY-FIVE

"How do you feel about his death?"

I hugged the couch pillow tighter to my chest as I sifted through all the emotions that surrounded that question. Glenda had the most comfortable couch, and the best couch pillows in the entire world. They were this kind of silky softness that put me at ease immediately. I looked up at the gentle rays of light that were filtering in from her large office window. Glenda had an elegant office, with plush white carpet on top of dark hardwood floors. Her desk was a pristine white, cleared of any clutter except a sleek, silver laptop, and a cutesy calendar you might find in a home decor magazine. There was also enough shiplap on her walls to justify an entire episode on *Fixer Upper*. I liked her office, I liked her. Glenda wore a beautiful blue romper that looked gorgeous against her ebony skin, and she had these hazel eyes that were stunning. She was the kind of pretty you might find in a magazine, the kind that you just wanted to stare at.

"Why do you think it's difficult for you to answer that question?" she asked gently. She knew that I was stalling.

I pulled my eyebrows together as I concentrated on the

floor. It didn't have any answers, but it was therapeutic in helping me avoid Glenda's gaze.

"It's not difficult... I just... I don't know how I feel," I admitted weakly.

Glenda crossed her left leg over her right one, and adjusted her pad of paper; her long, soft black hair was swept to the side by her movement. "So, then you feel happy about it?"

"No, not happy," I quickly corrected her. She did this with me. If I answered something while being vague, she would push until I clarified.

"Then what do you feel, Ramsey? You must feel something."

I picked at the pillow, and thought about it. I dug deep so that I was honest. I actually had no problem being honest with Glenda, I just really didn't know how I felt yet about Davis' death.

"I feel... relieved, I guess. I am glad that no one else will get hurt because of him. It feels like a form of justice, I think. I mean, there was a small part of me that thought if he did go to jail, then some connection that he had would get him out early." I rambled on while still picking at my magical pillow.

Glenda was writing, and gently kicking her foot up and down. She had perfect manicured toes that I could see through her nude, peek-a-boo heels. "Do you feel like you are allowed to feel relieved that someone died?" she asked, while still looking at her notepad. She knew that I didn't like direct eye contact while we were digging up pieces of my soul.

I furrowed my brows again. "I think..." I took a big breath and decided that I just wanted to let this part go, out of my body, out of my mind, for good. "I think so. I don't wish death upon anyone, but what he did, what he could do to someone else... I feel bad for feeling good about him being dead. Doesn't that make me a terrible person?" I asked, looking up at her.

She set her notepad aside and leaned forward, knowing I was finally ready to excavate some of this guilty dirt that surrounded my mind and heart. I loved that Glenda was always standing by with an emotional shovel.

"It doesn't make you a terrible person, Ramsey, it makes you an honest one. No one can judge you for how you respond to his death. You were the only victim in that room. Feeling anything about his death that you don't want to feel will only give him power over you."

I let that sink in. I didn't want him to have any power over me, I wanted to be done with this.

Glenda sat back and grabbed her notepad. "You hold the keys to your own freedom, Ramsey, remember that. No one can make you feel anything that you don't want to feel, and no one has the right to taint your own feelings towards the situation. It happened to only you, it's yours to own or to release," she said, while finishing her thoughts on her notepad.

At her words, I felt like a load had been lifted off me. Glenda set the notepad aside and got up to walk to her desk, to where her laptop sat open. "Let's discuss you going back to Belvidere, and our continued appointments once you go back."

A surge of excitement went through me at the idea of going back home. It was home to me now, officially, now that I had accepted the offer to own Sip N Sides, and now that Jimmy and I were… cleared up. This was me and Glenda's last session before I went back. We talked through my breakdown, and we talked about some ideas on how to control those impulses when I felt powerless. She made an official speculation that things would get easier for me once I was back home and got into the rhythm of things. Especially now that things with Davis were finalized, and I would never have to see him again; I hoped she was right.

"Can we do FaceTime or Skype appointments?" I asked while watching her look through her computer.

She looked up at me for a second and smiled. "I would enjoy that, Ramsey. I would really like to continue to meet at least once a week, especially as you become a business owner and take that on. Adding stress to your life might be tricky at first, and it will be important to know how to maneuver the stress around that. I want you to know that I consider myself on-call for you. If you need a quick chat, or conversation on your way to work, never hesitate to call me." She flashed her gorgeous white teeth.

I smiled back, and then released my pillow. I was half-tempted to ask her if I could take it with me, but then I realized that would be weird and normal people didn't ask to take pillows with them. I grabbed my purse and hugged Glenda, not really caring if she wanted one or not. She had gotten me through a really ugly period of my life, and I was thankful for her. She laughed and hugged me back. She scheduled me in for a FaceTime conversation for one week from now, then I headed back to the hospital to help Mom get packed up.

Mom was doing better. That's what they said anyway... I was happy with the news at first, then I realized that they hadn't changed her diagnosis at all but told me that Mom could still prove everyone wrong if she wanted. I felt better knowing that we gave her the best possible chance available.

Once I made it up to her room, I found her packing her own things. I smiled and moved around her to take over, and she didn't protest. She found a chair and relaxed while I packed her things up. I couldn't help but feel a sense of relief that we were finally leaving, and I knew that Mom felt the same way. She was so supportive when I told her about what had happened with the night club and my 'episode,' and she was also happy to hear about Jimmy and I reconnecting. I didn't tell her everything, just that Jimmy took care of me when I woke up. She must have seen my face flush at the memory of us together, because she had her own smile and started speaking in Cambodian about answered prayers.

I was excited to get home for so many reasons, but I was nervous to see Jimmy again. We hadn't stopped texting and talking on the phone, but we never spoke of what life would be like when I got back. Even though I spoke to the kids every night at dinner, they just put me on speakerphone while they ate, and acted like I was a part of their nightly routine. I felt happy, and full, but still, I was nervous. I checked my work calendar and noticed that he still had our little meeting scheduled for Friday night. I thought it was funny, since it was obvious how we felt about each other now, but he still wanted to go through with it. Maybe it would be considered our first date? I smiled again and finished packing up this particular chapter of our lives, eager to get back to the story awaiting us back home.

BELVIDERE WAS A BEAUTIFUL SIGHT AS WE PULLED INTO THE city and saw that the fall colors had completely taken over. The red and yellow trees lined the streets as we drove past the old city hall, and the old red brick buildings. We slowly headed towards our street, past the grocery store and the post office, and when we went past Sip N Sides, my heart about burst open. It took all my strength not to pull into the deteriorating lot, get out, and hug the building that was now mine. Well, almost. Theo and I still had a few things to sign and process, to make it official, and I still needed to train, but it was basically mine and I loved it.

Once we pulled into our driveway, there were a few things that I noticed right away.

First, our lawn was mowed and looked fresh. Our gravel even looked like it was fresh, if that were possible. There was a fall wreath on our front door, and a hay bale sitting next to our door with a few pumpkins sitting on and around it, making our porch look dreamy and festive. The next thing I noticed were the signs. There were two huge wooden signs resting in front of our door that were painted white, and written in dark blue lettering were the words:

Welcome Home, Ramsey

The second sign said:

And Ramsey's Mom

MOM AND I BOTH LAUGHED AS WE UNPACKED THE CAR. MOM only unpacked her light travel purse, and her pillows from the front seat, while I grabbed our suitcases and bags. We made our way inside to a sparkling clean house. There were fresh flowers in glass vases, covering every possible surface in the house. I knew it was Jimmy even before I saw the note, but I knew for sure it was him when I walked into my room and found a letter pinned under a massive vase of flowers.

WELCOME HOME, BABY. THE KIDS AND I ARE EAGER TO SEE YOU, but we know you might need some time to get unpacked and rest. When you're ready, please come visit us... or just me, whatever you feel like. I installed a security system for the house to make you feel a little safer at night. Something I should have done when you first got home from the hospital. Come see me when you're ready. - Jimmy

THERE WAS A NEW SILVER KEY ATTACHED TO THE NOTE, AS WELL as codes and instructions for the new alarm system. It made me smile that he had replaced his house key for me. We were slowly picking up the broken pieces of the last few weeks of our relationship. Later that night, after unpacking and showering, I contemplated on whether or not to use my shiny new key or not.

I decided that I would. Dressing in some loose-fitting jeans, and a cute black, off-the-shoulder sweater, I hurried toward my bathroom to do my hair and makeup. Internally I kept scolding myself that I didn't need to dress up, but deep down I wanted to. I wanted this to be a fresh start for us. Jimmy and I hadn't texted or spoken since I arrived home, so the anticipation was killing me. Once I was ready, I walked into mom's room, kissed her forehead, and told her goodbye. I also left her a note, letting her know I was at Jimmy's, in case she woke up and I wasn't here. Not that I was planning on spending the night with Jimmy but... just in case.

I got into my old SUV and headed towards Jimmy's. I had butterflies in my stomach and my breathing was ragged. I double-checked the dash clock and realized that it was the kids' bedtime, and he was probably putting them to sleep right now. I wanted to text him, but I also wanted to surprise him. I wasn't sure how he would feel if I just showed up. I bit my lip as I considered what I should do, all the while slowly making my way to his street. Then I was on his street, down to two houses left before I was in front of his house. Decision made, I would just go in, and see where this put us. Better to just find out.

Theo's truck was gone, but the lights in the house were still on, so I knew they were at least up.

I parked along the curb and slowly made my way up to his house, trying to brush off the last time I had done this, and had been rejected. I didn't want to use my new key, just out of fear that it wouldn't work for some reason and I would somehow be launched back into a world where Jimmy was shut out of mine. I shut my eyes tightly and tried the door knob. It was locked. I decided, since it was early, to knock.

I knocked three times, but no one answered. Reluctantly, I

used my key, and relished the sound of the few clicks it took to unlock the door.

The house was quiet, but there were lamps on in the living room and kitchen.

I took my shoes off, and slowly made my way into the kitchen—it was empty. I turned around and started heading upstairs. I walked past the kids' rooms because I didn't want to disturb them or to confuse them at me being there so late.

I found Jimmy's door and stared at it. I couldn't hear anything on the other side, so I knocked gently. I felt so weird, like an imposter, but he had told me to come and see him. Suddenly, I felt insecure and unsure, did he want me to call first? Was I invading his space? I was about to hyperventilate, when I just decided to open the damn door and figure it out. So, I did. I went in and closed the door behind me but looked around and found his room empty as well. The large bed was still made up, but his bedside light was on. As I made my way further in, I heard his shower on. Then I turned bright red and was glad no one was there to see it.

What was I supposed to do now? Obviously, there was a large part of me that was cheering my inner self on, to walk into that bathroom and let him know that I was here in a very memorable way. The more logical side of my inner self said; take it slow.

I stood there for too long before I heard the shower turn off, I was hyperventilating again. He had no door separating his bathroom from his bedroom and time was running out. I decided to physically cover my eyes with my hands, like a ten-year-old, and when I knew he could hear me, I yelled, "Don't come in here without some clothes on!"

I heard a little chuckle from the bathroom. *Glad he thought this was funny.*

I kept my hands where they were, until I heard movement and felt body heat in front of me. Then I felt hands gently touch the hand that covered my eyes and pulled to lower it. Jimmy stood in front of me, wet hair, lake green eyes, huge smile, and wearing nothing but black boxers.

I gulped. Literally gulped. Like a virgin.

My face flooded with heat and that only made him laugh harder. He must have felt how uncomfortable I was, because he walked over to his dresser and pulled out a pair of sweatpants and slid them on. I was mortified, not because of how he came out of the bathroom but because of my reaction to it. Why was I being so weird? Jimmy was probably wondering the same thing. Because I most definitely was not a virgin.

I decided that I was way too embarrassed to say anything about it, because I knew that deep down, it had to do with being insecure about him actually wanting me for me, not just something physical. We had some ways to go to build back up that trust.

I relaxed at that self-assessment and moved over to his bed, crawling onto it, then grabbed his TV remote and started flipping through channels. Jimmy walked around to the other side of the bed and crawled in until he was right next to me. We sat there next to each other, watching the beginning of a singing competition in silence. I felt like a teenager with how awkward everything was, but I didn't want to give any part of me to Jimmy until I knew for sure that he wasn't going to change his mind about us. After a few contestants won their challenges, Jimmy moved until he was sitting behind me, and I was resting back against his chest. We kept watching, as he bent down to kiss my forehead and then started playing with my hair.

"How was your trip back?"

I smiled, even though he couldn't see me. "Good, I really liked the signs that were waiting for us, and the beautiful flowers. It made it a nice homecoming."

I felt a little stupid for not saying something sooner. I was so focused on surprising Jimmy tonight that I wasn't even thinking of how his kids would feel if I didn't say something about the signs. He squeezed my shoulders then ran his hands down my arms, which I couldn't feel because of my dumb sweater. Then he bent to the side and kissed my bare shoulder. *Okay, sweater redeemed.*

He kept kissing my shoulder, all the way up the side of my neck. All I wanted to do was melt into him, to kiss him, to give into what we have both been waiting for, but I needed assurances from him before we went that far. I fought against every nerve in my body and kept myself facing forward, watching the singing competition like it was the most riveting thing in the world, but my body betrayed me. I didn't realize I was letting out little moans until I heard Jimmy laughing behind me. He moved our bodies, until we were laying further down in the bed and I was half-covering his chest.

Stupid betraying body.

He scooted himself to the side until he was completely out from under me. My heart was beating so hard, I thought he might notice. I was almost positive that he could see my pulse jump in my throat. I was screaming for us to press pause in my head, but nothing came out of my mouth except for more moans. *Damn it.*

He closed his eyes and gently ran his nose along the side of my neck, until he was hovering over my face. Then he kissed my lips, slowly. He caressed them like they were the most delicate thing in the world.

I reached up and ran my fingers along the sides of his face as I pulled him in towards me, deepening the kiss. Taking that as a sign that I wanted more, he let out a moan from the back of his throat and moved to lay on top of me, while moving his right hand up my back under my shirt. Things were escalating quickly, and I definitely needed to break this kissing fest and let him know that I wasn't actually ready to have sex with him yet. I would stop him. In a second.

He pulled me to his chest until we were flat, like two boards. His left arm held his body up, while his right hand was secured underneath me, bringing me off the bed by an inch or so; it was hot as hell. My arms went around his neck and we were kissing like it was the end of everything. His tongue, hot and desperate licked and kissed, demanding more and I was all too willing to give it. Panting like we'd run a half marathon, we continued our assault against each other. I felt his reaction hardening against my stomach, which caused the inferno in my belly to rage hotter.

Shifting us a bit, he slowly moved his knee, up until it was resting right in between my legs, right at my core.

We needed to stop. I needed assurances from him that he'd stay, that he wouldn't go away again when things were tense or hard. He had my entire heart in his hands and now he was burning through my skin. His fingers trailed up, cupping my breasts, pinching the hardened bud there. I let out a gasp, and tugged on his neck, until he was closer. My body took over, grinding all my softened places against his hard edges, it was screaming for release. My willpower was clearly nonexistent, it was getting weaker by the second. Every scorching kiss was stripping me of any reasons that we needed to wait. Right as two strong fingers dipped below the waist line of my jeans, searing a line of heat down my butt; the bedroom door creaked open. A small voice rasped,

"Daddy?"

Jimmy sat up quickly, throwing a pillow over his lap. I tried to follow his lead, slowly scooting further and further from his side while adjusting my shirt. Thank the Lord the TV was on, so I could pretend that I had been watching it, and no clothing was gone, except for Jimmy's shirt. But I was all clothed and really, that's all that mattered for the moment.

"What's wrong, buddy?" Jimmy asked, still sitting in his spot.

Sammy hung on to the door knob, while rubbing his eyes, as he replied, "I had a bad dream about an evil, green eyed hippo that was trying to eat us while we went swimming." Then he sniffled and started crying, "It got Jasmine."

He was crying, and I was holding back a laugh because it was the cutest things I'd ever seen. Jimmy, finally not worked up any longer, got up from the bed and knelt in front of Sammy, pulling him into a hug.

Sammy cried into Jimmy's shoulder, while Jimmy rubbed his back. After a few minutes, Sammy lifted his head and wiped his snot with the back of his hand.

Then looked at me, finally noticing I was there. I should have snuck out when I had the chance. I stilled as he pointed at me and asked, "Can I snuggle with you and Ramsey until I feel like the bad dream won't come back?"

I pulled the blankets down and waved him towards me. "Come on, buddy, we were just watching this singing show, wanna help us judge?"

Sammy jumped onto the bed, still sniffling, wearing his *Lego Movie* pajamas. He burrowed down into the pillows, next to me, then Jimmy turned the lamp off and got in on the other side of Sammy, and we sat there watching for a while. Jimmy slipped his arm up over the back of the pillows until his fingers found my hair, then he played with the tail of my braid. After a while, I snuggled down into the pillows, like Sammy. Before I knew it, I was drifting off to sleep, my only thought being about weapons one could use against crazy, hungry hippos.

FORTY-SIX

JIMMY

SOMETIME DURING THE NIGHT, I moved Sammy back to his bedroom, so that he would sleep better, and so I would sleep better. It was killing me that Ramsey was so close, and yet so far away. My whole body was still aching from wanting more from her tonight, from wanting everything from her. I felt like an idiot when Sammy opened my door, how could I have not locked it? I guess, in my defense, it wasn't like I normally had women in my bed at night that I was trying to seduce.

If that's what I was even doing. All I knew was that I wanted Ramsey, really fucking badly, but she seemed so hesitant. More hesitant than when we were in Jackson's house. Another place we were interrupted from taking, maybe not the next step, but steps still the same. I felt like I've waited my whole life for her, to be with her in every way. Still, I couldn't shake the feeling that Ramsey wasn't as ready as me in that department. Maybe it was because she was back home now, and things like taking that next step would change things between us. I wanted them to change.

Once I put Sammy back in his bed, I got back into mine and pulled Ramsey into my arms. We slept like that until my alarm went off at around six in the morning. I hated it, but I knew that she would want to go home as soon as she woke up, not wanting the kids to think badly about her. How could I even hold that against her?

The alarm beeped, and Ramsey stirred in my arms. At that moment, I was the happiest I had ever been, except for when my kids were born. I couldn't see Ramsey's face when we woke up at Jackson's house, so getting to watch her face first thing, was heaven. When she woke up, she had this tiny smile that started in the corner of her mouth. It slowly made its way up her face, until her eyes lit up with it. Like a sunrise.

I smiled at her as she registered that she had fallen asleep with me. Red flushed her cheeks and I knew she was remembering last night. I wanted to laugh because we didn't do anything blush-worthy last night, but I definitely wanted to, and I hoped we would soon. She started to get up and before I could think better of it, I leaned in and kissed her.

She relaxed against me, and smiled into my lips, then squirmed a little, which was my cue to let her go. I released her and she started to crawl out of bed. I got up with her and walked her downstairs, knowing she wanted to get out of here and get home to check on her mom. Once we were by the door, she leaned in for another kiss, which I gladly gave her, then she opened the door and left. I rubbed my chest absently, because watching her walk away was like watching a piece of my house get up and walk across the street. It felt foreign and wrong, like she belonged here, with me.

I let out a breath and decided I better get the day started, because I only had today to prepare things for our little six-week talk and share what was in our envelopes. We obviously knew how we felt about each other, but there was still so much to make up for, I wanted to turn the night into a declaration to her.

I went through the motions of getting ready and preparing

for the day. My mind was so full of things that needed to be prepped and planned for the restaurant to close for an entire evening that I hadn't even checked my phone until lunch.

No new notifications felt a little strange now, like nothing had changed with Ramsey and she was still ignoring me. It stung. Pushing through it, I was about to shoot her a text, when one of our vendors came into my office with an emergency. The craziness didn't stop and before I knew it, it was past nine at night and I was barely making my way home.

By the time I ate dinner, showered, did the kids' laundry, made their lunches, and caught up on bills, it was nearly eleven. I checked my phone before I plugged it into the charger and saw that Ramsey still hadn't called or texted. I pushed away the fear of her pulling away and decided that in healthy relationships people didn't have to talk every single day.

I tried to talk myself into believing that Ramsey just needed time to adjust to training for Sip N Sides and being home, but a huge part of me wanted to be that ridiculous, clingy couple that stayed on the phone all night listening to each other breathe. I crawled into bed and pulled the pillow that Ramsey slept on the night before into my chest and breathed in her scent, feeling hopeful for what tomorrow could mean for us.

FORTY-SEVEN

I PRESSED the button on my phone again, just to be sure that there weren't any new notifications. It was past eleven at night, but I was sure that Jimmy wouldn't end the day without saying anything to me, would he? I could simply text him and be done with this whole waiting thing that I've done all day, but I wouldn't.

Even through learning the ways of owning a bar, and going over finances for Sip N Sides, my mind was on Jimmy. We kissed and almost did more than that. We were moving forward, and it was wonderful. But because we had kissed and, in my mind, we were together, I found myself checking my phone, waiting to hear something from him. Maybe I was spoiled after all the texts he'd sent while I was in Chicago, but not hearing anything from him felt strange.

It was now past ten at night and I still hadn't heard anything from him. The mature side of me was saying to just text him, say goodnight. The immature, still very insecure, part of me wondered if he had changed his mind. Or if something had happened again, and we were out of each other's worlds again. I hated that we were still tainted by those days and hours apart, those weeks spent alone. My chest constricted at the thought of Davis having power over this part of my life still, but I couldn't bear the idea of Jimmy rejecting me again. So, I turned my phone completely off and closed my eyes, praying that I got past these insecurities with him, and soon.

The sun streaming into my window woke me after a fitful night of sleep. I knew my ticks by now, what my triggers were, and when to call Glenda.

I curled up on the living room couch with a hot cup of coffee while powering my phone on. While I waited, I looked around at all the flowers in the house, my heart softened, and I could feel the anxiety over last night start to leave me. Once my phone came back on, I gave it a second to catch up and load any missed calls or texts. I glanced back at a vase of white hydrangeas and exhaled as I felt my expectations start to rise.

I glanced back at my phone, and still, there was nothing. Pain pierced my heart, and I felt like a lost teenager. I hated how out of control my emotions were. I rolled my eyes at myself as I pulled up Glenda's contact information. It was barely past seven in the morning, but I knew Glenda started early.

A few rings later, I heard her pick up. "Hello, Dr. Stanza speaking."

I cleared my throat and tried to be as professional as her. I had never called her anything but Glenda, so I wasn't totally sure how to proceed. "Uh, hi, Glenda? It's Ramsey Bennington."

"Ramsey! I am so glad you called, I was hoping you would check in after a few days. How are things going?"

I couldn't keep the smile out of my voice. There's just something about someone being happy to hear from you that feels good. "Really good. Mostly… I, uh… I was wondering if we could chat really quickly about something that is triggering me?"

"Of course, what's going on?"

I could hear the concern in her voice, and I immediately cringed. I felt like Jimmy issues weren't on the same playing field as my abduction issues, but I needed some perspective.

"It's just my relationship with Jimmy... I thought we were on the same page, or moving forward, but after we nearly, uh... connected the night I came home, he hasn't communicated with me."

I rushed through it all as fast as possible, hoping not to sound as desperate and pathetic as I felt.

"I see, and his distance is triggering you? What exactly is it making you feel?" she asked delicately.

I thought for a second and wrestled with the intensity of what was going on in my chest.

"Powerless, breathless. I feel like it's all locked up in my chest. Like somehow, what we did at his house wasn't as real to him as it was to me, and he will just disappear again."

Thankfully, Glenda had a full rap sheet on Jimmy and all the stupid things he and I had been through, so she was all caught up.

"I see. And have you tried contacting him?"

"Uh... no. I feel like, if I do, and he doesn't respond, then I will have another episode. I'm terrified of feeling that lost again."

She exhaled and then softly continued, "Ramsey, you aren't being fair to Jimmy. You two have barely reconnected. You have to remember what responsibilities he carries, remember that you haven't been a part of his life in weeks. It will take some time adjusting, but from what you have told me, he seems genuine about his intentions."

I thought through what she was saying for a second. She was right, of course. But what if he did push me away again? Then what? How would I recover this time?

I didn't realize that I had stayed quiet until I heard her clear her throat. "You still there, Ramsey?"

"Sorry, yes, just thinking through some things. I knew before everything, that I would have been fine without any communication, but now it just feels so heavy between us."

"So, lighten it up. Reach out in a non-heart-threatening way. Maybe use work, or some other common ground that you have. If you are too worried to risk talking about your relationship, then start with something smaller. Don't let this have power over you, Ramsey. You are in control."

Just hearing it, I felt a weight being lifted. I knew she was right, and I began to actually believe it.

"Thanks Glenda. I appreciate it."

I could hear her smile as we said our goodbyes and hung up.

I took three large breaths in and out, then I pulled up Jimmy's contact info. Something light, and unattached to us. I could do that.

Just as I closed out the texting app and pulled up his email info instead, I heard a knock at the door. Mom was still sleeping, so I appreciated that they weren't pounding it down, but I jumped up quickly to answer just the same.

I pulled the door open and came face-to-face with Jimmy. He was wearing his motorcycle jacket, and his hair was messy. As his lake green eyes found mine, I couldn't help but feel like he was feeling the same way that I was. He had that same look in his eyes; that lost, cautious, confused look. I noticed a second later that he had a white paper bag in his hand and a coffee. I pulled the door wider, and he quietly stepped in and walked past me to the kitchen.

I stalked behind him with my arms crossed over my chest. I had on sleep shorts, a t-shirt, and a robe. Jimmy set the drink on the counter and started to open the bag, without looking at me. Then he started to softly speak.

"I was slammed yesterday up until almost midnight with stuff, sorry I didn't get a chance to talk to you. I'm guessing that you were pretty busy too? I didn't see anything come in from you through the day."

Heat burned my face, and I could feel my chest aching again. He sounded as hurt as me. We were so messed up to keep doing this to each other. I hated the cycle of dysfunction that we seemed to be caught up in.

I lowered my arms, trying to come off as less distanced. "Sorry, I... honestly am still really messed up by our distance and stuff, and I didn't know exactly where we stood... so I was just waiting to hear from you."

I chanced a look up at his face. His eyes looked past me, down at the counter, his face twisting with frustration and that damn jaw ticking. I hated that I made him look like that. He took a step away, and it felt like miles had just been put between us. I was doing this. Ruining us. Damaging us, again. Just like in Chicago.

Panic and fear had me stepping towards him, invading his space and gently placing my hands on his chest. He was hesitant when he looked down at me, those eyes, worried and confused. I had to fix this. I stood up on my toes and kissed him. He responded, gently, then wrapped his arms around me, and held me tight. He was like my new form of anxiety medication. His arms, a shield to ward off the fear and worry that consumed so much of my time these days. I broke the kiss and tucked my head under his chin as he continued to hold me. I didn't know that I was crying until I heard it in my voice.

"I'm sorry. I feel so insecure where you're concerned. I feel like at any moment you will just change your mind about me, or you will just disappear."

He was quiet, his arms still like two pillars wrapped around me in a cage of security.

I continued confessing to him, "Don't give up on me. I will

get there… it will just take some time."

He rubbed my back in gentle strokes, then spoke up in a soft tone, "What can I do to help?"

"I think talking about our relationship, expectations, what we officially are will help," I stated, trying to look up at him.

He continued to rub my back, then kissed my forehead. "Tonight. We will cover it all tonight. No more staying away though. Assume that I always want to hear from you. I can't carry it all alone though, Ramsey."

We separated, and he turned back to the bag as I absorbed his words. I felt foolish for assuming that he didn't want me again. Felt foolish for doubting him. I knew if he did it to me, that it would drive me crazy. I nodded my head in acceptance of what he said.

He handed me a bagel, then kissed my forehead again before heading back towards the front door. I followed after him, not wanting him to go, but knowing he was busy.

I stood at the door as he headed towards his bike, but before he started it, he yelled back, "See ya tonight, babe."

Then he winked, and my heart nearly burst open. Tonight… he would give me answers tonight, and I could finally have some peace as to where we stood and confirm exactly what we were to each other.

I MET UP WITH THEO AND WE WENT OVER THE CONTRACTS FOR me becoming the official owner of Sip N Sides. My face hurt from smiling so much, and I loved that Mom had come down with me, to see the place and to show her support. Jimmy was still a silent partner, like he always had been with his Dad, but Theo gave me the option to kick him off the contract. I chose not to; regardless of what happened between us, he was a good business partner.

Theo was also leaving the business bank account as-is. Meaning, every dime left to him from his late wife for the bar, he was leaving to me. It felt wrong, and as soon as I realized that it was happening, I fought him on it. We spent three hours arguing over it. Finally, he relented by saying that I could invest the money into other business ventures, or charity, but otherwise, it needed to stay with the business. It was any first business owner's dream. I decided that I would pretend the money reserve didn't exist. It gave me a more accurate idea of how well I might do. Then I decided that I would pay Theo out of the funds, as a 'business venture.' I couldn't wait to talk to Jimmy about everything, and I really wanted to get his opinion on some things before it all became official. Theo planned to stay on as manager for the next year, to help out with things. Honestly, I was relieved, it would give the customers time to adjust to me, since I knew for a fact that everyone in this town loved Theo.

It was almost time to head to Rockford to meet Jimmy. Butterflies were in my stomach all day but had only gotten worse as we got closer and closer to our meeting time. He had texted to let me know that a car would be picking me up, so I wouldn't have to drive. I appreciated that, because it would make it less awkward when we ended the evening. He texted that he was wearing a suit. So, I called Laney for advice and she told me to hussy it up as much as possible. I settled on a white, knee-length dress that hugged my body, and had little diamonds and beads knitted throughout the fabric. I paired the dress with white heels, and red lipstick. My hair, I decided that I would curl and then braid a small part off to the side. All in all, I looked beautiful and more importantly, I *felt* beautiful.

I checked my phone and saw the car should be there any minute, so I pulled the box from the back of my closet out and grabbed the manila envelope that Jimmy had mailed to me six weeks ago. It was still sealed and unopened. I ran my fingers along his name in the upper left-hand corner and hugged the envelope to my chest. It was finally time to open it. I had been dying of curiosity after I got the envelope in the mail. I almost mailed it to Laney to keep it for me, because I was so weak, but it got easier and easier not to open as Jimmy grew more distant.

I heard the doorbell ring and knew it was the driver. I grabbed a shawl to cover my shoulders and headed towards the front door. I kissed my mom on the cheek and told the nurse who I had secured for the evening about the dinner options in the fridge and freezer, then headed for the door.

The fifteen miles from Belvidere to Rockford went by fast. My stomach was in knots as the town car pulled up to the curb of Jimmy's. The entire entrance was dark, as opposed to the twinkle lights that usually lit the path to the door. There was a small sign near the beginning of the parking lot that said, 'Closed for Private Event' in what I assumed was Jessica, or Claire's, girly, cursive writing.

I grabbed my envelope, and purse, and pushed the door open . It felt a little eerie to be out at night alone. I pushed back the residual fear that always accompanied that thought and walked towards the entrance. The town car waited until I was safely inside before pulling away.

There were a few candle lit tables that illuminated the main bar area, but otherwise everything was dark. I could see through the large glass windows in the back, that Jimmy had set everything up on the patio. I walked towards the stringed lights that hung above the beams that darted across the top of the patio. I gently opened the glass door that was slightly ajar, and heard music playing. It was something like Mumford and Sons, or Kaleo. I heard a deep, earthy voice singing in another language, and it was methodic and beautiful and set my heart racing. I still didn't see Jimmy.

I looked around and noticed there was a table set for two,

right next to one of the fire pits, which was nice because it was freezing outside. I also noticed one of the wicker loveseats pulled close to the fire pit with a large, fleece blanket folded over it. Everything was perfect.

From the serving doors, near the kitchen, I heard Jimmy coming. I slowly turned and saw him approaching with a tray and a bottle of wine. He was in a slate gray suit, he had on sleek black shoes, and his hair was combed to the side. He was stunning, I felt tongue-tied for a second as he got closer. He wore a huge smile, that warped into something sly and devilish as his eyes raked over my dress and lingered near my neck line, that happened to be a bit lower than I normally preferred.

He slowly set the tray down and the wine, and I made my way to the chair that I assumed I was to take. Before I sat down, he skirted around the table until he was in front of me. Once we were standing toe to toe, he wrapped his arm around my waist and pulled me into him, then kissed me. His kiss was gentle and slow, like the music playing above us. He released me, then set his forehead against mine, and whispered, "Hi..."

I smiled, whispering, "hi," in return.

He caught my wrist, kissing my hand while pinning his gaze to mine then led me to my seat.

We had Rav's scones, and some steak sliders, along with one of my favorite salads, and stuffed mushrooms. Rav must have prepared all of this for us; it was all my favorite foods that he made. I smiled as we ate and drank our wine, and we laughed about the kids' response to us going on a date tonight. Apparently, they were more than thrilled.

Then I gushed over Sip N Sides and all the ideas that I had, and we talked about everything that Theo had told me and discussed what his plans were. Jimmy was supportive and excited for me. It felt genuine, and he made sure I knew that he was my biggest fan through this process, and I could ask him anything at all. I was all warm and relaxed, partly from the wine, but mostly from this moment. It was beyond perfect, and the knots in my stomach only grew as we neared the end of the dinner and Jimmy moved us over to the wicker loveseat by the fire. I had kicked off my shoes and brought my legs up under me, while wrapping the blanket around me. Thankfully, it was big enough that the other half rested over Jimmy's lap, so I didn't feel totally selfish.

He sat there, smiling at me, as he held his wrinkled manila envelope. His looked like he looked at it way more than I had looked at my envelope. It actually looked like it had been opened and then resealed.

Jimmy held it in his right hand, and I noticed that his leg was jumping a bit, it made me feel better to know that I wasn't the only one nervous.

"So, here we are. Six weeks of building a foundation. Maybe wasn't the best foundation, but at least it gave us some time to be sure of our feelings for each other," he said, his knee still bouncing under the blanket. I gently placed my hand on his knee and smiled up at him.

"Here we are. Thank you for giving me the six weeks, Jimmy."

His smile was sweet as he leaned in to kiss me. It was short and perfect. He pulled back just in time to start opening his envelope.

I noticed the tape that had sealed it was different than the one I had used to seal it. Don't ask how I knew that, but as an accountant, I noticed things.

I placed my hand over his to stop him. "Hey... this looks opened..." I stated, a little curious.

He blushed, and I knew I had him.

"Jimmy you didn't!" I practically yelled, forgetting how close we were. He started to laugh.

"Just hear me out, okay." He turned so that we were facing

each other a little better, then he rested his free hand on my thigh as he explained himself.

"When you went to Chicago, and you weren't talking to me, I was in a really dark place. I was worried that you wouldn't give me another chance. So, one night, when I just needed to hear from you, I tore it open and read it. Then I pinned it to my bulletin board, so that I could read it every day."

I blushed, because I slightly remembered what I put in the envelope but not entirely. I squeezed his hand, so he knew I wasn't mad.

"Read it to me," I whispered to him.

He opened the manila envelope and pulled out my journal paper, with the designs in the corner. He exhaled, then squeezed my hand as he read.

"Jimmy the Jerk and I have a very complicated connection. Not relationship, connection. I barely know him, but what I do know of him, is that he owns a successful bar that I would give anything to work at. I now know that his father was the sweet old man that gave me a job after my disastrous interview with Jimmy, I also know that Jimmy is a dad. I know this because I accidentally on purpose babysat his kids tonight. Jasmine and Sammy. They are perfect kids. I mean it too, completely perfect. Funny, and sweet, strong and independent.

Tonight, something changed in me, and it scares me because it's all too fast. If I'm being honest, it feels a little like fate. That sounds so corny, but who would have guessed that the house I went to tonight would be Jimmy Stenson's? I have to try and stop calling him Jimmy the Jerk, because tonight he really wasn't one. He came to apologize to me this morning and brought flowers. No one has ever given me flowers before, but I was a jerk and didn't even let him speak.

So, when I showed up at his house to babysit his kids, I was a little shocked. But here's the thing. I kept picturing my life in that house. I know it sounds crazy, but it felt like part of me was missing and I had finally found it in that house, with those kids, and yes, even with Jimmy.

The clincher for me, was the moment Jimmy came out onto the trampoline with us. I am pretty sure he ended his date early, but he came and watched the stars with us. It was this weird moment for me, where everything shifted. I looked over at him, and I just knew, somewhere deep in my bones, I knew. One day, I want to marry Jimmy Stenson. I want to be his wife, and I want to be a mother to his children. I want to wake up every day and make them breakfast, I want to sit around the dinner table with them, I want to sign my last name the same as theirs. I want forever with them. Even if I don't get a forever with them, they will always have a little bit of my forever. Because this is the first time in my life that I could see it all, the whole picture. With only them. Forever. Anyone else, and everyone else, will always be held in comparison to them."

I WAS FIGHTING BACK TEARS, BECAUSE I FORGOT HOW vulnerable that letter was. I couldn't believe how forward I was being by giving him that six weeks ago. If we had to choose letters today, I would definitely not declare that I wanted to marry him. Talk about walking right into rejection and asking it to slap me in the face. I let out an audible sigh, because I could only imagine what Jimmy was thinking. That I was crazy, or clingy, or a freak. But he'd read it every day... what did that mean? I was going through all of this turmoil in front of him. I felt him shift, and then he placed his hand on my cheek, lifting my flushed face to see his. He had this twinkle in his eye as he simply said, "Now open mine."

I was so embarrassed, his was probably stating that he liked me, or wanted to take me out on a date. This was six weeks ago, after all. I started breathing hard, as the shame and concern washed over me. I wanted to run, and hide, and get out of there. The perfect moment was gone. I stopped opening the envelope and hesitated. I had to come up with some excuse to leave. He must have sensed something because he gently placed his hand over mine, and said, "Open it."

Letting out another sigh and feeling the burn of tears threatening to fall from the edges of my eyes, I ripped open the envelope. Tears were blurring my vision, but I'm pretty sure what I saw inside was a small green firework. I pulled the mini, paper tank out and examined it. Not sure what to make of it, and with no other letter included, I looked to Jimmy for an explanation. His cheeks were red, and his eyes were glossy, but his face could have been the missing note with how expressive it was.

He was staring down at the tank, and then carefully said, "Ramsey, ever since I was little, I had heard this story from my parents about how you know you've found the one you love. They called it, the 'glimmer.' It was always a sweet story, that I never fully understood. Find someone that will always burn for you, not always be bright, or exaggerated in their fire. No, find someone that will burn, even when the darkness comes, find someone that will make you work to find her. To train your eyes to see her light, you'll find that she'll always lead you home. I always pictured the glimmer like a firework, specifically one of those tank fireworks. When I found someone, it would be like a lit tank rolling down the street, leading me home, never going out, just staying lit with a low flame rolling past, house after house. As I grew older, I thought it was a load of crap, until I met you.

"Ramsey, you burned so hot inside of me from the moment we met, that all I have been able to think about is making you mine, in every way. It happened too fast, too soon, so I got scared, but I knew that night too. The night of my date, I kept comparing her to you and I barely knew you. I carried your resume in my jacket pocket because it somehow made me feel closer to you. I was crazy about you. That night you were in my house, I pictured you there permanently. It was after the pizza night that I knew for sure I wanted to do this, when I stopped talking myself out of it, telling myself I didn't deserve you. Truth is, I'll never deserve you, Ramsey, but I'll always love you." His voice was starting to break, I watched his eyes as he gently closed them, then he whispered, "Now open it."

I gently shook the tank, and sure enough, something rattled inside. I found easy-to-open tabs at the top of the paper tank and began to pull it open. I dumped whatever was inside into my open palm.

Something cold, and shiny, reflected back at me. I blinked a few times to clear the tears and gasped at the silver ring, attached to a large, single diamond. I had no words; my hand was over my mouth as I tried to discern what exactly I was holding. I finally dared to look up at Jimmy and he was kneeling in front of me. When did he move? God, the tears. They were coming so fast now. I didn't say anything, because I was too scared to wake up, or to have some celebrity jump from behind a table shouting that it was all a prank. Jimmy gently took the ring into his hand as he finally spoke.

"You are my forever, you are my heart, you are my glimmer. You are the light leading me home, my own personal firework. Will you marry me, Ramsey?"

My heart was beating so hard, and my breath was coming in and out, too fast. He took the ring and slowly slid it onto my left ring finger as I vigorously nodded my head. Tears were clogging my throat and burning my eyes, but once the ring was on, I threw myself at him. Kissing him fiercely, dangerously. He was mine, and I was his. We were in this forever, all I knew for sure was that if he needed me to shine, then I would burn for him, for the rest of my life.

I would be his glimmer. He would be my life.

→

EPILOGUE

Jimmy
Two Months Later

"WILL I catch on fire if I walk down it?"

"NO, STUPID. JUST HOLD MY HAND AND WALK, AND STAY AWAY from the flames!"

"I DON'T UNDERSTAND WHY DAD HAS TO GLIMMER THE ENTIRE wedding. When I grow up, I'm not having a glimmer."

"SAMMY, STOP IT. IF YOU KEEP MOVING, YOU ARE GOING TO knock down those candles and catch the entire church on fire."

. . .

I WAS LISTENING TO MY KIDS WHISPER-FIGHT WHILE WE DID A rehearsal with real candles, trying not to laugh, I looked over at Jackson and could tell he was battling the same struggle by the hidden smirk on his face. The only person up here with us who didn't look amused was the preacher, but he'd been dragged out into a snowstorm to perform one last rehearsal at Ramsey's request, because she wanted Sammy to feel comfortable on the big day. If I didn't already ask her to marry me, I would just for doing that. I thought back to the night I'd asked her to marry me two months ago. It was the best memory I had of us; the night was beyond what I could hope for. The memory of her that night was burned as a memory I'd hold onto forever.

The way she walked over to the side entrance and turned off the lights, leaving us in darkness, save for the fire lights and few stars that were peeking out. She sauntered towards me, and like a fool, I just sat there and stared at her. The firelight made her glow, like she did that night when we danced together. I caught her eyes and saw a small smirk on her lips; they were still blood-red and ready for me to take them.

She slowly lowered herself in front of me, the music still playing softly in the background. I held my breath as she slid the sleeve of her dress down, then the other, all while watching me. She leaned forward and tugged on my tie, then pulled at my shirt buttons, her ring catching the firelight with every flick of her hand. I was sinking under the weight of her stare, of her love and devotion, and when she whispered in my ear, "Make love to me," I was done. We clashed together, as though every moment that had separated us would pay for its treason in keeping us apart. We shattered apart, beautiful and broken, every touch of skin, every second of pleasure just a stone being set into place for us, for our future, our eternity.

Just the memory of having her lay with me, wrapped in that flannel blanket under the stars, had me ready to find my bride-to-be and tell her we needed another closed night at Jimmy's.

At first, Ramsey was hesitant about setting a date. I

couldn't figure out why, but I knew with the way she kept looking off into the distance any time we talked about how many months out to take it, that it had to do with her mom. I remember the day we officially set it, so clearly.

We sat in my Tahoe, rain hitting the windows and leaves littering the ground. I had started picking her up from her house on our way to work after the night at Jimmy's. We had dropped the kids at school and sat on the side of the road on our way to Rockford. That highway so significant for us now, after everything. I had turned the car off and watched Ramsey as she trailed a raindrop down the window with her finger. She had been distant since I suggested a summer wedding, and that was after I had commented on how cool it was if we waited one year from when we got engaged. She was still kind and sweet, but distant. I was ready to get to the bottom of it.

"Is it me?" I asked, quietly.

She spun towards me, her eyes full of worry. "What?"

I searched her eyes for any sign of conflict, but all I found was genuine confusion. "Setting the date. Every time I mention it, you freeze up and get distant," I mumbled out my frustration and watched her face.

It went from confusion to concern, her eyes tilting down and her lips going thin. She was bothered by something, I just needed to figure out what. She played with a gas receipt that I had in the cup holder as she responded.

"It's not the date. I'm sorry I get distant. We could do a summer wedding. I know you mentioned that earlier, and I didn't really respond. I'm sorry." She sounded like she wanted a summer wedding, but her face and posture told me a different story. Her eyes dropped to her hands and her fingers kept tearing at the receipt, as if she was nervous. No, she didn't want a summer wedding, or a fall wedding. But I knew that she wanted to marry me, so what was—of course!

I reached forward and gripped the back of her head, tilting it so I could kiss her the way I liked. She responded, slowly but genuine. I let her go but stayed close, our breath mingling as she waited.

"Two months. Marry me in two months, just enough time to set every-thing up," I told her in a brisk whisper. She gasped and gripped my shirt.

"Are you serious?" She was eager, frantic, hopeful.

I nodded and kissed her again. "Yes. Marry me in two months."

She hugged me as tears slid down her face. She started whispering into my neck. "I just want her to see me get married, and you've given me that. I just don't know if she'll be here in a year, or by summer."

She choked on her tears. How could I have been so blind? I hugged her closer and kissed her again, our lips speaking louder than any words we could share, until it turned frantic and heated. She pushed me back against the seat and began to show me exactly how grateful she was to have set a date. A date that might just be in time for her mother to be a part of.

SEEING CARLA'S AND DAD'S REACTIONS WERE PRICELESS, AS were the kids. We invited Carla over for a big dinner, during which Ramsey flipped her bare, silver ring over to reveal the diamond. Carla nearly spilled all the drinks with how hard she slapped the table, then started praising the Lord in Cambodian, at least that's what Ramsey told me.

When we revealed to everyone that we had set a date for two months, Carla started to cry. In fact, everyone was crying, even the kids. While I knew Sammy wouldn't have any issues, I wasn't sure exactly where Jasmine stood on the issue, but as soon as we gave our news, her little face brightened, and tears of joy fell down her face. Dad hugged Ramsey with tears in his eyes, which moved a big piece of my heart around. I had only seen him cry over a few things in my life.

Jackson and Laney just laughed when we had told them and asked when to show up. So here we were, the beginning of January, in the middle of a snowstorm, rehearsing our wedding. Ramsey wanted it to be intimate, just a few people from work. Ramsey picked out a small chapel that had recently been renovated. It had all new wood flooring, white pews, and stone pillars. It was beautiful. She wanted it at night and she wanted candles. She said she wanted to create a picture of what my tattoo meant; an unwavering light to guide me home. She wanted the aisle lined with candles, so they would lead her to me, and she had those stringed, twinkle lights around every pillar and around the two makeshift pillars where we would stand. Everyone called it the glimmer effect, which is why we needed extra practice with Sammy. I looked back towards the closed doors, where I knew Ramsey would emerge, and my heart rate soared.

I knew this was practice, but even as I was standing there, wearing jeans and a t-shirt, it felt real. If Ramsey would let me, I'd marry her tonight, just like this. I know she'd do it too, if not for her dream to give her mom a real wedding before she passed. I counted and waited, then our song came on, the one she'd walk to: "There Will Be Time" by Mumford and Sons. She started walking, my dad holding her arm and leading her down the candlelit aisle. Even in yoga pants, snow boots, and a t-shirt, she was stunning. I tried to clear my throat as I began to choke up. Her hair was in one of her famous braids; the candlelight making her look angelic.

If I was this sappy at the rehearsal, I'd be a mess during the real thing. I only saw her, she only saw me. I could tell she was thinking the same thing about just doing this tonight, but I'd wait. I could wait one more day, but tonight, I didn't care about rules or tradition; tonight, she was sleeping in my arms. Besides, I had a little secret I had to share with her about our honeymoon. I had arranged everything so that her Mom was taken care of, as well as the kids.

After our wedding, we would have a car take us to Chicago, where we'd stay in a gorgeous hotel by the water. Once the winter storm passed, we'd fly to Hawaii. Neither of us had ever been, and I was desperate for some time alone with her. We would be gone for two weeks. So, I told my heart to slow down and be patient. It would wait for her to become mine, but the thought of having her with me tonight was driving me crazy. I couldn't handle seeing her like this without being near her; my heart wanted only her. My glimmer, my unwavering light.

RAMSEY

SIX MONTHS LATER

WAKING up to little elbows and feet shoved into my back and ribs was something I hadn't gotten used to yet. Most nights, the kids were fine and would stay out of our room, but after Jimmy and I had gotten home from Hawaii, we found at least one of the kids in our bed by morning; on occasion, it was both. Jimmy felt bad, saying the kids never did this, but honestly, I didn't mind. I loved it. All of it. My whole life had completely changed in a matter of months, and I loved every moment of it.

I slowly untangled Sammy's heel from my ribs and slid out of bed, I glanced at the clock on the nightstand and saw it was only a little past six thirty in the morning on a Tuesday, *the* Tuesday. I let out a sigh and pulled my robe from the closet, then glanced back at my boys, who were both asleep, piled under a mound of white blankets. Jimmy's golden hair was peeking out from the right side, and Sammy's little dark hair poked out from the top, both of them snoring. I smiled and felt my heart flutter in my chest; it had been that doing that a lot lately. I tied the robe around me and padded down the hall and peeked into Jasmine's room. She was still asleep, covered up by her million blankets. It was warm now, with summer in full swing, but Jasmine still loved those blankets.

I continued downstairs and started a pot of coffee. I liked that Jimmy and Theo liked the older kind of pot; plus, it made getting us all coffee in the morning a lot less time-consuming. Theo was still acting manager at my bar. That felt so weird to say, but yes, my bar. Sip N Sides was doing wonderfully. I had taken it easy the last few months, getting used to married life, and becoming a mother.

Yes, a mother. I had asked Jimmy if I could adopt the kids as my own. I knew that he would always be their dad, and nothing would ever change that, but I wanted to be more than a stepmother to them. I wanted them to be mine forever, especially if anything ever happened to Jimmy. He kissed me stupid when I asked, then got off early from work to surprise me at home, where he showed me exactly how he felt about that idea. I loved those moments; since we were both business owners, our schedules were freer than most. So, whenever we wanted a little time to ourselves without worrying about the kids or Theo, we would get off work early and meet up at home to make love.

I loved getting up before everyone else. I liked looking around the house and remembering how much I wanted this, just months ago, how much I wanted to be a permanent person in this family. Now I was, and it was everything I wanted and more.

I took out the eggs and bacon and started warming up the pans. Just as I clicked the burner over, I heard my phone ring. I smiled at the sound of my daily call. I walked over to where my phone was plugged in and swiped the screen to accept the FaceTime call. I held the phone up to show my face and saw my mother's cheek. She hadn't quite figured out where to hold the phone when we talked, so she always seemed to hold it to her face.

"Mom, move the phone away from your face, you Face-Timed me." I tried not to shout at her.

"Oh, honey, where are you, how come I can't see you?"

I rolled my eyes, thankful she couldn't see me.

"Mom, pull the phone away from your face and look at the screen!" I said, a bit louder this time.

Finally, a flash of movement, and I saw her smiling face. "Aww, there you are, sweetie. How are you doing today?" she said sweetly while smiling from ear to ear. Her purple track suit was showing, as well as her purple beanie.

"I'm doing good this morning, Mom, just starting breakfast. How are things over there? You still liking it?"

When I married Jimmy, we had planned on surprising her with our plans to add on an apartment for her above the garage, but Mom decided to give me her own surprise instead.

She sat me down and told me she was glad I had found someone, because she met someone while in the Chicago Institute. They were both terminal, but she and Larry wanted to spend as much time together as possible. I was floored, but obviously supported her decision to go and stay in the institute, where she'd get round-the-clock care and the opportunity to be near Larry.

"Oh, everything is fine, sweetheart. Larry and I watched a movie last night. I am really enjoying my time here."

I loved hearing that. I had felt guilty for so long being away from her, I almost cut my honeymoon short just so that I was close to her. I should have known then that something was up; she was staying at the Chicago Institute and didn't want me to come back.

"Good, Mom, I am happy to hear that…"

"Show me your belly!" she exclaimed, cutting me off, as she did every single day. Just when I thought we might have a normal conversation. I let out an exaggerated sigh and tilted the camera down to my robe, to show her that my stomach was still flat. She was persistent, I'd give her that.

"Mom, I am not pregnant. Just like I wasn't yesterday, and just like I won't be tomorrow. It's called birth control," I stated with another roll of my eyes because I had become a fifteen-year-old again apparently.

"Oh, hogwash. You know that you would wait to tell me until you were weeks along. The only way I can be sure is to see you every day," she said, with a little eye roll of her own.

I loved my mother, and I was so glad that I could let her see me get married before she passed away, but having a baby was where I drew the line. Jimmy and I would love to add to our lives, but not right now. I wanted to enjoy getting to know the two children I adopted as my own, and I wanted time with my new husband before adding a baby to the mix. I told my mother this, but she was convinced that Jesus was going to miraculously allow me to get pregnant just by her prayers alone.

I knew there was no use in arguing with her, "Okay, Mom, have your look and let's move on. I promise you, though, the second I know that I am having a baby, you will know right away."

She smiled, and we continued to talk about her treatments and her overall health. Her health hadn't really improved, but she looked happier than she had in years.

I finished my call with Mom as I finished the bacon and started on the eggs and toast. Just as I said goodbye, Theo came upstairs. He wore these cute glasses that sat on the bridge of his nose, and every morning, he read the paper while he drank his coffee. He came up to where I was standing in the kitchen and kissed me on the forehead, then walked to the cupboard to get his cup for his coffee. I plated him some breakfast and took it to where he sat every morning.

We usually didn't talk much, and I liked that about him; we

both enjoyed our silence in the morning. While he ate, I packed the kids' lunches. There were only five more days left of school before summer break, and I could hardly contain my excitement. We had big plans to travel this summer to go see Yellowstone National Park. I had my own plans to take the kids to the pool, play as much soccer as possible, and of course, sleepovers out on the trampoline.

I went back to warming up breakfast, checking the clock and saw it was nearing seven thirty. I was about to head upstairs to wake everyone up when I heard a few thumps on the stairs. I smiled as I heard the sweet sound of, "hey, Mom."

My whole heart soared at the sound of it. I turned to face Jasmine and pulled her into a hug as I kissed the top of her head.

"Good morning, sweetheart. Hungry?"

She nodded and shuffled over to where Theo was and sat next to him.

I got her food ready as I heard more thumps down the stairs, and knew my boys were up.

I was facing the counter, plating more food as I heard a raspy, "Mommy? Can you get me the orange juice this morning?"

My heart fluttered again. This must be what new mothers felt like with their newborns. I turned my head and saw Sammy with his messy hair, rubbing at his sleepy eyes. I walked over and pulled him up into a hug, then kept him on my hip like he was a toddler, as I set his food on the table. I kissed his cheek, then set him across from his sister. I walked back and grabbed two cups, filling each one with orange juice.

Jimmy was leaning against the counter, sipping his coffee, watching me. When he looked at me like I was his breakfast, it did things to me, but things like that needed to be saved for later that day, after everyone was gone. I walked over into his embrace and hugged him. I loved this. Loved him. I leaned up and kissed him, then sat down with my own food and coffee. Jimmy came and sat next to me, so close that we were practically in each other's laps. I knew why he was so close today, and I loved him for it. I was actually feeling pretty good for it being the day of the trial.

I had to go in today to testify against the two other men who had helped abduct and hurt me. I was surprisingly calm about it, but now that I had this life, I had Jimmy, it felt like the darkness from that day couldn't touch me anymore. My therapy sessions were nearly nonexistent now; Glenda was right about things calming down for me once I got into a rhythm. I grabbed Jimmy's hand under the table and squeezed it. The trial was going to be in Chicago, which meant after we dropped the kids at school, we would head that way and stay the night with Jackson. I felt peaceful about it. Those men would get justice, and then I could officially close that chapter of my life for good.

I sat at the table and looked around at my family—at my children, my husband, my father-in-law. I exhaled and leaned into Jimmy's shoulder as we laughed at a joke that Sammy made. Jimmy talked about how I was his glimmer, but he had no idea how he was my home, my everything, and now I had two children that were mine. Mine for always. It was moments like this that made any amount of darkness worth the effort, because now we would shine together, for each other, to always lead one another home.

The End

KEEP READING FOR MORE

If you enjoyed Glimmer, please consider leaving a review! It helps authors more than you could possibly know. If you aren't interested in reading the peek at Laney and Jackson's story, just drag the bar for the story length to the end and it will auto pop the review portion for you.

Thank you so much for reading!

Want to know all the details from Laney and Jackson's introduction and all the scenes left out of Glimmer? Continue reading for their origin story: At First Fight- and be sure to catch their full-length story Fade available to read through Kindle Unlimited.

AT FIRST FIGHT

PROLOGUE

Laney

Mama always said introductions were important.

She swore that within the first five minutes of meeting someone new, I'd know if they were the kind of person who would help me heal or help me hurt. I know, seems deep and complicated, but that's Mama. She has a saying for everything. I blame her southern upbringing; she blames her deep soul. Whatever it is, her little saying stuck with me.

I took it and tucked it away in my heart like a lucky rock to pull out whenever I needed direction. I called it my sixth sense. Sure enough, when I was out with a man, I knew within the first few sips of a martini, a handshake, or a heavy gaze if I was headed for hurt or healing. What I hadn't worked through yet was what to do when I found someone I'd be willing to hurt for. With me, it was only a matter of time. I attracted bad news like a fast-moving storm. So honestly, it was inevitable, one day I'd find someone who'd only help me hurt and I knew that on that day, I'd be the sucker handing him the metaphorical knife to slice me open....

LANEY

THE INTRODUCTION

It was September, and the beginning of a new work quarter, which meant we were busy, stressed, and irritable—some more so than others. I tried to brighten the mood by bringing in flowers... flowers I technically stole from my downstairs neighbor. She was in a fight with her husband... *again*, and he tried to win her over with flowers... *again*. She always dumped them right in front of her door, free for the taking. I wish he'd buy her donuts or real coffee, that would really brighten up the temperament of this place. Especially since Mr. Reed had been in a crabby mood for the last few weeks. Ever since he'd worked out, he actually needed all those accountants he fired from the fifth floor, he's been a real delight. *Not.*

Mr. Reed may not have been in the best of spirits, but he had nothing on my supervisor. If men had periods, Mr. Ashby had been on the rag for a solid eight weeks. Who knew what had crawled up his ass and died but I was over it. I was naturally an angry person, so it took extra effort for me to be nice. I had to take extra precautions to avoid any negativity that might push me into a fit of rage. Losing it at work would definitely be frowned up, but Mr. Ashby was testing my will power.

"Ms. Thompson, I need you in the boardroom immediately." As if on cue, Mr. Ashby shouted at me as his short, stubby legs carried him past the break room.

I glanced at the wall clock and saw I still had five minutes before I was *supposed* to be in the meeting, so I turned around and acted like I didn't hear him. Remember that willpower I was working on? Yeah, it was for his safety I ignore him.

I grabbed three sugar packets, tore them open with my teeth and poured them into my crappy, vendor machine coffee. I stood at the counter, stirring the sugar in with the cream, trying to get those few dust bubbles of dried creamer to dissolve. After accepting defeat, I let out a heavy sigh and tipped my head back downing half the cup of scalding liquid. It tasted bitter and like it cost me ten cents because it did. Vending machine coffee was hitting rock bottom for me, and the fact I had already hit rock bottom on a Monday pretty much sucked ass.

"Ms. Thompson!" Mr. Ashby screamed again. He gripped the door frame with his chubby white fingers and narrowed his frantic gaze on the coffee in my hand. Surely, he was scanning the fresh brown stains now splattered across the front of my white shirt, thanks to him scaring the hell out of me. That was my last dime too. *Asshole.*

"I told you, I needed you immediately," Mr. Ashby repeated and moved further into the break room.

Darcy, the intern, darted out through the opposite door, leaving me alone.

I took a calming breath and turned toward Mr. Ashby, "Sir, I realize you requested my presence earlier than what was on my calendar, but I would like to start this meeting out with my best foot forward. I'm sure you can understand." *There, diplomatic and professional.*

Mr. Ashby narrowed his beady eyes. "I don't give a shit about your feet or your best whatever the fuck." He whispered

angrily. "I need you in that boardroom now!" He turned around, leaving in a huff.

I shrugged and continued drinking what was left of my cheap coffee. After dealing with this for the past eight weeks, I had built up a bit of a tolerance to his little tantrums. They annoyed me but didn't exactly phase me. I tossed the paper cup, wiped my blouse and slowly sauntered toward the board room.

Before I even entered the meeting area, I heard men yelling. Not the fun, ass grabbing, cigar smoking, jovial yelling either. It sounded like some spoiled adult male was tearing into someone about his time being wasted. I picked up speed, not out of fear or concern but for my total obsession with drama and a good show. Especially if Mr. Ashby was the one getting his ass chewed. I maneuvered around the corner just in time to see Mr. Ashby, sitting at the large mahogany table, red in the face and looking like he was either going to cry or murder somebody.

"I'm grossly overpaying you, and you can't even manage to get your employees to a simple meeting on time?" A tall, gorgeous specimen of humanity reprimanded Mr. Ashby while standing near the front of the table with his hands in his pockets. I felt a tiny morsel of guilt for not attending this meeting the first time my boss asked for me, but at the same time, he was an egotistical jerk.

"I know, Mr. Tate, I'm so sorry, she should be here any second." Mr. Ashby stuttered in response, nervously loosening his tie. He glanced toward the door and saw me slowly making my way over and jumped out of his chair. "Here she is, she's right here. See, told you she was on her way."

I had the horrible aftertaste of cheap coffee in my mouth, and the very last thing I wanted to do was meet a handsome, rich, full of himself the asshole. My stomach flipped a few times as Mr. Tate's eyes drifted over me, starting at my hair and

gliding down the length of my body. He kept his hands in his pockets as the side of his jaw ticked. It was a strong fucking jaw too.

I drew closer and held out my hand, wishing I had time to breathe into my palm to test how horrible my breath was, but I didn't, so I just threw my useless hand out there for him to shake. "Hello, Mr. Tate, I'm Laney Thompson." I refused to apologize for being late because I wasn't.

I glanced up at the wall clock, and I still had a good two minutes before I was *supposed* to be here.

Mr. Tate took his hands out of his pockets, let out an exaggerated sigh, and shook my hand. His hand was warm and firm. His frozen, blue eyes pinned me in place while he assessed me. He had a closely shaved head that only made his sharp facial features pop and look more defined. He let me go a second later as an honest smile erupted on his face.

"Nice to meet you. *Mrs.* Thompson was it?" He smoothly asked, emphasizing the *Mrs.* Part. My chest burned at his question. Why did he need clarification of whether I was married?

I wiped my hands down my skirt and smiled. "Actually, it's just *Miss* Thompson." I clarified and changed that sketchy subject because *what the hell?*

"Let's get started, shall we?" I moved toward the laptop sitting open on the back counter and carried it over to where Mr. Ashby and Mr. Tate were. I swirled the black, rolling chair until I was positioned across from Mr. Tate, who'd unbuttoned his jacket and taken a seat. He wore a navy suit that fit him so perfectly it made me want to pull my phone out and snap a picture. It might also have been because he looked like David Beckham during that shaved head phase he went through. *Maybe if I angled my phone just right, people would buy it was the famous soccer player, and I could make some money from selling the picture.*

Focus, Laney!

My blood pressure was higher than it reasonably should have been as I began to pull up the portfolio we had set up for 'Singe,' the restaurant Mr. Tate was opening.

"Okay," I began. "So, we have a few things to go over here but before we begin, do you have any questions I need to address?" I asked while trying to talk through my teeth. For some reason it was insanely important he *not* smell my breath.

He leaned forward and rested his chin onto his clenched fist as he grinned, giving me a heated look. "None that are professional."

Okay…

I tossed my long hair over my shoulder and tried to hide the red that was likely engulfing my face. Mr. Ashby was on his phone, ignoring us. I wasn't even sure why he was here, but I was oddly glad he was.

"Let's begin then…" I began clicking file after file, not sliding my eyes toward Mr. Tate's, because I was afraid of what I might see there. My mind was somewhere else entirely though; *what was his question? How unprofessional was it?*

I cleared my throat, and moved the laptop mouse, so the data I wanted to share with Mr. Tate was up on the projector screen.

He was still staring at me, fist under his jaw, smiling. *Was he trying to intimidate me?* I've had my fair share of dates. The spectrum varies, but I've spent time with a few alpha A-holes in my time and have learned to read their ticks. But this wasn't drinks at a bar. It wasn't evening, and I wasn't in a cocktail dress, showing a decent amount of cleavage. I was in a stained shirt, my hair was sporting some decent frizz, and I had coffee breath for fucks sake. Yet, this guy had *"I'm all business but all kinds of fun"* etched into his rigid posture. Was he flexing his arms? I studied the defined lines of sculpted muscle, visible through his suit. He was totally flexing those biceps… *Who the hell was this guy?*

I resisted the urge to peek at his forearms and tried to focus on the task at hand; figuring out this jerk's flirtatious angle. He was busy staring up at the projector while I assessed him from under my lashes. The longer I looked, the more it hit me: He *was* trying to intimidate me. He probably had girls' trip over themselves all the time to flirt or slip him their numbers.

My fear regarding my bad coffee breath now felt more like a weapon, one I felt compelled to capitalize on. I opened my mouth and leaned in close to Mr. Tate, exhaling heavily. "Here we go, take a look at the screen."

He flinched and sat upright in his chair, immediately giving me a peculiar look.

I turned my face toward the screen, suppressing a smile. My brothers would be so proud of me right now. I didn't like rich jerks. I dealt with them all the time and having one who thought he could get me to fumble and mumble all over the place just angered me to no end. Mr. Tate, to his credit, actually treated me like I was qualified to go over the information regarding his startup after the coffee breath incident. He stopped smiling like an idiot, he stopped flirting, and finally started to ask me real questions.

Once we were finished with the small presentation, we all stood. I straightened my skirt while he buttoned his jacket. Mr. Ashby took a call, and left the room, leaving just the two of us.

"It's Jackson by the way," he smiled leaning into my space, so close I could feel the heat from his skin. I swallowed as his scent hit me. Holy Lord, he smelled dangerously good. Like, change my name-curl up in the trunk of his car-eat my hair and spy on him through his closet- kind of good. His eyes were so cold, and bright, a small smile started in the corner of his mouth, mesmerizing me. So much so that I didn't expect it when he exhaled directly in my face.

I coughed and leaned back a fraction. *Kill me...* I wanted to die from the odor, it was awful. He immediately broke into a

laugh as my face contorted and I tried to regain composure. He smirked, then quirked an eyebrow as he grabbed his brief-case and walked around me. *Touché.*

"I look forward to working with you *Ms.* Thompson. See you tomorrow." He emphasized the Miss part of his sentence again and left the room. Leaving me alone, confused and with the distinct impression he would most definitely help me hurt if ever given the chance… just like my mama said.

Good thing, I had no intention of giving him one.

JACKSON

THE PROBLEM

I didn't like being an asshole, it was just a necessary evil when I did business with people. I worked hard for every single penny in my bank account, so my standards for the people I employed were high. Call me a sexist, but if a company threw a hot piece of ass at me to "work" with, I usually saw right through the ploy.

The bigwigs thought a high-profile client who had a reputation for being a playboy might get distracted by a move like that and ignore how lazy they were; well, they were wrong. When it came to business, I didn't play around, and I certainly didn't mix it with any kind of temporary pleasure. So, when the pathetic mess of a supervisor, Mr. Ashby, brought in the new project supervisor for my startup, I saw right through it.

Long, thick red hair, a complexion so creamy and perfect, she could have been one of those porcelain dolls. She wasn't tall, but her legs were lean and muscular. Lips, red and perfectly plump. She was perfection incarnate. And assuming she was in on the idea to distract me from the money and work I'd be sinking into this endeavor; I bemused her.

Normally if I wanted to mess with a woman, it didn't take

much effort. I'd smile and flirt, they'd show a little cleavage, touch my arm a bit and try to slip me their number. At one point in my life, I'd be flattered at how easy it was to distract the fairer sex. Now, I held no such delusions because these women *knew* I was rich, and the fact that my face was symmetrical, and I treated my body like a temple was just a bonus.

So, when hot Ms. Thompson leaned in and deliberately tried to kill me with her coffee breath, I was taken back a bit. More than a bit but I wasn't quite ready to dive into all the reasons why her trying to kill me with that disgusting breath affected me so much.

I was only here at Dyson and Reed because I needed some help with my second restaurant startup. My first restaurant was currently a five-star establishment, but its success was superficial. I accidentally stole a popular chef from another successful restaurant. In my defense, I didn't know he was ready to quit. He was a friend of mine, and when I asked for some recommendations, he surprised me by giving his own name and quitting the other restaurant on the spot.

His fame and notoriety traveled with him, across the city to my little startup; 'Savor.' With the second startup, I didn't expect to get so lucky, so I ventured to get some help. Dyson and Reed offered a panel of marketing strategists, city and migrant specialists, a legal team and cost analysis experts. The full team was scheduled to meet today instead of just Ms. Thompson and Mr. Ashby from yesterday. He brought in Ms. Thompson because she's a veteran here at Dyson and Reed and currently working as a marketing communications supervisor as well as being a member of the legal team.

I walked into the same boardroom as yesterday and felt the smallest bit of anticipation stir in my gut. I kept checking the door to catch a glimpse of red hair, and I had no idea why. She was just business. She worked for me. Still, my eyes on their own accord went to the hallway every time I heard a female voice filter through it. I tilted my wrist and realized I was still twenty minutes early. I liked being ready and prepared for meetings. I liked making people feel the pressure to perform when they realized their high-profile client beat them to the meeting. I didn't expect Ms. Thompson to arrive early, especially since yesterday she had stretched her attendance to the last second.

Sure enough, as the room filled with overeager, hungry specialists and analysts, all jumpy with nervous energy, Ms. Thompson still hadn't shown, and there were only four minutes to spare. I smiled at my accuracy in pinning her habits already. Mr. Ashby stood at the front of the room, checking his phone while loosening his tie. He seemed nervous again and was likely worried Ms. Thompson might not be on time. I withheld the urge to laugh. Normally I'd be pissed but for some reason, I felt like her being exactly on time was a business strategy she used with her superiors. *Smart.*

Our meeting was supposed to start at nine a.m. and at exactly eight fifty-nine, Ms. Thompson walked in.

She had a flimsy, rather small paper cup filled with coffee, resting in her hand. I didn't really notice anything about her look except that she wore a tight gray skirt that clung to her thighs, and black high heels which did something to her calves that shouldn't be legal. Her lips were red, her eyes green and her hair was a curled, glossy mass of red. She was fucking gorgeous, and my stomach did all sorts of somersault gymnastic shit at the sight of her.

This was a problem.

I cleared my throat as Ms. Thompson started typing on the laptop at the head of the boardroom. She hadn't glanced my way once, so I thought I'd get her attention.

"Ms. Thompson, nice of you to join us," I tilted my head her way in acknowledgment. She looked up from the laptop as a few of the people around the room began to murmur amongst themselves.

"Nice to see you again Mr. Tate," she quipped with disinterest. Her lack of regard was grating my nerves and the fact that it grated my nerves, pissed me off.

"Let's get started everyone," Ms. Thompson said, starting the meeting. She stood in front of the room, using a PowerPoint clicker, while she dove into my business specifics.

"I'm assuming you all read up on our client." She gestured toward me with her hand. I hated how I noticed her fingernails were painted black and how good it looked against her creamy skin. "Mr. Tate is starting his second restaurant and has come to us for assistance with the startup," she continued. "We're honored to have been chosen by him, so let's make sure we show him exactly why he picked Dyson and Reed to handle this transition."

There was a small round of clapping for her little speech. She dipped her head until she was moving the mouse and clicking the screen a few times. Her red hair was like a curtain around her face. The urge to have her attention on me was heavy in my gut like a living creature ready to pounce. I needed her to see me.

I stood and cleared my throat. "Thank you, *Miss* Thompson." I waited for those viridescent eyes to land on me, but they didn't move. She focused on her peers around the table. I was still towering above her. "And for the remainder of our time here, let's get a little less formal. My name is Jackson, please call me that." This time she blushed and took a sip of her coffee. Amused with myself, I continued. "In fact, let's go around the room, and say our names, so I know each of you," I suggested, then sat down as I looked to the guy to my right. I didn't give a shit about their names, I just needed to hear my feisty redhead say hers again. I was fairly certain it started with an L, but I had to be sure, and I didn't have the energy to open the folder in front of me to try to find it.

"My name is Ryan, and I have worked here…"

"Just the first name is fine," I cut the blonde kid off in the middle of his sentence. He blushed and sat down as the person next to him got up. "Richard…" After I heard from the entire table, my eyes settled on the last person sitting. She stood and looked everywhere but where I was and said, "Laney. Now let's get started please."

Laney.

I pushed down the feelings I was wrestling and the warmth that spread through my chest at hearing her name. If I didn't stop acting like a fifth grader with a crush, I was going to fucking ruin this entire deal. I needed to stop watching her lips as she talked about projections and business models. Stop looking for that shorter piece of hair to fall across her forehead.

Stop trying to smell her when we stopped for breaks and walked around the room. I just needed to fucking stop. The last thing I needed was to get distracted right as I was about to start this new restaurant.

Click Here to Keep Reading

ABOUT THE AUTHOR

Ashley lives in Central Oregon with her husband and four children. A previous public speaker, and assistant director to a non profit; she now resides at home thinking up stories and writing them down in between carpool pick up, dinner, movie night and all the other tasks that come along with mothering four children. She loves assisting her husband with DIY Projects around their home, but more often than not can be found snuggling under a blanket, reading a good book.

You can find her most active in her reader group: Book Beauties where she over shares Gym Fail stories and teasers for works in progress.

ACKNOWLEDGMENTS

First and foremost, thanks to my creator and God who built the love of storytelling in me and has never been far from me during the writing process.

Secondly, thanks to my own 'Glimmer', Jose. You were my biggest fan and encouragement through this entire thing. Thank you for hearing my stories, reading my entire book and making suggestions on Jimmy's behalf. Mostly, thank you for loving me and allowing all my crazy binge reading purchases.

To my children; I love you fiercely, deeply and fully. May you always dream, create, and discover. Hopefully one day I'll be reading your own acknowledgment section in your books, where I better be properly thanked.

To my Mom and Eric, you've each placed stones of literary love inside of me and I wouldn't be who I am or where I am without you. I love you. Dad, I have no idea how heaven works as far as you seeing this but you were an integral part of this story. There were too many times where I'd stop and talk to you about an idea, or want to ask your advice about detective Gepsy and police work. I hate that you're gone and I hate that

I never got to ask you but I love that you lived a life for me to be proud of and I love that I caught you reading and writing the majority of my life. The world lost a powerful poet when it lost you.

To my sister Rebecca, thank you for all the hours and phone calls you poured into me and into this. I love you and thank God that he gave us to each other.

To Daniel, thank you for pouring over my words and encouraging me, for loving me, and for being in my corner and wanting the very best for me. To Amanda, Jon, and Haley, I love you guys and wouldn't have any ideas for stories without you.

Jess Hoeffer, you not only coach me to be physically strong but you took on this task of helping me improve Glimmer when I backed myself into a corner and needed help. I'm so thankful for you. Thanks to you, Jimmy is way less girly and I didn't use the term bulge when referencing his muscles.

To my beta readers, Rebecca Patrick, Ruth Hall, Mandee Franke, Leah Weybright, Kassie Dedmond and Kristin Moynihan. You guys. I can't thank you enough for your love and dedication to me and to Glimmer. I couldn't have done this without your eyes and your hearts.

Thanks to my editor, Amanda Edens. Glimmer wouldn't be something I would be confident sharing with the world without your creative editing.

To my cover designer, Dee Garcia. Thank you for being pure magic and finding the theme I needed to convey the message and feeling behind Glimmer.

Hazel Grace, girl you have been my own personal Yoda and I couldn't be more thankful for your help and always answering all of my millions of questions.

Finally, to my readers and hopefully fans. Please leave a review of this book, even if you didn't love it. I value your thoughts, your ideas, and your suggestions. If you have ever wanted to write, then just do it. I wrote over seventy percent of this book from my cell phone while I nursed, and held my newborn. There is no right way to write, just start writing and keep doing it. Take breaks to read great books, then get back at it.

Printed in Great Britain
by Amazon

62107346R00329